THE
GIRL
FROM
SILENT
LAKE

BOOKS BY LESLIE WOLFE

DETECTIVE KAY SHARP SERIES
The Girl From Silent Lake
Beneath Blackwater River

TESS WINNETT SERIES
Dawn Girl
The Watson Girl
Glimpse of Death
Taker of Lives
Not Really Dead
Girl With A Rose
Mile High Death

BAXTER & HOLT SERIES
Las Vegas Girl
Casino Girl
Las Vegas Crime

STANDALONE TITLES
Stories Untold
Love, Lies and Murder

ALEX HOFFMANN SERIES
Executive
Devil's Move
The Backup Asset
The Ghost Pattern
Operation Sunset

THE
GIRL
FROM
SILENT
LAKE

LESLIE WOLFE

bookouture

Published by Bookouture in 2021

An imprint of Storyfire Ltd.
Carmelite House
50 Victoria Embankment
London EC4Y 0DZ

www.bookouture.com

ISBN: 978-1-83888-985-2
eBook ISBN: 978-1-83888-984-5

ACKNOWLEDGMENT

A special thank you to my New York City legal eagle and friend, Mark Freyberg, who expertly guided me through the intricacies of the judicial system.

CHAPTER ONE

Silence

She watched him through a blur of tears, her heart thumping against her ribcage, plastic ties cutting into her flesh as she struggled to free herself. The man's back was turned to her while he arranged some objects on a tray, the soft metallic clinking a surreal omen that froze her blood and threw her thoughts into a whirlwind of sheer mindless terror.

She threw her daughter a quick glance, forcing herself to put hope and courage in her tear-filled eyes. Her eight-year-old daughter Hazel was bound on a chair only a few feet from hers. She whimpered, her little chest heaving with every shattered breath. When they locked eyes, Hazel's sobs became louder, muffled by the scarf he'd tied over her mouth, yet still loud enough to get the man's attention.

"Enough with it already," he ordered in a low voice. He turned and took a few determined steps toward Hazel, then stopped, his menacing eyes inches away from her little girl's.

Alison froze.

The man grabbed a strand of Hazel's long hair and played with it, coiling it around his fingers, then leaned closer and inhaled its scent. The girl's terrified gaze seemed to be amusing to him. He let go of her hair and wiped a tear off the child's cheek with his thumb, then licked the salty liquid with a satisfied groan.

"Don't cry," he whispered, "your mommy loves you so much, doesn't she?"

Hazel fell quiet, as if too scared to make another sound, but her tears flowed freely down her cheeks, soaking the fabric of the scarf. There was something eerie in the man's voice, in the way he'd whispered those words, a sense of foreboding that sent uncontrollable chills down Alison's spine.

"Please," Alison said, "she's just a little girl."

A lopsided smile tugged at the corner of the man's mouth. "She is, isn't she?" Then he added, sounding almost bitter. "They always are."

Then he turned his back to them, and the clinking of objects being placed on a tray resumed against the cold silence.

He wasn't the woods-dwelling, rags-wearing monster one would imagine capable of kidnapping a mother and her daughter and holding them hostage in a remote cabin. He was clean-shaven and smelled of expensive aftershave, well-dressed with new, expensive clothes, and the cabin where he'd taken them was clean and large. If there was something off about it, that had to be the complete absence of personal objects, although the cabin had clearly been lived in for a while.

He seemed comfortable and habitual about his activities, as if he'd done it many times before. No hesitation in his movement and no fear in his dark eyes when he looked at her, when he seemed to be studying her like he would a piece of furniture or art he'd want to acquire.

From the man's broad shoulders and raven-black hair, Alison's gaze moved on to the spotless white walls and tiled floor. In the far corner of the room, next to the door, the cement grout was stained, something reddish-brown discoloring the light gray, porous material. She couldn't take her eyes off that spot, where intersecting grout lines shared a stain that had to have been larger, like a pool of liquid advancing through the seams between the granite tiles and stopping at the wall.

He must've cleaned the tiles, but the liquid had permanently discolored the cement, in testimony of what had happened on that floor.

Blood.

Alison felt a new wave of panic taking over her brain. She willed herself into controlling it, into retaining some shred of command over her racing thoughts. She breathed slowly, holding the air inside her lungs for a few seconds before exhaling it.

The memory of her mother invaded her mind, the smell of cinnamon and the soft tones of her voice telling her, "Why go all the way to the Pacific Coast for a vacation? All by yourself, with a little girl, that isn't safe, sweetie. Not these days. Not anymore. Why don't you and I take Hazel to Savannah instead?"

The sound of her mother's voice resounding in her memory made her eyes burn with fresh tears. Had she known what was going to happen? Maybe she'd seen one of her uncanny warning signs, a bloody moon or a stained sunset, signs Alison had always waved off indifferently, attributing them to her mother's Cajun roots, nothing more than baseless superstition.

Oh, Mom, she thought, *do you see a sign of us coming back home?*

She inhaled forcefully once more, steeling her will. She tugged against her restraints, wincing from the pain where the zip ties had cut her skin around her wrists. She sat on a wooden chair, her hands bound behind the straight, narrow back of it. Her ankles had been secured against the square, thick legs of the chair, and no matter how much she forced herself to bend her ankles and snap the ties, all she did was cut even deeper into her flesh.

When he turned and approached her, she whimpered and shook her head, despite her decision to maintain her calm for as long as possible, for her daughter's sake. Panic roared through her body with every step the man took toward her, her eyes riveted on the silver tray he carried, then on the four-legged stool he pushed between her chair and Hazel's, setting the tray atop it.

She looked straight at him, trying to read the expression in his dark pupils, the meaning behind his cold smile. As she started to understand, uncontrollable sobs shattered her breath, while the terror flooding her body turned absolute, merciless.

He was never going to let them go. Death was written in his eyes, a silent sentence he was about to execute, welcoming it with a blood-lusting smile and the casual demeanor of a man engulfed in a pleasurable Sunday afternoon activity.

My poor baby, she thought, *this can't be happening. I can't let it happen.*

She frantically fought to free herself. She threw herself to the floor, hoping the chair might break under her weight.

She fell hard, the fall knocking the air out of her lungs for a moment. He pulled her back up with ease, grabbing her with unforgiving fingers that crushed her flesh.

"No, no," she pleaded, choking on her own tears. "Please, let us go. W—we won't say a word, I swear."

He didn't reply; his only reaction to her words was the widening of his smile. Alison fell silent.

Grabbing a bone-colored comb from the tray, he combed her hair, taking his time, until it crackled. Her mind raced, trying to anticipate what would come next, grateful he was focused on her and not Hazel.

If he'd only let her go, she thought, clinging to the surreal hope like a drowning man clutching at a straw.

He parted her hair in the middle, from the front all the way to the back, and separated her long strands into two equal sections. Every time his fingers touched her hair or brushed against her skin she shivered, her teeth clacking, her entire being revolting, not knowing when the blow would come, and how. She only knew it would. Soon.

He started braiding her hair, slowly, patiently, seemingly savoring the activity, quietly humming a lullaby. Watching him move, seeing him transposed by the experience, feeling his fingers against her scalp was a living nightmare, one she'd stopped hoping she'd ever wake up from.

"Why?" she whispered, slightly turning her head to face him.

He tugged at her hair to keep her head in place. "Sit still. We're almost done."

When he finished the braid, he secured it with an unusual, handcrafted hair tie made from what seemed to be leather and adorned with tiny feathers. Then he moved over to her left side and started braiding again, humming the same familiar tune.

For a while, she didn't recognize the tune, only that she knew it. But then her frantic mind started imposing lyrics over his hums. Following her gut, she swallowed her tears and started singing softly.

"If that mockingbird won't sing, Mama's gonna buy you a dia—"

She froze, seeing his reaction to her singing. Instead of softening him up, like she'd hoped, his features had turned to stone, rigid muscles knotting under his skin, his stare intense, burning, his knuckles cracking as he clenched his fists.

"Sing," he ordered, but only a whimper left her lips. "Sing, damn you," he shouted, grabbing her half-finished braid and forcing Alison to turn and face him.

Hazel screamed; a short, muffled scream quickly drowned in tearful sobs.

Alison's voice trembled as she sang out of tune, but he didn't seem to mind.

"If that diamond ring turns brass, Mama's gonna buy you a looking glass," she managed, then sniffled and whimpered, "Please, I'm begging you."

"Sing," he shouted.

She quivered, the lyrics she knew so well suddenly gone from her memory.

"Sing," he repeated, his voice uncompromising. He was almost done braiding her hair; then what would he do?

Please, God, don't let him touch my baby, she prayed silently. Then, her voice more a whimper than a song, she sang through the rhyme. "And if that looking glass gets broke, Mama's gonna buy you a—"

She stopped when he wrapped the hair tie around the end of her braid. She was shaking badly and felt cold, frozen, despite the late-afternoon sunshine coming through the window. In the deathly silence, she heard the birds sing outside the window, oblivious to the nightmare contained between the walls of the isolated cabin.

He looked at Hazel for a long, loaded moment, then reached out and touched the little girl's hair. He seemed to be thinking what to do next.

Alison held her breath, her thoughts frantic. *No, no…*

As if hearing her plea, he walked over to Alison and stopped right in front of her. He studied her face for a long moment without saying or doing anything else.

She swallowed, her throat constricted with unspeakable fear, and forced herself to sing some more. "And if that horse and cart fall down, You'll still be the sweetest little baby—"

Without warning, he ripped open her blouse. She gasped, trying to pull herself away from him by pushing with her feet against the floor, but he held her in place, his hand searing against her bare skin.

"Please, not in front of my daughter," she pleaded. "I'll do anything you want."

If only Hazel didn't have to witness what was going to happen. If only she didn't have to see her like that.

His laugh reverberated against the empty walls. He leaned closer to her face, so close she felt his heated breath on her face.

"I know you'll do anything I want," he replied, still laughing. "Are you ready?"

The blue jays that had been filling the valley with their chirping fell silent all at once when her scream ripped through the clear mountain air.

CHAPTER TWO
Home

The last hour of the drive home was just as enchanting as Kay remembered, the perfectly straight concrete strip of the interstate running through the flat and deserted dust bowl gradually replaced by meandering curves sloping gently, cutting through the thick woods of the national forest. Then, as the elevation increased, foliage faded, favoring evergreens, while the slopes were more abrupt and the curves tighter, unforgiving. The October leaves were turning, a display well worth the drive into the mountains north of San Francisco, even if for no other reason than to take in the colors of the beautiful California fall.

She cut the flow of conditioned air coming from the Ford's vents and opened a window instead, letting the wind play with her wavy blonde hair and bringing the almost-forgotten scent of fallen leaves, of morning dew on green blades of grass, of waterfalls and pine needles and the promise of snow.

She was going home.

Not a trip she wanted to make, not ever again.

She sighed, and, without realizing, touched the side of the cardboard box she'd placed on the passenger seat with long, thin, frozen fingers that would've made any concert pianist proud. The white box bore the insignia of the Federal Bureau of Investigation, and contained her personal belongings. A few hours earlier, she'd cleared her desk and gathered everything that had made one of the desks on the fifth floor of the San Francisco regional office her own. A coffee mug with a cartoonish figure of a sniffing dog, a gift from a colleague of hers. A couple of books, one on investigative psychology and the other on profiling violent crimes, both riddled with red and yellow Post-it notes inserted between their pages. A photo of herself, fishing on the Pacific Coast, off the rocky shore at Sea Cliff. A desk nameplate in brushed gold on solid walnut, her name in block letters preceded by her title, SPECIAL AGENT KAY SHARP. Just the sound of those words in her mind used to make her straighten her broad shoulders and put a spring in her step, adding about an inch to her height and making her delicate chin thrust forward with confidence.

All that was now in the past, and she was going home.

She remembered how painful it had been to collect all those items and pack them in the box borrowed from evidence storage, to step out the door knowing she wouldn't be back there come Monday. She'd held her head up while saying her goodbyes, fighting back the sting of tears as she looked at the bullpen one last time and then rushed to the elevator, shook one more hand while going down five floors, before walking out of the building. Pulling out of the parking lot in her white Ford Explorer, she'd given the high-rise building one last look, as always noticing how the perfectly blue sky reflected in the mirrored windows. Then she turned left, heading north.

Heading home.

Just because Jacob couldn't control his damn temper.

Her shy, little brother Jacob had grown into a rather bulky man, his arms and back ripped with muscles he'd built working construction during summertime, whenever he could find work. Jacob had always struggled; he didn't relate well to others, and apparently had anger management issues too. Those were new; she'd always known him to be gentle, withdrawn, a man who wouldn't hurt a fly.

When he'd called her a few days before, his voice was fraught with shame and regret.

"I'm going to jail, sis," he'd said, jumping straight into the core of the issue, like he always did. "I—I don't know how it happened. He provoked me, threw a bottle at my head, and I only hit him once. But I decked him." He paused, cleared his voice, then said, speaking almost in a whisper, "I never expected the judge to give me time to serve, that's why I didn't tell you about it."

"How long?" she'd asked, while tears flooded her eyes. Her little Jacob, in jail. Despite his stature, he wasn't built for prison; he wouldn't last long. His kind nature, his shy demeanor would invite abuse from career criminals who knew their way on the inside. If he'd only told her, she would've appeared to testify on his behalf, to speak for his character, and maybe the judge would've considered a suspended sentence.

"Six months," he replied after a long moment. "But I could be out—"

"Jeez," she reacted. "How could you—"

She stopped herself from continuing. It made no sense to pound on him; he was already aware of what he'd done and all the implications, and by the sound of it, he was drowning in guilt.

"You know what that means, sis," he added. "You have to—"

"When do you report and where?" she cut him off.

"This coming Friday, at nine a.m., at High Desert."

High Desert State Prison was only a few hours' drive from home. She'd be able to visit, maybe put in a good word with the warden, as a professional courtesy maybe, if something like that was ever extended to former FBI agents. And she'd want to speak with that judge, and ask why he'd felt compelled to give jail time to a first-time offender for what seemed to have been nothing but a bar brawl.

She'd take it one day at a time, and make the most of each day. The mantra of an existence rife with adversity.

Nevertheless, come that Friday evening, she had no choice but to be back home.

And that meant leaving her career behind, all the hard work she'd put into her role as a profiler for the FBI in the past eight years down the drain, soon to be forgotten.

Meanwhile, she was supposed to go back to living in a place she'd sworn she'd never see again. She was to build a life for herself there, in a town haunted by memories she'd spent years trying to forget.

One stupid, drunken punch, and her career had come to an abrupt stop.

She wiped a rebel tear from the corner of her eye and cursed, her words swallowed by the wind as she drove with her windows down, inviting the chilly mountain air to cool her heated forehead.

Damn it to hell, Jacob. How could you do this to me? To us?

It was almost dark when she drove past the sign that said, MOUNT CHESTER, ESTABLISHED 1910. POPULATION 3,823. She took the first exit, then it took her about thirty minutes to pull up in front of the old ranch, and that included a five-minute stop at the Katse Coffee Shop for a fresh brew and some butter croissants.

It was just as she remembered it.

She hadn't been back since her mother's funeral, ten years ago, but she remembered the house clearly.

Approaching it, driving slowly, she pulled onto the driveway and cut the engine, but left the lights on. Seeing it from up close, Kay didn't recognize it anymore, even if it was shrouded in darkness. The lawn was overcome by weeds and littered with junk, the paint was cracked and chipped, and the porch needed new decking to replace the rotten, weathered one. Several baluster spindles were missing, while others were broken yet still hanging in there.

She cut through the grass and instantly regretted it when she tripped on a rusted truck rim hidden in the weeds, and flailed to regain her balance. Then she braced herself, and climbed up the five squeaky, wooden steps leading to the front door.

It wasn't locked. Why would it be?

Shivering, she pulled at the long sleeves of her black turtleneck until it reached her fingers, then entered, feeling the wall for the light switch. Doused in the pale, yellowish light coming from a broken ceiling fixture, the house welcomed her with unwanted memories. Some things never changed, choosing to survive the passage of time undisturbed, either as enduring bits of routine or as mementos of a forgotten past. The smell of stale foods and dirty dishes fueled by the pile littering the sink. The stink of mildew that came from the walls, from the bathroom, from everywhere. The stained rug in the middle of the living room, seemingly unvacuumed for a long time. A family photo taken when she was about ten years old and Jacob nine, their parents standing behind them. It hung crookedly above the cracked fireplace, framed and protected with thin, broken glass. The kitchen table littered with empty beer cans, old newspapers, and frozen dinner wrappings.

"Jeez, Jacob, what the hell?" she muttered, while walking slowly through the empty house, the creaking of the floors the only sound she could hear.

What did she expect, leaving that house to be cared for by a man, by Jacob, no less? He'd never been too practical or too good with his hands. Even if he worked construction in the summer or ski-lift maintenance over the winter, up at the resort, Jacob had never been the kind of man she could count on to keep things running smoothly. Jacob was broken, and she knew why. For the most part, it was her fault.

She opened a few screened windows and turned the lights on everywhere, inviting the evening mountain breeze to chase the shadows away. She took the garbage out, putting the bin by the front door, afraid to cross the lawn in the dark to find the can. The floors needed a good scrubbing, and if there was a working vacuum in the house, she needed to put it to work. But not now. Tomorrow.

She cringed, a shiver coursing through her slender body, realizing she needed to sleep in that house, and, for a long moment, she considered sleeping in her Ford Explorer instead. It was clean and smelled of new leather and fresh croissants. But sleeping in the car was a cowardly move; she had to embrace her new reality, the sooner the better.

Wandering from one room to the other, she wondered where she could settle for the night. Jacob's room was littered with dirty clothing scattered all over the floor, and the bedsheets hadn't been changed in a while. His bathroom had toiletries and toilet paper, but it wasn't in a usable state by her standards.

The door to her parents' bedroom was closed, and she held her breath before opening it, almost expecting her father to scold her for waking him up. The bed was neatly made with the same linens and pillows she'd put on it after her mother's passing. Jacob hadn't touched it, and she wasn't about to. She couldn't bear to think about her mother; despite the passing of time, the pain was still raw. She closed the door gently, as if to not disturb the memories sheltered in that space.

That left her old room, and she stared at the narrow bed from the doorway, unwilling to enter the space that had witnessed so many of her tears. She closed the door gently, then went back to the kitchen. Maybe a hot cup of tea would change her outlook on life, on living in her old house, with so many old memories, for the foreseeable future.

The fridge held beer, liquor, and frozen TV dinners, the only exception being a small jar of mustard. She shrugged off her hunger and closed the fridge door, then grabbed the coffee maker pot and made herself a cup of tea that smelled of stale coffee grounds. Holding her mother's old mug between her frozen hands, she stood at the window and stared at the backyard, barely visible in the dim light coming from the house and the haze-filtered moonlight. It was unkempt, just like the front lawn was, with overgrown, knee-high grasses and weeds, and it seemed that Jacob hadn't set foot out there in a long time. But it was just as she remembered it, a wide grassy area leading to the woods on one side, and the willows by the river on the other.

The weeping willows had grown, their leaves brushing the ground, their crowns touching one another above the massive trunks. Their sprawling silhouettes loomed ominously against the dark sky, their moonlit shadows large, moving with the wind, almost touching the house.

Shivering, she closed the window with a loud thump, then pulled the curtains shut.

"Oh, Jacob, you really had to throw that punch, didn't you?" she whispered, and only the wind replied, whooshing against pine needles and long, weeping willow branches.

She finished her tea and placed the empty cup on the table, then opened the folded newspaper she found there. It was yesterday's local paper, and the first thing that caught her eye was a title in big, bold lettering, DETAILS EMERGE IN CUWAR LAKE FOREST MURDER. Intrigued, she pulled a chair and sat, not minding the grime staining the seat, not taking her eyes off the small print, barely visible in the dim light, reading every word intently, forgetting where she was.

When she finished reading, she brought the laptop from the SUV and started typing a letter, while biting hungrily into a fresh butter croissant.

CHAPTER THREE

Captive

She'd lost track of days, although she tried to keep count, constantly reminding herself how many times the sun had risen since they'd been taken. But the brain is a fragile thing, creating alternate realities when the real one is too painful to endure. Alison's mind was no exception; after several days spent locked in the basement, with only a crack in the wooden panel that boarded the small window to see if it was light or dark outside, she'd finally accepted she wasn't going to know which day it was. Not anymore, not with any degree of certainty.

She'd scratched short, vertical lines on the wall to keep track, but when she woke up from her agitated, terror-filled sleep she couldn't remember if she'd fallen asleep last night or an hour earlier. She knew to listen for him, for the sound of his car's engine, fearfully anticipating his return, knowing what it would bring.

Every day, right after dusk. Some days, earlier.

She still had time until his arrival, or at least she hoped she did. The sun was still up, because she couldn't see it setting through the crack in the wooden window board, and that meant she could hope to find a way out before he returned.

It wasn't like she hadn't tried to escape before. She had, pushing herself against the massive door, scratching at the boarded window until her fingers bled, pounding on every inch of wall. She'd done all that in the first day she spent in captivity, and then every day after that, some days more than once. She'd done it even when her body ached so badly she could barely stand.

But today was different. She was frantic, desperate out of her mind to get away, more desperate than she'd ever been. Because last night she'd heard Hazel scream.

It had happened while he was still there and had just left her lying on the barren cement floor, bleeding. He locked the door, then she heard his heavy footfalls climb stairs, not one flight, but two. A few minutes of tense silence ensued, during which Alison didn't dare to breathe. Then she'd heard it, the piercing wail of her daughter, distant yet heart-wrenching, ending in sobs.

She was still there, her baby girl, and she was still alive. At least that much she knew, as of last night. But why did she scream? What did he do to her?

They had to get away. And it had to happen today, before he could get near her again. No matter what it took.

Shaking and sobbing, Alison threw herself against the door, not minding the pain that shot through her side, the memory of how the man had stared at Hazel fueling her agony. How he'd played with her daughter's hair, how he'd touched her face and tasted her tears.

The echoes of Hazel's scream reverberated in her mind, over and over.

She took two faltering steps back, then ran and slammed her thin body against the door again, only to fall to the floor in a heap. That door wasn't going to budge.

Turning her attention to the sliver of light coming from the window, she pounded against the wooden board with both her fists. Out of breath but not giving up, she grabbed the sill with one hand to reach higher, and struck it with the other hand as hard as she could.

Nothing.

She let herself slide to the floor, sobbing hard, hugging her knees with bleeding hands. Weeping until her tears ran dry, she clasped her hand over her mouth to stifle her sobs, afraid Hazel might hear them just as Alison had heard her little girl's scream the night before.

Then she jumped to her feet, realizing she'd been pounding on that wooden board all this time, when she should try pulling it toward her instead. Maybe there was a chance that way.

She managed to slip her finger inside the crack enough to get a grip and yanked, and a few wood shards came off, widening the crack. Now she could slip two fingers in there. Minute after minute, the crack widened and her grip grew stronger, pulling the wooden board with the nails that held it in place, slowly, while more light found its way to fill the bleak room.

She could see the rusty nails almost entirely now, and beyond the crack, a section of the window frame, fragile, easy to break. She took a deep breath and pulled again, her fingers raw and bleeding, and the board gave way to another fraction of an inch of rusty nail length.

One more time, and the board came loose so suddenly it hit her forehead, but she didn't care. Shocked, she stared at the window, now fully exposed, a mere eight-by-ten-inch hole in a concrete wall.

She was never going to fit through there.

A heavy sob swelled her chest and she let it out, covering her mouth with bleeding hands while she dropped to the floor. Suddenly, she heard laughter. She opened her eyes to find the man staring at her, cackling loudly.

"You've been busy, I see," he said, then laughed some more.

"No, no," she whimpered, pushing herself away from him until she reached the corner of the room.

"No?" he replied, amusement still lingering in his eyes. "What if you could see Hazel tonight? Would that change your mind?"

"Y—you mean it?"

He placed his hand on his chest in a gesture of mockery she chose to ignore, too desperate to believe him. "I swear." Amusement was gone from his eyes, leaving them as cold and as dark as she'd grown to know them.

Tears streamed down her cheeks. She felt pathetically grateful to the man who had kidnapped them and had been torturing her for days. The thought of it made her sick to the stomach, but she didn't care; she was going to see her daughter soon.

Alison closed her eyes, imagining Hazel running toward her with her arms wide open, laughing, squealing with joy.

As she heard him undo his belt buckle, she didn't open her eyes. When he grabbed her ankle and dragged her on the floor, she didn't resist.

She was going to see her precious girl tonight.

CHAPTER FOUR

Cuwar Lake

Kay knew she should've spent the day getting herself organized in her old family home, since she was going to live there until Jacob was released. She owed that to her little brother; they only had each other, and in a world where billions of people lived, they could only rely on each other. Once the word of his incarceration swept the town, it would've been a matter of days until everything he owned would've been ransacked or stolen. The thought of strangers trampling through the house made her sick to the stomach. Well, not on her watch.

Instead of getting her new life a head start, she found herself obsessing about the body found at Cuwar Lake Forest. Who was she? How did she get there? How was she killed? She'd pored over the newspaper article twice, but knew better than anyone that many critical details about a crime were often left out from police statements to the media, a strategy most investigators used to weed out false testimonies and fake confessions. The only usable detail the article mentioned was that the body had been wrapped in a blanket; the rest was sensationalizing filler.

She'd known about the murder since before she'd left San Francisco, and she'd read everything the media had published about it. More than a week before, the body of a young woman had been found buried at Cuwar Lake Forest, only yards away from the lakeshore. The reports described the woman as a twenty-eight-year-old brunette with long hair and brown eyes who'd been brutally strangled. The article spoke of significant bruising to her body, most likely associated with the equally brutal sexual assault the local reporter was describing in vivid, editorialized detail. Yet since the first mention of the young woman's body had appeared in print, no official statement from the medical examiner had corroborated the reporter's take on the crime.

But it was enough for her to start putting the puzzle together.

She'd always kept an eye on her hometown's news; she had every reason to want to stay in touch with the goings-on of the small community, especially when it came to crime. Of course, back then she could use her FBI credentials to access information, but now she no longer had access to those systems, and that was a source of annoyance keeping her from her planned activities.

She eagerly waited for dusk, walking around the property and making a mental list of things she needed to get done, then immediately forgetting about it, her mind busy visualizing the details of the unsub's elaborate ritual. Fragments of the unknown subject's actions appeared clearly in her mind, shards of a broken image she needed to uncover and paste together, many pieces still missing, still hidden from view. Only a few miles away, at Cuwar Lake Forest, a few such pieces waited for her to uncover them, to cast them into the light, bringing her one step closer to unveiling the unsub's identity. But she wasn't a fed anymore; just Jacob's sister, returned home to house-sit while her brother did his time. All she could do with her findings was write letters and send them to the investigators, hoping they'd be read before landing in the wastepaper basket. Yet she couldn't let go, she couldn't resist the urge to hunt for that young woman's killer, because deep inside she knew he wasn't done.

He was just starting.

She picked the occasional piece of junk from the front lawn and carried it over to the curb, hoping the service would collect it, happy to postpone the moment she'd have to go inside. But mainly she was out on the lawn watching the sun go down, unhurried, achingly slowly.

The moment it disappeared behind the mountains, she climbed behind the wheel of her Explorer and set out to drive to Cuwar Lake.

The article didn't specify where exactly the body had been found, but she knew the lake like the back of her hand. When she was growing up, a day spent on the sandy beaches of the lake was the closest she'd come to a real vacation. And there were miles of those beaches, flanked by dense woods that provided the much-needed shade in the summertime. Deer oaks, bigleaf maples, and cottonwoods provided the local kids with year-round entertainment. Acorn treasure hunts, tree-climbing contests that had given her plenty of scars to show off proudly, and necklaces made of double-winged samaras kept the kids busy all weekend long, while the parents caught a little bit of rest.

Sometimes.

When she was lucky enough, she was invited to join her best friend's family for an outing to the lake. Judy's family was lots of fun, she recalled with a sad smile. She hadn't seen them in a long time, and she couldn't bring herself to understand why she hadn't called them.

She turned onto North Shore Road and slowed, wondering how she'd be able to locate the place where the body had been buried. Maybe the yellow, do-not-cross tape was still in place, and it would be that easy, if only she could spot that in the dark.

Several paths led from the road to the lake, eager tourists driving trucks or SUVs blazing new ones each weekend, in search of a stretch of deserted beach they could call their own. The article said the body had been found close to the beach but had mentioned Cuwar Lake *Forest*, not just Cuwar Lake. That meant she had to drive a little farther and reach the southern limit of the national forest.

Rolling down her window, she pointed a flashlight toward the forest, darkness already thick, impenetrable from the road. When she was about to turn around and try her search again from the lakeshore, a flicker of yellow tape caught her eye in the distance. She turned onto the path and drove slowly, then stopped a good twenty feet away from the open grave.

After cutting the engine and killing the lights, she gave her eyes a few seconds to get adjusted to the darkness, then approached the grave. Shielding the beam of the flashlight in the palm of her hand, she kneeled by the graveside and examined it inch by inch. It had been dug with a flat shovel, the lines left in the edges long and parallel, suggesting methodical approach and upper body strength. A man in his prime. It had been dug about three feet deep, not a hasty job but a carefully executed task by someone who cared enough to take his time and risk getting caught only to give the victim a proper burial.

Remorse?

Probably.

She needed to see the crime scene photos to be sure.

Kay kneeled at the far side of the grave and projected the beam at the bottom of the excavation, seeing something that didn't belong. A double-winged seed samara leaf, when all the fallen leaves around the grave were oak, not maple. But a samara is nature's design for a seed meant to fly far from the tree in the gentlest of winds, spinning around and gaining momentum, in search of fertile grounds where it can grow.

It was probably nothing.

She spent a few minutes looking at the many tire tracks visible on that path, wondering if the sheriff's office had taken molds of any of them. There were very few sections of barren ground where the tire tracks had left discernible impressions. October foliage covered almost every square inch, and tire tracks on leaves were as ephemeral as the wind.

She heard an owl hoot and smiled at the sound, unafraid, although in the local culture the owl was a symbol of death, a bad omen people feared. But death had been there already, had taken its grim toll. The owl was just a bird, nothing else, one of the many thriving life forms one could find on the north shore of Cuwar Lake. The only thing the owl foretold was the presence of mice on the ground, its favorite prey.

Standing, she ran her hands against her jeans, brushing off the dirt and leaves, and looked around. She could barely see the lake's shimmering surface under the moonlight, through the thick forest. As far as body dump sites went, this one wasn't badly chosen; the victim could've stayed buried for years without anyone finding her.

How was she discovered, anyway? The newspaper article didn't say.

She climbed into the Explorer and started the engine, frowning when she saw in the headlights the many footprints she'd left at the side of the grave. Thankfully, by morning, they'd all be gone, scattered by wind, a fresh layer of falling oak leaves covering the ones that bore her mark.

Putting the SUV in reverse, she drove away slowly, careful not to hit anything on her way out of the woods. Her eyes, riveted to the rearview camera, didn't notice the man who watched her from a distance, arms crossed at his chest, leaning against his car.

He'd been there a while.

CHAPTER FIVE

Elliot

Kay had spent her second night after returning to her childhood home dozing off at the kitchen table, with her head nestled on her arms, her face touching the latest local newspaper. The light of dawn and its accompanying concert of chirps and eagle cries found her stiff and unrested, but happy the darkness was finally gone.

She could bear to look at the house in broad daylight, when the ghosts of her past seemed defeated by the sun. With daylight as her ally, she started cleaning the house methodically, thinking ahead of the days and nights she had to spend there.

She started with the survival trio, as she liked to call it, kitchen-bathroom-bedroom, the bare necessities of any dwelling. She began with her old bedroom, not a room she wanted to sleep in, but out of the existing alternatives, the lesser evil. The task, which should've lasted no more than a couple of hours, ended up taking the bulk of her day.

The only vacuum in the house was dead, and replacing it took a trip to Mount Chester's only Walmart store, a thirty-five-minute drive. On the way in, she used the opportunity to grab some breakfast at a pastry shop, glad to see no one recognized her. She wasn't up for conversation, just happy to be anonymously on her way as soon as possible. Once at the store, she decided to stock up on some fruit and vegetables, and added cleaning products, household consumables and a new set of bedsheets to her cart.

Then she returned to the ranch, mad as hell she'd forgotten to get air fresheners and shampoo.

Approaching the house at high noon was a different experience than it had been the night she'd arrived. The ranch was less menacing, looking frail and shabby, as if about to fall apart if the winds picked up. Before unloading her shopping, she walked the front lawn, deciding what to do first. Yesterday's list forgotten, she opted for giving the tall weeds outside another few days of life, in favor of cleaning the living spaces inside to a level that she could tolerate.

She dove right back into cleaning the bedroom, and when she finished vacuuming, wiping all the surfaces and making the bed with the new dark green sheets, it looked almost livable.

Kay took the old sheets to the laundry room and loaded the washer, only to storm back to Walmart a few minutes later. The thing hadn't been in use for months, judging by the thick layer of dust settled on its command panel, and was not powering up. Three hours later, a well-built, bearded man by the name of Joe finished installing the new washer-and-dryer combo, took the old ones to the curb, and gratefully accepted a twenty-dollar tip with a smile colored by chewing tobacco stains on his crooked teeth.

The next few days were spent scrubbing the floors, cleaning the windows, running laundry load after laundry load, until the acrid smells were finally replaced by the lavender scent of dryer sheets. But scrubbing the kitchen floor took its own special kind of toll, and she found herself throwing up after finishing that section of hardwood, bent over the weakened rail of the front porch. When the heaving relented, she rinsed her mouth with some bottled water and slammed the door behind her, car keys in hand.

"Screw this," she muttered a few moments later, from behind the wheel of her Ford, peeling off in a cloud of dust and pebbles.

Twenty-five minutes later, she was unlocking a room at the Best Western downtown. There, she immediately ran herself a bath, immersing herself in blissful, cleansing peace until the water turned cold. A few hours later, her senses soothed by the warmth and cleanliness of everything that surrounded her, she found the willpower to leave behind the promise of a good night's sleep, and headed back to the ranch.

She couldn't afford to leave the place unguarded for one single night.

That had been two days ago, and she couldn't believe she'd arrived almost a week earlier. The fridge was clean and held some real food, not just beer and frozen dinners, although she couldn't bring herself to cook yet. Maybe later… maybe never. Deli meats, sliced cheeses, strawberries and apples made up her diet, and the croissants she kept getting from Katse Coffee Shop, over the mountain.

A couple of times she'd tried calling Judy, but got her voicemail. She couldn't find the words to leave a message. How could she explain not having called her best friend for all those years? As soon as the cleanup was done, she'd drive by and speak to her in person. That was a promise she made to herself, a promise that made her smile with fond anticipation, the bitter guilt for being out of touch for so long starting to dissipate.

Once the scrubbing and cleaning was done for the most part, she'd found herself with nothing to do, yet, for some reason, postponing the planned visit to see her best friend. Instead, she looked for jobs, but there were none in Mount Chester, population 3,823. She was willing to do anything, even wait on tables at one of the local diners, but nobody was hiring until the start of the winter tourist season, only a month away. And she couldn't bring herself to visit with old acquaintances and ask for their help. That would trigger more unwanted memories, questions, and gossip. Better to go at it alone; she'd done it before. Thankfully, her savings account could handle her living in Mount Chester for six months until Jacob was released and she could return to her real home, in San Francisco.

She ached to speak with her brother and planned a visit to him. He couldn't take calls; no inmate could, unless, of course, the caller was a federal agent, which she wasn't. Not anymore. She thought of him almost every moment, wondering how he was surviving behind bars and dreading the conversation she was going to have with him, if she had no answers yet. No solution, no promise of an earlier release, of an appeal that would move fast enough through the system to make a difference.

Not a day too soon, little brother, she thought, then suddenly wondered if the 3,823 people noted on the town's sign included her or not, or when it would include her again, if ever. Hopefully, she wouldn't be there long enough for that to happen.

The first knock on the door barely registered in her mind and she quickly dismissed it, thinking it must've been a woodpecker, busy at work up in the old oak tree looking for some grub. But the second, louder rap had a rhythm to it, strong evidence it was generated by a human.

She wasn't expecting anyone.

Frowning, she wiped her hands on a paint-stained rag and headed for the living room, feeling for the weapon holstered at her hip, under her loose shirt. Then she opened the door, tentatively at first, then widely, as soon as she saw the badge the stranger was holding at her eye level.

"Detective Young, Franklin County Sheriff's Office," the man said, and his Texas drawl made her smile. "May I come in?"

Her frown returned. "Um, sure."

He didn't look like any Franklin County detective she'd seen, resembling a Texas cowboy who'd boarded the wrong flight. In worn-out jeans and a navy-blue T-shirt stretched over well-defined muscles, he looked nothing like a detective would, especially during business hours. Usually, the sheriff departments all around the country required business casual attire—slacks, shirt, tie and a jacket—but this detective apparently had not received that particular memo. The black, wide-brimmed hat and the Lone Star belt buckle were statements to that effect.

He took off his hat entering the house and remained standing by the door. Without the shadow cast by the dark felt, she could see a tall forehead littered by unruly, light brown hair, slightly furrowed above blue eyes that looked straight at her, inquisitive, restless. A hint of a smile tugged at the corner of his mouth while he studied her openly, without trying to hide his gaze.

Irritating as hell.

"What can I do for you, Detective?"

"I heard one of the top FBI profilers had returned home," he said, giving the living room the typical cop once-over. "I figured I'd stop by and introduce myself."

She refrained from fidgeting, from showing how uncomfortable his presence made her, especially when she noticed how carefully he examined his surroundings. Had he been inside the house before? She had no way of knowing, but one thing was certain: she didn't believe a single word he'd spoken since he stepped over that doorsill.

She forced her smile to look sincere. "Well, now we've met, Detective. Anything else?"

He leaned against the wall and crossed his legs at the ankle. "Ms. Katherine Sharp, is that correct?"

"Kay," she rushed to correct him. "Everyone calls me Kay."

"Uh-huh," he replied, a hint of a smile touching his blue eyes. "So, what's a hotshot fed like you doing in a place like this?"

The man was nothing if not direct, but she wasn't going to answer his baseless questions. Surprised, Kay took longer than a split second to reply. "I don't see how—"

"You burned out or something?" he asked, his smile touching the corners of his lips as he sized her up. "Or does it have something to do with your brother being in jail?"

Angry, she propped her hands on her hips and took one step closer to the door. She knew the type well, having encountered them frequently in her years as a fed. Nosy cops on a fishing expedition, when the days were too peaceful to justify their existence on the taxpayer-funded payroll. "I believe I can't be of any real assistance with anything, Detective, and I have work—"

"Oh, but I believe you can," he replied, his Texas drawl prevalent, a constant reminder he didn't quite belong. He pulled a folded piece of paper from his back pocket and handed it to her. "I believe you can help me sort out what's written in this letter. Make some sense out of it."

She took the crinkled, typed letter and swallowed a curse. She recognized the font she'd used, the layout of the page. Even before she read the first few words, she knew it was one of the letters she'd sent. Yet she pretended to read through it, while thinking of how best to handle the situation. If she wanted to have a conversation face-to-face with the detectives investigating the Cuwar Lake murder, she would've signed the damn thing.

"Seems pretty clear to me," she replied, folding it and holding it out for him to take back.

He didn't.

"Ma'am, I'm just a Texas lawman who landed up here, trying to make a living. I'm not as smart as you are. Why don't you explain what it says, in plain English, words I can understand and use while hunting for the son of a bitch who murdered that woman?"

She stared at him for a quick moment, wondering if he wasn't actually playing dumb. She still didn't buy a word he was saying, but decided to play along.

"The letter suggests the killer is experienced in taking lives, and especially in disposing of the bodies in a manner that speaks to experience, to routine. And there's a reference to a certain ritual, as seen in the way the victim was buried. The positioning of the body, the blanket he wrapped her in, that speaks of remorse."

"Anything a simple cop from Austin can actually use?" He shifted his weight from one foot to the other, still leaning against the wall.

"The letter suggests this might be the work of a serial killer," she added, then stood, waiting. She wanted him gone, out of the house as quickly as possible. Somehow, having a cop inside her home turned her into a nervous wreck, although if the same situation would've happened in San Francisco, she would've invited the fellow law enforcement officer to stay for coffee and she would've gladly discussed the case.

Then she realized she was making a mistake, behaving differently from what she would've normally done in the city.

"How about some coffee, Detective?" she asked, changing tack, turning and stepping over to the kitchen counter.

His smile widened into a full-blown grin. "How about we drop the anonymous letter act? And how about some beer instead?"

Damn. And it's not even eleven o'clock in the morning, pal. That's how they do law in Austin, Texas? With a cold one in hand?

She held her breath until her back was turned to him, while she took two cold beers from the fridge. Then she let herself exhale, her frustration muted and lengthened until it sounded like normal breathing.

"What do you mean?" she asked, handing him the bottle.

He popped the cap with a quick gesture, then looked around before locating the trash can and sent it there with a precise shot across the room. He whistled when the cap landed neatly in the trash, then held the bottle up to hers, though without touching it.

"Cheers," he said, then gulped down thirstily almost half the contents. "Well, let's see. You're the only criminalist with a psychology degree within a hundred-mile radius. I also know this isn't the first letter we received from you, even if you just moved back here. Coincidentally, the other letters had a San Francisco postmark. You've been keeping an eye on the local events, now, haven't you?"

Of course, she had. It was her hometown. Her skeletons.

The drawl was still there, but the simple-boy-from-Texas routine was completely gone. She weighed her options for a while, then decided to own it.

"Guilty as charged, Detective," she replied without smiling. "But last time I checked, writing letters wasn't illegal in Franklin County." She sipped her beer slowly, savoring the cold flavor.

"No, but interfering with an active investigation is," he replied calmly. "You see, now we can do one of two things. I can listen to what you have to say, or I can put you on notice to stay away from the investigation. I'm not afraid to arrest a former fed, Ms. Sharp, keep that in mind."

She raised the bottle at him before taking another mouthful. "It's Dr. Sharp, by the way. Cheers."

He looked at the ceiling for a quick moment, the male, head-involved equivalent of an eyeroll. "Of course, it is," he muttered. "I knew that. I know a few things about you."

Kay gestured at one of the chairs around the kitchen table and sat on another. "Sit at your own risk," she said quickly, embarrassed by the state of the furniture. "Again, what can I do for you? Seems to me you understood everything I wrote in there quite well."

He scratched the back of his head with a quick gesture. He seemed a little uneasy now, maybe frustrated too.

"You've worked serial killers before?" he asked, avoiding her eyes.

"Yes, eight wonderful years of putting away the region's sickest, most disturbed murderers," she replied, adding some dramatic flair to test his reactions.

He remained serious. "Well, I haven't. All my murder collars have been simple, mostly motivated by greed or passion, jealousy,

B&Es gone bad, stuff like that. But twisted minds like this one…
I can't get myself to think like him, that's all. And I've been a cop
for thirteen years."

"Where, in Texas?"

"There, then here," he replied. "I moved up here a few years ago."

"Why?" Kay asked, the first question she was really curious to
know the answer to. What would make an Austin cowboy choose
to live in a place covered in snow for six months a year?

"Ah, long story." He waved her curiosity off with a hand gesture.
"But never mind me," he said. "Tell me how to get in that killer's
mind, that's what I need to know."

She stood, pacing the space between the kitchen and the living
room, and he allowed her the thinking time. "It's not that simple,
Detective."

"Call me Elliot," he replied, "at least that should be simple
enough."

She smiled. "Elliot, okay." She continued to pace, wondering
how she could condense her years of training and experience into
information she could convey while he finished his beer. Because
there certainly wasn't going to be a second bottle.

Taking her seat back at the table, she made her decision. "Why
don't you tell me about the victim, Elliot? Let's start there."

Kay expected some hesitation, being how law enforcement is
usually reluctant to share details of an active investigation with just
about anyone, but Elliot replied right away, making her wonder
if that wasn't really what he'd come prepared to do from the start.

"The victim is Kendra Marshall, twenty-eight years old, a legal
assistant from New York City. She was here on business. She was
going to meet with the Christensen family on a matter regarding
an inheritance. She never made her appointment."

"Thanks," she said, thinking what little that information told
her, despite it telling her something he had probably missed. "I

could start by telling you things like you have a predator who doesn't stalk, but rather seizes the opportunity and has a quick and effective manner to grab victims without being seen. He has mobility and means. He knows how to cover his tracks, and his victim's tracks as well. He's local, or used to be, because he knows his way around this place."

"Yeah, that's useful," he replied.

"Or I could tell you I spent years training to be a doctor in psychology, and more years in the field, working these types of cases, seeing these monsters operate, interviewing them, understanding the sociopathic mind better than most law enforcement can."

"You're saying I can't do my job worth a pinch of sundried manure?" he reacted, pushing himself away from the table with a loud screech of wooden chair legs dragged against ceramic tiles. "Is that what you're saying, *Dr.* Sharp?"

"Whoa, hold your horses, cowboy," she replied, laughing, entertained by the textbook display of bruised male ego. "All I'm saying is that teaching you how to think and feel like him would take time, and with this killer, you don't have the luxury of time. He will kill again, and soon. So, I'm offering to work this one with you."

"In what capacity? You're not a fed anymore."

"True, but I'm an educated and experienced civilian, a qualified consultant, for lack of a better word."

"How much do you want to charge the taxpayers for this gig, Dr. Sharp?"

"Nothing, I'll do it for free. And you can call me Kay."

He frowned, wrinkling his forehead while he considered her offer.

"Why Kay? What's wrong with Katherine?"

"Ah, long story," she replied, hoping he'd give it up.

"I got time," he said, staring at the remaining inch of beer on the bottom of his bottle.

She pretended she didn't notice the unspoken request. "I just hate the name, that's all. I only kept the initial, K. That reads Kay, right?"

"Who would hate a name like Katherine?" he muttered, then downed the rest of the beer and placed the bottle gently on the table. "Thank you. Where do you want to start?"

"At the coroner's office, as soon as possible."

"How about now?"

Speechless, she gestured toward the empty bottle, but he didn't even blink. Resigned, she reached for her jacket. "Perfect, I'll get us some breath mints."

CHAPTER SIX

Autopsy

Elliot wandered through the overgrown lawn looking for something in particular, while Kay pretended to lock the front door. She didn't have a key; Jacob probably hadn't locked that door in years.

"There," Elliot said, then bent over and picked a few leaves from a small bush. "Black peppermint," he clarified, putting one of the leaves in his mouth and chewing enthusiastically. "Does wonders to hide the smell of beer. Want some?"

"I'll pass," she replied, climbing into his unmarked SUV.

"Your loss," he replied cheerfully, tossing the remaining leaves into his mouth.

"You know your herbs," she commented, unwilling to let the silence ignite the wrong questions. He was smarter than he let on, and that kind of intelligence was dangerous. Cops like Elliot often developed a strong intuition, a mix of instinct and rapid thought process that steered them in the right direction despite the apparent lack of evidence. Last thing she needed was Elliot Young snooping through her life.

"Yes, I do," he replied, turning onto the state highway, on the way to the county morgue. "It's a shame you don't, being that you grew up here. How come?"

"I know some," she replied cautiously. "I just don't happen to like herbs that much. Not all of them, anyway," she added, looking at the in-dash clock and knowing it was going to take him a while to get to the morgue, on the other side of the mountain.

"Tell me one you like," he asked.

"I like eastern hemlock tea," she replied. "I love that tea on a cold fall morning."

"Hemlock is a tree, not an herb," he laughed. "I thought you knew the difference, Dr. Sharp."

She turned and saw the amusement in his voice was matched by a genuine smile and not the least bit sarcastic.

"No kidding," she laughed. "I like rosemary too," she added. "If you were a shrink you might go off on a tangent exploring my fascination with needle-shaped leaves in plant life."

"But I'm not, so I won't," he replied. When he spoke, she could pick up a hint of his minty breath. "But I will ask you, for the sake of passing the time, why are you really back here, Kay?"

She pressed her lips together until all the oaths that flooded her mind stopped being at risk of blurting out of her mouth. When her anger subsided, she remembered she had experience talking serial killers into revealing their burial sites or the names of their victims. For sure, she could handle a deputy from Texas, regardless of how smart he was, and throw him off whatever scent he'd picked up.

Start with the truth was a valuable trick she'd learned early in her career. *Build an iceberg: the truth you can use above the surface, where it can be easily seen, verified, then everything else under the water surface, where no one will think to look. With that, you can sink any suspect's ship.* Those had been the words of her mentor, the head of the Behavioral Analysis Unit, Aaron Reese, during one of the advanced criminalistics lectures he sometimes gave to agents who showed promise in the field.

Of course, Aaron Reese would've been appalled to learn she was about to use his deflection techniques on a fellow law enforcement officer.

"My brother is the only family I have," she said eventually, just as Elliot was starting to frown. "He's the kindest man you'll ever meet, and he wouldn't intentionally hurt anyone."

She paused, seeing if Elliot would be satisfied with that tiny morsel of truth she'd laid out in front of him.

He wasn't.

"And?" he pressed on. "Still, why are you here?"

"I'm looking into what caused him to be given such a harsh sentence over a bar brawl. Those happen every night, as far as I recall, and nobody gets sent to jail over it. No one died; no one was even injured badly or needed stitches. It just doesn't make sense." She looked at the trees lining the highway, taking in the rapidly moving landscape for a moment. "He won't do well behind bars, Elliot. He's not equipped for life on the inside."

"And how is your presence here going to help him, exactly?" he asked.

It was a legitimate question, yet it deepened her concern. "I'll be close to him, taking care of his house, of what few assets he has in this life. I'll speak to the judge; I've already asked for an appointment with him. And I'll speak with the warden, if he'll see me."

"You could've been better off staying an FBI agent to do all that, don't you think? Why not take a leave of absence, instead of leaving the bureau?"

Huh, she thought, *that went way beyond a casual question.* It was time to turn the tables on the nosy deputy.

"How do you know I'm not? Have you checked up on me?" she asked calmly, forcing her voice to not convey the anger and angst she was feeling.

"I made a few calls," he replied casually.

He sounded unapologetic, well within his rights, and maybe she'd caused that with her damned letters. If she'd only minded her own business, she wouldn't have one Elliot Young sniffing at her heels. But she couldn't do that; not when a killer was out there, most likely getting ready to kill again. Men like him never stopped killing.

"And what have you learned?" she asked calmly, forcing herself to smile with feigned amusement.

"Quite a lot," he replied. "I learned you left the FBI with minimal notice, but it would take you back in a heartbeat. I heard you're the best the San Francisco field office has seen in decades, no other profiler having the capacity to understand criminal behavior like you do. And I figured I had a valuable asset by my side, one who chose to write anonymous letters instead of talking to me directly, for some twisted reason."

"And?" she asked, holding her breath.

"Hey, I'll take what I can get, and I'll be grateful for it," he replied, keeping his eyes on the sloped, winding mountain road.

Again, she didn't believe him for one second. She'd failed to throw him off her scent.

"Your turn now," she said. "Why are you here, in Mount Chester, instead of Austin? Did you develop a sudden interest in winter sports?"

He clenched his jaw briefly, enough to let Kay know she'd hit a nerve.

"I screwed up on a case," he eventually said. "Back in Austin. My partner and I, we should've told our boss to reassign us; well, it's a long story. And I left. I wanted the stink of that screwup as far away from me as possible. If I'd stayed in Texas, it would've clung to me like muck on a pig."

"Strange," Kay reacted. "You don't strike me as the kind who runs away from the fallout of his mistakes."

"We're here," he announced, his words followed by a poorly disguised sigh of relief.

He held the door for her as they entered the county morgue, then, after a brief exchange with a lab technician wearing green scrubs, they entered the autopsy room.

"Hey, Doc," Elliot said.

She thought she recognized the silhouette of the man washing his hands at the stainless-steel sink. When he turned around to meet them, she smiled widely.

"Dr. Whitmore," she said, "what an unexpected surprise."

He apologized with a gesture for his dripping hands, and proceeded to wipe them on a towel, but Kay didn't care. She hugged him, and enjoyed the brief warmth of the bear clinch the doctor offered in return.

Stepping back, she noticed Elliot's surprised frown in passing, and she studied the medical examiner like one does a good friend who's been absent for a long time.

Dr. Whitmore had been the San Francisco County medical examiner for the first five years she'd been an FBI agent, their paths crossing often at crime scenes and in the autopsy room. She'd heard he'd retired and regretted not having had the opportunity to say goodbye, but here he was, just as she remembered him, leaning over the autopsy table, quietly whispering notes in his voice recorder and speaking soothingly to the victims as if they were alive and eager to be left alone, to find their peace at last.

He'd aged, but gracefully. His beard was entirely white, and so was his hair. He hadn't lost his hair like most men his age. He'd added a couple of pounds around his waist, but seemed the same as she remembered him, including his dark-rimmed glasses and jovial smile.

"It's been what, three years?" she asked.

"Yeah, about that long," he replied. "Time flies. How's life in San Francisco?"

"Same old," she replied. "Busy and more interesting than we'd care to have, but that's what happens when you're in the state that holds the crown for the most serial killers in the entire nation. I thought you retired," she added.

"I did," he replied. "I *am* retired. We have a house here, up on the mountain, by the ski slopes. There aren't many deaths happening here, thankfully, but when there are, they call me in. It's usually tourists getting in accidents; nothing like this."

"How about the county coroner?" Kay asked.

"You know just as well as I do, coroners aren't even required to have a college degree, not to mention an MD. But medical examiners are a different story. This case isn't one we can fumble with."

She approached the stainless-steel table, where a woman's body lay covered with a white sheet. The warmth of the reunion dissipated abruptly, leaving behind the chill of metallic instruments and X-rays affixed to the wall lightbox. She felt a shiver travel up her spine as she drew near the girl's body, as if the coldness that had engulfed her was somehow touching Kay's soul.

"What can you tell us about her?" she asked, her eyes drawn to the dark locks of hair that had slipped from underneath the sheet.

Dr. Whitmore uncovered the victim's face gently, peeling down the sheet until her neck was entirely exposed.

"This is Kendra Marshall, twenty-eight years old," Dr. Whitmore said, his voice loaded with sadness. "The official cause of death is asphyxia by manual strangulation."

Kay could see the discoloration where the killer's hands had crushed her throat, leaving bruising behind, and petechiae around the girl's eyes.

"Broken hyoid?" she asked, knowing that a fracture in the hyoid bone was an indicator of how forceful the strangulation had been.

"Yes," he confirmed. "Crushed trachea, shattered hyoid, actually. The killer was enraged."

"When did she die?" Elliot asked.

He'd stepped closer to the exam table, looking a little pale in the fluorescent lights.

"I'd put time of death about ten days ago, based on decomposition and insect activity," Dr. Whitmore said. "It's been cold, the perfect temperature to slow the decay of a body, and that widens the margin of error. I'll write it down as eight to twelve days ago, to be sure."

"I was about to ask if the autopsy report is done yet. I believe that means it's not?" Kay asked.

Dr. Whitmore sighed. "This is not San Francisco, and I'm not an official ME anymore, just a retiree no one rushes tox screens for. This is a preliminary report. I'll narrow down time of death in a couple of days."

Kay was starting to see how different things were, now that her badge was gone; the absence of her official status made a world of difference. It was probably the same for the retired doctor.

"Tell me everything you can, and we'll work with it," she offered.

He peeled off the white sheet completely, leaving Kendra's bruised body fully exposed under the strong lights. Pale. Vulnerable. Cold.

Kay repressed a shudder.

"Whoa," Elliot reacted, stepping back as if he'd seen a ghost.

Kay found his reaction strange. He must've seen dead bodies before, including Kendra's at the crime scene. She took a mental note to ask him what that was about, maybe on the drive back.

Kendra's body was covered in bruises and cuts, some older and some perimortem. The same type of bruising Kay saw around her neck was visible on her arms, her shoulders, her thighs.

She pointed at a cluster of such bruises, yellowish, almost healed. "Are these his fingers?"

"Exactly. He forcefully held her in place and handled her roughly. She was beaten, sexually assaulted, and tortured extensively for days; I'd say at least one week. That's how long it takes a bruise this deep to heal and turn yellow."

"Any assailant DNA?" Elliot asked.

"None, I'm afraid. He was thorough and careful about leaving any trace evidence on the body. I'm thinking he might've washed her body before burying her. The blanket she was wrapped in was moist, but that could've been from soil seepage."

"Not even under her fingernails?" Elliot insisted, earning himself a quick, disapproving glance from the medical examiner.

"There are no defensive wounds," he clarified, "at least not any new ones. It was as if she'd given up fighting. I've scraped, but I don't anticipate the lab will find anything we can use."

An out-of-town, apparently random victim; a killer who knew how to take forensic countermeasures; and tox screens that took more than five days to run. Not the trifecta Kay was hoping for.

"How was she found?" Kay asked.

Dr. Whitmore pulled up some crime scene photos on the large monitor hanging on the wall by their side. "She was buried face up, hands folded on her chest, completely naked and wrapped carefully in a new blanket," he said. "I found pieces of maple leaves and a couple of seed samaras on the blanket, but they could've been picked up from the surface or the soil. Fibers and source of the blanket are still pending."

The images on the screen showed Kendra's body neatly wrapped in the blanket as if she were a newborn baby, then the position of her arms folded at her chest after the ME had unwrapped her body at the scene. There was something deeply disturbing about how she was laid to rest, something Kay couldn't put her finger on.

"This looks ritualistic. Remorse?" she asked.

"Definitely," he confirmed. "The grave was shallow, but it was sheer luck she was discovered. Just a tourist whose dog wouldn't take no for a command."

He flipped the images on the screen. A couple of closeups of Kendra's head were displayed, showing her hair braided and tied with Native American hair ties.

She approached the screen and squinted. "Pomo," she said, referring to a Native American tribe with roots in the region. The local population still held a couple of hundred Native families, most of them Pomoan, although the Shasta tribe was also represented.

Kay had grown up immersed in the remnants of the local Native American culture and she could distinguish between the various tribes' cultural differences, no matter how minute.

"Not Shastan people?" Dr. Whitmore asked.

"I don't believe so," she replied. "See how the hair tie is braided from leather strips, my guess calf skin? That's Pomoan. And the feathers are waterfowl, not raptor."

Dr. Whitmore extracted a transparent evidence bag holding the hair ties. "I'm sending these to the San Francisco lab today, as a special request. Maybe it can find epithelials from the killer on the ties. Hopefully, he handled these with his bare hands, which means some skin cells might've adhered to the leather. I couldn't see any skin cells under the 'scope, but I don't have much of a lab here," he added apologetically.

Elliot took a photo of the hair ties with his phone.

"How about her hair?" Kay asked. "In the photos I see it was braided, but now it's not."

"I combed carefully through every strand. If the killer had braided it himself, we might catch a break. Epithelials found in her hair are pending DNA, but don't hold your breath; it could be all hers."

Kay squinted at the headshots again. The pale figure with the braided hair tied with the Pomoan hair ties seemed oddly familiar. *Where have I seen this before?* she thought. *Other than most powwows, that is.*

"Were her braids started low, behind the ears?" she asked. The photos weren't detailed enough to show. "Or here, above the ears, like Caucasian women would do it?"

"The braids started low," Dr. Whitmore said, pointing behind Kendra's right ear. "Then they were tucked behind the ears and drawn forward, to her chest, the feathers of the ties laid carefully, as they would hang naturally if the woman were standing."

"Again, Pomoan," Kay repeated her earlier finding. "This is his signature. Tell me about this blanket, the pattern on it, how dirt was laid out around her body, any boulders he might've used," she asked. "I want to see everything you have on how she was found. Maybe there's something in his signature I could use to generate a profile."

"You're thinking serial killer?" Dr. Whitmore asked.

"Yes. I know this is the only victim you have so far, but I'm willing to bet there are more out there. A serial killer isn't necessarily defined by the number of victims; the pathology of the kill is the telltale evidence. You can see his pathology in the way he tortured Kendra, in how the bruises line up on her body. He was methodical, sadistic and prolonged the pleasure he derived from overpowering her."

Dr. Whitmore exchanged a quick glance with Elliot.

"That's why you're the best," Dr. Whitmore replied. "You've always had a nose for these killers and their handiwork. No one could mislead you."

"What are you saying?" Kay asked, looking intently at the doctor.

"We found another woman's body," Elliot replied, "relatively close to where Kendra was found. But this vic had been dead for months. We have no identification yet."

"Yes," Dr. Whitmore said, pulling open a refrigerated drawer where he stored the bodies before and after the autopsies. The drawer held a woman's corpse, covered with a blue sheet. "Meet Jane Doe. All I could determine so far was the manner of death, also manual strangulation, supported by a shattered hyoid bone."

He exposed the victim's almost entirely decomposed skull and stepped aside.

Kay studied the body for a moment, then looked at Elliot impatiently. "I need to see the burial site."

CHAPTER SEVEN

Scream

He'd kept his word for exactly five minutes, not a second more.

He let her see Hazel, even allowed her to hug her little girl, while their tears mixed on their touching faces. He even had the decency to let her get dressed before bringing her daughter to see her.

"Mommy," Hazel had said, touching Alison's face with trembling fingers. "Don't cry," the girl had pleaded, while Alison folded her in her arms, afraid any moment he could yank Hazel away from her and lock her upstairs somewhere.

She forced herself to break the embrace and studied her baby's face, her hands, her arms and her legs. There was only one bruise on her forearm, but Hazel seemed shocked, staring into emptiness when she wasn't crying.

She'd wiped her tears and smiled, looking at Hazel's red, swollen eyes. "I won't cry, baby, I promise." She hugged her again, so tightly she tried to wriggle free. "What do you do all day, sweetheart?"

"Nothing," she replied, and Alison felt a wave of relief hearing her reply. "There's a boy here too."

Alison felt a pang of fear. "How old is that boy, baby?"

"He's little," Hazel replied, holding her hand at her shoulder level.

Alison let out a breath.

"When we go home, can we take him with us, Mommy?"

"Of course." She wiped her tears with the back of her hand. "He could be your little brother."

"When can we go home, Mommy? Can we go home now?"

There were no words, only tears springing from her eyes. She hugged her daughter again and buried her face in the girl's hair, just as the man returned and yanked her away.

"No, no, please don't take her," Alison begged, "give me one more minute, I'm begging you."

But he didn't even bother to respond. He dragged Hazel out of there kicking and screaming. She could hear her fighting him all the way upstairs, punching him with her little fists.

"Don't fight him, baby," she whispered, although Hazel couldn't hear her. "It will only be worse."

Hazel's sobs slowly faded until she couldn't hear them anymore, and regardless of how intently she listened, she couldn't hear the man's steps coming back downstairs.

What was he doing up there, alone with her daughter?

Was he touching her? Was he doing to Hazel what he'd been doing to her? Fear drove a hot knife through her gut.

"Oh, God, please, no… please don't let that be true. I'm begging you, watch over my baby."

She stood and started pacing the room, oblivious to the pain each step was causing her. She limped slightly and her belly hurt badly, but at least she wasn't bleeding anymore.

But where was he? Why wasn't he coming downstairs already?

She wanted him to come back to the basement, although she knew exactly what to expect from his presence. But she would do anything to keep that monster away from her daughter, even if for a minute.

Was he hurting her, and she couldn't hear it because he was gagging her, like he'd done on the first day? What if she's—

No… she couldn't think like that. Obsessive thoughts circled in her mind, running over the same terrifying scenario in wide, incessant loops of pure horror. No. Her daughter had to be fine. They both would be fine, and they would soon go home. They'd both escape, any moment now.

But what about that boy? Where did he come from? Was his mother like her, a prisoner in the basement? Since she'd been there, hers were the only screams she'd heard. Her own and Hazel's.

Out of her mind with despair, she paced the room like a caged animal, mumbling prayers and senseless words, conjuring a future where Hazel and she would be back home again, safe and secure together. Eating dinner. Watching cartoons on TV. Doing all those things they'd done together that she'd taken for granted so many times before.

Finally, the lock turned, and the door opened, letting the man enter. Whimpering, she rushed to the opposite corner of the room and crouched on the floor, her back against the cold concrete bricks, watching him standing there, staring at her.

He wasn't some crazy mountain man she couldn't hope to communicate with. With an immense effort, she willed herself to study him, to try to understand him. He was dressed cleanly, in slacks and a blue shirt, starched and pressed. His shoes looked new and expensive. His skin seemed soft except for his bruised knuckles, acquired when he'd pounded on her. Swallowing some rising bile, she admitted he seemed almost attractive if it weren't for that sickening blood lust in his terrifying eyes.

She forced her lungs to fill with air and stood, unsure on her feet and shaking badly, to be closer to his eye level.

"It's a shame this is happening," she managed to articulate, then ventured a timid smile. "If you'd asked me on a date, I would've said yes."

He laughed heartily, the echoes of his voice reverberating eerily against the basement walls.

Blinking away her tears, she continued, her voice breaking as she spoke. "We could've had dinner, talked, and—"

"You think I want a date?" he asked between cackles. "You think I want to hear you speak?" He took a step closer and she flinched, ready to run back to her corner, but he was faster. He grabbed her and whispered in her ear, "All I want is to hear you scream."

CHAPTER EIGHT

Site

It was a relatively short drive from the morgue to the northeast tip of Cuwar Lake, and Kay immersed herself in her thoughts, absently looking at the stunning landscape. The road to the lake, a narrow and winding strip of asphalt bordered by tall firs and the occasional oak or maple, used to be her favorite road trip before she moved away. It seemed like a lifetime ago, the last time she'd visited the lake without looking for a body dump site; a different age, an innocent age, although at the time she would've vehemently objected to that label. She'd stopped being innocent a long time ago.

Elliot chewed on a piece of straw he'd picked from the front lawn of the morgue and stared a little too intently at the road ahead, as if trying to avoid her scrutiny. Maybe it was time for him to get a taste of his own medicine.

"So, what was that all about in there?" she asked.

"I sure don't know what you're talking about," he replied morosely.

She didn't back down. "You, acting like you've never seen a corpse before?"

He removed the straw from his mouth, studied it for a brief moment, then lowered the window and threw it out. The crisp fall air filled her nostrils with the scent of fallen leaves, of wet tree bark and moist earth.

"Not like that, I haven't," he admitted, visibly embarrassed.

"Ah," she reacted. Things must've been peaceful in Austin. If she remembered correctly, Elliot's hometown hadn't seen a serial killer since the Servant Girl Annihilator, who preyed on the city of Austin between 1884 and 1885 and was never caught. Austin held the infamous honor of having been the city to produce the first serial killer in the history of the United States, but since the Annihilator, no other serial killer had called the emerging metropolis home. "It can be off-putting," she added, choosing her words carefully. "But I thought you'd seen Kendra's body before, at the lake?"

"Not, um, like that," he mumbled.

He probably meant not naked under the cold, merciless neon lights, her body covered in cuts and bruises all over, each bearing testimony to her terrible ordeal.

"What do you think about the way she was buried?" she asked, satisfied to see his shoulders relaxing a little when she changed the subject. "Have you seen this before?"

"We found the other vic, and she was wrapped the same way."

"I meant, outside of these two body finds," she clarified.

"N—no, can't say that I have." He glanced at her quickly, enough for her to catch his raised eyebrow.

"I haven't either," she replied, speaking slowly, deeply immersed in thoughts. "It resembles old Native American burial customs, but mixed and matched, not like a single tribe's custom. More like the killer took something from one tribe, something else from another, and so on."

"You recognize them?" He made a vague gesture with his hand.

"Some of it, yes," she replied, still thinking, gathering pieces of the ceremonial puzzle. "Some Native American tribes wrap their dead in blankets, together with jewelry or other possessions, things the spirits would need in the other world. Was anything else found with their bodies?"

"Nothing else, nope."

"But they never wrap the bodies like that," she added, continuing her previous chain of thought. "Not at an angle."

Based on what she'd seen in Dr. Whitmore's crime scene photos, the body had been laid on the blanket diagonally, head at one corner and feet at the opposite corner. One corner of the blanket had been folded above her feet, then the sides brought over the body, left side first, then the right side. Like swaddling a baby, except the head corner had been folded to cover the victim's face.

To cover? Or to protect from dirt?

Guilt? Or shame?

"The braiding of the hair also speaks of Native American customs," she added.

"That part I figured," he replied. "What do you make of it? Neither victim was Native. Doc Whitmore said Jane Doe was Caucasian."

She shrugged. "Looks familiar to me, but I can't place it."

"I'm sure you've seen women wear their hair like that before, haven't you? This is Native country."

She smiled, a distant childhood memory filling her heart with a swell of warmth. The smell of mutton on the spit, sage sprinkled and burned, eastern hemlock tea served in ceramic mugs against a backdrop of a lonely canyon flute invoking the spirits and asking for rain. She had the privilege of growing up close to the Native peoples of the region, many times thinking she belonged more to their tribe than to the white man's. And in a Native household she'd found refuge and solace many times, which was lacking in her own home.

But this was different. Eerie almost, in the way it felt personal, for some reason that was not evident. As if Kendra's hair was not hers, was someone else's.

"I've seen braided hair before," she replied, choosing to keep most of her thoughts to herself, and all of her memories. "But this particular style of braiding, and the hair ties he used, obviously handmade, remind me of something specific."

He frowned, glancing at her quickly, then turning his attention to the road.

The forest was starting to clear; they were nearing the northeast corner of the lake, where the road was closest to the water. Only two or three minutes to the burial site, which was off the North Shore Road, about one mile after passing the viewpoint, right on the southern limit of the national forest. She knew very well where that was, but didn't feel like sharing that particular bit of information.

"Like what?" he asked, probably knowing he wasn't going to get an answer.

"It will come to me at some point," she replied, stretching her legs.

They had arrived.

The place looked different in broad daylight. Lengths of yellow police tape still clung to the trunks of several trees, moving gently in the evening breeze, although they'd been torn when the sheriff's office released the scene. Two separate sections had been cordoned off, but she didn't need to see that to know where the bodies had been buried. Park services hadn't been by, apparently, to clean up and restore the illusion of normality to the area.

She'd seen Kendra's grave the night before, when she'd visited by herself and crossed the police tape, then uncut, to study the open grave from up close. Back then, in the cone of her flashlight, she'd noticed the fallen maple leaves and samaras, but hadn't thought much of it. She hadn't noticed the large maple tree the night before, and she hadn't seen Kendra's body yet. She hadn't seen her braided hair, and the leather and feathers hair ties. She hadn't seen the pattern on the blankets, a Shastan geometrical motif on dark brown, framing a centered design featuring feathers tied together with a blood-red leather twine and carried by an arrow.

As if their bodies had been laid to rest on a bed of feathers, to shield and protect them from all evil.

Like in the old days, when a tribe mourned the death of a loved one.

Except for one tiny detail.

Kay took a few steps back and looked at the maple tree above Kendra's grave. Its crown was wide enough, and the thick branches ramified low enough to create a natural platform.

"Take off your belt," she asked Elliot, while removing hers with quick moves.

"Whoa," he said, laughing, his eyebrows raised above his amused eyes. "Really?"

"Don't get your hopes up, cowboy," she replied. "I need to climb up there," she said, pointing a finger at the tree's massive crown.

"Oh," he replied, all amusement gone from his face, replaced readily with embarrassment and a bit of gloom. "Why the hell would you want to do that?"

"Because the only thing that doesn't add up is the burial," she explained. "Many Native tribes use a burial tree and place the bodies of the deceased at the fork of that tree."

He sized up the tall trunk and frowned. "Are you sure? Putting a body up there would take some serious doing," he added. "Above average strength, or maybe a rope system with pulleys. But she was buried, right? We dug her out of *there*," he added, gesturing with his hand toward the open grave that gaped wide and dark only a few feet away.

"Yes, and that burial is the only piece that doesn't fit."

He took off his wide-brimmed hat and scratched his head, then put it back on. "Fit what?"

"The old Native burial rituals," she replied calmly.

Many Native tribes believed that contact with the deceased's body could bring sickness, misfortune, or even death, so burial was a simple, quick process, attended by very few. Some tribes burned the possessions of the deceased; other tribes, like the Seminole, would throw all the deceased's possessions into a swamp, then relocate their entire settlements to move away from the place touched by death. But there were also tribes who buried their dead in burial mounds, mostly the Ohio River Valley peoples.

"I'll do it." Elliot hesitated, considering the best way to climb to the tree fork, and then took the leather belt she was offering. He removed his, then attached the two belts together. He then looped the extended belt around the tree trunk and his body, securing the end through the buckle, and trying it with a couple of vigorous tugs.

"What am I looking for, up there? 'Cause the view don't interest me worth a truckload of manure on fire."

She turned away to hide her smile. He was as colorful as he was smart, that was for sure. "Fibers. Evidence that she was laid to rest there, for any length of time. Better take these with you," she added, offering several small evidence bags and tweezers from his field kit.

He took them and shoved them into his shirt pocket, then started climbing the tree, testing the resistance of the belts only a couple of feet off the ground, leaning heavily against them. They held.

Nevertheless, Kay held her breath all the time it took him to get to the fork. When he was safely there she breathed, while memories flooded her mind. The first time she'd seen a Native burial. How the tribe selected burial trees, and where they were usually located. How she'd cried at the root of one, looking up through the branches at Grandma Aiyana's body and calling her name until Grandpa Old Bear had covered her mouth with his warm, withered hand and taught her to never call the dead, to let the spirit be on its way, undisturbed by the grief of the living. They weren't her grandparents, they were Judy's, but they'd raised her just as much as her own parents had, maybe even more.

"You were right," she heard Elliot's voice above her head. It startled her, tearing her away from fond memories and immersing her into the cold reality. She looked up and saw him waving an evidence pouch in the air. "I found blanket fibers."

"You can come down now," she shouted. "If we need more, we can borrow a platform truck from the power company and get a crime scene technician up there to pore over every branch."

"Hate to disappoint you, but here in the boonies we do our own evidence collection," he said, starting to climb back down carefully. "There is no crime scene technician."

"Wait," she said, and thought she heard a muffled oath. "Take a look around, see if you can spot another burial tree nearby. They're large, have a wide fork where the body can be placed, and they're deciduous." He stared at her without a word, but she understood his unspoken question. "The only trees fit to be chosen as burial trees are ones that shed their leaves every fall, mimicking the cycle of life, death, and being reborn, resonating with the sacred ritual in every aspect."

He looked around, shifting carefully to get a 360-degree view of the area. Then he climbed down and found her near Kendra's grave, studying the access road, the tire tracks in the soil.

"There might be other burial trees," he said apologetically. "It's hard to tell with all the foliage. We'd have to walk the ground looking up, I guess. But I found where he roped her up to the tree fork, if that's helpful."

"What did you see?"

He waved a couple of evidence pouches in front of her eyes, smiling. "Right next to the fork, the bark was torn off a branch, and fibers from a rope still clung to it. I got us some samples."

Everything was helpful in an investigation, every tiny sliver of evidence could become a piece of the puzzle that, when completed at least in some significant measure, could help her visualize who the killer was. Because everything he chose to do or not do spoke about the processes in his mind, about his obsessions, his compulsions, his fantasies.

"He brought her here by truck," she said, "and the earth was disturbed around both burial sites. Was it like this when she was found? Or did the crime unit disturb the ground like this?"

"The ground was disturbed when we found her," he confirmed, "but here the climate is tough, and any ground disturbance disappears in a week or two at the most. We have rain, sleet, snow, wildlife, the works."

"Gee, I didn't know that," she replied sarcastically. "I'm new to the area, you know."

He shook his head, mumbling something she didn't hear and probably didn't want to. She walked quickly to the other gravesite, and, looking up, found what could've well been the other burial tree. This time an old oak, with the fork much larger and much closer to the ground, but a thicker trunk that would've made climbing more difficult.

She looked at the path he'd taken to reach the site. As in the other location, many tire tracks could be seen, turning the forest trail into a two-rutted path that would've been difficult to travel after rainfall.

If she remembered correctly, many of these paths cut through Cuwar Lake Forest, one of the most popular tourist attractions in the area during summertime. Young couples looking for solitude, families camping and fishing by the lakeshore, tourists looking to spend an afternoon in the gentle sun, all drove from the main road toward the lake, seeking such unpaved roads or creating them in their large, off-road vehicles, cutting new trails through the forest.

That's how he got to the oak tree fork. He'd driven his truck all the way to the tree, then climbed on the cab holding her body in his arms. From there, he could've easily lifted her and set her on the fork. Even an SUV would've worked, not as easily as a truck, but still.

She walked slowly, looking at the base of the tree, searching for a tire track that almost brushed against the trunk. The weather had already taken its toll, heavy rainfall dumping fresh leaves and washing away dirt.

"He took a different path for each girl," Kay said, frowning. It was almost dark now, and a strong chill dropped from the mountains, making her shiver. "Can we get cadaver dogs, here in the boonies?" The moment she'd voiced the request, a shiver traveled down her spine, triggered by the smell of damp, leaf-covered earth.

"We sure can," he replied, sounding almost proud, as if the K9 unit was his own accomplishment. "Do you think there are more?"

"I'm willing to bet there are," she replied, hints of her grim thoughts coming across clearly in her voice. There was no way of knowing how many without help. Walking the forest looking for burial trees and disturbed ground made no sense; some of his victims could've been laid to rest a long time ago.

Leaning against a large Douglas fir, Elliot adjusted the brim of his hat. "You didn't tell me, why bury them in the ground, if the ritual called for this tree burial instead, and he'd done that already?"

She'd wondered that herself. "The spirit should be able to escape easily, that's the main reason why the bodies are placed up in the trees, to be closer to the stars. But after the spirit escapes the confines of its human form, the body can be buried in the ground. It rarely was, back in the old days." She sighed as she cleaned the dirt off her hands as best as she could, then ran her hands against her arms a few times, to warm herself. "But I believe he did it as a forensic countermeasure. He didn't want the bodies to be found, and so he buried them. He couldn't risk tourists looking up and seeing the bodies up there, above their heads."

"Smart guy, this one. I wonder what he does with them during winter, when the ground is frozen like a desert boulder," Elliot said. He'd been silent, not offering much in terms of dialogue, but she could tell his wheels were turning.

"That is, if he really killed more than the two we've found, but I guess we would've heard something by now," he continued. "What does he do? Stops killing for the season?"

"I'll tell you what he does," she replied calmly. "Remember how the autopsy showed new and healed wounds? He keeps them hostage and tortures them until the ground thaws enough to bury them. How long has Kendra been missing?"

CHAPTER NINE
Sheriff

"What the hell were you thinking?"

Franklin County Sheriff Stephen Logan rarely shouted, but Elliot had probably pushed one of his buttons without even knowing it. Logan stood behind his desk in the posture he usually assumed for video conferences or interviews, against a backdrop of the stars and stripes and the California Republic bear, his native state's colors.

Logan leaned forward, planting his palms flat on the surface of his desk. Elliot maintained eye contact and cleared his voice.

"Boss, I thought she'd be useful, that's all. Being she is who she is."

"And who is she, exactly? A civilian. You coopted a civilian into the investigation and didn't think I needed to at least know about it ahead of time?"

"Sorry, boss," Elliot replied, lowering his gaze for a moment. "She's done this a lot, and she can help us get ahead of this guy. I didn't think you'd mind."

"If I wanted the FBI's behavioral analysts involved, I would've given them a call. Why do we need one of them, and not even an active one, to help us catch a killer? Can't you do your job?"

Elliot asked himself the same question. What was it, really, that had led him to visit Kay Sharp the day before? He was a good cop, with a decent case-solving record, who knew how to catch a killer. It wasn't as if he needed handholding or anything.

He raised his eyes, meeting his boss's glare. "Damn sure I can," he replied. "But none of us has dealt with a serial killer before, and she has," he added.

"What serial killer?" Logan asked, his voice a little quieter, as if afraid the words might leave the confines of his office and spread like wildfire in the community. "We have two bodies, last time I heard. Not more."

"She said it's about the pathology of the kill, not the number. It used to be five kills, before, then three. That's what I knew. But she said—"

"Drop it with what she said, already," Logan snapped, then sat in his leather chair with a groan of frustration. "This place has never seen a serial killer. Hell, we haven't even seen a *murder* since nineteen eighty-nine, when Dick Joshua came home drunk and found his wife in bed with the plumber. Are you sure it's a serial killer?"

Elliot nodded, the brim of his hat accentuating the movement of his head. "That's why I thought she could help, FBI badge or not."

Rubbing the root of his nose between the thumb and index of his right hand, Logan kept his eyes closed for a moment. Then he traced the lines flanking his mouth with the same two fingers, as if to wipe away the tension keeping his features frozen in a grimace of tiredness, despite the early morning hour and the almost-empty coffee mug on his desk.

"We can't have a civilian involved in the investigation," Logan said, his voice now back to the normal that Elliot knew well. "If this gets out, it will be hell to pay; the people and the media will be all over us. How much time do you need to sort through this mess?"

With how little he knew about catching serial killers, Elliot had no idea what to answer. He'd seen enough crime drama on TV, but the timelines of real-life crime policing were entirely different. About forty percent of murders remained unsolved, especially those with random victims who couldn't be linked to their assailants. And if not solved in the first few days, a murder case stood a great chance of turning cold.

"I need a few days, four or five," he said. "By then, we—"

"You have two days," Logan replied coldly.

He knew it was pointless to argue.

"Yes, sir." Elliot took two steps toward the door when Logan stopped him with a hand gesture.

"I hope you're doing this for the right reasons, Detective. I've seen good people getting fired over less."

Elliot nodded and left, then walked straight to his car, wondering if he *was* doing it for the right reasons. The woman drove him nuts anyway, with her questions, her assumptions, and the way her mind worked. What made it worse was she was right so darn often, and that made him think he maybe didn't deserve to carry the gold-starred badge in his wallet, not when a serial killer was at large. The woman had a brain the size of a big ol' pickup truck, and attitude to match.

Up a tree? Really? Not in a million years he would've thought to look there for probative evidence. That spoke to her abilities as a profiler, of which he was in absolute awe. It was the way she'd written her letters, addressed to "The lead detective investigating the Cuwar Lake murder," that had drawn him to knock on her door the day before. She'd been articulate, to the point, offering a fresh perspective and some angles he hadn't thought of before—and all that had been before he'd actually *met* Dr. Kay Sharp. Since then, since she'd opened her front door the morning before, in her paint-stained jeans and an oversized shirt that probably belonged to her brother, he'd been able to think of not much else but her.

And the last time he'd experienced that, it ended badly.

He'd just made detective in Travis County, Texas, and he'd been assigned a partner, a rookie he was to train on the job.

Charlene Sealy.

There had never been anyone more wrong for the job of detective in the entire history of the Lone Star State.

Or more fitting.

She was the stunning, twenty-five-year-old daughter of a Texas farmer. By farmer, Elliot understood someone raising cattle on a twenty-acre ranch, while she had meant the farmer who owned a large portion of central Texas and an entire vertical of food industry operations, from meat packaging plants to meat processing, food manufacturing and distribution.

At first, he didn't correlate his new partner's last name with the most expensive brand of T-bone or ribeye cuts on the shelves at local stores.

When he did, he tried to understand why a multimillion-dollar heiress would choose to chase perps in the scorching, dust-filled heat for a measly detective salary. It seemed, though, that her entire life, Charlene had dreamed of becoming a cop and had prepared for it, breaking the gilded hearts of her parents. She'd graduated cum laude from Texas University with a criminal justice degree, and she was smart. Brilliant. There was a cunning about her that enabled her to anticipate the moves of the most hardened criminals, and with looks like hers, their defenses dropped down enough for her to read right through them, then read them their rights.

It was impossible not to fall in love with Charlene Sealy, and Elliot had resisted for the longest time, knowing he had little in common with the Sealy empire heiress, other than a passion for the job. Soon though, he could think of little else but her, and counted the hours before the start of a new shift.

When they were assigned a case involving drug trafficking over the Mexico border with ramifications on both sides, they jumped on the opportunity. A large drug bust would be a career maker, and they both believed they could make a difference in the war against the white death.

When their investigation took them to a distant relative of the powerful Sealy clan, they discussed it for a moment. Elliot, as the senior detective, had suggested they inform the sheriff and see if he wanted them reassigned. But Charlene was one hell of a cop who didn't want to let go; she knew they were close to making a bust, and didn't care that a distant uncle was using his family home as a coyote hub, charging them one kilo of cocaine per transit.

But the DA cared, and so did the Travis County sheriff, when the case against Charlene's distant relative blew apart in court with the help of an expensive team of defense attorneys who exposed the family connection and claimed the investigation had been tainted by a vendetta dating back generations over a large piece of farmland.

The only thing that had saved their jobs was that they had worked the case by the book, in all aspects except for not disclosing Charlene's personal connection to one of the main suspects. The other defendants in the case were all sentenced accordingly, which made little sense in the grand scheme of things, considering Charlene's distant uncle walked.

In a meeting with the sheriff Elliot couldn't forget, they were both given the terms under which they could continue to serve the county as detectives. Swallowing tears of frustration, Charlene stated that the moment her uncle ran a traffic light or rolled through a stop sign, she'd be there to bust him, but ended up signing a letter saying she was to keep her distance from all family members involved in criminal activities, and immediately report such activities to her sergeant. Elliot earned himself a letter of reprimand on his permanent record, and was assigned to the night shift for the foreseeable future.

And they weren't going to team up together anymore. It was written.

Before the end of the meeting, Elliot resigned. Outside, feeling cold in the mid-July heat, he hugged Charlene and left, responding to her wall of objections with a shake of his head and keeping his eyes hidden under the brim of his hat. He walked away without having told her how he felt, without having held her except for that last goodbye embrace.

A few months later, he took the detective job in Mount Chester, grateful for the frigid climate, because everything having to do with heat reminded him of Charlene. Her sleeveless white tops she wore at work. Tiny droplets of sweat forming above her upper lip. Her smile, the way she threw her hair back and looked at him over her shoulder, saying, "Hot dang, partner, are you coming? Can't afford to keep those perps waiting in this heat, now can we?"

Mount Chester had been peaceful for him with its frozen winters, pristine white snow covering the mountains six months a year and crystal blue skies like he'd never seen anywhere else. He'd established himself, with a solid record and good case closure rates, and had earned the respect of his adoptive community.

Then Kay Sharp had appeared, with her letters, her profiling skills, and an unexpected vulnerability he perceived to exist disguised under her appearance of strength. And he could think of little else but her.

Last time he was so eager to start work each day it ended up in a raging ball of fire, burning him so badly he had to leave his beloved Texas behind and chill his heart in the frozen mountain winters to forget about Charlene. Getting work mixed with personal issues was a terrible idea, and he knew that better than anyone else.

This time, the sheriff had stepped in and had set a time limit to his collaboration with Dr. Kay Sharp, although he wasn't kidding himself as to the real reason why he hadn't given his boss the heads-up about bringing Kay in on the case.

"So, there, go shoot yourself in the foot again," he mumbled to himself when he got behind the wheel of his SUV. "Let's see where you move to this time. Alaska?"

Still, as he peeled off, heading out to meet Kay, he was smiling.

CHAPTER TEN

Broken

Elliot was quiet for most of the drive, and Kay wondered whether she had anything to do with his silence. He'd picked her up as planned, to visit with the Christensen family, but had hardly spoken a word since he'd said, "Howdy," with a tip of the hat.

It was a mild October day, when the sun still showed it had the power to defeat the night's cold shadows, and the drive over the mountain to the Christensens was an unexpected joy. She didn't think she'd feel that way about any aspect of her life back in Mount Chester, but she had to admit there had been things she'd missed about her hometown. The scents filling the air when the sun hit the dew-covered grass on a fall morning. The chirping of the jays and warblers, interrupted at times by eagle cries that scared them all into silence for a while, fearing the predator circling above their heads. The snow-covered crests of the mountain, staying forever white, a postcard view against the California blue sky.

"They helped us identify Kendra, you know," Elliot broke the silence as he turned onto the street where the family lived. "They saw the TV ad we were running, and called it in."

"Uh-huh," she replied, her mind piecing the puzzle together. A legal assistant from New York, who was about to visit a family in Mount Chester about an inheritance. Yet they recognized her from a TV ad? "Where had they seen her before? If they'd never met?"

"To recognize her, you mean? They didn't."

"You just said—"

"They called and said the person they were supposed to meet with never showed. We took it from there."

Elliot pulled up at the curb in front of the modest ranch and cut the engine. She approached the front door, but didn't get a chance to knock. A middle-aged woman with a pleasant smile opened the door, inviting them in.

"You must be the detectives," she said, and Kay didn't think she needed to clarify her status. "Please, come in. We were expecting you."

Stepping inside the Christensens' home was like visiting another chapter of her childhood. The quilt-covered sofa, clean but a little worn out, was a mainstay in every local living room. A fresh pot of coffee, ready to be served, waited for them on the dining room table, set on a silver tray and surrounded by simple white ceramic cups. Mrs. Christensen busied herself with the cups, then rushed to the kitchen to bring sugar and milk.

A man stood with visible difficulty, walking over to greet them with a bent back and an extended hand. He had the build of a day laborer, but kind eyes and a warm, baritone voice. Straightening his back, he smiled, the smile not touching his grim eyes. "Paul Christensen," he said, shaking Kay's hand, then Elliot's. "Please, make yourselves at home."

He looked at them with unguarded curiosity, rubbing his hand against his three-day stubble. "This is an unfortunate occasion, but if you don't mind me saying, we like having people over."

Kay smiled. "Thank you for having us, Mr. Christensen."

"Please, call me Paul," he replied simply.

It was hard not to like him. He was fifty-four years old, and had worked for the US Forest Service all his life. His wife, Madeline, was a nurse, and she was five years younger than him. That was the extent of the information police records were able to provide about the couple. That, and the fact that they had no criminal record and had always filed their taxes on time.

"And you can call me Maddie," the woman said, offering Kay a cup of coffee.

She took it with a nod. There was something pleasant about the woman, almost motherly. Her hair was short, but that didn't take away from her femininity; quite the opposite. And there was a warmth in her eyes, almost like a glow. Kay had only seen that in people who really loved what they did for a living. Instead of the harshness the years of labor can bring over one's features, there's a sense of accomplishment, of achievement, of having made a difference. Maddie's interior warmth was a testimony to that, although nursing was never an easy job.

Intrigued, Kay asked, "Maddie, please call me Kay. And that's Elliot, over there."

She nodded, and her smile widened.

"What do you do for a living, if I may ask?"

"I'm a neonatal nurse," she replied with pride in her voice. "I work in Redding. It's a bit of a drive every day, tough to do in winter, but I get to work with babies, and that makes it all worthwhile."

That explained it. Kay looked around the room and didn't see photos of a large family; only Maddie and Paul in a couple of instances, but that was it. The couple probably didn't have children of their own.

"We have a few questions about Kendra Marshall," Elliot said, accepting a cup of coffee from Maddie's hands. "Thank you, ma'am."

The woman's smile vanished. "What an unspeakable tragedy," she whispered. "And right here, in the heart of our community, where we've always felt safe."

"What do you need to know?" Paul asked.

"Anything you can tell us," Kay replied. "How did you come to know Kendra?"

Maddie pulled out a chair and sat, then took a sip of coffee from her mug.

"We didn't know her at all," Maddie said. "She called us sometime mid-September. She worked at a law firm, um, what was it called?" She turned toward Paul with an inquisitive glance. "It was Abrams, DeSanto, and what?"

"Parsons, I think," Paul replied. "Yes, Parsons."

"Yes, them. Poor Kendra called to say Paul's estranged father had recently passed."

"I'm sorry to hear that," Kay offered. "Please accept my condolences."

"Thanks," the man replied, his glance sideways for a moment. "I haven't seen him since I was in high school. But I guess these lawyers tracked me down here, and sent Kendra."

"Why was she coming to see you?"

"To review his estate documents with me," Paul replied, "and those were her words, not mine. No idea what that really meant."

"Was your father wealthy?" Elliot asked, evidently wondering if there could've been a financial connection to the murder. But even if old Mr. Christensen had died a rich man, the killer had taken the life of a legal assistant, not the heir of the Christensen estate.

"I don't have a clue," Paul replied with a shrug. "When he left my mother and me, I never expected to hear from him again, and, honestly, I never thought anything of worth would come out of that man, least of all an estate."

So, no love lost there, with the passing of Mr. Christensen senior. But all that was probably irrelevant to the case, Kay determined.

"When was the last time you spoke with Kendra?" Elliot asked, looking at Paul first, then at Maddie.

"I spoke with her, I'd say about a week or ten days before she was supposed to get here," Maddie replied. "She seemed like a nice person. She sounded helpful, willing to travel all this way just to meet us and walk us through what the probate process would entail."

"When was she supposed to meet you?"

"On the thirtieth," Maddie replied. "It was a Thursday. We waited, but she didn't call us either way. We just assumed something had delayed her arrival, and didn't worry about it." She covered her eyes briefly as she spoke, running her hand across her forehead.

Shame, or maybe guilt, Kay observed. But for what?

"Either way?" Kay asked.

"Kendra told us she'd call us when she arrived and got a hotel room. She had tickets to fly in the day before. The appointment for the thirtieth was tentative; she was supposed to call to firm up the time."

That had been three weeks ago. Apparently, she had arrived in the area on September 29, and Dr. Whitmore had estimated she died around October 10.

"Did you call the law firm to ask what was going on?"

Maddie stood and walked over to Paul's armchair, then sat on the wide armrest, leaning slightly against her husband's shoulder.

"No," she eventually replied, lowering her gaze and clasping her hands together. When she looked at Kay, her eyes were filled with tears. "You have to understand, we didn't think anything of it at the time. It wasn't as if we were eager to deal with Paul's father's estate, you know." She paused for a moment. "Now we blame ourselves. If we would've said something, or called the law firm to say she didn't make it, maybe she would be alive today."

Paul reached out and grabbed Maddie's hand, squeezing it tightly. He stared at the floor, the grim expression on his face carving deep lines on his forehead. When he spoke, his voice was filled with bitterness.

"We live in the age of indifference," Paul said, "where people don't care about people anymore. We watch TV, and pretend we're social on the internet. I thought we were different, Maddie and I, but seems that, when put to the test, we have proven we're not. We are really sorry," he added, squeezing his wife's hand again and looking briefly at Kay, then at Elliot. "We are just as much to blame for her death as that sick bastard is."

"That's not true—" Kay started to say, but Maddie cut her off.

"I hope you catch him, before he does this to someone else."

They left the Christensen residence and drove in silence for a while, Paul and Maddie's guilt weighing heavily on Kay's mind. Were they right? Had the age of indifference spread its shroud over humanity, darkening the very essence of society's fabric? What else could explain that no one had reported Kendra missing with the local authorities, when she was supposed to arrive on the twenty-ninth, and at least her employer had to have known her destination? And, since she'd probably flown into San Francisco, how did she get to Mount Chester? Where did the killer set his sights on her?

"Something doesn't add up," she said, breaking the silence halfway to the town. "Why don't we go back to my brother's place? I need to make some calls and we might as well grab a bite to eat."

"Uh-huh," he replied, shooting her a quick glance. "What's on your mind?"

"She'd been missing for seventeen days when her body was found, and yet no one had filed a missing person report with the county. Her employer should've tracked her down. I'm pretty sure the company paid for her travel expenses, most likely with a corporate card. We need to speak to someone there."

He acknowledged her with a nod, then turned to her briefly and asked, "How about Jane Doe? She wasn't reported missing in the area either. If she was like Kendra, a traveler from a different part of the country, it makes you wonder."

"What?" she asked, not sure she followed his train of thought.

He pulled in front of her house, and she cringed, seeing the state of the lawn. If he was put off by the state of the property, he wasn't letting on.

"All that stuff Paul Christensen was saying, about the age of indifference. How can these women disappear, without anyone looking for them? People just falling through the cracks like that, it's not normal."

She wondered if she should share the story of the man who had died at his desk, in the open office he shared with over twenty other people, and no one around him noticed for several days. She'd read his story in the *New York Times*, but the man's sad demise was no surprise to her. It wasn't the age of indifference, like Paul had stated; it was the age of self-absorption and of informational overload, driving people crazy with the stress of an excessively demanding life and corroding the core values of humanity.

"Right," she replied instead, opening the front door, reluctant to take the first breath of air inside the house. It wasn't as bad as she'd found it when she'd arrived from San Francisco, but she should've plugged in air fresheners anyway. "I'll get some coffee started, then we'll take it outside on the porch while I make some calls, all right?"

Elliot stood in the doorway, hat in hand, watching her move around the kitchen with a curious expression on his face. She smiled briefly and shot him an inquisitive glance, while pouring water into the coffee maker. "Penny for your thoughts?"

Running his hand through his wavy hair, he pushed it backward, away from his forehead. "Just wondering why you came back to live here, that's all," he replied, and she instantly regretted asking him. "No one in their right mind would leave what you had there to come here to this," he added, underlining his words with a vague hand gesture.

"Huh," she chuckled quietly, keeping her face turned away from him while loading the machine with a fresh filter and a few spoonfuls of ground coffee. "No offense taken," she added, sprinkling a little humor in the tone of her voice.

Thankfully, he stopped with the questions, resigning himself to lean against the wall, hat still in hand, as if eager to get out of there as soon as possible. That part she could relate to.

She opened a cupboard and pulled out two mugs, but then froze. One of them had a broken handle, the remnants of the handle sharp and weathered like broken wisdom teeth, dark crack lines running across them like spiderwebs. Feeling the color draining from her face, she grabbed the mug and threw it in the trash, so forcefully it shattered into countless pieces, the loud noise startling her.

At least she won't have to see *that* again.

Not ever.

CHAPTER ELEVEN

Shards

Her father was at it again, and, by the sound of it, it wasn't going to end well.

Swallowing her tears, Katherine grabbed Jacob's hand and dragged the little boy behind the sofa, where they both crouched down, waiting for the storm to be over.

Sometimes, that happened quickly. Other times, her father's bellowing would rattle the windows for hours in a row.

"Goddammit, Pearl, what did I say to you, huh?" he shouted, every other word an oath. "How many more days do I have to come home to snotty brats and uncooked dinner?"

He threw himself on the sofa, and the old piece of furniture groaned under his weight. Katherine and Jacob withdrew into the corner of the room, behind an armchair, putting more distance between them and their enraged father.

"Gavin, please," their mother said, her voice loaded with unshed tears. "It's not like I don't go to work every day."

"And do what?" the man replied with venom in his thunderous voice. "Sit on a comfy chair and shuffle papers all day long, while I break my back laying concrete to keep you and your brats fed?" He wiped his hands against the front of his sleeveless undershirt, leaving trails of sweat and grime against the worn fabric. Then he ran his hand against the surface of the coffee table and held it in the air for

his wife to see. "How long has it been since you wiped this damn table, huh? Is it too much to ask to eat on a clean table?"

Pearl dropped what she was doing and rushed to clean the table with a wet rag. She cleared the table of all the items, the TV remote, a couple of wine glasses from the night before, and the dirty plate from that morning's breakfast.

Watching, Katherine wondered why her dad didn't put his plate and his wine glass in the sink, just like she and Jacob did with their own dishes.

Her mother started to wipe the table, when her father leaped and snatched the rag from her hand, then threw it in her face.

"You're wiping my table with this? *You're cleaning the toilets with it! Are you trying to kill me, woman?"*

Trembling, Pearl faltered back, a tear rolling down her cheek. "No, Gavin, I use the blue one for the bathroom, you know I do."

"I know a liar when I hear one talkin', that's what I know," he shouted, standing and taking two menacing steps toward her. The floor creaked under his heavy footfalls. "I know I'm forced to live in a pigsty, because you're a lazy, good-for-nothing bitch, damned be the day I met you!"

"I'm sorry, Gavin," she whimpered, wiping her tears with her sleeve. She'd walked backward until she hit the wall. "I'll make it up to you, I swear."

"How will you make it up to me, huh? Is the food ready?"

Her panicked eyes shot a quick glance at the stove, then toward the wall clock above the TV set. "In a few minutes, Gavin. I just got home from work."

For a long moment, her father stayed silent, choosing to stare his wife down with unspeakable contempt.

"Why don't I pour you some wine while you wait?" Pearl asked in a pretend-cheerful voice that made Katherine shed quiet tears.

"Yeah, do that, before I wipe you off the face of this earth," he said, raising his hand as if he was going to strike her. She cowered

and whimpered, holding her arms raised to shield her face from the blow that was to come.

He laughed and lowered his hand. "You stupid bitch," he muttered, then took his place back on the sofa, waiting to be served.

Pearl straightened her back and shot Katherine a quick glance, not even trying to hide her tears anymore. "Get me a mug for your dad, one of the white ones, will you, sweetie?" she whispered, holding on tightly to the fridge door handle for balance.

Katherine left the corner where she and Jacob had taken refuge and rushed to the kitchen with skittish steps, keeping as much distance from her father as she could. Thankfully, he'd switched on the TV and was watching some sports game. For a while at least, all his curses and anger would be directed at some strangers who'd chosen to play ball for a living and who weren't there to take the brunt of his rage in person. But if his favorite team lost, that rage could turn against Pearl and the kids again, at a moment's notice.

With trembling hands, Katherine opened the cupboard. Standing on the tips of her toes, she reached for a mug and grabbed it. It was heavy, and it slipped between her sweaty, shaking fingers, falling to the floor with a loud, shattering sound.

"You goddamned, worthless piece of shit!" her father shouted, leaping across the living room and rushing into the kitchen like a madman.

But her mother was faster, stepping in and shielding Katherine with her body. "No, Gavin, she didn't mean to. It was an accident, I swear."

She couldn't see her father, concealed as he was by her mother's body, but heard the telltale sounds of his belt buckle being undone, then the belt was yanked forcefully from his pants.

"Do you think I'm made of money?" he continued to shout, trying to get at Katherine, the heavy belt folded in two and held high in his hand, ready to leave its marks. "Have you ever earned a lousy dollar in your entire life? You spawn of the devil, piece of sorry-ass shit. I'll end you where you stand!"

With each word, her father grew angrier, and Katherine wished she had the courage to face him, to take the beating so that he'd be done already, satisfied by the blood he'd drawn, drinking his wine and letting them survive another day.

"No, no," Pearl pleaded. "Please, Gavin, she's just a little girl."

"Get out of my way, woman," Gavin demanded in a low, menacing tone that brought shivers down Katherine's spine. She grabbed fistfuls of her mother's skirt and sobbed loudly, no longer caring if her father heard her cries and saw her weakness.

"No, Gavin, please," her mother pleaded, fear raising the pitch of her voice. "Don't hurt my baby, I'm begging you."

Gavin shifted the belt in his left hand, and with the right he struck Pearl across the face hard, throwing her into the side of the cupboard. Then a second blow came, and the woman cried as she fell to the floor, shielding her face behind her bent elbows.

The belt found its way back into his right hand as Katherine fled screaming. He hit Pearl twice with the looped belt, then grunted and grabbed the mug from the floor. He studied it intently, while Katherine held her breath in the opposite corner of the living room.

"It's still good," he muttered, seeing that only the handle had broken off.

Then he took a bottle of cheap wine from the fridge and poured, the gurgling sound and acrid smell making the bile rise in Katherine's throat. He gulped thirstily, then topped off the mug and took his seat back in front of the TV.

"Go, Niners!" he screamed, pounding his heavy fist against the table surface, rattling the remote and the mug. A few droplets of wine found their way out of the cup and onto the stained surface of the table.

He didn't seem to care. He sat on the edge of the sofa leaning forward, his eyes riveted on the ball, throwing cusses and cheers in a constant barrage of drunken shouting that pierced Katherine's ears.

Rushing to care for her mother, she left Jacob whimpering, scared out of his mind, still hiding in the far corner behind the armchair.

She found a clean towel and drenched it in cold water, then squeezed the excess water out of it and applied it gently to her mother's face, where the swelling had already closed her left eye. She'd done it before... too many times than she cared to recall.

As she hurried by the sofa to bring her mother an Advil, her father grabbed her wrist and she cried in fear.

"Come, sit with me," he said. "Let's watch the game together."

CHAPTER TWELVE

Jeep

"What was that all about?" Elliot asked, approaching the trash can and studying the shattered object of Kay's rage.

She shrugged, shaking off the unwanted memories she wanted thrown into the garbage along with the ceramic shards. "Nothing," she replied, painfully aware of how pathetic her lying was. "I just hate that Jacob holds on to all this trash," she managed to improvise. "Broken furniture, cracked dishes, torn carpets, and that stupid mug. I can't change his furniture, but at least I got rid of that."

She finally dared to lift her gaze from the remnants of the mug and met his, briefly enough to see in those blue irises she hadn't convinced him one single bit. The shadow of a frown furrowed his brow while he was studying her without trying to hide it. But what she saw in those eyes was concern, not the excitement of a cop who'd picked up a scent and was ready for the chase.

"Why don't we drop the subject of my brother's housewares and focus on Kendra?" she said, injecting an enthusiasm she didn't have to fake into her voice, and inviting Elliot with a gesture to pour himself some coffee. Catching Kendra's killer was by far more important than obsessing over things that were ancient history. Especially if her worst fears were to be proven correct, and the unsub had grabbed another woman before or right after he'd killed Kendra.

Elliot held the door for her, and they went outside to the front porch, where she found herself standing with the coffee pot in one hand and the bottle of milk in the other, at a loss in the absence of a table where to set them down. The old wrought-iron table she remembered was still there, rusted and dirty, in no condition to serve its purpose. Out of options, she set everything down on the porch handrail, hoping the rotted wood would hold.

The same went for chairs; there was her mother's old rocking Adirondack, with the yellow paint all peeled and weathered, and covered in dust so thick it looked like mud. The other seat was the last of the wrought-iron set that had included the table, its legs so rusted it posed a risk to whoever dared to sit.

"How about the backyard?" Elliot asked.

"No," she replied, a little too quickly. "That's even worse, I guess," she added. "I haven't been back there since I arrived. A girl can only clean so much in a day."

"Can't say that I blame you," he replied, then helped her pour the coffee into the two cups. "We could always sit out here Texas style," he added with a quick smile. Demonstrating, he took a seat on the top step of the wooden stairs that led to the porch. "Care to join me?"

At least the rain had washed those steps clean of dust and grime once in a while, and they seemed like the best choice under the circumstances. She sat and leaned back against the balusters, but Elliot grabbed her elbow and helped her regain her balance when one of the balusters gave with a snap.

"Bad idea," Elliot said, and she thanked him with a nod, finding herself appreciative of how he didn't judge, not raising an eyebrow at her living conditions. He posed questions, and she couldn't hold that against a good cop, to ask questions when things made little or no sense at all.

Pulling out her cell phone, she ran an internet search for the law firm Paul and Maddie had mentioned.

"Found them," she announced, "Kendra's employer. We should map every step Kendra took since she left New York until she disappeared."

"Do you think the killer saw her in New York? Maybe followed her here?"

She thought for a moment before replying. Any good profiler takes statistics into account when formulating theories, especially when few victims are identified, and victimology cannot be determined with any level of certainty.

"If we find out that our Jane Doe is also from New York, I'd be willing to consider this theory," she replied. "Otherwise, based on what we've learned about the place and the manner in which he disposed of their bodies, I'd maintain he's local. Everything we've learned about him so far points to that. The knowledge of his surroundings, the Native American influence, the way he blends into the environment, managing to remain unnoticed by everyone here, in such a small community."

"Then why Kendra?" Elliot asked. "I can't wrap my mind around that. If she'd been here so little time, when and where did she manage to get his attention?"

"Unfortunately, seventeen percent of all serial killer victims are chosen at random, which makes catching the killers much more difficult. If the victims are random, you can't establish the commonalities that qualify the victims, and in missing that, an important piece of the profile is also missing. We'll have to compensate for that," she added, dialing the number she'd located for Kendra's employer.

A receptionist took the call immediately, and located a senior partner for them, Mr. Abrams himself, the first billed in the company name. When hearing what the call was about, he was quick to refer them to Kendra's boss, a junior partner by the name of Mitchell Gallagher.

"Mr. Gallagher," Kay said as soon as he picked up, "I'm Dr. Kay Sharp, and I have Detective Elliott Young here with me, from Franklin County Sheriff's Office."

"Yes," he said, "this is about Kendra, right?"

"That is correct," Kay replied. "We have a few questions for you. Is this a good time?"

She always tread carefully whenever lawyers were involved. With them, she never knew where she stood, and Kendra's law firm was an important lead in the investigation. But the last thing she wanted to do was waste precious time flying to New York and fighting the system to pry the information out of them.

"Yes, please go ahead."

"We're learning that Kendra had been missing since the twenty-ninth, yet you didn't report her missing. How could that happen?"

"She took two weeks' vacation," Gallagher replied. "She wasn't due back until Monday the eighteenth, and you called and notified us about Kendra on the fourteenth."

That was convenient, or maybe true, in its undeniable simplicity. Occam's razor was supporting Gallagher's explanation, but she still had to check. Kay was a big fan of the problem-solving principle, one that had at least as many definitions as spellings of its name, but in essence it conveyed one simple meaning. All things considered equal, the simplest, most straightforward solution tended to be the correct one, and the problem solver should choose the option that involved the fewest number of assumptions.

"And you have paperwork to support that?" Elliot jumped in.

"Sure, we do. We have more than that. Our executive assistant booked her travel with the return flight on the sixteenth," he replied calmly. "Like I said, we had no reason to worry about Kendra."

"Tell us about her family," Kay asked, although she knew the answer. "Was she married? Any kids?"

"Not as far as we knew," Gallagher replied. "There was no one in her life, not since she broke up with her boyfriend last year. She was studying to become a lawyer, working, and preparing for her bar exam. When you do that, there is no personal life."

"But she decided to spend two weeks of her time in the middle of nowhere?" Elliot pressed on.

"No," Gallagher replied. "She was going to meet with the client, then travel the entire California Coast, from San Francisco to LA and back. She was very excited about it, and this business trip gave her the opportunity to do what she'd always wanted to do but couldn't afford. We were covering the air travel, her car rental, and a few nights of hotel stay."

"What car rental company do you use?" Kay asked.

"We have a VIP account with Enterprise," Gallagher replied. He covered the microphone of his phone, and all they heard for a moment was some muffled conversation and papers being shuffled. "I have her itinerary in front of me," Gallagher added when he came back. "She caught a redeye into San Francisco, and arrived there on the twenty-ninth, right before noon. My assistant checked; Kendra picked up her car on schedule. Her plan was to drive to Mount Chester, spend the night, discuss with the client, then drive along the West Coast."

"And you were okay footing her vacation bills like that?" Kay asked, frowning. Her employer's generosity seemed unusual, especially for a law firm.

"We have weekly rates with Enterprise; it wasn't a big expense. And Kendra was one of our best. She put in sixty, seventy hours every week, and we don't pay overtime. At least that much we could do for her, like we do for all our associates. Call it an unofficial perk for an employee who will be missed."

There was a moment of silence, while Gallagher waited patiently for more questions. Kay and Elliot exchanged a quick glance, then

Kay asked, "Does your assistant happen to know what kind of car she picked up from Enterprise?"

"I'll ask her to find out for you," he offered, and the muffled conversation returned for a few seconds. "Until then, is there anything else I can help clarify?"

"How about her hotel? Where was she going to stay while in Mount Chester?" Kay asked.

"Um, she was going to stay at the Best Western, right there in town."

It made sense; it was the only decent hotel in the area. Kay wondered if Kendra had checked in before disappearing, but that was easy to find out.

"Do you know of anyone who might've wanted to harm Kendra?" Elliot asked.

"N—no," Gallagher answered, his hesitation brief, yet natural for an attorney who was probably considering all the implications of a statement before making it. "She worked the back office, and rarely engaged with the clients we are defending in criminal cases. And we always win," he added proudly. "Our clients have no reason to hold grudges or hurt our people."

"Thank you, Mr. Gallagher," Kay said. "If you can think of anything else, please don't hesitate to call us."

"Consider it done," he replied. "Before you go, I have the information you asked for. Kendra was driving a red Jeep Grand Cherokee."

Kay thanked him and ended the call, then looked at the distant edge of the forest, where the treetops were moving slightly in the afternoon breeze. Then she turned to Elliot and asked, "Now, where the hell is that Jeep?"

CHAPTER THIRTEEN
Another

This gal sure knows her way about the world, Elliot admitted to himself, yet feeling frustrated with how Kay had taken the lead on the investigation while he resigned himself to be the third wheel, the silent partner, or whatever other name for deadweight he wanted to give himself. She was supposed to consult, and even that unofficially. Instead, she was ahead of him all the time, thinking of things that didn't cross his mind, and one step ahead at what he thought was his game.

Darn serial killers and who brought them onto this earth, he swore in his mind, while holding on to the door handle on the passenger side, another first in many years. Kay wanted to drive, promising she'd deliver the fastest trip to San Francisco International Airport, and so she had. Of course, she had. She'd driven like a racetrack driver, weaving her way through traffic and beating his best time by a long shot, showing absolutely no respect for the double yellow line marked on the asphalt or any road sign for that matter.

Yet he sat in the passenger seat looking at her and barely containing a smile, more taken with her than he cared to admit, even to himself, even in the confines of his own thoughts. Kay had spunk, and could stare into the abyss of the darkest, most diseased minds without feeling the slightest bit of fear or revulsion, only a deep desire to rope her killers and bring them to justice, like any good cop should feel. Maybe she was a bit too fascinated with the inner workings of serial killers' minds for his taste, and maybe she enjoyed her job a little too much. But watching her work was well worth driving in the passenger seat, even figuratively when it came to his own investigation.

Even so, there was something about Kay Sharp he didn't understand. Sometimes he felt as if he was getting close to uncovering something about her, something important that she guarded carefully, that she didn't want to share. It was in her cautious demeanor, in the way she veered her eyes away from his when he asked certain questions, in her unusually jittery reactions to certain words he said. He was sure that she had a secret, something that made Kay Sharp who she was or maybe risked destroying her. Not his secret to know, most likely, but his nature drove him to leave no stone unturned until the entire truth was exposed. Because there's one thing about the truth: it always comes out into the light, and when it does, some of the shadows it casts can throw some people into darkness forever.

"What are you frowning about?" Kay asked, shooting him a quick glance as she turned onto the ramp leading to San Francisco International Airport.

"Just thinking this is the only road sign you actually obeyed," he replied, glad he was safe from her scrutinizing gaze. If she didn't have to focus on driving on the ramp at the same speed she'd been driving on the highway, she'd probably see right through him. And he wasn't ready to have that conversation.

She chuckled, and that was her only reply, her long fingers gripping the steering wheel tightly as the tires of the Ford squealed, turning into the Enterprise customer parking lot. Moments later, she'd worked her magic with the folks at the car rental office, and they were eager to help, all without warrants or flashing the badge she no longer had.

"Hey, guys," she'd said, as if she'd known them her entire life. "This is Detective Elliot Young, and I'm Dr. Kay Sharp. We need your help with an investigation. Who can assist us?" Then she smiled widely, making eye contact with all three attendants, even those busy with customers willing to drop everything to help her.

"I can do it," a young man said, leaving his station and approaching the desk quickly. He wore a white shirt and a black ballcap, and his name tag read, RODERICK—MANAGER.

"Thank you, Roderick," Kay replied, her beaming smile still turned on. "You could save us a ton of time, and we appreciate it. Where can we talk a little more privately?" she asked, lowering her voice just a little.

"Please, follow me," he replied, inviting them to step behind the counter and into his small office in the back. They took seats on black canvas chairs, while Roderick sat behind his melamine-coated desk and unlocked his computer, then took his ballcap off. He had buzzcut hair and looked young, maybe not even twenty years old, somewhat nerdy after he'd put on black-rimmed glasses. "Now, what can I do for you?"

"A Ms. Kendra Marshall leased a Jeep Grand Cherokee on September twenty-ninth," Kay said, and as she talked, Roderick's fingers started to dance on the keyboard.

"Yes, I have her here," he replied. "The rental is still active."

"Isn't this vehicle supposed to be back?" Elliot asked, seeing where Kay was going.

"No, it's not," he replied calmly. "The car isn't due back until later today. It was taken out for three weeks."

"That's strange," Kay reacted. "Ms. Marshall's flight back was on the sixteenth."

"Oh," he reacted, a frown promptly furrowing his brow. "It should've been back in that case."

"Isn't it unusual to book the car for longer than the total stay?" Elliot asked.

"Not with corporate VIP accounts on weekly rates," he explained. "You see, if you book the vehicle for two weeks and four days, it would cost more than the full three weeks. Did something happen to the vehicle?"

His fingers found the keyboard again and clacked loudly.

"We don't know—" Elliot started to say, but Roderick cut him off.

"The vehicle's GPS pings here, in the SFO parking lot."

Elliot looked at Kay briefly. Her eyebrows shot up in surprise.

"Was the car picked up?" she asked.

"Yes, it was signed off our lot on the twenty-ninth, at twelve forty-three p.m., and now it shows in the long-term parking lot." Roderick stood and locked his computer. "Can I ask what this is about?" Then, without waiting for an answer, he turned and accessed a large vault, searching for something. He came back with a car key labeled with a long serial number, and the color, make and model. "Do you want to see it?"

Kay stopped him with a gentle touch on his arm before he could leave the privacy of his small office. "We're investigating the death of Kendra Marshall," she disclosed in a low voice, making Elliot shake his head in disbelief. She shouldn't've shared that information with a civilian, not without clearing it with him first. Soon it would be all over the San Francisco tabloids. "We need this matter handled with the utmost confidentiality," she continued, and a wide-eyed Roderick nodded his approval. "You cannot disclose anything to anyone, you understand? It would be a criminal offense."

"Mum's the word, I swear," he replied quickly, then rushed out the door with the two investigators in tow.

He invited them to climb into an SUV bearing the company insignia, and drove them straight to the long-term parking lot, starting the search for the red Jeep. It wasn't difficult to spot; Roderick had brought along a handheld device that showed the car's position with unexpected accuracy, the only element missing being the altitude. It was on the third floor, right where the device had indicated it would be, and Roderick was quick to unlock its doors with the spare remote.

"Let me check if—" he started, but Elliot put a reassuring hand on the young man's shoulder. "This Jeep is now part of an active investigation. Could you please wait here, in your vehicle? We won't be long."

Roderick nodded, and Elliot joined Kay as she circled the vehicle, studying it carefully. She'd put on gloves already and held a compact flashlight in her hand. Nothing in her demeanor said that she was no longer active law enforcement; maybe when she'd turned in her badge, she'd held on to what used to be her routine as an FBI agent. Elliot knew he would, if he were in her shoes.

"Do you think he'll keep his word and not spill the beans?" Elliot asked quietly.

"I believe he will," Kay replied. "I know you've already released Kendra's death to the media, but that was locally, in Mount Chester. I'm hoping the San Francisco media won't learn about it for another few days, just in case I'm wrong and the killer is here, somewhere."

"I was surprised you shared anything with him," Elliot said. "And a bit pissed, to be honest."

She looked at him briefly, taking her eyes off the driver's door handle for a quick moment. "Oh?" Kneeling by the side of the vehicle, she examined the undercarriage carefully, shining her flashlight over every nook and cranny.

Her reaction made him take a step back. "I'm not used to having a partner. Haven't had one for a while."

"Is that what we are?" she laughed. "All right, partner, let's look inside. I don't see any wires or anything to indicate the risk of explosives."

"Explosives? Why think that?" His voice had climbed up a notch or two. Kay's mind went places he just couldn't follow.

"No reason, just being cautious. I've seen a lot, and this car, dumped here, right back where it originated, rings a loud bell for me."

"Why is that? Because she didn't drive it outside of the San Francisco airport?"

"We don't actually know that she didn't," Kay replied. "No… it reminds me of an old riddle I knew as a kid. Where do you hide a green-eyed elephant?"

"I don't know, where?"

"In a herd of green-eyed elephants," she replied, gesturing at the vast parking-lot floor, filled to the brim with cars.

She opened the driver's side door gently and listened intently, while Elliot held his breath. Roderick was watching every move they made from his car; he hadn't budged since he'd been told to stay put, but seemed intrigued by their activities.

"The question is," Kay said, "if Kendra was killed in Mount Chester, how on earth did her vehicle make it back? Or did she hitch a ride with someone else, leaving the car in the SFO long-term garage? Maybe with the killer?"

Inspecting the car, Kay noticed that a cell phone was in one of the cup holders. She picked it up. As expected, it was dark; it probably had run out of battery a long time ago. She took it and dropped it inside a small evidence pouch, then sealed it and put it in her pocket.

Elliot opened the trunk and said, "Her luggage is still here."

"Maybe he abducted her from the parking lot? But why stop here, if she'd just taken possession of the rental car, she should've driven off the airport, right? Did you notice how you have to leave the airport completely when you leave the car rental terminal, and then re-enter to get here? It makes no sense."

Elliot circled to the front of the Jeep and looked inside, then said, "She didn't hitch a ride with the killer. She made it to Mount Chester."

"How do you know?"

Elliot picked up a paper coffee cup from the second cup holder and held it up with two gloved fingers. He removed the lid and sniffed the dried, moldy content. "Iced tea," he said, "from our own Katse Coffee Shop. See this awful daisy pattern? I don't believe Starbucks sells their iced tea in these."

"You're right," she replied, "I've never seen this anywhere else either. That means she was there, and she drove back? Or did the killer drive back the rental, to hide it where no one would look for it?" She grinned, removing her gloves with a snap of the nitrile. "That means we have some leads, partner. Katse is one, and *that* is the other," she replied, pointing at the video surveillance camera installed on the ceiling of the parking garage.

She's like a dog with two bones, Elliot thought, entertained by her excitement. "Katse, what an interesting name for the coffee shop," he said, searching the storage compartments in the vehicle. Rental agreement, mints, a small bag of Oreos.

"Katse is Pomoan for black," Kay replied. "The name translates as Black Coffee Shop. Just like Cuwar Lake is, in fact, Silent Lake. Cuwar means moon in the language of the Shastan people. Well, it also means sun; I know that's difficult to comprehend, but I guess it means a well-lit object in the sky," she added with a wide smile. "From there, the jump to silent isn't that farfetched, if you start from moon, and the moon is visible at night, when everything is silent, including the lake."

He'd been living in Mount Chester for five years, enough to know the nearly four-thousand-resident town inside and out, but didn't interrupt her. He liked to hear her talk, and that had nothing to do with the case or his knowledge of the Native roots of the community he now called home. No; it had everything to do with her.

"What do you think?" she asked, catching him lost in thought.

"About?"

"Can you see why they call it Silent Lake?"

"Absolutely," he replied, a little too quickly.

He noticed she held back a chuckle, then she turned all serious and said, "Let's have this baby impounded. Roderick?" she called, and the young man lowered his window.

"Yes?"

"We need to have this towed to the sheriff's office in Mount Chester," she said. "We'll sign the documents right now, if you'd like, and we'll be on our way. Thank you for all your help, you've been amazing."

"Sure, I'll arrange it," Roderick offered. "Oh, by the way, we have another rental unit gone AWOL, in case you're wondering. It was on this morning's report. Someone else takes care of unreturned recoveries, but I thought I'd locate it and guess what? It's pinging here, in the same garage."

CHAPTER FOURTEEN
Return

Roderick had arranged towing for Kendra's rental Jeep, and while they waited for the tow truck to show up, he went ahead with Elliot and located the other vehicle on level five. Then Elliot texted her that he had to run back to Roderick's office to get the spare key for the Nissan Altima.

Kay could barely control her anxiety. Since Roderick had mentioned the other vehicle, she'd had this unusually strong sense of apprehension, as if she was about to discover something terrible that went far beyond what they already knew. What could be more terrible than finding out that the unsub had taken another woman?

But other questions whirled in her mind, driving her to pace the stained, concrete floor of the garage impatiently. Could this unsub have taken two different women who had rented cars from the same car rental company, at the same airport, both going to Mount Chester? What were the odds of that?

Infinitesimal. So close to zero they didn't even matter.

Nine different rental companies operated on premises at the San Francisco International Airport. An average of over twelve hundred flights landed or took off from that airport every day, servicing over one hundred and fifty thousand passengers daily, or fifty-seven million passengers each year. How did he conveniently pick the women headed to Mount Chester, out of those vast numbers? Was he someone who worked for the airport, one of the airlines, or maybe even the car rental company? At which point on her route would a traveler like Kendra disclose her final destination as being Mount Chester? Quick answer: she wouldn't. Travelers landed, picked up their rental cars, then disappeared. But maybe car rental companies kept an eye on the locations of their vehicles, and could tell when a car was headed to or had arrived in Mount Chester. A car rental employee could be the killer they'd been hunting for.

Just as that thought passed through her mind, Roderick returned and stopped his SUV at some distance from the tow truck.

She gave the young manager a long look, wondering, but then dismissed the thought. The young, freckled man didn't fit the profile one iota. If the unsub was a car rental employee, it had to have been someone else. Someone older, stronger, who could lift a body up a tree. The fact that she was pacing restlessly in the SFO long-term garage didn't mean any man who crossed her path was who they were looking for.

She could barely wait to see what was going on with the vehicle on level five, and as soon as the tow truck driver finished loading the Jeep onto the platform, she told him to follow them to the fifth floor and wait until she finished with the other vehicle. She wasn't going to let that Jeep out of her sight until it was safely locked inside the sheriff's office impound in Mount Chester.

Roderick led the way and drove to the fifth level of the parking garage, where she found Elliot studying the undercarriage of a white Nissan Altima.

"Bingo," he said, when she jumped out of Roderick's SUV before it even came to a complete stop. "I believe that's a Katse daisy cup in there."

Roderick pressed the remote and the Nissan unlocked with a chirp and a four-way flash.

Slipping on a fresh pair of gloves, Kay opened the driver side door and looked inside. The cup was there; when she removed the lid the smell of stale, moldy coffee filled the vehicle.

The driver of the white Nissan had visited Mount Chester.

Then she noticed something else and felt her heart sink.

The passenger side seat and floor mat were littered with crumbs, as if someone had eaten crackers without the tiniest shred of consideration for the cleanliness of the car. A kid.

"Her suitcase's here," Elliot said. "Same as the other one."

"Elliot," she called, feeling her stomach sink and a wave of dizziness grab hold of her. "Look," she pointed at the open glove compartment with a strangled voice. "Gummy bears."

Rushing to the back of the vehicle, she shone her flashlight on the back seat, then on the floor. *Oh, no*, she thought, reaching out and grabbing the plush teddy bear from the floor. *Please, don't let it be true.*

"The bastard's got a child," she said, a wave of rage strangling her to the point where her words struggled to come out. "He's got a child this time, Elliot. I didn't profile that. I didn't see it coming."

"Maybe he—" Elliot started, but she cut him off, turning her attention to Roderick.

"Who leased this vehicle?" she asked, her words coming out with intensity, causing Roderick to fluster.

"Um, Alison Nolan, from Atlanta," he replied. "I have the scan of her driver's license, if you—"

"Yes, of course I need it. How old was—um, is she?"

"Twenty-seven," Roderick replied, then cleared his throat.

"When did she arrive?"

He checked his device and typed on the small keyboard, each key giving a quiet beep when pressed.

"On October fifteenth," he replied. "She was supposed to drop the car last night."

The fifteenth was only a few days after Kendra had been killed. Dr. Whitmore had estimated she'd been dead since as early as October 8 or as late as October 12. And after only a few days, he'd taken someone else. He'd taken Alison Nolan from Atlanta and her child.

"Who processed Alison's rental?"

"I did," Roderick replied, a slight tremble in his voice. He looked paler in the dimming light, and sweat popped on his forehead despite the evening chill. "I remembered her when I saw her driver's license photo."

"How many children did she have with her?" Kay asked.

He hesitated for a brief moment, closing his eyes for a moment. "Only one, a little girl with long brown hair, about seven or eight," he replied. "I'm sure of it."

"How come you remember?" Elliot asked, a frown visible above his inquisitive eyes. "You must see thousands of people every week."

"I remember her because, um, she looked like my girlfriend," he said. The words came out quickly, while his cheeks lit on fire. "While I was processing her, I was thinking this is what Abby would look like with a kid, and I liked that."

While Elliot was on the phone with his boss to bring him up to speed, Kay asked Roderick for the key and returned to the vehicle. She turned on the engine and studied the media center, ignoring all the chimes and the lights that came on across the dashboard. The vehicle had GPS, and if they were in luck, the system had memorized the places where Alison had traveled and stopped.

"We need to impound this one too," she announced, beckoning the tow truck driver.

"I figured," Roderick replied. "Are they, um, will they be okay?" he asked quietly.

Kay touched his forearm. "Not sure, but we'll do everything we can to get them back safely."

He seemed scared, as if being a part of the investigation had put him in danger. It was what she called the doom contagion effect, the foreboding that people sense when death drew near, even if someone else's, even if at arm's length.

Kay's focus shifted back to the Jeep, loaded and secured on the tow truck's platform, visualizing Kendra's arrival in San Francisco, her trip to Mount Chester, her disappearance. Where? Where did her journey end, and her captivity begin?

"Does the Jeep have GPS?" Kay asked.

"All our vehicles do," Roderick replied, his words sounding rehearsed. He must've spoken the same phrase at least a few times each day.

"We'll probably need to take those navigation units apart. We need to figure out where these vehicles have been, and when they got back here."

"No need to take them apart for that," Roderick replied. "May I?" he asked, half-opening his door.

Kay nodded and handed him a pair of gloves. He leaned into the Nissan without sitting behind the wheel and started operating its navigation unit.

"You go to *navigation*, then *history*," he said. "You can select to see the routes on a map, where the stops will be marked with blue circles, like this," he said, touching the screen with the tip of a gloved finger.

The lines on the map showed the Nissan had traveled to Mount Chester, and the Katse Coffee Shop was marked by a blue circle, confirming the evidence found in the car.

"Strange," Roderick said. "There's no return route."

"What do you mean?" Elliot asked, staring at the screen from behind the young man's bony shoulders.

"I mean, she drove the car to this point here, a few miles from this Katse place, and then nothing. There's local traffic in the SFO airport, so many overlaid routes that we can't really tell when those happened without going into the line-by-line data. Our customers don't know or don't care about erasing their GPS history, and every one of them has driven this car here, at the airport, either leaving or returning the vehicle. But there's no return route from Mount Chester to San Francisco."

"How can that happen?" Kay asked, frowning. If the unsub had tampered with the vehicle's GPS unit, none of the data that was left was worth anything; it was only what he wanted them to find.

"If someone can figure out how to delete partial navigation data, I guess," Roderick said. "Maybe you do need to take this unit apart. I watch crime shows on TV," he added. "I know cops have top-notch computer people who can do pretty much anything, right?"

"Right," she replied, while Elliot locked eyes with her, surprised. Maybe in a previous life she would've had access to FBI's top analysts who could take the unit apart and figure out every secret it held inside. But that was then. Now, they had to figure it out on their own.

An unsub knowledgeable enough to alter the GPS data in rental vehicles changed the game. That, and the fact that this time he'd taken a woman and her child.

CHAPTER FIFTEEN
Stolen Life

He cherished the memories of his mother, the way she'd been with him at first, when he was little and she didn't have other children, only him. They were faded and distant and barely recognizable, washed over by the blur of time, but they were the most precious he had.

Him, sitting on the floor at his mother's feet, helping her tie little feathers with strips of calf leather she then used to decorate the dreamcatchers she made. His sister was a swaddle of gurgling sounds and whimpers back then, and his brother a bump in his mother's belly. From there, at her feet, her hair seemed to surround her head like a halo against the sunlight, making him wonder if she was an angel, while she sang about little babies and mockingbirds, over and over, in a soft, love-filled voice.

She wasn't, she'd explained many times, nor was she a spirit. She was just his mother, a woman he loved more than anyone else. And with her by his side, his entire world made sense.

When he was about five years old and his sister had started grabbing hold of his finger with her tiny hand, he was thrilled to put her in the stroller and take her outside in the gentle summer breeze, pushing it slowly if she was asleep, or as fast as he could run if she was awake, until she laughed hard and squealed. But one day the stroller overturned when its front right wheel hit a pothole, sending his sister flying through the air. She landed hard on her back, her piercing wails instantly drawing his mother outside, still wearing her kitchen apron.

But he didn't see her coming. His eyes were riveted on his little sister's naked body. The blanket she'd been swaddled in was still clinging to the side of the stroller's canopy, and her diaper had become loose. She was kicking and flailing, arms and legs in the air, powerless, and yet her vulnerability stirred him up inside, rendering him stiff, frozen, his eyes fixed on her pale skin, unable to move.

That was the first time his mother hit him, the memory of her heavy hand across his face searing, even in the distant memories dusted by the passing of so many years. She'd rushed outside, picked up her daughter ever so gently, and quickly checked to see if she was all right. Then she'd turned to him in a rage and shouted, "Don't come near her again! You hear me? Get out of my sight... I can't even *look* at you right now."

Turning, she went inside, his sister in her arms still wailing, leaving him alone in the yard, lost, a flood of tears burning his eyes. He'd never wanted to hurt the little girl, but who would believe him, if his own mother wouldn't?

He heard his father's truck pull up in front of the house. Panicked, he realized his dad would soon learn about the entire story and he probably wouldn't be too pleased. Quickly, he put the stroller back on its wheels, then ran and hid inside the barn, wishing the earth would open already and swallow him whole.

That night, he didn't go inside the house, not even for dinner when his stomach had started growling fiercely. He didn't believe he deserved food or the warmth of his home, and terrified to face his mother again, he preferred to curl up on the straw and pretend he didn't hear the mice munching on loose grain.

It was his father who came looking for him eventually. Instead of hitting him or shouting at him, he'd sat on a square bale of straw by his side and explained that his mother had been scared and upset, and didn't mean all the harsh things she had said. She wasn't upset anymore, and she waited for him to join the family for dinner.

Head hung low and hands clasped tightly in front of him, he followed his father inside, then ate dinner without saying a word or lifting his eyes from his plate. His mother didn't speak to him either, busy as she was with feeding a toddler and an infant, his little brother. He went to bed without a word spoken to him and lay awake until the early morning light. He remembered that well, because it was the day that had marked the first shift in his mother's love for him.

After that unfortunate incident, he was only allowed to play with his younger siblings under his mother's strict supervision. She seemed afraid of him, of what he could do to his brother and sister. "Don't play rough, you'll break her bones," she'd say, raising her voice to carry over the large yard. "Watch it, she's not as strong as you are." Or worse, "Don't be an animal."

Gradually, but beyond any doubt, she'd stopped loving him. The last time he remembered her being affectionate was right before his twelfth birthday. She'd dressed him up for church, just like she always did, and gave him a hug after he was done, a warm embrace that resonated in his entire body, awakening him in ways he wasn't familiar with. Then she'd pushed him aside abruptly, not looking at him anymore. Maybe it was something he'd said, or maybe he'd never know what it was he'd done wrong.

Around that time, with that day as a first, he'd started to change, his own body betraying him. Unwanted thoughts troubled his mind during the day and his dreams while he slept. It was as if his entire being had decided to embarrass him. His voice was undecided if it was going to stay high-pitched like a child's, or turn baritone, more like his father's. One night, he woke up drenched in his own urine. Another time, he couldn't leave the dinner table because he was afraid everyone would see his erection. But the tiniest, most innocent gestures triggered his body to react in the most unusual, embarrassing ways. His mother, cutting a piece of chicken breast on her plate to share among the children. The way the word *breast* sounded on her lips, when she'd asked him if he wanted a piece. The way her dress contoured the shape of her full chest, the red fabric in contrast with the warm shades of her skin.

That night, he found himself passing through the hallway when his mother was in the shower. As if drawn by a powerful yet invisible hand, he'd crouched in front of the bathroom door and looked through the keyhole. He didn't see much, only the shape of his mother's body under the flow of hot water, blurred behind the steamed shower curtain, but where his eyes couldn't see detail, his mind was quick to imagine it. His father almost caught him, but he'd heard his footsteps and managed to rush back into his room, his hands held in front of his body to cover his painful hardness.

There, in the solitude of his room, he touched himself for the first time, to relieve the pain, to study the part of his body that so frequently acted against his will, to learn how to control it or to regain some sense of restraint over his urges.

The exact opposite happened.

He discovered pleasure, the reward he didn't expect to find at the end of so much misery and humiliation. That initial exploration of his sexuality, the deeply satisfying bonanza of emotions and feelings, forever changed who he was. Instead of running away from his body, from the things that turned him on, he started seeking the thrills, compelled to indulge again and again in the death-like pleasure.

At all costs.

He stopped feeling guilty when his body responded to seeing his sister and her friends in their short dresses, their budding breasts pushing through colorful fabrics. He didn't avert his eyes when his mother reached over the table for the saltshaker and he could stare down her cleavage. Come summer, he loved hanging out near the picnic areas, where tourists often took their clothes off to get some sun. Every opportunity he had, he enticed his body to respond, seeking the fleeting pleasure of release.

That didn't, in any comparable measure, compensate for the loss of his mother's love. As time passed, she pushed him away more and more, but still didn't seem satisfied. She did her best to keep everyone away from him, a cruelty he didn't understand.

He was about fifteen when he gathered his courage and asked his mother, "Why do you tell everyone to stay away from me?" To his deepest shame, his lower lip quivered under the threat of tears, a threat he hadn't foreseen when he was rehearsing the conversation in his mind. His wishful thinking had his mother saying, "Oh, darling, I'm so sorry you feel this way! It won't happen again."

The reality proved vastly different. His mother stared coldly at him and replied, "I don't know what you're talking about. Have you said your prayers?"

Ever since he could remember, when his mother, who'd been baptized Catholic at twenty-six years of age so she could marry his father, wanted to avoid a conversation with any of the family members, she brought up prayers.

That night, he'd given up trying to understand why his mother was rejecting him, but spent countless nights obsessing over every single thing he might've done wrong to upset her, to push her away.

He decided to fight for her affection, to earn it all over again. He took up more house chores without her asking, and got his school grades up so fast his teachers commended him, yet she didn't let him anywhere near her heart. A year or so later, he wasn't even allowed to be in the backyard with his little sister and her friends when they played. He was supposed to stay at a safe distance, like a vicious animal, while he yearned for their company.

Even so, she wasn't satisfied.

One such night, after his sister had gone to bed, his mother had grabbed him by the arm and took him to the door, while his father watched with sad eyes. She opened the door and shoved him out of the house, calling him an abomination and telling him he was never to come back.

His mother, the woman he loved more than life itself, had thrown him to the curb like a heap of garbage.

The memory of that night almost twenty years ago still crushed his chest as if the weight of the entire world had condensed into a single thought, unbearably heavy, merciless, and cold.

That bitch…

What had he ever done to her?

Nothing, unfortunately, but oh, how he regretted that.

Through the one-way mirror, he looked at the little girl, seeming sad and frightened as she sat on the edge of the bed. She sometimes cried, other times she just sat there or curled up on her side, her eyes squinted closed. Hazel was her name, yet she reminded him of his sister, the tiny fragile thing he wasn't even allowed to look at, as if he were a leper.

But now he was in control, he had the power to do whatever he wanted, and that girl couldn't call for her mother anymore. He'd made sure of that.

A wave of images and thoughts swirled through his mind, setting his body on fire. He welcomed the fantasies taking over and leaned back into his armchair, relaxing, letting them carry him away. He invited them to conquer his consciousness, dreaming with wide-open eyes, getting ready for the perfect family evening, when he was going to make the bitch in the basement pay for the life she'd stolen from him.

Again.

And again.

CHAPTER SIXTEEN

Question

It was almost three in the morning when they reached the sheriff's office in Mount Chester, driving the safe limit for the tow truck that hauled the two rental cars. All lights were on, and Elliot recognized Sheriff Logan's car in the parking lot, among at least half a dozen others.

Elliot instructed the tow truck driver where to go to unload the two rental vehicles and asked a uniformed deputy to assist, then escorted Kay inside. She rushed straight for the coffee maker, someone had thankfully taken the time to run, and poured two large cups.

Sheriff Logan didn't wait for them to reach his office. He rushed toward them with two deputies by his side.

"How sure are you?" he asked, jumping straight to the core of the matter.

"Positive," Kay replied, although the question wasn't addressed to her. "He took another woman and her daughter, and I believe we might still be able to find them alive."

Sheriff Logan frowned, not taking his eyes off Elliot's.

"We have both of them leasing the vehicle and leaving, we have evidence that the child has been in the vehicle," Elliot replied. "And no one has seen or heard from them since."

"That was on the fifteenth? A week ago?"

Elliot had called Logan from the San Francisco airport parking garage and filled him in, yet he wanted to go over each detail, thoroughly.

"First, we have to make sure they're really missing," Logan said, and Kay raised her eyebrows at him. He didn't seem to notice or mind.

"They weren't on their flight back to Atlanta the night before last," Elliot replied. "We checked with the airline before leaving San Francisco. Local police already spoke with Alison Nolan's mother."

"In the dead of the night?" the sheriff asked.

"When Alison and Hazel didn't return on time, she tried to reach them, then filed a police report. She said it wasn't like her daughter to be out of touch for so many days, but she knew she was traveling in secluded places, so she didn't worry. But Alison always called before boarding her flight."

"Did she give us anything useful?"

"Not really," Elliot replied. "The last time she spoke with Alison was on the fifteenth, after they landed in San Francisco." He shifted his weight from one foot to the other. "She also said she had a bad feeling about this trip, but her daughter wouldn't listen."

"Great," Logan mumbled. "That's going to help a whole damn lot."

Kay was studying the sheriff, thankfully not intervening much. It seemed every word she had to say, even her presence there was irritating his boss, and he wondered why. Was it her youthful appearance? She was twenty-nine, and by that age she'd accomplished a lot. Maybe the seasoned sheriff disliked that, maybe it made him feel insecure. That had to be it, because Elliot hadn't noticed a gender bias in his boss in the five years he'd worked for him.

"Action plan?" Logan asked, and two other deputies drew closer to hear the details.

"We've organized search parties that will start working the grid at first light."

"Did you center that grid at the point of her disappearance?" Kay asked.

Three pairs of disapproving eyes focused on her.

"And how would we know where that is, if you don't mind me asking, Miss—?"

Kay grinned for a split second, then turned serious. She was going to eat him for breakfast without toast on the side.

"It's *Dr.*, if you don't mind. You can call me Dr. Sharp. And you should start at the last point where Alison's rental vehicle recorded its location on GPS, which is just over the ridge, north of Katse's. That is, of course, if Sheriff Logan agrees."

Logan nodded. "You can start there," he said. "But what's that I'm hearing about the GPS units having been tampered with?"

"We're looking into that," Elliot replied. "The unsub—"

"Where do you get off with this unsub business? We're not FBI," Logan reacted, angry all of a sudden.

"It just makes sense to call him that, an unknown subject," Elliot explained calmly, although his patience was running thin. His boss was being a pain in the rear, totally blinded by his aversion to Kay's presence. "He's Kendra's killer, but Alison and Hazel's kidnapper. What would you like me to call him?"

"Ah, don't get cute with me," Logan slammed him.

He knew to let it go. The boss was probably tired, a sleepless night far more demanding at Logan's age than at his.

"As I was saying," he stated calmly, a calm he was now struggling to display, "*he* might've tampered with the GPS, but this bit of information is still the best lead we have, when it comes to starting a grid search."

"Okay, start there. I want hourly reports," he said, pulling out a nearby chair and sitting with a groan. "Until then, let's round up the usual suspects. Bring in Tommy MacPherson first. The name of his coffee shop is all over this investigation. There has to be a connection."

Kay looked at Elliot with an unspoken question.

"MacPherson is the owner of Katse Coffee Shop," he clarified quickly. "He's got a rap sheet a mile long. Assault, battery, breaking and entering. He's an angry fellow with a short fuse, but is not a registered offender."

"An unsub this organized wouldn't draw attention to his own coffee shop, Elliot," she replied. "The profile doesn't fit. He's not the person we're looking for. But he is a strong lead; maybe, if we apply the right pressure, he'll share something about Kendra and Alison, and what brought them to Katse before they vanished. Sheriff, if you don't mind, let us interview him instead. He might be more cooperative in his own setting."

"Thank goodness we have Dr. Sharp here, to teach us how to do our jobs," Logan said, the sarcasm in his voice heavy.

"I mean no disrespect, Sheriff," Kay replied. She seemed composed, but he already knew her well enough to guess she was boiling under the surface of that perfectly balanced politeness. "I was under the assumption that we're working together as a team, under your leadership, with the goal of saving the lives of two innocent people and catching a dangerous killer who will not stop. If I was wrong, I apologize."

Logan was slack-jawed for an embarrassing moment. Kay knew precisely when to cut short.

"I am your resource, Sheriff. Use me as you would any of your deputies."

"Sure," he said, then swallowed with difficulty and cleared his voice before continuing. One of the deputies turned away to hide a smile. Their boss had been taught a lesson he wasn't going to forget anytime soon, like a rodeo bronc saddled for the first time with calfskin-gloved hands. "Who else do we have? Is Eggers out of jail?"

"Yeah," one of the deputies replied. "His last number was assault, and he did his time up at state. Got out last year."

"Who's Eggers?" Kay asked.

This time, the sheriff had an entirely different demeanor when he answered. "Our very own registered sex offender. He's done time for statutory rape, rape, aggravated assault, the whole bag of beans."

"He's not our guy," Kay replied. "If you don't mind," she added, and paused to let the sheriff weigh in. He invited her to speak with a hand gesture. "We're looking for someone who's highly organized, smart, and has the technical abilities to tamper with a car's navigation system. He's able to abduct women without being seen, and dispose of their vehicles quickly and effectively, choosing—at least from the cases we know—to return them to a place where they go undiscovered for the longest possible time. He's a sadistic, sexually motivated serial killer who takes his time inflicting pain. He demonstrates a detailed, ritualistic manner in disposing of his victims' bodies that reflects a strong, trauma-based motivation, most likely childhood or early adulthood trauma. Is that who Eggers is, Sheriff?"

Logan shrugged before replying, probably an involuntary reaction he most likely regretted. "No, but we'll bring him in, nevertheless. Maybe he's seen something."

The darkness outside the window had started lifting, a signal that the search for Alison and her daughter could finally start.

"I believe the most important question we should answer right now is, how does he get those cars back to San Francisco?" Kay said. "If we learn that, we might get him on camera somewhere, although I don't imagine he'd make such a mistake. But maybe we get lucky; maybe there was a camera he didn't know to avoid." She paused for a moment, while the sheriff coordinated with the deputies. They had requested assistance from the neighboring counties, and their units were starting to pull into the parking lot. The excited bark of a German Shepherd police K9 came across loud and clear, signaling to the deputies it was time to begin the search.

"Deputy, um, Hobbs," Kay said, reading the officer's name off his tag. "Ask the teams to look for any evidence, anything that could tell us where he grabbed them from, and how."

"Yes, ma'am," Hobbs replied, then rushed out the door.

Elliot grabbed the door, holding it for Kay.

"Before you leave," the sheriff called, "I have a message from Dr. Whitmore; it just came in. DNA came back on the other victim. Her name is Shannon Hendricks," he said, after reading the notes on a piece of paper. "She was thirty-two years old, a mother of two." He suddenly looked tired, as if the dark circles surrounding his eyes had deepened as he'd read the notes. He ran his hand over the back of his head, easing the stiffness that tensed his back, but he obviously wasn't done breaking the news.

Elliot and Kay waited for him to continue, standing in the doorway.

The sheriff added, his voice low and strangled, "Her missing person report says she disappeared last November with her five-year-old son."

CHAPTER SEVENTEEN

Search

The sun hadn't risen yet when they reached the focal point of the search grid, determined with accuracy from the Nissan's GPS records. It was an isolated spot over the ridge, about a mile down from Katse Coffee Shop, where Kay's latest-generation smartphone didn't get a single bar of signal. A gently sloping stretch of two-lane road, it led to a valley between mountain ridges, the entire length of it probably a cellular blind spot.

The road was bordered by thick woods on both sides, while the distant landscape was breathtaking; rocky mountain peaks covered in snow, touched pink against a glowing light show in deep purple, bright orange, and the promise of a perfect azure sky once the sun was up. Not a hint of the tragedy happening somewhere in the thickness of those woods, not a shred of evidence to speak of the place where a young woman and her daughter were being held.

Kay held close to the K9, waiting impatiently for the officer to leash his dog, a large Malinois with a work vest was tagged, NINER. Unzipping an evidence bag, she offered the dog the plush teddy bear recovered from the Nissan. The Malinois sniffed it thoroughly, obeying short commands given by his handler, then whimpered, signaling he was ready to trace. Niner lifted his nose into the air at the side of the road, turning and seeking the scent where it was stronger, then decided to lead them uphill.

The deputies had started the grid search, and were headed into the woods on both sides of the highway. Other than the two of them, the K9 officer and his dog, no one else was on the road, blocked with hastily deployed barriers on both ends. But she could hear voices coming from the woods, calling out Alison's name, sometimes Hazel's. While they walked briskly on the asphalt behind the Malinois, the voices faded farther into the woods.

Neither Alison nor Hazel had answered, the silence of the woods the only witness to their whereabouts.

Niner stopped and angrily sniffed a certain area, walking in circles and whimpering quietly. Tire tracks were still visible where a car had pulled over. Niner's handler pulled him away and patted him on the shoulder.

"This is where the trail goes cold, Detectives," he said, assuming Kay was there in an official capacity.

Kay pulled out her phone and studied the photo she'd taken of the Nissan's navigation history. The blue dot in the car's system was barely two hundred yards from where they stood.

After taking out his phone, Elliot put it back inside his pocket with a sigh of frustration. "No signal," he said. "Let's get an impression lifted off those tire tracks," he told the K9 officer.

"That won't tell us much, just confirm our theory," Kay replied. She was crouched by the side of the road, studying every inch of the shoulder carefully. She could visualize what had happened. For some reason, Alison and Hazel had pulled over, then decided to walk toward Katse. Was that when Alison had bought the coffee whose moldy remnants were found in the Nissan? "We know whose tire tracks they are."

But why did they stop in a no-cell-phone-service area?

Because they had to, she thought. It was the only logical answer.

She stood and closed her eyes, to shield them from the piercing sun and focus on the image of the Nissan's dashboard, the way she'd seen it when Roderick had started the engine. She rewound the images burned into her memory, then played them back again. The young man had started the engine for her, triggering lights and chimes on the dashboard that she ignored, fixated as she was on the media center and the GPS.

In her recollection, she focused her attention on the dashboard and what lights had come on when the engine started, the way they normally do to show drivers the respective sensors worked and could be relied on. Then they all turned off, after being on for just a second.

Not all.

One had stayed on. The check engine light.

She opened her eyes and looked at Elliot. "Her car broke down," she said, already starting to walk downhill toward his SUV. "That's why they were on foot in the middle of nowhere. It's time to visit Katse Coffee Shop and its ex-con owner. Although he doesn't fit the profile, I believe he could've sabotaged her car when she stopped there for coffee, coming from the airport."

A short walk to the car and an even shorter drive later, Elliot pulled up on the gravel in front of the coffee shop just as the owner, a bulky man who looked about fifty, was unlocking the rusted padlock that secured the place overnight. He wore a dark blue shirt with white stripes, but that did little to help him conceal a potbelly worthy of a champion eater.

"Thomas MacPherson?" Elliot asked, showing his badge.

Fear flickered in the man's eyes for a brief moment, and he flinched almost imperceptibly, as if getting ready to run.

"Don't even think about it," Elliot said, his drawl heavier, his hand on his sidearm.

The man shook his head with a sad smile. "I'm not an idiot," he replied. "You'd catch me in no time. It was just an impulse, man, what can I say? Once you've been on the inside, cops scare the shit out of you, even if you haven't done anything."

"Aren't you going to ask us inside?" Kay asked. "After all, the coffee shop is now open, right?"

He muttered something, but stepped out of the doorway to let them in. Elliot gestured to him and he led the way, sighing a lungful of frustration. "What do you need, officers?" he asked, demeaning Elliot's rank on purpose, but he was too smart to let that get to him.

"One of your customers has gone missing," Elliot said, and his statement set MacPherson off like a can of dynamite.

"Oh, so now I'm a suspect?" he asked, slamming the kitchen utensils he'd pulled out to warm up some bagels. The implements clattered loudly against the stainless-steel sink behind the counter. "This is about the bodies you've been digging up at Silent Lake, isn't it? I won't let you pin those on me!"

"Why don't you come on over here," Elliot said, "and keep your hands where I can see them?"

MacPherson obeyed, the glint of hatred in his eyes tangible and sharp as a hunter's blade.

"There, happy?" he asked, once he was a few feet away from them, standing with his pudgy hands propped on his hips.

"Now take a seat," Elliot commanded, pointing his finger at a nearby chair.

He pulled the chair out and sat, mumbling profanities under his breath.

"Thank you," Kay said. It was a little late to try to build rapport with the man, but it wasn't impossible. "And no, Mr. MacPherson, you're not a suspect," she confirmed, earning herself a quick look from Elliot.

"Good, 'cause I ain't done much but work my ass off since I got out of the joint and built this place up on my own. And it ain't much." He sounded a little relieved, but still wary.

"It's the only coffee shop between Redding and downtown Mount Chester, isn't it? It's got to have some customers, right?" Kay probed.

"I can barely afford to keep the lights on, and I sleep in the back room, with the supplies, so that I'm not stargazing at night, if you catch my drift."

"Seems to me you could've done something else with your life, if this isn't what you wanted," Elliot said.

"No one would hire me, with my record. No one cares I've been on the straight and narrow since I got out five years ago. You make one mistake and that's it, your life goes down the drain."

He'd made more than one mistake, at least three different ones for which he'd been charged with a felony and convicted, but Kay wasn't about to argue. Instead, she lowered her voice to almost a whisper and said, "I understand, and I appreciate your willingness to help us, especially under these circumstances."

"Uh-huh," he muttered, "so, what do you need from me?"

"Like my partner said, one of your customers never made it aboard her flight, and she'd been here before she vanished. Maybe you remember her, a twenty-seven-year-old woman with long, curly hair? She came in with her daughter, maybe," Kay added, thinking that Alison could've asked Hazel to wait outside.

MacPherson ran his fingers across his three-day stubble, scratching his chin thoroughly, as if considering whether to *remember* them or not. "Yeah, I remember them," he eventually said. "She said her car broke down, and she had to walk for a mile to use my phone. No cell phone coverage in the valley, you know. She bought something, can't recall what, made her call, and left. End of story."

"Had she been in here before?" Kay asked. "Maybe on her way in from the airport?"

"When was this? Last Friday?"

"We didn't say, but that sounds right, yes," Elliot replied.

"She could've been here earlier, and I didn't notice her. On Fridays I have help. We get busy with weekend traffic. If she didn't need to use the phone the first time, I probably didn't see her if she stopped by."

"How about outside? Did you step outside while she was here, to notice what kind of car she was driving?" Kay asked. She knew that asking direct questions rarely got her anything other than defensive behavior from people, especially those with a long and impressive rap sheet.

"No idea what car she drove," he replied without hesitation, without the tiniest spark of fear in his eyes. "I can barely take a bathroom break on a Friday, we're so busy. I have to keep the bagels and donuts coming. I work the oven nonstop; make the coffee, sandwiches, and omelets and take care of any customers who sit at the bar instead of a table."

She could see he was telling the truth.

If he didn't sabotage Alison's car, how did the Nissan break down in that conveniently secluded, no-signal stretch of road? Did the unsub sneak into the café parking lot and sabotage it, knowing it would fail in an area where his victims were helpless and vulnerable? How precise could someone be, to get that kind of result? Was the location of the breakdown an act of chance or of expert engineering skill? The questions swirled in Kay's head.

"Has anything like this happened before?" Kay asked, returning to the point where she'd left off before. "Women coming in here, saying their cars broke down?"

"A few times, and not only women," he replied. "Cars break down when coming off the mountain. Them city drivers have no clue how to go down these mountain roads, keeping their foot on the brake pedal until it smokes. Every month we get one or two of them, more during winter." He laughed heartily, his raspy voice echoing in the empty coffee shop. "Lucrative piece of business, if you were to ask me. They walk in here, ask to make a phone call, then sit and wait while ordering stuff. Then they tip well. Can't complain."

"Really?" Kay reacted, laughing with him. "How about frequent customers, locals maybe? Do you have a lot of repeat business?"

"I have a few," he replied hesitantly, probably not willing to share that much about his regulars. "But most of my business comes from tourists. Them, and the folk who own cabins up on the mountain."

"Thanks," Kay said, visualizing what must've happened with her eyes closed. Alison had stopped here for coffee, driving in from the airport. Then she drove another mile, when her car broke down. That's why she walked on foot back here, to Katse, with Hazel, and made a call. It made more sense to imagine she'd waited here for whomever she'd called, than to assume she'd walked back to the car, coffee in hand. But she couldn't be sure.

She smiled, looking at Elliot, then she turned to MacPherson and asked, "Who did she call?"

But Elliot replied before he could. "Tow truck."

"Uh-huh," MacPherson said.

"One more thing," Kay said, getting ready to leave. "Did she wait here for the tow truck?"

He scratched his chin again. "For a while she did," he said. "Then the tow truck guy called and said she should meet him at the car. She left by herself, just her and her kid."

As they left the coffee shop, piercing rays of the sun brought a little warmth to the morning chill. Kay's smile widened.

"I know how the cars made it back to SFO without the GPS showing anything."

"Yup," Elliot replied, "tow truck."

CHAPTER EIGHTEEN

Play

Kathy loved playing at Judy's place. It was close to her home, and her parents let her cross the street and walk down the road the four houses over to Judy's, all by herself, making her feel like a grownup. If it got late, Judy's mother would make the girls dinner, and her food was delicious. She sometimes secretly wished Judy's parents were her own, but then felt guilty because she loved her mom very much.

She was about twelve, that sunny September afternoon, when leaves had just started turning up on the hills and the evening chill had grown sharper. She told her mother she was going to Judy's, but instead of just letting her go with a kiss on her forehead, her mom told her to wait a few minutes. Then her father had taken her reluctant hand in his and walked her there, joining Judy's dad, Mr. Stinson, on the porch for beers.

Bummer.

Being away from her father was half the reason why she enjoyed being at Judy's so much. It meant she was safe from the screaming and the beatings. But maybe he'd behave with Mr. Stinson there, watching.

The two men chatted on the covered porch, while the girls played in the front of the house. Judy had drawn some circles on the asphalt in yellow and green chalk, while Kathy hung like a monkey from Mr. Stinson's tow truck. She loved climbing on the rear of the vehicle, grabbing on to all those rods and cables and chains, and then jumping back down again.

"Get off that truck," her dad called, and she sadly let go and walked away. Mr. Stinson's truck was bright red and had something that looked like a cross in the back. That's where she liked to climb, up on the platform, hanging on to that tilted cross and dangling by the cables.

But she obeyed, just as her father, short-fused as always, had gotten off his chair to come and get her down himself.

She went over to the driveway and found Judy waiting, a fistful of pebbles by her side. In the corner of her eye, she saw her father sitting down next to Mr. Stinson, uncapping another bottle of beer. For a while at least, he'd let her be.

Picking up some pebbles, she started throwing them at the circles Judy had drawn. Their game was simple, nameless, and lots of fun. For each pebble that missed the circle, she had to obey Judy's command. Then it was Judy's turn, and for each of her misses, she got to give the commands and watch them being executed, while both of them laughed and laughed until they couldn't breathe.

Kathy threw each pebble carefully, weighing it in her hand to make sure she didn't over- or undershoot. Still, a pebble bounced right out of the green circle, after it had landed squarely inside.

"No," she squealed, then looked at Judy, waiting for her sentence.

"Lay flat in the dirt," Judy ordered.

Without a word, she lay on her back by the driveway, her arms folded under her head.

"Face down," Judy insisted, laughing.

"You didn't say!" Kathy replied, jumping to her feet and brushing some of the dust off her dress.

She picked the pebbles from the circles and gave them to her friend, then took her position to the side. Judy missed, and Kathy was quick to order, "Do a cartwheel."

Her eyes wandered while Judy threw her pebbles, and saw Nick in the distance, by the barn. He was looking at the two girls, and Kathy waved.

"Why can't Nick play with us?" she asked.

"Mom said he has to do chores."

Her smile waned. She liked Nick. He must've been about sixteen; he went to high school, and Judy got to brag about her older brother all the time. She also had an endless supply of homework already done, from four years ago when Nick had gone through the same assignments. All his notebooks were saved in a box under his bed, and he readily shared when asked. Nick was cool.

She waved at him, but he didn't wave back. Instead, he showed her the rake he was holding, lifting it up in the air and pointing at it in an exaggerated way, then went behind the fence, to work. He threw her one long look, clearly feeling sorry he couldn't play with them.

"Nick!" Mrs. Stinson called. "Get in the barn and lay the straw already. It's almost dark."

She waved at him one more time, but he didn't see her. Then she felt her father's sweaty hand grab hers and jumped out of her skin.

"Let's go home," he ordered, the stench of booze heavy on his breath. "You and Judy can play at our house tonight."

She turned to her friend, who seemed just as confused as she was, and then to Mr. Stinson, who smiled and said, "Go on, girls, have fun!"

CHAPTER NINETEEN
Offender

They stopped at the Chevron gas station on the way back to the sheriff's office, and Kay rushed inside while Elliot filled up the tank. A few minutes later, she came out carrying a box of fresh donuts and some coffee and found him wrapping up a phone call.

After they climbed into the vehicle and Elliot started the engine, he took a bite from the donut she had offered. He chewed quickly, then said, "It was a no-show."

"What are you talking about?" Kay asked.

"Alison was gone by the time the tow truck driver showed up," he clarified. "He checked at Katse and drove the valley both ways, but she was gone."

She was quiet for a moment. If Alison was gone by the time that tow truck got there, the unsub must've moved very quickly. He'd grabbed both Alison and Hazel, and—

"Was the Nissan still there?" she asked.

"Nope," he said, then whistled and made a hand gesture mimicking a car peeling off at high speed. "Gone."

She frowned. How were they supposed to find Alison and her daughter if every single lead they had disintegrated, leaving nothing behind? That car was supposedly broken down. How the heck did it disappear?

"Mr. Stinson, right?" she asked, sadness gripping her throat for a brief moment. "The tow truck driver?"

"Right," he replied, shooting her a quick look. "How did you know?"

"His daughter was my best friend growing up. I haven't had a chance to pay them a visit since I got back, but I believe the tow truck involvement theory just crashed and burned. There's no way Mr. Stinson has any part in this; he's the kindest man I've ever met."

Elliot took another bite of donut. "I agree. I worked with him long enough to know it's not him. He's my go-to guy for DUI tows and traffic accidents; with so many tourists driving under the influence, he and I have been crossing paths a lot. But it made sense, the idea that the unsub is towing the cars to San Francisco. It's simple, no one would've stopped them on the way."

"Is Mr. Stinson still the only towing service in town?"

"Other than him, the closest one is in Redding, and that's almost an hour away. And there's no other towing capable truck registered to anyone in the area."

She stared at the road ahead silently, lost in memories she'd almost completely forgotten. Judy and her, playing by the tow truck. Judy's mother, setting the dinner table. The two girls, sharing a sweet sixteenth birthday, and talking about boys in the back of Judy's yard. Then she moved away to college, while Judy stayed behind. They'd emailed for a while, spoken on the phone, but soon fell out of touch, although Kay's heart still ached when she thought of Judy. She missed her friend.

"I'd completely forgotten about them," she said softly, her voice loaded with tears she didn't expect. "They were my second family, sometimes closer than my first, and I—"

"You moved on and built a life for yourself," he replied. "That must've taken some serious work, I bet."

"It wasn't easy, that's for sure," she chuckled, wiping off a rebel tear from the corner of her eye. "Do you know I used to play on that tow truck? And still, when we interviewed MacPherson, it didn't click. It didn't come to me. I was so sure we had the unsub's signature figured out, but no. We're back to square one." She bit the tip of her index fingernail for a brief moment, a long-forgotten gesture that calmed her frayed nerves.

It couldn't've been Mr. Stinson; she would lay her life down on that. But the tow truck theory made so much sense she couldn't just let it go. It was elegant, cop-proof, anonymous. How many cops pull over loaded tow trucks? Zero. Most of them transport vehicles with accident reports or in collaboration with police, like impounds or illegal-parking removals. The unsub knew he wouldn't get stopped. He had a way to grab the broken-down vehicles when they couldn't be driven anymore. Vehicles, because Kay had no doubt in her mind that the technician would soon call them and confirm the Jeep had broken down also. But if the tow truck had really been involved in the disposal of the victims' cars, then it should be on camera at the San Francisco long-term parking garage. As soon as she got those videos she'd know for sure.

"Not necessarily," Elliot replied, after wolfing down the rest of the donut and licking the sugar off his fingers. "We have Eggers in custody. You know, the local sex offender. I'd say he's by far more likely to have kidnapped and killed these women than your best friend's dad, don't you think?"

She let out a short yet loaded sigh. "Honestly, I think we're wasting our time. He's a disorganized sex offender, one of the grab-and-rape types, not the man we're looking for."

"Still, Logan has him chained to the table in an interview room," he said with a wide grin. "All yours to play with, while I get a warrant to search his house."

"We're wasting time, Elliot," she said, aware she'd raised her voice. "I'm telling you, it's not him."

"And I'm telling you, I have a boss and I have to work for a living," he replied calmly, but she knew better than to buy his appearance of composure. "It makes sense, from a police procedure perspective," he added. "Stuff you might not give a horse's rear end about, but might end some good cops' careers if things go bust and we can't even say we rounded up the model citizens of the neighborhood."

She didn't reply; there was nothing left to say. Instead, she spent the little time she had before the Eggers interview analyzing the unsub's signature.

It was uniquely complex, requiring agility, both mental and physical, strength, knowledge and means. She didn't separate the burial ritual from the vehicle disposal, including them both in the signature, because they'd both been orchestrated by the same man. By definition, the signature of a killing included the particular elements that are not necessary in the committing of the crime, but speak to the killer's compulsions and fantasy-driven rituals. The vehicle disposal might've been a forensic countermeasure and nothing else, allowing him to hide the cars without risking leaving particulates and fingerprints inside. But she believed that there was more to it than just excellent planning and even better execution.

The time frame he had to grab Alison and Hazel and hide the car before the tow truck got there was incredibly narrow. Now that she remembered Mr. Stinson, she no longer suspected the tow truck driver of involvement in the crime, but still felt strongly she should talk to him, not only to catch up, but also to build an accurate timeline of events. What time did he get the call from Alison? Even if he didn't remember exactly, phone records could be obtained. How long did it take him to respond? What time did he get to the vehicle, to find Alison was gone?

But maybe, she had to admit, she was obsessing over the vehicle disposal part because she didn't have a solid lead; not anymore. If she wanted to find Alison and Hazel alive, she had to find a shortcut somewhere, because the road that led from the SFO video surveillance analysis to the tow truck business phone records was a long and meandering one, not guaranteed to succeed but guaranteed to take days, if not weeks.

Alison and Hazel couldn't afford that. The unsub had killed Kendra after only ten days of captivity, and he'd already been holding Alison for seven days. Time was running out.

As soon as Elliot pulled into the sheriff's office parking lot and cut the engine, Kay rushed inside. A few minutes after nine, she entered the interview room to find a skinny man stinking of alcohol. The early morning hour didn't seem to matter, because for Eggers the party didn't seem to stop.

Kay had just reviewed his record, while he waited with a smirk on his face, when Elliot joined them. She decided to cut it short, the formality that it was, and went straight for the critical question.

"Mr. Eggers, where were you on October fifteenth, between two and six in the afternoon?"

"How am I supposed to remember?" he replied morosely. "Let me ask my secretary," he added, sarcasm dripping from his venom-loaded voice. "Oh, now I remember, I was on a fishing expedition with a bunch of loser cops."

"I suggest you remember," she insisted. "It's in your best interest."

"Yeah, like you care about my best interest," he replied, leaning back in his chair as far as the handcuffs chained to the table allowed him. "You know what's in my best interest? A damn lawyer, that's what. And take these damn chains off of me, 'cause I'm not under arrest, am I?"

Elliot looked at Kay briefly, then removed Eggers's handcuffs. The man rubbed his wrists vigorously, then interlaced his fingers behind his head in a defiant posture.

"You're not under arrest, Mr. Eggers," Elliot replied. "We need you to answer a few ques—"

"You need to pin something major on me, don't you, Texas Ranger? Aren't you a bit far from the O.K. Corral?"

Elliot tried to speak, but was quickly cut off again. "That's in Arizona, not Texas. Mr. Eggers, there's no need—"

"There's a need for what I say there's a need for, and that's a lawyer. I know my rights."

"All right," Kay replied, "you'll have your lawyer. Can you afford one? Or should we get one of those young folks, fresh out of college, to seal your fate?"

"The greenest of lawyers will know to tell you I'm not talkin' to no cops." He spat on the floor, inches away from Kay's foot. She didn't flinch.

"Until your lawyer gets here," Kay said, "if you needed a tow truck, where would you get one?"

"From the *Yellow* fuckin' *Pages*, that's where. No more questions without my lawyer; don't try to trick me."

Elliot beckoned Kay to follow him out of the room. As soon as the door was closed behind them, he said, "We'll storm his house and find Alison and Hazel, if they're there to be found. Don't pave this guy's road to a release over a Miranda technicality. He's asked for a lawyer. We're done."

"I'm not law enforcement," Kay replied with a weak smile.

"Yes, but I am, and my presence in the room guarantees his rights."

"Can't you just, um, go out for coffee?" Kay asked. "He's not the unsub, Elliot, I promise you that. But maybe he's heard something out there, maybe I can get him to talk. Thing is, we don't have much else to go on. It's like Alison and Hazel vanished into thin air."

"There's no way, I'm sorry," Elliot replied. "Logan would fire me on the spot, and whatever we'd find out during the questioning would be fruit of the poisonous tree; he'd walk. You know that, partner."

Yes, she did. She hated it, but the law was clear, and today didn't seem like the day she could bend the rules a little.

"All right. Let's see what the search yields, maybe we can get some leverage and question him again. Because I'm telling you, Elliot, we won't find those girls in this man's basement."

CHAPTER TWENTY

First Kill

The first few minutes after his mother had thrown him out of the house, he stood there in a daze. It wasn't happening; it couldn't happen. She must've been joking, and she'd soon open the door and invite him back inside, give him a hug and run her fingers through his hair, arranging it neatly like she used to do when he was little.

She didn't. The house remained silent, and the front door locked.

About twenty minutes later, the porch light was switched off, leaving him alone in the unwelcoming darkness.

He banged on the door, begged and pleaded, but no one seemed to hear him. He swore he'd be good, although he didn't understand what he'd done wrong. Then he crouched on the ground, hugging his knees and leaning against the door, the night's chilled air freezing his blood.

But she didn't open that door.

At the crack of dawn, his father came out and said, "Son, you're old enough. You'll be fine out there. You have to go. I'm—um, really sorry." And he shoved a couple of twenty-dollar bills into his son's trembling hand. Then the door was locked again, this time for good.

He understood, although he had no idea why. He understood his mother didn't love him anymore, maybe she never had. He realized his father was never going to take his side. And he walked away, burning tears flooding his eyes.

His first stop was the church. He knew the priest helped people in need; that's why all his old clothes and things the family didn't need any more were donated to the congregation. But Father Reaves had listened to his cry for help with distance in his demeanor, then said to him he wasn't welcome at church anymore.

"Pray to the Lord for forgiveness, and He'll show you the way back from the dark realm of concupiscence," Father Reaves had said, spewing words he didn't understand. "Then the community will open its bosom for you, my little lost sheep."

"But, Father, what have I done?"

"You have chosen the wrong path, my son, a path serving Satan through selfishly inward carnal fervor, and it's a terrible sin," the priest said with a long sigh. A couple of elderly women entered the church as he was saying those words, shooting worried glances at him, then at the priest. "Search your soul, and find the path back to righteousness. And pray to the Lord to guide you." He then grabbed his elbow lightly but firmly, and showed him out the door. "Go with God, my son. I'll be praying for you."

It seemed his mother had poisoned the entire community with lies about him. He couldn't stay and face the disdain; he was always going to be a pariah in the town he once called his home. No one would help him, no one would take him in or give him food scraps to eat. He had to leave.

That day, he hitched a ride to San Francisco on an eighteen-wheeler whose driver took half his money to drop him off at the foot of the San Francisco-Oakland Bay Bridge, after questioning him thoroughly about his age. He swore he was over eighteen; he was still a year and several months shy of that milestone, but San Francisco's Tenderloin neighborhood had very little against adding one more panhandler to one of its street corners, especially one as young as him. The ill-famed neighborhood was home to some theaters and entertainment, but also to the majority of the city's deviants, sex workers and vagrants; its squalid conditions, street drug trade and illegal strip joints having earned the neighborhood its name, a reference, many say, to a hooker's tender loins. Others believed the neighborhood, a cultural and societal duplicate of the New York City Tenderloin district, had earned its name from the fact that cops working that beat made so much money on the side that they could afford to eat tenderloin every day. Regardless of which shady practice had earned the neighborhood its name, there wasn't a better place for him to lose himself and start his new life in the streets.

In a few days, he'd figured out where to sleep and how to get his aching belly full every day, and which dumpsters were worth diving into. The days were long, and he ventured outside the Tenderloin, looking for wealthier people willing to put some more change in his hat. He'd quickly learned how to avoid cops, after narrowly escaping a patrol that caught him loitering in front of the wrong building. And three days after he'd arrived, he'd snatched the sleeping bag from underneath an elderly hobo, realizing he felt absolutely no remorse. Three nights in the cold San Francisco fog had made his priorities crystal clear.

He was two months shy of his eighteenth birthday when he was raped for the first time.

He'd found himself a quiet corner behind a restaurant, and had been sleeping there for the past few weeks. After closing time, the restaurant staff took the garbage out in the back, then locked the doors and went home. Behind that building was the back of a three-story manufacturing building turned warehouse, secured by tall fences. Tucked in that dark, dead-end alley, he'd felt safe.

Until that night.

The fog had dropped thick, engulfing the city and all its sounds in a milk-like substance that put cold moisture into his bones. When the SUV pulled over, he just pulled back a little farther, hoping he wouldn't be seen.

But the three men came looking for him. He recognized them; they'd put some spare change in his hat earlier that day while making all sorts of comments about his body, his mouth, his tight ass and the things they wanted to do to him, laughing loudly with raspy voices loaded with lust. He didn't think much of it at the time; since he'd been a Tenderloin resident, abuse had been no stranger, especially that of a verbal kind.

He didn't stand a chance, a young and malnourished boy against three strong men in their mid-twenties. When the three assailants finished with him and peeled off in their blue Cadillac Escalade, he just lay there on the cold asphalt, swallowing tears mixed with blood.

He moved that day, hurting with every step and hauling his worldly possessions tied in a bundle, found another dead-end alley where he hoped he'd be safe for a while. He started eating more, denying the revolt he felt for the food he retrieved from the trash. He made it a priority to find decent dumpsters that serviced better restaurants, then drove other homeless people away from that area, using them as punching bags whenever he could, knowing he would one day need to be able to fight better than the last time.

Later that month, when the three men returned, he thought he was ready for them. He was surprised they'd found him again, but they must've been stalking him because they didn't seem to hesitate when they pulled into the dark alley, laughing loudly.

He fought them as best as he could, landing a few scrawny punches that only got the men more excited, hollering their lustful frenzy in the all-engulfing fog. Then they took turns until they were spent and lost all interest in the boy who lay inert at their feet in a pool of his own blood.

He knew they'd come back. They'd always come back, because he was there, an easy victim, someone who couldn't file a police report, someone who no one missed, and no one cared about.

This time, he didn't move, he didn't search for a better corner of the Tenderloin to hunker down in. This time, he had a plan, and when they returned, he was ready for them.

He shanked the first two men quickly, with a lightning-fast series of stabs into their abdomens, using a carving knife he'd found discarded in the dumpster behind the restaurant. He had to chase the third down the street for a few hundred feet, but he was fast and caught up with him eventually. When he did, he sliced the man's throat from behind, grabbing a fistful of his hair and holding him in place, without a moment's hesitation. Then he let his body fall on the sidewalk with a thump that mimicked the beats of his racing heart. He dragged him back into the alley and threw him into the dumpster, then checked on the other two, who were still alive, agonizing in a growing pool of blood. Just like they'd left him a few weeks before.

A sense of exhilaration, of superlative power coursed through his veins, injecting liquid euphoria in every drop of his heated blood. He breathed deeply, filling his lungs with the salty fog and feeling reborn, as if the lives he held in his hand synergized with his own.

He stood tall, wondering if he should finish them off or let them die on their own, to get a taste of their own medicine. They weren't going to last long, anyway, but they deserved to suffer. Then he wondered why the third man hadn't taken off in their luxury car. The answer was right there at his feet, in a puddle of rainwater that was stained red. A fancy keychain and a key bearing the stylized mark of the coveted brand, that he must've dropped as he ran down the alley.

He bent over and grabbed the key, holding it in the palm of his hand for a long moment, seizing the continuing feeling of freedom, of complete and exhilarating power he felt for the first time in his life. Now he knew what he wanted.

Power.

At all costs. Without limits. The power to survive, to thrive. To kill.

CHAPTER TWENTY-ONE
Ranch

Kay waited outside, while Elliot and the deputies thoroughly searched the Eggers property, an old, rundown ranch sitting on a couple of acres of land, and a large shed on the other side of the potholed driveway.

Alison and Hazel had been missing for a week, and they'd just learned of Shannon's little boy, Matthew, who was also missing since last November. The thought of Matthew made her wonder how many other missing children she might find if she ran a database search. But the sad reality was that only the year before, over seventy-six thousand children had been reported missing in the state of California alone. Needles in a very large haystack, and no way to correlate any such report with the unsub. She was better off following the evidence where it led her.

But what were the odds of finding them there, at that desolate ranch, and still alive? She looked at her watch impatiently. It was almost noon, and they still had nothing, no hope of finding Alison and the kids.

Oliver Eggers stood a few feet away, flanked by his attorney, a young woman who couldn't've been more than twenty-seven, maybe twenty-eight years old, but who had proven to be articulate and astute, getting Eggers released without delay.

Coming out of the house, Elliot beckoned Kay. She approached him quickly, already knowing what he was about to say, visible clearly in his hung head, tight lips and the hand he clenched in a fist and buried in his pocket.

"They're not here," he said. "We should've listened, and not wasted any more time. They were never here," he added, pointing at the K9 team. Niner was sitting calmly in the shade of a large oak, a sign that Hazel's scent wasn't there to be picked up and traced.

"Detective," one of the deputies called. He'd been searching Eggers's truck in minute detail, and he'd just opened the cargo space in the back, covered with a black plastic cover bearing the Dodge Ram logo. He pulled out a large, dirty towing strap with D-rings attached at both ends and showed it to them.

"Could he have towed the vehicles to San Francisco with this?" Elliot asked.

"Hardly," she replied. "The cops would've pulled him over fifteen times on the interstate. He would've never made it to the city."

Two deputies had cut the padlock and were opening the shed's corrugated metal double doors. She didn't pay attention to what they were doing; instead, she kept looking at the towing strap. There were lots of innocent reasons why people living in rural areas owned such a strap. To secure farm or garden equipment on a trailer. To tie up large loads to the bed of the truck. But towing another vehicle for large distances wasn't one of them.

Unless…

"Detective," a man called from inside the shed, "you need to see this."

They rushed inside, and after her eyes adjusted to the darkness, she saw a large utility trailer, the kind that has a ramp built in at the back that lifts and locks into place. The wooden surface of the trailer showed signs of repeated use over the years. It wasn't new; far from it. The wood was partly rotted, and pieces of it were missing, exposing the metallic structure underneath.

"Do you think that Nissan could fit onto this?" she asked, but Elliot pulled out his phone instead of answering.

After a brief moment, he lifted his eyes from his device and said, "That Nissan Altima model is one hundred and ninety-one, point nine inches long. Let's see. Anyone have a measuring tape?" he asked, raising his voice to be heard outside the shed.

Someone rushed in with a tape, and Elliot grabbed the end of it and pulled, attaching it to the far end of the trailer. "Sixteen feet," he announced. "That is, I'll be damned, one hundred and ninety-two inches on the mark."

Kay approached, studying the dirty flatbed. Multiple tire marks were showing, staining the old wood with black, ragged lines in various patterns. Maybe one of the most recent ones was a match to the Nissan's tires.

"How about the Jeep? Does that fit?"

Elliot checked, then said, "With room to spare. The Jeep is one hundred and eighty-nine inches long. It's also taller, exceeding the height of the front bulkhead. You could easily haul that Jeep with this trailer. All you need is a—"

"A strap, to secure it in place," Kay said, pointing toward the truck. "Can you call the office and ask the technicians to see if there were scratches on the Nissan's fenders? It would've fit very tightly, with no room to spare. Maybe it got scratched in the process."

Hearing a commotion, she rushed to the house, followed closely by Elliot, who was on the phone. Two deputies were booking Eggers formally, reading him his rights, while his attorney shouted, "What is my client being charged with?"

One of the deputies held a small packet of white powder with two gloved fingers. "Cocaine. I guess it's small enough to be simple possession, without intent to distribute, but we'll let the lab weigh in on that." He laughed curtly, showing two rows of yellow, crooked teeth, probably entertained by his own pun. He sounded like he'd made that joke at least a few times before. "With his priors, it will be a while until your client can see daylight again."

"This is bullshit," Eggers screamed, wrestling the two deputies who held his arms while a third clinched the handcuffs on his wrists. "You put that in there, motherfucker, I saw you!" He spat at one of the deputies, then charged toward him. "You framed me, and I'll kill you for it."

"Mr. Eggers, I must advise you to remain silent," his lawyer intervened. "Not another word, and stop resisting."

Eggers spat again and cursed while the deputies loaded him in the back of their Interceptor, but at least he seemed to take some of his lawyer's advice to heart.

His arrest opened some possibilities, and Kay was quick to jump in and seize them. She approached the lawyer and said, "We might work a way around this issue, if your client is willing to cooperate."

"What do you have in mind?" the lawyer asked.

"Let's discuss it later," she replied, quick to end the conversation before Elliot approached.

"There aren't any scratches on the Nissan," he announced. "The Jeep shows the same check engine light when powered on, and both vehicles return the same codes, depleted coolant and overheated engine. But both have their coolant up to the mark. Now they have to take the cars apart and figure out how they broke down."

Great, she thought. *Can't we get a bloody break?*

This unsub had the knowledge how to sabotage vehicles quickly, in a manner that caused them to fail, yet befuddled the technician. That rounded up his skillset nicely, right there with the ability to grab victims quickly and unseen, and make vehicles disappear without a trace, only to appear three hundred miles away, parked neatly where no one could think of looking.

"We'll sweat him, don't worry," Hobbs said, pointing at Eggers. "I bet he'll be willing to spill his guts by the time we get back to the house."

"The house?" Kay asked, intrigued.

"We call the sheriff's office the house, short for the White House. It's white, you know, and our president lives there," he added with a quick wink.

"Do your best," she said, looking at Eggers. "Find out if he hauled any vehicles for someone, or if he loaned the trailer to someone recently. Offer him a deal if he talks." Eggers seemed to have had the ability to tow the vehicles back to San Francisco, but everything else about him was wrong. She wasn't holding her breath; the killer was still out there, holding Alison Nolan and two children captive, torturing them.

If they were still alive.

Elliot's phone buzzed, and he looked at the screen. "They're stopping the search," he said, his voice tinged with sadness. "It's almost dark, and they need to start again tomorrow. They're bringing bloodhounds from Sacramento."

She kept her gaze on the horizon the entire time, as if not hearing him. What was she going to do? Go home and watch TV in that sad living room, while Alison endured the unsub's torture, hour after endless hour? Eat, shower, sleep, like a normal person would at the end of a workday, because there was always tomorrow?

What if Alison and those kids didn't have a tomorrow?

Elliot touched her arm gently. "Come on, let's go. I'll buy you dinner."

"Listen, if you're tired, you can go home," she said, squeezing his forearm, "and I know what I'm asking is against regulations, but I need to borrow your SUV. I need lights and sirens where I'm going."

"And where exactly is that?"

"San Francisco," she replied. "I want to visit Shannon Hendricks's family. If I step on it, I could be there by ten."

"Why?" he asked, already rushing toward the vehicle. He tossed her the keys and took the passenger seat.

"I don't know what to expect, but there aren't any other leads we could follow tonight." She started the engine and peeled off, throwing pebbles and dust up in the air.

Maybe this time she could catch a break.

CHAPTER TWENTY-TWO
Found

Kay drove as fast as she dared on the interstate, taking advantage of the lighter traffic, while Elliot had dozed off on the passenger seat, leaning back. His cowboy hat covered his face almost completely, shielding his eyes from the red-and-blue flicker of the flasher bar she hadn't turned off since they'd left Mount Chester.

She hadn't slowed down, nor stopped the entire time. She wanted to ring the doorbell at Shannon's house as early as possible, on the most difficult day that family had gone through. After having already skipped on one night of rest, tiredness had taken over, forcing her to drive with her window down, counting on the cold air to whip her senses back into high gear.

Shannon had been gone since November, and so had her five-year-old son Matthew. Almost a year had passed since they'd been taken. She vaguely recalled seeing TV coverage of their disappearance, back when she was still in San Francisco, working at the FBI regional office, but she didn't recall all the details. There had been numerous theories at that point, just thoughts and ideas passed around between investigators, no more. But none of them came close to explaining why Shannon, a stunningly beautiful divorcee, had vanished without a trace.

Kay recalled Shannon's driver's license photo. She was a blonde with long hair, at least in that picture and the ones her mother had shared with the media to use in the ads and appeals for her safe return. Digging into the system, Kay had found the AMBER Alert, still active, but showing a couple of modification records, which meant the content of the alert had been changed since it had originally been issued, probably as more information had become available.

And still, recalling Shannon's physiognomy only posed more questions. Kendra had been Caucasian with long, sleek hair in a dark, reddish shade of brown, and brown eyes. Alison's raven-black hair was a mane of long, unruly curls, her skin was pale, and her eyes also dark brown, almost black. But Shannon was a natural blonde with blue eyes. If these women were surrogates for the object of the perpetrator's rage, there was no pattern she could readily notice.

However, she held on to the hope that maybe Shannon had been the unsub's first kill. That could potentially yield valuable information, because most serial killers start close to home, by choosing a target who crosses their path. Someone they see on a daily basis, or someone they have some sort of a relationship with. Maybe if she understood Shannon's background in detail, she could find some clue to the unsub's identity.

With Shannon's identity only discovered early that same morning, victimology was far from being complete, but Kay knew not to expect much. Kendra was from New York City, Alison from Atlanta, and Shannon from San Francisco. It was a safe bet to assume the women had little, if anything, in common, and it seemed that they didn't even share a physiognomy type. Other than age and race, Kay couldn't think of any common trait the three shared. Alison and Shannon were mothers and had been taken with their children, but Kendra was not a mother. The only commonality was that all of them were between twenty-five and thirty-two years of age, with Shannon being the oldest. That, and the fact that all three women had traveled to Mount Chester.

Victims of opportunity, maybe, Kay wondered as she pulled in front of Shannon Hendricks's residence. Did the killer think travelers in the area would be more difficult to trace back to Mount Chester?

She cut the engine and nudged Elliot in the shoulder.

"We're here," she said. "Wake up, cowboy."

Frowning, Elliot took his hat off his face and looked around, squinting. They were parked in front of a two-story townhouse in Glen Park. It didn't look like much from the outside, but Kay knew it was valued at about 2 million dollars, and the views from the upper floor must've been spectacular. It was built at the top of a hill, facing northeast, overlooking a part of the San Francisco downtown area, and the bay in the distance. From records, Kay knew Shannon had lived there with her mother, Joann Hendricks.

There wasn't anything worse than having to discuss the circumstances of a child's death with the mother. Kay felt a chill and rubbed her hands together, inhaling sharply.

"It's nine thirty," Elliot commented, after taking a drink of water from one of the plastic bottles he had stocked up on in a small cooler in the rear seat. "How fast were you going? You drove four hours' worth of interstate in barely three. Did you put our lives in danger, Dr. Sharp?"

"I'll plead the fifth," Kay replied, rushing to the front door. The lights were still on, and as soon as she rang the bell, she could hear footsteps coming down the stairs, and approaching the door.

A woman in her sixties opened the door. She'd been crying; her eyes were red and swollen, and tears welled up when she looked at Elliot's badge.

"Did you find Matthew?" she asked, her voice filled with hope that Kay was about to shatter.

"No, ma'am, we have not," she replied gently. "May we come in?"

Joann Hendricks invited them to take a seat on a couch, and she sat on one of the two opposing armchairs. She was petite, but the way she carried herself, even when grief stricken, showed internal strength. She wore her hair naturally gray and cut short, speaking of her direct nature.

"My apologies," she whispered, patting the corners of her eyes with a tissue. "I've just received the news of my daughter's death this morning. I—I'm not ready to deal with life yet."

"No need to apologize," Kay replied. "It's rather late, and I want to thank you for taking the time to speak with us tonight."

"I just can't come to grips with the situation," she said, her voice strong at first, before trailing off in a stifled sob. "I won't be able to, for a while at least."

"I can only imagine how you must feel. If you need more time, we could—"

Joann dismissed Kay's question with a gesture of her hand. "Tell me, what do you need to know?"

"When's the last time you saw your daughter?" Kay asked.

"On November twenty-seventh, last year," she replied, "the Tuesday after Thanksgiving." She paused for a while, hugging herself and leaning forward, her head hung low. "We had such a nice time. She was just starting to be happy again, after her divorce."

Tears began rolling down her cheeks, while a stifled whimper escaped her lips, escalating into a sob before she could control herself.

A piercing, blood-chilling wail came from upstairs.

A moment later, Kay saw a young girl standing on the second-floor landing, pale and seemingly in shock, her blue eyes staring into emptiness. She wore a long, white nightgown stained with fresh tears.

At the sight of the child, Kay held her breath. The girl looked just like her mother, a much younger and distressed version of the beautiful blonde with long, curly hair that could be seen in many photos on the wall.

"Oh, no, Tracy," Joann whispered, rushing to the child. She climbed the stairs as quickly as she could, then sat on the top step and talked to the girl in a low whisper. After a while, the little girl allowed Joann to take hold of her hand and they both climbed down, slowly, one step at a time.

Joann sat in the armchair, the girl curled up in her lap with her knees tightly against her chest. After a while, under her grandmother's gentle caress, her shattered breathing normalized, and the child finally fell asleep.

"My poor baby," Joann said, still caressing the girl's hair. "My little miracle. It's a wonder she came back to us."

Kay looked at Elliot for a brief moment. He seemed just as stunned as she was. Came back? From where?

"What do you mean?"

"Don't you know?" Joann asked, her voice a barely audible whisper. "Wasn't that in the, um, police reports, or something?"

"I'm not sure what you mean," Elliot said, sounding apologetic, almost embarrassed.

"When Shannon disappeared, she had both children with her," Joann said, lowering her voice even further. "Tracy was found wandering the streets, here, in San Francisco, a couple of weeks after they'd all vanished."

Kay sprung to her feet, but quickly sat again, when Joann's firm gaze met hers. She couldn't believe there was no mention in the missing person report of the other child. She looked briefly at Elliot. He was checking something on his phone, already retrieving the report from the system.

She remembered it word for word, because she'd read it many times, each time hoping the report was wrong, hoping Shannon had been taken alone, and that her son was home, safe. Each time she read the same phrase, "Last seen leaving her home in Glen Park, in a blue Subaru Forrester, together with her son Matthew, age five." Then the report listed the corresponding AMBER Alert activation number. No mention of Tracy anywhere.

"Tracy isn't listed in the missing person report," Elliot said, confirming her recollection of the facts. "I'm not sure how—"

"She spent a few weeks in foster care, poor child," Joann said with sadness. "It took them a while to identify her, although I had given them DNA samples for all three. But because she was found lost, in the street, they couldn't assume she'd been taken with her mother and her brother, I guess. No one bothered to tell me anything; why would they?" The bitterness in her voice was unmistakable.

"When could we speak with Tracy?" Kay asked.

"She hasn't said a word since they found her," Joann replied. "Don't you think I would've said something, if I'd known anything, any little detail that could lead to finding Shannon and Matthew?"

"Have you tried speaking with a psychiatrist?" Elliot asked. "Sometimes they're able to reach children like Tracy."

"You mean, children traumatized beyond words?" Joann replied. "Yes, I've tried. I took Tracy to a Stanford University professor, who saw her every day for weeks. He tried hypnosis and other methods, but Tracy seems too shocked to be able to speak, and he recommended we don't push her. At some point, when her brain will be able to handle the trauma, she will start remembering and she'll tell us what horrors she witnessed."

She choked on the last word, and the little girl shifted in her sleep, whimpering quietly.

"No one knows how she came to be lost, or where her brother is," she added. "She just screams when she hears me cry, and it's been incredibly difficult, especially today."

Slack-jawed, Kay looked at the two of them, broken-hearted and frail, rocking gently in the leather armchair. A million questions whirled in her mind, most of them having to do with the police investigation into Shannon's disappearance a year ago. "What did the cops say, after Shannon and the kids disappeared?"

Joann breathed deeply before answering, as if gathering her strength before bringing up painful memories.

"Shannon wanted to teach the kids how to ski," she said, wiping a tear from her eye with a quick touch of her finger. "She just packed them up in the Subaru, winter clothes and everything. On a Tuesday, no less," she added with a sad chuckle. "It wasn't something she'd planned; she just waited for the first snow to fall, so it would be nice, but not crowded, and not very cold. Shannon hated the cold."

"And then?" Elliot asked when the woman stopped talking, biting her lip hard to control her tears.

"She was supposed to call that night, and she didn't. I called her, and got voicemail. Then I rang again the next morning, but I didn't panic until about lunch. I started to call the hotel, the resort, asking if anyone had seen her. Then I phoned the police."

They'd only known Shannon's identity for a few hours; reviewing the investigation findings with the San Francisco Police Department was something she now wished she'd had the time to do before meeting with Joann Hendricks.

"What did they say?" Elliot asked calmly.

"They went back and forth for a while," Joann replied, "as if they didn't know what they were doing. They kept asking questions about Larry, Shannon's ex. He lost custody of both children and they assumed he was vengeful, or had kidnapped them himself."

"Is he a violent man?" Kay asked, wondering if he could be who they were looking for. If Shannon had been his first victim, it was possible the unsub had a personal relationship with her. The divorce and lost custody battle could've been the trigger, setting him off on his rage-fueled path of killing women. Everything fit, except the Mount Chester connection.

"He's an addict," Joann replied coldly. "He was snorting cocaine to perform at his high-paying job, and was driving my daughter insane. She was able to do the same job without drugs, and raise two children, but him, no. An addict and a loser, that's who Larry Pickett really is."

"Was he upset about the custody? As a man, that had to hurt, not being allowed to see his kids," Elliot said.

"I don't believe he cared enough to feel hurt," Joann replied, contempt seeping from her words. "He found himself some girls he could do cocaine with and started living the life, forgetting to send in his child support checks. A couple of months after the divorce, he was fired from his job, and he spiraled from there. I was happy that Shannon didn't get to see him in the office every day; that was terrible, an awful situation. They worked together, both of them were analysts for that major investment bank, um, Rolfe Sanders Trust."

She whimpered quietly, evidently heartbroken to use the past tense about her daughter's job, her life.

"Where is he from?" Kay asked. Another key piece of the already paper-thin victimology had shattered when she'd learned that Shannon had driven her own car to Mount Chester, meaning the car rental thread that Alison and Kendra had in common was just a coincidence, and so was the connection with San Francisco International Airport.

"Not sure, but I can tell you where he is," she replied. "In jail. Where he belongs. And as sad as I am to know my grandkids will grow up knowing their father is a convicted felon, I believe this is better for everyone."

"Since when?" Kay asked.

"They arrested him in May, I believe. He was high, and propositioned an undercover cop, offering her drugs and money for sex."

If he was in jail, Larry couldn't've killed Kendra, or abducted Alison and her daughter. Another dead end. Kay repressed a sigh of frustration.

Tracy shivered and started shaking in her sleep, mumbling unintelligible words. Joann wrapped her arms around the child and whispered in her ear, "Shh, baby, I'm here, and you're safe. You're at home, and I love you. Shh… sleep now, baby." After a few heart-wrenching moments, the little girl settled.

"That's how she's been," Joann said, gently touching the girl's hair. "She cries or she shakes; she has night terrors and she screams; and she never relaxes. Who knows what happened to my poor baby, what that monster did to her?"

There was a brief moment of silence. Kay kept thinking how she could hope to unlock the secrets buried inside the girl's traumatized memory, while Elliot seemed to be preoccupied with something else, given how he kept reviewing his notes.

"You were telling us about the police investigation," he said, whispering so quietly she could barely hear him.

"Yes," Joann replied. "They didn't do much, and I believe they weren't so sure she was kidnapped. You see, at first, they kept obsessing about Larry. Then they found her car—"

"Where?" Kay asked.

"In the airport's long-term parking lot, out of all places," she replied, frowning. "Subaru did a number with a technology it has, STARLINK I believe it's called, and located the car. The police conveniently assumed she left by plane, although her luggage was still in the car. Even her coffee cup was there, untouched."

The airport. One common thread that remained true, the unsub's favorite method to dispose of the victims' vehicles. She checked the time and realized it was almost midnight. Tomorrow morning, when she would see the case photos, she'd be able to establish if the untouched coffee had come from Katse Coffee Shop in Mount Chester.

"Where's the car now?" Kay asked. She wanted to see if she'd find it with the check engine light on, returning the same error codes as Kendra's Jeep and Alison's Nissan had.

"The police have it. Honestly, I have no idea why Shannon drove to San Francisco International Airport," Joann continued. "She left for Mount Chester Ski Resort; that's north of here, not east."

"Did the FBI investigate?" Kay asked, knowing it was the norm for the bureau to deploy the Child Abduction Rapid Deployment or CARD team for missing children of Matthew and Tracy's ages.

"Yes, they all worked together, but didn't, um, couldn't find them. Then Tracy was found, and they said there was a strong possibility Shannon abandoned her children and flew out of San Francisco under a false identity, probably to meet a lover. They let the case grow cold," she said, while tears pooled in her eyes. "They gave up on them. On us." She cleared her voice quietly. "My daughter would've never abandoned her children. Never."

CHAPTER TWENTY-THREE
Monogram

Alison had lain on her side, unable to move, for what seemed like hours after he'd left. She couldn't distinguish where the pain was coming from anymore; her entire body ached. But worst of all was she hadn't seen Hazel, not for two days. She hadn't heard her either, although she often held her breath hoping she'd hear a sound, no matter how tiny, just to tell her that her daughter was okay.

She'd asked him earlier, but he'd just laughed and said, "You and your little girls... aren't you something?" When she'd asked again, he was instantly enraged and grabbed her by her braided hair, pulling her back. He sunk his teeth into the flesh of her breast, hard, until his teeth pierced the skin and she screamed, as much as she'd sworn to herself she wasn't going to scream again.

Because Hazel could hear.

Then, lesson learned, she'd just let herself be inert in his hands, not fighting anymore, knowing it was useless and would only hurt more. He'd been fuming and violent, more than usual, saying senseless things like, "So much for that mother's instinct of yours... you only care about your little girls, not your boys. Screw the boys, right? Well, screw you!"

She knew better than to ask what that was about. She endured, swallowing her tears, trying to think of something else, of Hazel playing in the hot Atlanta summer sun in the backyard of their house. Of the day when they'd both walk through that grass again, barefoot, enjoying the morning dew against their feet.

When he finished with her and left, she didn't dare to move, fearing the new pain she would discover as soon as she tried to stand and walk. But only moments later, the dreaded footsteps approached, and a part of her clung to the hope he might be bringing Hazel to see her. Because she'd been good. She hadn't fought him back, hadn't clawed at his face, to force him to tie her up again. The fact she could eagerly await the return of the man who'd been raping her every day since she was taken messed with her head and nauseated her, eroded her inside like a cancer seeded and watered every day by her captor.

She raised her head a little as he stepped inside the room, only to see he was alone.

"Hazel?" she whispered through fresh tears.

He laughed, a short laugh that turned into a lopsided grin. "Not before you clean up this pigsty."

He set on the floor the bucket he'd brought with him, filled three quarters with foamy water smelling of bleach and detergent. "There's a rag in there," he added. "Scrub everything clean, the floors, the walls, everything you've touched and stained. Under the mattress too, and the bathroom floor."

Then he left, locking the door behind him and climbing up the stairs whistling that sickening lullaby.

She didn't realize how much time had passed since he'd left. She slipped in and out of consciousness, weakened by the blood loss, traces of which lined the inside of her thighs and the soiled floor tiles. After a while, the tiniest sliver of hope started fighting the darkness in her mind, making her wonder if he really meant it when he'd promised she could see Hazel after finishing up the cleaning. Maybe he spoke the truth. Maybe she should hurry.

She forced herself to her knees and fished the rag from the bottom of the bucket, then squeezed it with trembling hands. As she scrubbed and scrubbed, dried blood stained the soapy water, the foam turning pink, an innocent color that didn't belong in hell.

How much longer would she endure?

For a while she'd thought she could escape. That hope had died quickly, after a few days in which she'd tried everything she could think of to break free. Then she hoped he'd get bored with her and set her free, or maybe the cops would break down the door one day and rescue her, like she read in the media and saw on TV. She'd just seen such a story of a man who chained nannies to the bed and kept them as sex slaves. They caught that guy and set those women free. Who would set her free? And when?

What if no one came?

Tears started rolling down her cheeks, dropping onto the floor as she scrubbed her way across the room.

If no one came, what would happen to her? Would he keep her for years and years?

She reached the corner where the mattress, lying directly on the floor, took almost a quarter of the room. She scrubbed all the way to its edges, then lifted the corner with trembling fingers, to see if there was dirt underneath it.

A torn pair of panties had been shoved under there, the cream silk contrasting with the dark tiles. She took them, carefully, as if not to disturb the woman who'd once worn them. They'd been torn at the seams and had bloodstains on them where several drops had reached the luscious fabric.

She felt something in the fabric and turned them on the other side to find some embroidery, the name *Janelle* in cursive silk thread. Who was Janelle, and what had happened to her? Did he grow tired of her? Did he set her free?

Was the little boy upstairs Janelle's child?

As realization started creeping into her weary mind, she threw the panties on the floor and crawled backward until she hit the wall, as if the contact with the other woman's garment was somehow fateful, Janelle's cruel destiny about to engulf her.

"No, no, no," she whimpered, shaking her head. "Oh, God, no."

Janelle was gone, and soon she would follow, to make room for someone else.

Soon.

CHAPTER TWENTY-FOUR
Ghost

Kay remembered very little from the journey back. She'd been more than happy to let Elliot drive while she mulled things over in her mind, dozing off at times, or discussed aspects of the case with him, trying to sketch a useful profile with such limited information. Back home, she'd collapsed on her bed, thinking she'd sleep until the alarm went off, but at day's first light, she was up.

She rose and fixed a fresh pot of coffee, then took the steaming mug by her bedroom window and opened the curtains, letting the sunshine in. Taking big, throat-burning swigs, she looked at the backyard with critical eyes. The lawn was overgrown, out of control, weeds knee high, an embarrassment. The job needed to get done, whether she liked it or not.

The strong brew injected fresh energy into her weary body. Checking the time, she realized she had about an hour until Elliot picked her up. They'd discussed the case at length on the way back last night, and had agreed the best use of their time was to review the San Francisco police and the FBI's notes on the Hendricks missing person investigation. Maybe something in those pages could give them an inkling of information that would help them find Alison and the missing children.

The thought that Alison and her daughter had spent another night in captivity forced the bile to rise in her throat. Was Matthew still alive? Had the unsub let him go somewhere, only to become lost or victim to another predator? She mumbled a long curse while putting on a pair of old, ripped jeans, then went outside to the garage, where she'd spotted the old lawn tractor. She hoped it still worked.

Opening the garage door, she kicked a few scattered pieces of junk out of the way, rusted tools; an empty, cracked bucket; a few pieces of firewood. Then she started dusting off the seat of the old tractor with a rag she'd picked up with two reluctant fingers from a nearby workbench, hoping no spider had chosen to call that rag home. Cautiously, she grabbed the tractor's wheel and slid onto the seat, then turned the key in the ignition, instantly filling the garage with loud, sputtering pops and the smell of gasoline.

"Howdy," she heard Elliot's voice behind her. She turned the tractor's key back and the sputtering engine fell silent. Glad he was early, she climbed off the seat and ran her hands against her pants, sending swirls of dust into the crisp morning air.

"You're early," she said, unable to contain a smile of relief. He looked fresh, as if he'd slept eight hours, not the three he'd had time for. He wore a black T-shirt, a hint too tight on his well-built torso, and white wash jeans. The way he looked at her would've normally made her smile widen and her eyes veer sideways, shielded by her long eyelashes. Instead, her smile waned, and her eyes met his directly.

"Could it be possible this unsub tortures and kills the women, but lets the children live?"

"Could be," he replied, pushing the brim of his hat upward a little with his index finger. "Maybe he lets them go at some point. But then, why take them? And how many has he taken that we don't know of?"

"They're witnesses," she replied, although she knew it had to be much more than that. "Maybe he let Matthew go, but he was never found," Kay continued, sounding unconvinced. "We can't count on that, though. We should still act as if the serial killer has Alison and the two children, and they're all still alive."

She stood in the garage door for a while, hesitant to invite him inside the house, where his refreshing presence collided so badly with her memories. It was as if the sadness of her past could stain him somehow, could rub against him, making her see him in a different light.

The simplest definition of insanity, she thought, turning around and beckoning him to follow. Her memories were hers only, deeply buried inside her mind. They couldn't touch anything from her present or her future, not unless she invited them to. "There's fresh coffee if you'd like."

"I could help you with this lawn," he offered, "but first we should go back to the morgue. The cadaver dogs discovered two more bodies at Silent Lake last night."

Her step faltered. "Please don't tell me it's the kids," she whispered.

"The ME doesn't seem to think so," he replied, grabbing an apple from the basket on her kitchen table and looking around for a knife. "They're adult women, and they've been dead for a while."

She released a breath. Maybe there was still a chance to find Alison and the kids alive.

Elliot leaned against the wall in what had become his favorite spot, over by the door, and held the apple in the air. "Knife, please?"

Taking a couple of steps to her left, she reached the knife block on the counter, then froze. All the knives were in their places, except the largest of them, the dark slit that used to shelter its blade gaping menacingly, as if it was about to reveal its secrets.

Elliot approached and reached for the smallest knife, his elbow brushing against hers and sending a shiver through her body. "May I?"

She nodded, her throat constricted and dry. Swallowing with difficulty, she stepped aside. "Sure."

He removed the small knife and deftly cut the apple in quarters, then offered her one. She stared at the apple slice, suspended midair in the palm of his hand.

"What happened?" he asked. "You look like you've seen a ghost."

CHAPTER TWENTY-FIVE

Memories

Katherine had just turned thirteen, her birthday a joyless celebration rushed by her mother who'd made her a small cake that she and Jacob ate quickly before their father came home. She understood why her mother didn't want to remind her father it was Kathy's birthday, and she was grateful to avoid the wet smooches he would place on her cheeks and his sweaty embrace that left her body stinking of his booze.

A few days of relative peace had followed Kathy's thirteenth birthday, each one a miracle in its own way, although Pearl and the kids didn't know for sure a day was going to be peaceful until it ended. The fear was always there, rattling their lives and making all three jumpy, eager for the day to be over and another one to start, so they could go back to school, and Kathy's mom to work. Where they'd be safe.

But that day was bound to be different. Her father came home from work late, already drunk and enraged. He'd celebrated a coworker's retirement or something; there was always a reason for his drunken outings, although the overarching reason Kathy now knew well. Her father was an alcoholic.

He'd come home at about eight that night, landing heavily on the sofa, in the place where the fabric was permanently stained by his sweat, right in front of the TV, and switched on the sports channel. He barely threw a look at Pearl, who was busy cleaning the kitchen after having cooked dinner. Kathy and Jacob had been playing Go Fish on the living room table, but when their father's truck had come to a stop in front of the house, they quickly collected their cards and found refuge in the far corner of the room, on the floor behind the armchair.

Pearl brought a plate with beef stew and set it quietly in front of Gavin, who barely acknowledged her. Then she brought a fork and a glass of water, and set those down too, before quickly withdrawing to the kitchen sink.

The kids had resumed their game, whispering quietly to each other, when their father's heavy footsteps drew Kathy's attention. She peeked from behind the armchair and saw Gavin approach her mother, then grabbing her by the hips and pulling her toward him.

"Come here, baby," he said, his voice raspy, loaded with years of smoking cheap stuff and drinking heavily.

"Hush, Gavin, not in front of the kids," she whispered, wiping her hands on her apron and pushing him away gently. Then she opened the fridge and took out a bottle of wine, pouring the remaining liquid in a glass she barely filled halfway. "Here you go," she offered, and Kathy hoped her father would take the wine and sit back on the sofa to watch his game.

He gulped the wine down in one mouthful and set the glass down on the table noisily. "That's all you can spare for your man?" he asked, his voice menacingly quiet. "That's all I deserve after a long day at work?"

"Sorry," Pearl whispered, shooting a quick glance at her daughter, as if to see if she was far enough from the brewing storm. "We're out of wine, and there's no money until Friday when you get paid."

"And what the hell are you working for, huh? Do you ever get paid?" he shouted, and Kathy heard Jacob whimper quietly.

"Yes, Gavin," Pearl replied, sliding out from his renewed embrace. A sense of resignation, of acceptance of the pain that was to come was seeping into her breaking voice, bringing burning tears to her daughter's eyes. "I got paid on the fifteenth, and I paid the rent and insurance and all, then I bought food with the rest of it. There's only so much—"

"Shut the hell up, woman," he shouted. "You're telling me there's no more wine left?"

"Yes, Gavin, there's no more wine left," she replied, her voice strangled, looking at the floor.

Kathy needed all her willpower to not jump out of hiding and tell her father off, but she knew she couldn't defeat him; it would only make matters worse.

"How about the cellar?"

"You drank it all," Pearl whispered, raising her hand to shield her face, expecting a blow. Her left eye was still swollen from the last time Gavin had struck her, the bruise now yellowish, but still visible.

Her mother looked tired, drawn, her eyes surrounded by dark circles and her stare hollow, as if something inside her had broken, had been damaged beyond repair. Her gaze lit up only when she saw her children, when she spent time with the two of them. That's when, for the briefest amount of time, Kathy felt she had a family.

"Come on, give it to me," her father pleaded, grabbing Pearl by the neck and pinning her down against the wall, while he groped her with his other hand.

"Gavin, please, no," she whimpered, trying to free herself from his hold.

"You must have a little bottle hidden somewhere, maybe you're saving it for Christmas or something," he pleaded. "It's only two days till Friday, and I'll buy it back for you."

"I really don't have anything left to drink, Gavin," she whispered.

Her words made him instantly angry, as if her double rejection had fueled his rage, fanning the fire burning already inside him. He slammed Pearl against the wall, and she fell to the ground, seemingly too weak to withstand his attack.

Kathy jumped to her feet, and Jacob with her. They both rushed to their mother's side, and Jacob tried to draw his father's attention away from his mother.

"If you want, I can go ask the neighbor if he can spare a bottle for you," the little boy offered in a slightly trembling voice.

"Uh-huh, you do that, son," he replied, turning to stare at his daughter and licking his lips, his eyes bloodshot and lustful. "I bet this young thing won't say no to me," he said, his clumsy fingers struggling to get his belt buckle undone. "Kathy, pretty Kathy, my sweet Kathy, Daddy really loves you," he said in a sing-song voice ending in a coughing spell. "Come on over here, Kathy, love your daddy back."

Kathy stared at him with wide eyes, not sure where to run. Pearl moaned but managed to stand again, holding on to her daughter for support, then shielding her with her weakened, aching body.

"It's your own daughter, Gavin, your own flesh and blood," she pleaded. "Don't you touch her."

Gavin unzipped his pants, his mind seemingly made up, and took two steps toward Kathy, but Pearl pushed the child out of the way and stood in front of him, trembling.

"Here, take me," she offered, undoing the top button of her shirt with hesitant fingers.

Shoving her to the side, he reached for Kathy, mumbling words that the little girl didn't understand. Letting out a short scream, Kathy bolted and found refuge on the other side of the room, by the dresser, where she desperately looked for something to use as a weapon, fear rendering her fingers weak, trembling, useless.

Kathy turned her eyes briefly away from him, going through the drawers as quickly as she could when she heard a commotion. In the corner of her eye, she saw her mother hit her father on the head with a frying pan.

He barely flinched.

He let out a raspy roar of laughter, and then, as if incited by Pearl's actions, he lunged toward the kitchen where she'd taken refuge by the counter and hit her hard, sending her tumbling to the ground. Then he turned and grabbed the largest knife from the block and raised his arm, ready to deliver a fatal blow.

"I will end you, scum of this earth," he bellowed.

"No," Kathy shouted, her hands going through the top drawer in a trembling rush and finding the pistol she knew he kept there.

Her hands shook badly, and the gun seemed heavy, too heavy for her to hold. She grabbed it with both hands, the cold metal chilling her to the bone, but then dropped it before she could take aim, the loud thud echoed by Gavin's scornful chuckle. She grunted loudly, then, as her father's raised blade descended on her mother's defenseless chest, she dropped to her knees, reaching for the fallen weapon, sweat-covered palms extended as far as she could reach, sweeping in a frenzy under the table.

She fired just as Jacob had charged with his baseball bat, the bullet barely missing her little brother. Horrified, she screamed, but then saw Jacob backing away from the line of fire, the bat clattering as it fell from his hands. He was still standing, unharmed.

Her father groaned, the knife still in his hand, coming down forcefully toward Pearl's chest.

She pulled the trigger again.

CHAPTER TWENTY-SIX
The Others

Kay was grateful to see they'd arrived at the morgue. It had been increasingly difficult to field Elliot's questions and hide her rebel tears. She couldn't blame the detective, though; her recent behavior would make any decent cop want to throw her into an interrogation room and push her until she unloaded all her secrets, broken, indefensible.

Or maybe not... Regardless of how jumpy and irrational she might have appeared, it didn't warrant too much suspicion, not of a law enforcement nature, anyway. Maybe of a personal one, from a man who might've found her attractive, who might've wanted to know her better. As good a cop as Elliot was, he had no way of knowing what monsters lay hidden in her past.

Still, she flinched when he touched her elbow and asked, "Really, what was that all about?" He looked straight at her with the unyielding focus she'd seen in countless cops when asking critical questions of a suspect. He'd parked the vehicle in front of the morgue, and there was no escaping him.

"It's nothing," she said, her broken voice betraying her. "It's about my mother. She, um, bought that knife block, for Christmas, a few years before I left. She got a coupon in the mail, and—" Kay let the welled-up tears flow freely, no longer preoccupied with hiding them. "It's just that being there, in the house where she lived, where she died... I didn't expect it would be so difficult."

He squeezed her hand gently, the intrusiveness in his gaze softened. "I'm so sorry," he said, his gentle words soothing, threatening to weaken her more. She inhaled sharply, reminding herself she'd just lied for the most part, and he'd probably behave entirely differently if he knew the whole truth. She couldn't afford to let her guard down; not now, not ever.

"Thank you," she whispered, then gently removed her hand from his and climbed out of the SUV. When her feet touched the asphalt, feeling the firmness of the earth supporting her and knowing she was safe from scrutiny—at least for a fleeting moment—only then did she breathe. She hadn't realized she'd been holding air trapped in her lungs, as if letting it out would've risked exposing all her secrets.

She entered the morgue, the chill and fetor of the air inside sending shivers through her body and calling all her senses into high alert. All three tables in the morgue were taken, the thin, bony silhouettes on each of them covered with white sheets that seemed to glow under the fluorescent bluish lights. Seated in front of the microscope, Dr. Whitmore prepared a number of slides, and as he put one under the powerful lens, a magnified image displayed on the wall screen, colorful yet unmistakably lifeless.

"Not what you had in mind for retirement, Doc, I could bet on that," she said, approaching the table covered in small trays and sample holders. She touched his shoulder, and he turned only briefly toward her with a hint of a smile.

"Not at all," he replied. He put another slide under the lens, then sighed and continued, "I'd expected to be bored and have time to read the entire works of Tolstoy, followed by some Steinbeck and maybe re-read Jules Verne, my childhood favorite." He saved a few images, then changed the slide again. "But no, there's a sick son of a bitch out there who's keeping me chained to the autopsy table." He saved a few more images with mouse clicks that echoed strangely in the cold silence of the morgue, then turned to her.

"Please catch the bastard, Kay. I promised my wife I'd take her to Cancun for Thanksgiving."

He stood and walked over to the first table, and beckoned them to follow.

"I have all our guests ready for your visit," he said, offering Kay a small jar of Vicks VapoRub. She rubbed a little ointment under her nostrils, then passed the jar over to Elliot, who took it with a grateful nod.

"I thought you didn't use this stuff, Doc," she said, returning the jar with a lopsided smile.

"I finished the part of my exam where my sense of smell is critical," he replied. "But you two shouldn't have to put up with this. These poor girls have been in the ground for a while."

Dr. Whitmore pulled back the sheet from the remains lying on the first table. "This is Shannon Hendricks—you met her Wednesday, right?"

"Uh-huh, yes," Kay replied, reluctant to open her mouth at first. Elliot had pulled back a couple of steps.

"I was able to confirm a few things since the last time we spoke," he said, sitting on a four-legged stool on casters, then he rolled closer to the exam table. "Her tox screen was clean; she wasn't poisoned or drugged, not in the last few days of her life, anyway. I have a few strands of her hair at the San Francisco lab for a detailed tox history. Her hair being so long, we have a great deal of information built into each fiber, a history of all the chemicals she was exposed to. It might help you pin down a location."

"When can you expect the results?" Kay asked.

"Not before the end of next week," he replied. "I have revised the time of death to the end of May—"

"This year?" Elliot asked, covering his mouth with his hand as he spoke, probably as reluctant as she was to inhale the air filled with the miasma of human decay.

"Yes, this year," Dr. Whitmore replied, furrowing his brow slightly. "She was reported missing on November twenty-seventh last year, you said, and that means she spent at least six months in captivity."

"It confirms your theory," Elliot said, "that he keeps them until the ground is soft enough to dig the grave."

"Maybe," Kay replied, studying the remains closely. Her throat still bore the signs of the brutal strangulation that had brought her demise. "How about the others?" she asked.

She pressed her lips together, swallowing a curse. She should've been at the scene when they dug up the other bodies. But she hadn't, and that was it. She had to rely on crime scene photos again, instead of all her senses.

Dr. Whitmore exposed both bodies. The state of decomposition was visibly more advanced.

"We don't have an ID yet; fingerprints didn't return any result," he said. "I had to rehydrate the remaining skin to take an impression of their prints, and I was hoping, by now, we'd know who they are. I rarely find skin on the fingers after so much time in the ground. I was surprised."

"How did they die?" Elliot asked.

"We'll get there," Dr. Whitmore said. "I'm not finished with who they are. About the same age as the other two, but that's where the commonalities stop."

Great, Kay thought. She was hoping for more commonalities, not fewer.

"Based on bone structure, this one was Black," he pointed at the middle table, "and the other one Asian. My guess, Chinese, but that speaks to race, not nationality. Her teeth are impeccable, speaking to an affluent life lived here in the US. That goes for both women, actually."

His first two victims had been white, and so was Alison. One more piece of the victimology puzzle was falling apart; the unsub was crossing racial lines. Only a small percentage of serial killers did. If he didn't kill substitutes for the object of his rage—women who reminded him of that someone in his past who had inflamed him, that had done him wrong—why did he kill these particular women? What made him choose them? She had to rethink the entire profile.

"This one, Jane Doe One," Dr. Whitmore said, pointing at the table on the far right, "the Asian, had given birth, but not recently. Jane Doe Two was nulliparous." He noticed Elliot's glance, and explained. "She'd never given birth."

"How were they found?" Kay asked. "Was the signature similar?"

"No," he replied, "it was *identical*." He displayed some photos on the wall screen, and she approached as close as she could to see the details in each photo. "They were wrapped in the same type of blanket, also new, in the same Native design. I'd venture to say, same provenance. Their hair had been braided and tied with the same leather and feather hair ties. And there were enough samara leaves to indicate these two women might've also been given a tree burial first, at a time in the year when seeds were prevalent." He cleared his throat and smiled with sadness in his eyes. "What an interesting idea, Kay, to look for burial trees. I'm happy I'm not in your shoes, trying to think like these killers do. I would lose my mind."

Kay smiled back just as grimly. She might've lost hers already, a long time ago. Maybe that's why she understood killers so well. Because she was one of them. Yes, she'd defended her mother's life, her own and Jacob's, but she'd taken the life of her father. She still remembered how she didn't hesitate, nor did she feel any remorse, not for a long time after the shots had stopped echoing in her mind. She still recalled the coldness of the trigger under her finger, the loud bang of each shot, and how she had to fight to control the urge to unload the entire magazine into the lifeless heap bleeding on the floor.

"Cause of death the same, Doc?" she asked, feeling her throat parchment dry.

"Yes, forceful manual strangulation in both victims, with shattered hyoid and crushed trachea. Due to the advanced stage of decomposition, sexual assault is likely, but not forensically bulletproof."

"When did they die?" Elliot asked.

"Sometime last year. I'll need more time to narrow down the window, but if I had to guess, and you know how much I hate guessing, I'd say that Jane Doe One was killed last summer, around July sometime, and Jane Doe Two, a few months later, but before winter. Let's say, October."

Dr. Whitmore continued to walk them through his findings, displaying the slides he'd captured before, presenting samples of tissue that had been damaged by blunt force or sharp force, all in various stages of healing, showing the same pattern of continuous abuse. But Kay's mind veered off, at what remained from the initial profile she'd started to sketch. Not much was left, as if she'd drawn her profile in pencil and the wave of evidence had rubbed most of it off, leaving the sheet almost entirely blank.

But then a chill rushed through her blood, remembering what the doctor had said about Jane Doe Two's time of death.

October.

Before the winter set in, and the ground was still soft.

Her gaze landed on the wall calendar Dr. Whitmore still kept, although most modern devices showed the date. October 23.

Would the unsub keep Alison until next spring? Or kill her now, quickly, before the earth froze? How about the children? What would he do with them over the winter?

She looked out the window at the gray sky, remembering the chill she'd felt in the air that morning, the bite in the northerly winds, the tall weeds on her lawn stooped by overnight frost. Small, isolated flurries danced, setting down and clinging to the landscape for a minute or two before melting away.

They were out of time.

CHAPTER TWENTY-SEVEN
Evidence

"You were right," Elliot said the moment they'd climbed into his SUV and closed the doors. "I have to say I haven't really bought your serial killer story, not one hundred percent, not until now. I hope you'll forgive me."

She chuckled, a quick, sad reaction to his words. "For what? For being a strong believer in the 'five vics to make a serial' rule? That used to be the norm, but it's obsolete. It's not wrong; only not very accurate anymore." She rubbed her forehead for a split moment, her cold fingers bringing relief to the early signs of a migraine that had tightened a vise around her temples. "Even serial killers evolve," she added, then immediately corrected herself. "Or, better said, our understanding of them."

Leaning her head against the cold window, she closed her eyes. What next? How could they find Alison and the kids, before their time ran out? In the distance, if she listened intently, she could hear the distinctive barks of bloodhounds at work, the experimental K9 team from UC Davis. They'd been searching since the break of dawn, and if anything had been found, any trace of evidence or any trail scent, Elliot would've received a call.

Most likely, after taking Alison and her daughter, the killer had disposed of the Nissan, and the two victims had been transported somewhere by vehicle, probably the unsub's, and that wasn't something the bloodhounds could track.

Elliot and Kay remained Alison and the children's only hope, and the lives of all three weighed heavily on her shoulders.

"Don't hold back," Elliot said. "Tell me what you're thinking. Where do we go next? What do we do?"

She pressed her lips together, while her brow furrowed. "The FBI will probably take over—"

"Don't give me that steaming pile of manure," he reacted. "You know better than anyone that it's up to you. By the time the feds get up to speed, he'll kill them all, and we'll find them who knows where." He touched her frozen hand and spread warmth in her body. "You've done this before, Kay. Let's nail the bastard, you and me, together."

She took a breath, having to concede certain arguments he'd made. She understood the unsub better than anyone new on the case would have the chance to before the time ran out. She felt she was close to figuring out his profile, and some of that profile seemed within her grasp, like a forgotten word that sits on the tip of one's tongue, refusing to come into focus, but clearly there, used, known, familiar.

"Usually, by victim number five I'd have a clear victim type, but I don't," she said, hesitant at first, but her voice caught speed as she entered the familiar territory of criminal profiling. "Some were Caucasians, while others were not. Physically, all they had in common was their age, and the length of their hair, long enough to allow this ritualistic braiding."

"Ritualistic?" he asked. "Why do you think it's more than just a simple signature?"

"Signatures are never simple," she replied. "They're the materialization of fantasies or yearnings the unsub has, and they're almost always complex, layered, speaking to the hidden drivers of their compulsions. This is the only clear part of the profile, so far. There seems to be a strong connection between the unsub and Native American life, their customs, their beliefs."

"You said you think he's local. Could he be Native, then?"

"I don't believe so," she replied. "He's definitely local, judging by the level of comfort with the surroundings, with the area in general. Something makes him kill here and bury his victims here. That something has to be a strong tie, either with the place he was born and maybe raised, or the place he still calls home. But he mixes various Native customs in his rituals; he's not true to one single tribe, like a real Native would be."

"Then?"

"He's got close ties to the Native peoples of the region in a way that is significant to his rituals, to his fantasies," she replied. "He has strong emotional ties with one or more tribes and their members."

She started thinking about the correlation between the victims' races and his ties with the Native people. What if the victims were of random races because they were placeholders for Native women? He braided their hair as if they were Native, Pomoan to be exact, and maybe it didn't matter to him what race they were, as long as they weren't Pomoan.

But then, why not hunt Pomoan women? Maybe because there weren't that many left in the tribe, or because killing them would strike too close to home, would paint a target on his back. He was too smart for that. He'd known how to stay undiscovered for the longest time, and he would've continued to kill without anyone being the wiser, if not for one tourist's curious dog.

"Yes, he's definitely local," she affirmed, "and the object of his rage is a Native American woman of twenty-five to thirty-two years of age. I believe he's white, based on the population makeup of the area, but it's a statistical assertion, nothing more."

"Should I write this down?" Elliot asked, the smile in his voice unmistakable.

"You might want to share this with your colleagues, so, yes, but I'll be there to answer questions."

"That means you have a profile?"

"A partial one," she admitted. "This type of predator is a power or control killer, and these killers normally have a type. The absence of a type could speak to the fact that his desired type is unavailable or too risky for him to touch so close to home."

"That type being?"

"Most likely a Pomoan woman," she said. "Sometime in this unsub's past, a Pomoan woman has done him wrong, defied him, or hurt him in a significant measure. But he won't go near the tribe to hunt, because he's also adept at avoiding being caught."

"Do you think he's opportunistic?" Elliot asked. "Is he waiting for tourists to venture here, then he attacks?"

"He's highly organized, and organized killers rarely leave any detail of their process to chance. I believe there's a precise method to his abductions, and that's why he was able to abduct, torture and kill here, in this area, without getting caught."

"Then, if not here, where do you think he hunts for his victims?"

She didn't answer right away. First and foremost, power-motivated killers had a strong compulsion, even if that compulsion wasn't lust. There's an urge in them to satisfy their need for absolute power over another human being, usually a symbol or a stand-in for the object of their rage. But how did those people hunt?

Some planned in detail their next abduction, choosing wisely and carefully victims who couldn't lead the investigators back to them. Others chose from high-risk victim pools, like prostitutes or street children, people who usually weren't missed. But she'd never before encountered an unsub with the level of cunning and of planning this one had. His victims came from all over the country, making correlations difficult when the victims were reported missing. He disposed of their vehicles in a place most likely to not raise any suspicion, and point only at the victim, not him. The only risks he really took were ritual driven, having to do with the burial of the women. It was as if he couldn't avoid following his compulsion, no matter how much he risked, by elevating victims in trees, then revisiting the area to bury them, all of that in a place where tourists ventured quite often.

"He can't avoid following his compulsion," Kay said, "no matter how smart he is, and he is very smart. I believe he has knowledge of forensics and criminology, given the level of concern with hiding his tracks and preventing us from profiling him." She paused, realizing she hadn't answered Elliot's question. "I don't believe we have enough information to figure out *where* he chooses his victims, but we know for sure he disables their vehicles and preys on them when they're at their most vulnerable." She thought for a moment about the missing children, and the power-motivated profile.

She felt a shiver traveling down her spine. Having a child increased a mother's vulnerability by an immeasurable factor. And yet, the unsub had let Tracy go. However, he'd held on to Matthew. Or had he? Where was Matthew Hendricks? Her head was spinning with all the possibilities, all the scenarios that stemmed from the killer's unusual actions and twisted rituals, behind them an intricate maze of fantasies he'd built over time, getting lost deeper and deeper in the abyss of his compulsions.

"This unsub is someone who has been, or *believes* he has been, abused, even tortured in his childhood. He carries with him the unhealed injury of that abuse and feels compelled to reassert his dominance over placeholder victims, over and over again, while nothing he does, no amount of suffering he inflicts on his victims will relieve the burning sense of powerlessness, of inadequacy he endures on a daily basis."

"You're telling me this unsub comes from an abusive family?" Elliot reacted with a scoff. "This area is one of the poorest areas in California; financial hardship and abuse go hand in hand."

"I know that," she replied harshly, his statement cutting a little too close to home. "But this is the profile, and I need you to understand it. Especially when I'm going to say that the best lead we have is those cars, and how he got them back to San Francisco."

"What lead, the tow truck?" he asked, his raised eyebrows wrinkling his forehead. "Eggers had nothing to do with those cars; following your idea, Hobbs offered to overlook his cocaine possession charge completely, but Eggers still couldn't tell us what we wanted to hear."

"I didn't expect a man like Eggers to be part of the unsub's plan," she replied. "I'd *hoped* he was, but never really expected him to be."

"Why?"

"This unsub is sophisticated, highly educated, knowledgeable of technology, of how to discreetly sabotage vehicles without your technician being able to figure it out on the spot, quick to act without leaving a single trace." She stopped for a moment, letting her words sink in. "Now, with this image in your mind, put Eggers next to him and tell me what you think of the two of them working together."

Elliot bowed his head for a moment. "Yeah, not gonna happen," he mumbled. "He's not our guy."

She stared in the distance, at the tips of the windblown trees against the gray sky. There was no way of knowing where, in the vastness of several adjoining national forests, the unsub could've built his den. Millions of acres of forested slopes and rocky peaks expanding beyond the tip of the Sierra Nevada mountain range, and not a trace of Alison and those two kids.

But he'd always, somehow, taken their cars back to the San Francisco airport, without their GPS showing any evidence of that trip.

"Where do you think he'll bury his next victims, now that we've found his burial site?"

"More like we desecrated it," Kay replied, checking her messages. "He won't stray far from Silent Lake. There's relevance to his choice of burial site. There's an old Native legend that says Silent

Lake, or Cuwar Lake in its original name, was formed from the tears of Native women crying for their dead." As she spoke, she realized the burial forest might've expanded way beyond the area they'd uncovered. "There are several paths that lead to the lake, most of them accessible to a four-by-four truck. This part of the ritual is critical; he'll be compelled to continue—" She stopped abruptly, seeing the email she'd been waiting for. "San Francisco Police Department Airport Bureau came through," she said excitedly, opening it. Soon they'd be able to see which tow truck had delivered those cars, maybe capture a plate or an image of its driver.

The email loaded painstakingly slowly, due to the size of the attachments. One by one, photos captured from surveillance videos appeared on the screen. She brought the phone closer to Elliot so he could see them, and pulled back a little when their heads came near each other, almost touching.

The images were grainy and had already been enhanced. In chronological order, the stills showed Shannon's Subaru, Kendra's Jeep and finally Alison's Nissan, all being driven into the parking lot by a man who knew how to cover his face with a ballcap and a hoodie.

All the vehicles had been driven there, not towed.

As soon as the unsub had pulled into the respective parking lots, he'd locked the cars and left, not spending one moment tinkering with their GPS to erase all records of the trip from Mount Chester.

Then how? How did he do it? How did he manage to disable the vehicles enough to get their drivers to stop and call for assistance, before driving them right to SFO without any issues?

The stills had time stamps, showing all three cars had been returned mere hours after the victims had last been seen. Not only was he precise in his execution, but he was fast. It also meant something else.

"He leaves them alone somewhere," Kay said. "He's got an isolated place where no one can find them or hear them scream."

Elliot shrugged, gesturing with his hand toward the wild scenery surrounding them.

She read the message from the SFO airport administration, signed by the chief of the San Francisco Police Department Airport Bureau, then read it again, in disbelief.

"Unfortunately," the message said, "there isn't a single camera view that captures the suspect from a better angle, although he passed through highly surveilled areas as he left the airport parking structure. We have tracked his movements on each of the three occasions, and we can confirm each time he took the fastest way out of the parking garage, then walked off the premises. He didn't take a cab or a shuttle. No person matching his description was seen leaving the area in a vehicle, as shown by all video cameras servicing the main access points to the local highway system. He just vanished."

CHAPTER TWENTY-EIGHT
Cadillac

He recalled driving around in that blue Cadillac, filling his lungs with the scent of fine leather and his stomach with the first decent meal in months, paid for with the parking change he'd gathered from the center console cup holder. He drove all night, enjoying the fog that had more than once been his enemy, because now the thick layer of ground-touching clouds was his friend, protecting him and concealing the bodies he'd left back in that Tenderloin dumpster.

He drove in circles all night, the SUV's vents blowing warm air on his shivering body, music loud, and nothing he'd ever felt before compared, not even remotely. He was safe in that Cadillac, as he once used to be in his mother's arms, before she'd turned on him and threw him out like yesterday's garbage. He felt warm, powerful, invincible. Every now and then he turned onto a side street to get out of the way of a patrol car, his heart thumping loudly against his ribcage, but no red-and-blue lights flashed behind him that night. People who drove cars like that rarely got pulled over, and never without cause, because people like that had powerful, bloodthirsty lawyers who fought hard for them, who protected them.

At about four in the morning, he drove all the way up to Twin Peaks, and looked at the city as it lay at his feet, a blanket lit up in a million lights covered in cotton, like snow-covered Christmas trees back home, in Mount Chester. He lounged on the car's hood, the heat coming from the engine keeping the night chill at bay, and stared at the dense fog layer, knowing his freedom couldn't last.

From there, he drove to Battery East park, where he pulled over by the side of the road and looked at the Golden Gate Bridge, a ghostly appearance in yellow sodium lights and red metal, shrouded in thick, heavy mist that captured the gilded glow and spread it across the water like a vision of the road to paradise. Only beyond the bay, somewhere across that bridge, the sky had already started to capture the dreaded colors of dawn.

Soon, the sun would rise, and, under its powerful rays, the fog would burn and vanish, exposing him, revealing the bodies of the men he'd killed. Heavy-hearted but knowing exactly what he had to do, he drove the Escalade one last time to a Tenderloin shop famed for its shady deals. He waited about an hour for the man who owned the place, a man he'd heard whispers about, hushed and scared rumors about how he'd earned the tattoos that adorned his skin and how he'd become a legend while he'd served his time. For manslaughter.

If anyone could understand, that man would. But he had no intention of sharing his problems; only of selling the Cadillac.

He negotiated badly, not used to the games the shop owner was routinely playing on people like him, and believing his threats about calling the cops on him. He barely refrained from jumping him, and he did so only because the man's bulging muscles told him he didn't stand a chance, not even with a blade in his hand. Out of options, he settled for whatever the ex-con was willing to give him for the stolen Cadillac.

When he left the shop, the sun was high, and he was clasping in his sweaty hand four thousand dollars in a thick roll of used, dirty bills, less than a tenth of the car's worth. He ached for the feeling of a car key nestled in the palm of his hand, but that money opened the door to his future life.

His first move was to head as far away from the Tenderloin dumpster as possible. He bought himself a Caltrain permit and rode the train past San Jose, until all he could see out the window were crop fields. Then he found a small room to rent in the back of an older couple's house, and a few days later, he got himself a job.

All the questions he'd encountered while trying to set himself up he remembered clearly. Did he have a driver's license? How about a résumé? References the employers could call? One by one, he tackled all those obstacles, learning from each experience just how far his world was from the realm of men who drove Cadillacs. And with each piece of knowledge, each document, and each line on his résumé, he drew closer to who he wanted to be.

A year later, he was admitted to college.

He worked days and studied nights, a gargantuan effort for the boy who used to live on the street, and had never finished high school. But he'd studied on his own and got himself a GED, then convinced the admissions office he was a great candidate who would make the university proud, because he was an orphan without means but immense determination to succeed.

The university bought his story. All of it, every word of the yarn he wove, without bothering to verify anything. The counselor even made it possible for him to be considered for a sports scholarship, and, after requesting two weeks to prepare, he aced all trials. The door to a better life was opening widely for him, and he could freely fantasize about his future, no dream out of reach.

He soon became the university poster child. He was articulate and could make an argument stick, no matter how flimsy. He had an air of vulnerability about him that women, regardless of age, fell for indiscriminately. And there had never been the slightest rumors of any relationships; he was too busy for that. Yet he found no pleasure in his academic success; to him, it was all a means to an end. His homeless days were behind him, but never forgotten, his wounds still bleeding inside his tormented soul.

All that time, there were two things very difficult to endure for him. Not driving a Cadillac, and not killing anyone. Some of his colleagues could testify they'd seen a glint of something in his eyes, something they couldn't name but that curled the fear of him deep inside their hearts. They had no idea how close they'd come to meeting his blade or having the life snuffed out of them by his bare hands wrapped around their throats. As for girls who'd tried to get a date with him, there were a few. However, none would admit the intensity of the primal arousal wave they'd felt when he laid eyes on them, sizing them up from head to toe, his eyes lingering in all the wrong places. Yet he never went past that lingering gaze, although they could've sworn they'd seen the signs of male interest in him; he just walked away, leaving them unsatisfied, frustrated, feeling rejected. As for him, he preferred to take his arousal home, where he could fantasize and find release his own way, unseen by anyone, not having to bother with someone else's feelings.

Meanwhile, the mystery surrounding him grew, together with his grade point average. He became a legend.

He knew to keep his distance from coeds, as well as the men who crossed him, because he understood just how lucky he'd been for not getting caught after his last night in the Tenderloin. He realized luck like that couldn't be pushed nor taken for granted. The three men he'd killed had been found the next day, but the case had remained open, now cold and forgotten by most.

Never by him.

Driven by an unyielding compulsion, he promised himself sweet relief the one evening he'd struggled the most to keep from killing a guy who'd tripped him on purpose during a game. But that relief wouldn't come without an immense price tag, unless he learned how to do it right. That man's name was on a list he'd started in his mind, of people he'd have to revisit when things would be just right.

He chose a major in forensic science, preparing for a career in criminalistics. As such, he'd learn how to hunt without getting caught. He'd gain access to knowledge, people, and systems to hone his skills as close to perfection as possible, while harnessing moments of blissful release. The one true calling that kept him up at night was the only thing he couldn't ignore. The only one worth striving for.

And one day, soon, he'd drive another Cadillac.

CHAPTER TWENTY-NINE
Backyard

Kay woke up and squinted in the bright morning light, wondering how she'd forgotten to pull the bedroom window curtains closed the night before. She'd been so tired she'd paid little attention to the familiar surroundings, letting herself drop on the bed and feeling grateful for the new linens smelling of lavender and cleanliness. The rest of the room looked just as she remembered it, small and crowded with mismatched furniture and all the objects her mother had stored in there after she'd left. The old desk she'd done her homework on throughout her school years still bore the scratches she'd left by accidently writing heavily with a ballpoint pen on a single sheet of paper. Those scratches had earned her a couple of slaps across her face from her father, another memory that invaded her space like a haunting, relentless hydra with thousands of heads.

She blinked a couple of times to get her eyes used to the light and chase the unwanted memories away, then she checked the time and sprung out of bed. Only forty minutes left until Elliot would be there to pick her up; she barely had time for a shower. They were meeting the sheriff and his team to deliver the profile, even if she'd never felt less prepared to do so in her entire career. But she hoped that what little she knew about the unsub could be released into the law enforcement community and provide enough insight as to get the killer identified. And maybe that would mean finding Alison, Hazel, and Matthew still alive.

She'd stayed up the night before until about three, playing with the pieces of the puzzle in her mind, trying to make them fit and draw the picture of the fearless predator who had been one step ahead of them the entire time. Who was this man? How could he be local and have strong ties with the Native community, yet no one seemed to know of him? Was the profile entirely wrong?

She wanted to go into the sheriff's office earlier than planned, to speak with the motor pool technician. He'd inspected all three vehicles and had taken the Jeep's engine apart piece by piece, trying to find out how those vehicles had been disabled. He didn't have a definitive answer yet, but she had a few questions she wanted to ask him anyway.

Distant noise grew closer as she filled up the coffee maker, a somewhat familiar buzzing. She was about to dismiss it, thinking it must've been the neighbor, when she looked out the window and saw Elliot riding on the lawn tractor, cutting large swaths through the overgrown greenery. She groaned, wondering in passing how he'd opened the garage door, and thinking she must've seemed pitiful and hopeless in the man's eyes, enough to earn her a mercy lawn mowing at the crack of dawn. He'd been at it for a while; the front lawn was almost entirely done, only the occasional heap of yellowed, mulched clippings, clumped together, was left behind.

Then the noise faded, as Elliot turned the corner behind the house and went to mow the backyard.

Her blood froze, the icicles in it prickling her skin and bringing waves of cold sweat.

She threw on a pair of jeans and a sweater, and rushed to the back patio. From the open back door, she saw Elliot weave his path by the willow trees, putting his arm out to keep the long branches from whipping his face or snatching the hat off his head. He'd done the perimeter first, mowing by the book, and now was weaving a path around each tree trunk, carefully approaching it for a close trim. Pale and shaking, she watched him go around the first willow tree trunk, then the second, riding back and forth a couple of times to mow the stretch of lawn between the trees and the edge of the woods. Hand to slack-jawed mouth, it took Kay every bit of strength she had to not shriek and run away, far, as far as she could go.

Elliot looked toward the house and waved. She waved back, but couldn't bring herself to smile or say anything. He turned off the blades and drove to the house, then stopped the roaring engine. Deathly silence fell heavy for a beat.

Swallowing the knot in her throat, she managed to sketch a smile. "Do you do this often?" she asked, aware her voice sounded strangled, unnatural. "Doing charity work for women who can't pull their own?"

He pushed the brim of his hat up a bit with his index finger. "Only in return for coffee and bagels," he replied cheerfully. But the effervescence in his voice didn't match his eyes. They'd turned tense, scrutinizing, a hint of worry showing in his blue irises.

He didn't say another word, and she couldn't think of anything to reply, not even to say she didn't have any bagels, or thank him, at the very least. Her eyes remained affixed on that grassy stretch of ground between the willows, where the thick, yellowing grass had been neatly cut, now showing quickly disappearing tire tracks from the tractor.

Was the ground frozen already? Kay found herself wondering, unable to take her eyes off that spot. For the past couple of nights, the temperatures had dropped below freezing, but to her, the ground seemed moist, saturated with water from recent rain, about to split open and show its secrets.

Does he know? She studied him for a moment, the way he drove the tractor, whistling a tune she couldn't catch under the engine noise and chewing on the occasional piece of straw. *He can't know; there's no way,* she decided, while her eyes veered back to the willows, to the freshly cut blades of grass that lined up that particular area.

He wrapped up the chore and drove past her with a wave and a playful smile, while she went inside and poured two cups of coffee, keeping one of them clutched tightly between her frozen fingers. She took a big swig, not caring if it burned her throat, eager to stop shaking before he came inside.

Better.

The hot liquid spread its warm healing throughout her trembling body, but her mind refused to stay in the present. Lured to go back, to immerse herself in memories she hadn't revisited in many years, she barely heard him come in.

"I've been doing this for a while," he said, taking his hat off and putting it on the kitchen table, "rescuing damsels in backyard distress, but I've always had the opposite effect."

Still trembling, she stared at him as if she'd seen him for the first time, unable to articulate a single word. All she could do was take another sip of coffee, shielding her eyes from his inquisitive glance.

He frowned almost imperceptibly and continued, "You know, cheerfulness, bagels, or something. Had I known I'd upset you I would've left those weeds alone. What's going on?"

CHAPTER THIRTY

After

"Nine-one-one, what's your emergency?" a woman asked at the other end of the line, and hearing her voice, Kathy broke down in bitter sobs.

She was kneeling by her mother, holding pressure on a gushing wound in her chest with a towel, while Jacob, pale as if he'd seen a ghost, stared silently at their father's body, fallen inches away from Pearl on the kitchen floor, the knife still clutched in his hand, its blade dripping blood.

"Please, come quickly," she managed to say, "it's my mom. Please, don't let her die. She's—"

She dropped the phone and used both her hands to apply pressure to the wound, but the towel quickly soaked through. Her mother's eyes remained closed, and color had left her cheeks, replaced by a sickening shade of gray.

"Mom," she shouted, tears rolling down her cheeks. "Mom! Please wake up. Mom!"

A distant voice was heard from the phone, abandoned on the floor a couple of feet away.

"Emergency teams are on the way. Are you safe? Hello? Ma'am, can you hear me?"

"Mom," Kathy cried, her face touching her mother's. "No, Mom, please, don't go. Don't leave us."

Pearl shifted slightly and opened her eyes, then called her name in a weak whisper. "Kathy?"

"Yes, I'm here," she said quickly, running her sleeve across her face to wipe her tears.

"Hang… up the phone," she whispered, struggling to point a weak finger at the fallen receiver.

Jacob grabbed the phone and ended the call.

"Take me… to the front room," she said, her voice barely intelligible. "They can't come in here. They can't—um, see him."

"Yes, Mom, we'll do that," she said, desperately looking around for something to use to carry her into the other room without hurting her. "Jacob," she called, and he came by her side without a word. "Here," she said, taking her brother's hand and putting it on top of the blood-soaked towel. "Press hard, like this," she said, and Jacob nodded, pale as a sheet.

She stood and rushed over to the cabinets, where she found a large tablecloth her mother rarely used, because they hadn't had guests in years. She laid that alongside her mother's body, gently pulling one edge of it under her, until she and Jacob were able to grab the corners and carry their mother into the front room in a makeshift gurney. Then she ordered her brother to go outside and guide the first responders to use the front door, not the side one leading to the kitchen where her father's body lay in a thickening, dark pool of blood.

Removing the tablecloth from underneath her mother's body, she hid it under a sofa pillow, and kneeled next to Pearl, holding pressure on her chest like she'd done before. Seconds later, she was sobbing hard, unable to control herself any longer.

She felt a gentle touch on her face and saw her mother's hand reaching out. Grabbing it, she kissed her frozen fingers. "Mom, please, stay with me. They're coming, Mom, soon."

"Don't let them see him," she said weakly, closing her eyes again. "My poor baby," she whispered, as red lights filled the darkness of the windows. "Don't worry about a thing. I'll… clean up when I come home."

"Uh-huh, yes, Mom," she said, ready to spring to her feet the moment the paramedics rushed through the door. "They're here, Mom, stay with me."

A cop was the first one to come in, followed by a man and a woman wearing paramedic vests in bright orange with the star of life embroidered on their backs in reflective white, with a gurney loaded with kits and equipment in tow.

"What happened here?" the cop asked, and Jacob, standing right behind him, seemed he was about to faint.

"My father," Kathy said, sobbing hard, "h—he stabbed her and ran."

The paramedics pushed her away, then kneeled by Pearl's side and started to work quickly, efficiently. The cop started looking around the room, pointing his flashlight at certain areas of the carpet, although the lights were on. Then he headed toward the living room, and Kathy's heart sunk, beating frantically.

"She's critical," one of the paramedics announced. "On the gurney, stat."

The other paramedic sprung to his feet and pulled the gurney closer to her body, while the cop walked past the living room and toward the kitchen. Her father's body would soon come into his view. It was over.

"Kathy," she heard her mother's weak voice calling her. "Tell that officer I want to speak with him."

Rushing after the cop, Kathy caught him by the sleeve just as he was about to turn into the kitchen. "Please," she said, "my mom wants to say something to you."

He approached Pearl just as the two paramedics were loading her onto the gurney. An IV line was already in place, the needle taped to Pearl's arm, and one of them lifted the bag, holding it at his shoulder level.

"Make it quick," the paramedic said.

"He's going to Phoenix," Pearl whispered, touching the cop's hand. "My husband… he's gone to Phoenix."

"Arizona?" the cop asked, and Kathy wondered how many other Phoenixes there were.

Then she breathed, seeing him climb into his car and peeling away.

As the paramedics loaded the gurney into the ambulance, she hugged Jacob tightly and whispered in his ear, "Don't go in there, little brother, okay? Just, um, watch TV or something. Or come with us to the hospital."

"No," he said, pulling himself away from her. He'd grown up overnight; she was looking at an adult. A pale and jittery one, but an adult, nevertheless. "I have to stay here, just in case." He looked around and made sure no one could hear them, then whispered, "No one can know, sis. I can't lose you."

Kathy rode in the ambulance with her mother, holding her hand and whispering encouraging words in endless phrases that made little sense.

Then they rolled her away and she waited for a while, curled up on a weathered couch that reeked of disinfectant while her mother was in surgery. She'd dozed off, exhausted, when she felt someone touching her shoulder. Startled, she stood abruptly, fearing the words that were about to come from the man dressed in green surgical garb. But there was a promise in the man's eyes, a smile she guessed touched his lips, hidden by the surgical mask.

"Your mother is going to be just fine," he said, then lowered his mask, and the smile was there. "She was lucky, having you by her side. I heard you applied pressure like a pro."

Tears rolled down her face as she struggled to find words.

"I've arranged for you to sleep in her room," he said, inviting her to follow him. "And tomorrow you can both go home. She insisted we release her at the earliest."

When Kay returned home the following day, supporting her mother's arm, she talked her into taking a seat on the front room sofa and wait there, until she figured things out. With Jacob by her side, she entered the kitchen holding her breath, and found nothing.

The floor had been scrubbed clean, and only a couple of small smudges remained where the linoleum tiles met the side of the cabinets. She searched her brother's eyes, unable to ask the question.

His eyes veered toward the living room window, the one facing the backyard. Silently, she walked over there and put her hands on the windowsill, as if to seek support to keep standing.

Outside, between the two willow trees by the far edge of the yard, the ground was disturbed, and the grass had been laid in large, ill-fitting chunks.

She didn't need to ask why.

Searching her brother's hand, she squeezed it hard. He reciprocated, and the both of them stared at the willow trees for a long, silent moment, hand in hand.

"The knife?" she eventually asked, her voice a whisper.

"That too," Jacob replied.

Those were the last words any of them had spoken about it.

Just like Kathy had done, Pearl had entered the kitchen most likely fearing what she was about to see, then seemed to understand everything without words, her tears the only visible reaction. Later that night, after everyone had gone to sleep, Kathy scrubbed the floors over and over, stopping occasionally to gag and dry heave, her empty stomach unable to give her the relief she needed.

By the following spring, the ground between the willow trees had settled, and new grass replaced the old, seamlessly, sealing the secret buried below its roots forever.

CHAPTER THIRTY-ONE
Weapon

There was no way she could begin to explain to Elliot what was going through her mind, how if she closed her eyes for only a blink, she could see nightmarish images of the ground splitting open to swallow the lawn tractor and its rider, the roar of her father's rage shattering the house and everyone in it.

Kay knew what she was dealing with; post-traumatic stress, augmented by a guilty conscience. In theory, she was well prepared by her formal education and experience as a doctor in psychology to deal with any case of PTS, but not when it came to her own person. She'd thought she'd resolved these issues a long time ago, but it seemed she'd only blocked them, tucked them away in a secret drawer in her mind, together with the distance she'd put between herself and the house she'd grown up in. And still, regardless of the distance or how deeply she believed she'd buried her trauma, it had kept her away from her home for all those years. Whenever she thought of going home to visit, she saw the haunting image of her father's body lying on the kitchen floor in a pool of blood. Her bullet nearly killing Jacob. The patch of lawn between the willows. Her mother, barely alive, finding the strength to lie to protect her children.

And she'd stayed away, hoping the bad memories would fade.

She'd left Mount Chester as soon as she'd finished high school and rarely came back, even if she missed her mother dearly. Jacob brought Pearl to San Francisco to visit on occasions, but that was mostly it. She couldn't find the strength to go back to the house, and no one, not her mother and not Jacob, had ever questioned her reasons. They both understood; they'd been there. But she'd found time to call her at least twice a week and spend real time with her on the phone, cringing in fear her mother would ask her to come visit, yet knowing she would never.

As a criminalist, she knew quite well that the shooting of her father was defensible as justifiable homicide, the ending of his life being unavoidable to save her mother's. Pearl would've testified to that, Jacob too. But that fateful night when she'd pulled that trigger, Pearl had urged her to lie, to hide what she'd done, probably afraid she'd lose her daughter to a legal system that often misfired, especially when people without financial means were involved. Kay too was afraid; she hadn't just shot him once, enough to stop him. She could barely bring herself to admit it, but she'd pulled the trigger twice more after that, and there was no possible way she could justify it, other than the fact that she was a thirteen-year-old scared out of her mind.

It would've held in any court, granting her the not guilty verdict that could've cleared her conscience and put her mind at ease for the rest of her life.

But not after Jacob had buried his body in the backyard. Not after Pearl had given that cop a false statement. No, there was no turning back, not without doing irreparable damage to her mother and her younger brother. She had to bear her cross, no matter what.

Eight years later, her mother lost a long battle with breast cancer, a disease Kay blamed on her father. It must've been his blows, the pain he caused, the physical and emotional bruises that had seeded the tumors in her body. When Pearl died, Kay cursed her father's name for the last time, but found she couldn't bring herself to attend the funeral. She drove all the way to the cemetery, then, frozen in grief that bore no witnesses, watched from afar, between streaming tears, how her mother's body was laid to rest. Before anyone could see her, she'd driven off, swearing she'd never come back to the place that had broken her heart, and swallowed her tears.

With her mother resting beneath the tall pines of Mount Chester's only cemetery, she wanted to come clean, to rid herself of the burden and face whatever consequences she had to for the shooting, for what had happened afterwards. But at which point could she walk into her boss's office, at the FBI, and say, "Just wanted to tell you, a few years ago, I killed a man. He's buried in my old backyard."

She'd played the scene countless times in her mind, and there was no way it could end well. Over the years, both Jacob and she were asked by the police if they had heard from their father, still a wanted man for the stabbing of his wife, but they continued to lie, even after she'd become an FBI agent, an officer of the law, and that changed things dramatically.

There was no turning back, especially not now, not with Elliot's suspicions kindled by her unusual behavior.

"I have a terrible headache," she eventually said, looking at him only briefly, afraid he'd see right through her lie. She knew she wasn't controlling her body language and her facial microexpressions correctly, but she just couldn't. She had no energy left. Watching Elliot drive the lawn tractor over her father's grave had left her weak, lifeless almost.

"I'm sorry to hear that," he replied, a hint of concern in his voice, and another of doubt. "Anything I can do for you?" he asked, putting down the coffee cup and grabbing an apple. This time he went over to the knife block and took the small knife himself, using it to cut the apple in quarters, like he'd done the day before. Then he rinsed and dried the knife and slid it back into its place. "Want one?" he offered a quarter of the red fruit, but she declined with a hand gesture. She was happy he'd stepped away from that knife block, where only five black, riveted handles could be seen, instead of six that used to be.

"You've done enough," she said, "with the lawn, I mean. Thank you for that; you didn't have to. I know it, and you know it, but… thanks." She forced some air into her lungs, aware she was losing track of her thoughts and babbling like an idiot. She needed to focus. "I've been procrastinating," she added, managing a weak smile. "Mowing is my brother's job. He's always done it. I guess I was thinking maybe I could work out a deal and have him released earlier, and maybe he'd do it." She looked at him briefly, then lowered her gaze and ran her hand across her forehead, painfully aware it was exactly what most liars did in an interrogation. Avert their eyes, run their hands over their face, subconsciously hiding. "Doesn't make much sense, I know," she added with a quiet chuckle.

"Don't worry about it," he replied, taking a big, crunchy bite from the apple quarter he'd offered her. "We all do—"

His phone rang, and he frowned briefly at the display before taking the call.

"Howdy, boss," he said, and Kay understood it was the sheriff himself calling at that early hour. She held her breath, waiting, hoping the search teams might've found something, some trace of Alison and the kids.

He listened intently, then said, "Got it, we're on our way." Ending the call, he slid the phone into his pocket. "They have another body, this time a fresh one."

She exhaled, feeling a sense of unspeakable dread.

"Where? At Silent Lake?"

"Yes, you were right," he said, with a hand gesture mimicking a salute. "He just chose another path leading to the lake. But he changed his ritual; he didn't put her up in a tree first; straight into the ground, it seems."

Her mind embraced that new piece of information like a vine, wrapping itself around it, building around it, grasping it from all directions. He'd changed his ritual. Why? What did that mean? Was he afraid he'd get caught, with the entire community up in arms about the bodies found at Silent Lake? Or was he afraid that tomorrow's forecast of -10 °F would make his ritualistic burial impossible?

One thing seemed certain; the perpetrator had been rattled to the point where the most important part of the killing, his signature, had to be modified, altered to fit new circumstances. And she knew well that a rattled unsub meant an escalating unsub, likely to kill more, to torture more viciously. And to make mistakes.

She grabbed a jacket from the other room and rushed outside, where Elliot had already started the engine. She didn't bother to pretend to lock the door, just pulled it shut after her and climbed into the SUV.

"There's more," Elliot announced, turning onto the main road. "There's a witness. Someone saw a suspicious vehicle pull out of the lakeshore woods just before the light."

"Where's this witness now?" she asked. Finally, a lead, a shred of hope. Although that hope was strangled, thinking who might've been buried at Silent Lake. Was it Alison? One of the children?

As if reading her mind, Elliot said, "They confirmed it's an adult female, recently deceased. That's all I have for now." Then, probably realizing he'd skipped the answer to her question, he added, "He's at the office, waiting for us."

If it was Alison Nolan, Dr. Whitmore would soon be able to confirm it, being they had Alison's driver's license from the car rental company. Soon, they'd know. Maybe within minutes of unbearable tension.

The witness waited for them in the interview room, his rifle leaning against the wall, outside the room. Kay raised her eyebrow, and a deputy clarified, "He said he was out there hunting. He's got a permit and all."

They entered the room and Elliot introduced both of them. The witness, a scrawny guy in his thirties named Mitchell Pettus, shook their hands firmly and took his seat, ready to start talking. His face was covered in a three-day stubble, a little more pronounced where his mustache would've been if he let it grow. His face was grimy, as if he'd spent days in the woods, not hours.

"Mr. Pettus, thank you for calling us," Elliot said. "But, before we start, what were you doing at Silent Lake so early in the morning?"

His lips tensed in a controlled grin. "I could tell you I was huntin' for wild pig, 'cause that's year 'round, but it ain't true." He scratched his head and continued, "I was hunting for *him*."

Elliot's eyebrows shot up in surprise.

"For whom?" Kay asked.

"For the bastard who's been killin' those women. I'd say season's open for that mother—" He stopped, lowering his head, embarrassed. "Sorry, it slipped."

Kay smiled encouragingly.

"My kids play by that lake, ma'am," he continued, running his hand over his disheveled hair. "And you might be thinkin', what's this dude gonna do by himself out there, right?"

Kay nodded.

"It's not just me," he added, lowering his voice as if sharing a well-guarded secret. "It's twenty-three of us, standin' watch all around Silent Lake. We figured the sheriff ain't got enough people for it."

"What, like a crew of vigilantes?" Elliot asked.

Pettus stood, visibly insulted. "Not vigilantes, sir, uh-uh. Concerned citizens, that's all. We called the cops, didn't we?"

"You're absolutely right," Elliot said, "and I apologize. Please go on."

He took his seat and settled his hands on the scratched surface of the table. "He came around four, in an SUV, and he just stood there, looking at the water, for a while. Then he started digging. I figured that out later, 'cause when he was doin' it, it was too dark to see anything from where I was."

"Why didn't you call us then?" Elliot asked.

"There's no signal over there, and I didn't dare to make a sound, afraid he'd hop in that car and drive off. He would've heard my truck's engine; it's a piece of crap." He swallowed. "Sorry, ma'am."

"Okay, so what exactly did you see?" Kay asked. "Were you able to see his face?"

"No, ma'am, sorry. But I saw him take this large bundle out of his car and put it in the ground, right at the crack of dawn. By then it was enough light for me to see that much. I was afraid he'd see my truck, but he didn't. He drove by only ten, fifteen yards from it and didn't stop."

"What kind of car was he driving?"

"One of those big, fancy SUVs, new too. Blue, or dark green. But I didn't see it clearly, and it was still kind of dark when he left. I only saw headlights, vertical and straight before they completely lit up, and I saw the way it shined under the moonlight. It was new, and big."

"SUV for sure?" Elliot asked. "Not truck?"

"No, sir," he scoffed. "I know what a truck looks like."

"How about the brake lights, when he came in?" Kay asked. Since the car industry had embraced LED lights, brands competed to create distinguishable designs in their headlights and brake lights. Back in her FBI days, there used to be a comprehensive database of all vehicles and how they looked in the dark, from all directions.

"I saw those clearly, ma'am, and they were fancy," he replied. "Straight and narrow."

Elliot gave him a notepad and a pencil, and he sketched what he'd seen in a childlike, stick-figure manner, but it was enough for her use. She made a call, asked a favor and in a few minutes, her phone buzzed with the text message response. *Cadillac Escalade.*

Elliot rushed to run a search for locals registered with that particular brand, while Kay thanked Mitchell Pettus for his help and let him go about his business. If they had any more questions, Mr. Pettus would be eager to help.

Then Elliot returned with a puzzled look on his face.

"We got zilch, not even one here, but I'm not surprised," he said. "I ran the search in the entire county, and there are a few Caddies in Redding, but none is an Escalade. Could he have been wrong?" he asked, pointing at the sketch drawn by the witness. "I doubt there's another vehicle that looks like the Escalade when seen from behind."

Or maybe her profile was wrong, and the unsub wasn't local after all.

"I'll ask anyway," she replied, just as both their phones chimed. She checked her message at the same time Elliot checked his, then their eyes met, puzzled.

The message was from Dr. Whitmore and read, *Positive ID— Alison Nolan. Murder weapon found with the body.*

They hadn't found her in time. Kay had been too slow, not nearly fast enough to catch up with that monster. And now Alison was gone, and nothing she'd done had been good enough to save her life, while the killer had thrown them another curveball from his sickening playbook.

"What murder weapon could there be in a manual strangulation?" Kay asked. "Has he changed his MO?"

CHAPTER THIRTY-TWO
Hunter

Almost the entire sheriff's department was there, standing, commenting in low voices, anxious to hear what Kay had to say and be gone. Most of them had been pulling double shifts, their faces and their irritable moods showing it. She drew breath sharply, steeling herself. She was ready to deliver the profile.

Or was she?

It seemed that the moment she started believing a certain part of the profile was rock solid, that part crumbled and vanished like remnants of a nightmare under the blazing rays of the sun.

The room fell silent when Sheriff Logan walked in hastily, shooting the wall clock a frustrated glance. It was almost eight in the morning.

"We're ready for you, Dr. Sharp."

She cleared her throat, surprised at how uncomfortable she was, doing what she'd been doing for the past eight years, delivering suspect profiles and answering questions. "This man is in his mid-twenties to late-thirties, and highly organized," she started. "He's technically astute, capable of disabling vehicles quickly and unseen, and erasing GPS information. He leaves nothing to chance. Every aspect of the abduction, murder and disposal of the bodies is carefully planned, thought through in obsessive detail. The burial aspect of his killings is part of his signature, and we consider it highly relevant to identifying and catching this suspect."

"We?" one of the deputies asked, smiling crookedly and shooting Elliot a sideways glance. A couple of others snickered.

"I," she corrected herself, feeling her cheeks catch fire. "However, Detective Young and I have been working closely together on this case, and I believe he contributed in no small measure to the generation of this profile." Then she realized she hated being cornered like that, and still remembered she knew better than to let the giggles and bad jokes continue. "Any other questions?" she asked in a firm voice, enjoying the ensuing silence for a moment.

"Carry on, Dr. Sharp," Sheriff Logan said.

She nodded. "We believe the unsub is local, or used to be, and has strong ties with the local Native American community. His knowledge of Native customs is far above average, as is the importance he places on Native rituals, essential to his signature."

"Are we assuming he's white?" a deputy asked, holding her notepad in the air as a journalist would at a press conference.

"We are," she admitted, "although the prevalence of white serial killers out of the total number of serial killers in general is barely above fifty percent. However, if we add to these factors the racial makeup of the population in this area, we believe it's safe to assume he's Caucasian."

"Not Native?" another deputy asked. "If he cares so much about Native stuff, why not?"

"His signature contains elements of multiple Native cultures, not a specific one, as we would see in the case of a Native American unsub." She paused for a moment, waiting to see if there were any other questions, then continued. "He crosses racial lines in his abductions, and he is a power-motivated killer. Contrary to what some of you might think, due to the sexual assault aspect, it's not lust that drives this unsub. He's gratified exerting power over his victims, and the ritualistic aspects of his signature tell us he could potentially be reenacting a situation from his past, where he was mistreated, abused or made to feel inadequate. He then overpowers, tortures and kills a surrogate for the object of his rage, the woman who'd done him wrong, in fact or in his imagination."

"Was the woman Native?" Deputy Hobbs asked.

"Excellent question," Kay replied, turning toward him. "We believe it's a strong possibility, yes. She could've been a mother, a sister or a lover. Because we profiled him to be Caucasian, we believe a lover is most likely."

"Um, I'm sorry, but that's not a whole lot to go on," another deputy said, a pot-bellied man with a handlebar mustache.

"I'm not finished," Kay replied. "We have a witness placing him at the dump site of another victim last night, and we believe he's driving a Cadillac Escalade, blue, or dark green."

"That's more like it," someone mumbled, and a couple of other people agreed.

"If you do traffic stops for Escalades, this man will most likely have a Native object on display, a dreamcatcher or something like that. Look for someone successful and composed, someone who's integrated well into society and seems sure of himself, although, beneath the surface, he is deeply insecure and likely to snap if pushed. Be very careful approaching; this man doesn't hesitate to kill."

"Is there evidence he's killed men too?" the female deputy asked.

"Not that we know of, no," she replied. "But based on the nature of the attacks on his victims, on the duration and extent of the assaults, we can ascertain he's easily insulted, and will most likely retaliate for any injury, real or perceived. Remember, with this unsub, it's all about control, about overpowering his victims, about maintaining the illusion of superiority at all costs. He's a malignant narcissist, patient, nonchalant, charismatic. And merciless."

A moment of silence, then the female deputy asked, "If he's not driven by lust, do you think he's, um, what do you think he does to the children he's holding?"

Deputy Farrell, per her name tag, apparently couldn't bring herself to say the words that had been on everyone's mind.

"I don't believe the children are being sexually assaulted, no. First of all, cases when perpetrators have assaulted both adult women and prepubescent children are exceedingly rare. I believe only one has been documented in the history of the Federal Bureau of Investigation. Because this unsub assaults his adult victims, it's safe to assume he doesn't sexually assault the children." She breathed, at the same time as her audience did. "There wasn't any evidence of sexual assault in Tracy Hendricks's case. Unfortunately, Tracy remains in shock and cannot tell us what happened during her captivity."

"Is the SFPD sure she was taken with her mother, then released by the unsub?" Deputy Hobbs asked.

"That is a strong probability, yes," she answered. Truth was, there wasn't any evidence to prove the contrary, and Kay believed Joann Hendricks when she swore Shannon would've never abandoned her children. "I believe these children play some kind of role in the unsub's fantasy, but Tracy Hendricks didn't show any signs of physical trauma, sexual or otherwise."

"Do you think he'll release Hazel Nolan, Alison's daughter, like he did Tracy?" Deputy Farrell continued to ask interesting questions She was probably one of the smartest in the group.

"It's a possibility we have to consider, but can't count on," Kay replied. "Don't forget, Matthew Hendricks, Shannon's five-year-old son, is still missing since November of last year, and we also have no IDs yet for the two bodies found yesterday at Silent Lake." She stopped short of voicing her concern. Maybe other children were missing, children they had no idea about. Hopefully, soon they'd know. "As far as the children are concerned, the profile is far from complete. But we have advised SFPD and Atlanta police to be on the lookout for Hazel."

"Why Atlanta? Do you think he'll take Hazel there?" Deputy Hobbs asked. "That seems rather extreme."

"He took Tracy to San Francisco, and we can't be sure he chose that city because that's where he operates, that's where he returns their vehicles, or because that's where Tracy was from. But the search for the missing children must continue as a top priority," she added, looking at Sheriff Logan.

The sheriff nodded, looking grim. "We'll do everything in our power to locate these children," he said. "Double shifts will continue until further notice, and we have neighboring counties pitching in with people and dogs. The FBI has deployed two CARD teams, one in San Francisco and one in Atlanta, and we are coordinating with them. But it's our turf, people, our backyard. You know it better than anyone else. Think of what you know. Where could he be hiding those kids? Who has a cabin in those woods and matches this profile?"

The deputies started to fidget and huddle closer to the exit, waiting for a sign from the sheriff.

"One more thing," Kay said, raising her voice a little, to cover the growing chatter. "The answer to finding this man is in the way he hunts. Where does he see his victims? How does he get close to them? How can he take them without anyone being the wiser? Look for anyone who doesn't belong, who lingers, who seems to wander without a specific task at hand."

"Tourists have started to pour in since first snow," Deputy Farrell said. "They'll all be wandering around soon. How can we tell the suspect from innocent tourists?"

"He'll linger, but seem edgy," Kay replied. "He'll have a cold look in his eyes and tension in his jaw. He'll be alone, not with family. And when you make eye contact with him, you'll feel an uneasiness, something unfurling in your gut. That's your instinct, telling you you're in the presence of a homicidal sociopath, a predator. A hunter."

CHAPTER THIRTY-THREE
Bloodthirst

He'd cut the first slice of cake and everyone cheered. He smiled and gracefully accepted the help of a coworker who took the knife from his hand and portioned the rest of the cake quickly, putting each slice on a Styrofoam plate and handing it out to their colleagues in the Forensic Services Division of the San Francisco Police Department.

He tasted the cake, savoring the feeling of family, of appreciation, of being valued. It was his second-year work anniversary; SFPD celebrated work anniversaries, not always people's birthdays, especially when said people didn't want their age or birthdate to become common knowledge.

He savored the creamy wedge to the last crumble and smear of icing on his plastic spoon, while his smile slowly waned.

"Want some more?" his helpful colleague asked.

"No, thank you," he replied, his eyes cold again, his smile completely gone. "I believe I've had enough."

And that was true from more than one perspective. He'd been a forensic scientist for two years and he'd had enough.

It was a dead-end job.

He'd learned all the systems that the SFPD Forensic Services Division team members used, their procedures, how they handled evidence and what they looked for in a murder investigation. He'd learned how quickly such investigations progressed, and where they got stumped and turned into cold cases, piled up in virtual basements, never to be solved. He'd identified all the limitations of the system, and realized all those movies and TV shows where people obsessed over a beetle, and turned in full tox panels or a bunch of DNA samples only to have the results returned to them the very next day were nothing but fiction. In reality, most investigators had piles of cases to work on, details slipped through the cracks all the time and beetles were rarely paid any attention to, unless one would venture on a wall somewhere, bother someone and quickly be killed with a swat of a handy object. DNA and full tox panels were costly and took a lot of time, and the brass frowned on indiscriminate use of departmental budgets. They preferred suspects rounded up and interrogated, fingerprints analyzed, and little else done. And little else was ever done, especially because a bunch of other cases would immediately pile up on top of the existing ones while the fierce fight for resources and time continued.

Only sixty-one percent of murder cases got solved. Smart killers never got caught.

Now he knew.

It was time to move on.

He was suffocating there, enduring the attitude of everyone, a mix of entitlement and arrogance that stepped on his nerves so often he could barely make it through the day, although he was appreciated, as attested by the fresh cake with custom messaging he'd just enjoyed. He was the first to volunteer to go to crime scenes, the gorier the better, and his coworkers were grateful to skip the fieldwork. Seeing the spilled blood of countless victims calmed his frayed nerves. If he let his imagination run, and if the victim was just right, he could pretend he'd been the one who stabbed her. Strangled her. Shot her. Drowned her. Vicariously, while examining untouched crime scenes, he could feel what the killer must've felt, the rage, the compulsion, the unbearable urge to take the life laid in front of him begging for mercy and getting none, and the earth-shattering release that came at the very end.

It was time to move on, and the direction to take was not that difficult to figure out. During his two years as a criminalist, he'd met all sorts of people from various walks of life, from hourly workers to businesspeople, from doctors to engineers, but no one wielded more power than the people of the law.

All this time, the only people he'd seen driving Cadillacs were lawyers, and he was going to become one. The best, most powerful lawyer in the state, maybe one day in the entire country. As a lawyer, people's lives would be neatly tucked in the palm of his hand, from where he could set them free or close his fist around them and extinguish their life force slowly, in endless agonies spent behind bars, caged like animals. As a lawyer, he'd discover all the secrets of those who put people like him on death row. And he knew he had it in him to succeed. The gods would smile on him from above, because he was ruthless enough to open a path for himself without hesitation or remorse.

But first, he had to go back to school for a few years, and it would be tricky. Law school wasn't the kind of degree one could get while working a full-time job. But the gods didn't let him down and smiled immediately, a wide grin in the form of a cocaine bust that came with a trunkload of cash in ten-grand bundles, shrink-wrapped together in hundred-thousand stacks. He kept his greed in check and detoured only one hundred grand from the bust, while his colleague was relieving herself at a gas station, after apologizing profusely for her urgent call of nature. Of course, the fact that her coffee had been spiked with a couple of water pills was not something she'd ever become aware of.

He'd been carrying the diuretic with him for a while, and other pills too, because gods always smiled on people who were prepared and always ready to seize opportunity.

A few weeks later, he announced he was going back to school, and retained part-time status with the Forensic Services Division. After all, seeing the occasional crime scene was helpful to keep his urges in check, and it was nice to access all the systems while learning how to become an attorney, how to dismantle the evidence found in them. It was like playing for both teams, prosecution *and* defense. He always won.

He wasn't greedy, and didn't spend the hundred grand on a new Cadillac, although the pining thought had crossed his mind. He'd grown smarter than giving in to impulse, and had learned the value of delayed gratification and its exhilarating rewards. He even took student loans, to cover all the bases, if anyone would think to inspect his finances. But having a stash of cash as a safety net did wonders for his morale, for his peace of mind. It was the guarantee that he'd be able to finish law school, that he'd never end up living on the street again.

He loved studying law, and enjoyed most of his time as a student, with the exception of those times when women judges or professors would challenge him in public, would chastise him for minor mistakes, for something he got wrong or for no reason whatsoever. Those times he struggled the most to keep his cool and abide by the self-imposed rule to not take another life until it would be safe enough to do so and he could savor the long-awaited moment.

When he graduated from law school, his grades were so impressive and his experience as a forensic scientist so valuable, he had his choice of venues. But the choice, again, wasn't difficult. After all, he only wanted money and power, with no thought given to employer or law specialty. And the legal profession held countless treasures for ambitious, young people like him.

As soon as he passed his bar exam, he started treasure hunting with endless resilience and the mental acuity of someone who'd climbed to success through his own strengths. He had street smarts, stamina and a sharp, analytical mind, and he couldn't be intimidated. He changed jobs often, every year or so, looking for that perfect mix of money, power and freedom that would bring him the ultimate satisfaction, the license to do what his entire body ached for.

He sometimes visited his family home, staying hidden in the shadows across the street, watching his mother, his sister and his father go about their business and never wanting to speak to them again. But every time he saw them, he struggled not to lose control and yet he couldn't stay away. He watched his family from a distance, silent, while his heart ached raw, the wound fresh, unhealed by the passing of time. While his monsters raged, locked inside his chest.

After one such visit, he'd tossed and turned the entire night, morning finding him drenched in sweat and filled with rage, but he took a cold shower and went to work. He was delivering an opening argument that morning in a capital murder case and he had to be at the top of his game.

The judge was a woman who took an instant dislike to him and chastised him every chance she got, sustaining every objection formulated by the opposing counsel with a hint of a smirk on her wilted lips, as if she knew exactly who he was, *what* he was. And right there, in the middle of a courtroom filled with people, he felt his old urge swell inside him, unforgiving, imperative.

He'd anticipated that moment for years, dreamed of it, planned for it, and now the time had come. He knew exactly what he had to do.

He'd smiled at the judge that day, accepting her hostile rulings with dignity and class, finished the session, and later found someone who could quench that bloodthirst.

CHAPTER THIRTY-FOUR

Kids

Kay didn't waste any time; as soon as she finished delivering the profile, she found Elliot and pulled him aside, out of passing deputies' earshot. He seemed a little flustered and avoided her glance.

"You ran out of there faster than a jackrabbit," he said. "I thought by now you'd be used to handling a bunch of hillbilly cops."

"I thought so too," she smiled, a little embarrassed, yet relieved to see the tension between them was easing off. "Let's start with the morgue," she said. "We'll come back and speak to the technician right after."

"Doc Whitmore just got his hands on that body two hours ago," he replied.

"Exactly," she said with a quick wink, then headed for his car. "I want to hear his first impressions and spend some time with him at the morgue." Elliot's face was rigid, frozen in a grimace of nausea. "Trust me, it's time well spent."

Dr. Whitmore disagreed, in tone of voice and body language. They found him bent over the body, face shield on, examining every inch of Alison's skin under powerful lights. He let out a long sigh of frustration as they walked into the autopsy room, then propped his gloved hands on his hips and straightened his back.

"I'd've thought you'd give me a few hours, at least, Dr. Sharp," he said, probably singling her out because of their history together. "What could you possibly expect from me at this point?"

"Any preliminary findings would be great," she replied, speaking softly, trying to appease him.

He sighed, this time sounding less frustrated than before, almost resigned. "I'd have to conduct a preliminary exam to give you preliminary findings, and I haven't had the time to do that yet."

"No rush," she said, "just wanted to see her, that's all." Kay approached the exam table and took the shield and gloves offered by Dr. Whitmore.

Elliot kept his distance, but put on gloves and a face shield too, under Dr. Whitmore's uncompromising scowl. "No one comes near her without gear on," he explained.

Kay studied Alison's skin under the exam lights. She had numerous bruises around her throat, some recent, some yellowish. Petechiae were present on her face, around the eyes, and on her throat, where the pressure of the strangulation had caused capillaries to rupture. She'd been strangled multiple times, in a sickening game of strangle-and-release that must've continued for days.

"May I?" she asked, pointing at Alison's eyes.

"Uh-huh," Dr. Whitmore replied, continuing his detailed exam of her body.

Gently, Kay lifted her eyelids to examine her conjunctive membranes and found more petechiae, some recent, some almost healed. "I think I know how she died."

"You do, huh?" Dr. Whitmore mumbled.

"Same as the others, manual strangulation, forceful, filled with rage," she said, feeling like an intern again. "I'm a little confused, because your message said something about a murder weapon being found?"

"I should've said torture weapon, not murder," he replied, sounding both apologetic and a little angry with himself. "This is why you should never rush a medical examiner." He pointed at several cuts on Alison's skin. "She was cut in various places, but these cuts were meant to inflict fear and cause pain, not death.

They're superficial, but not tentative. I counted thirty-seven of them, all done in the past twenty-four hours, all in locations bound to yield lots of pain but limited bleeding." He inhaled sharply, then continued, "The bastard probably didn't want her weakened by hypovolemia until he was done with her." He studied one of the cuts with his gloved fingers, bringing his face close to the wound. "What's remarkable is that he used a rusted knife, but that's preliminary. I'll have to confirm."

"Do these cuts match the knife you found?" Elliot asked, approaching the exam table.

"At first glance, yes, but I'll take a mold to be sure." He lifted her arm and examined her ribs, her axillary region, and the underside of her arm. "By the way, I was able to lift usable prints off that knife," he added. "There were several clear ones on the handle."

That was not the unsub she'd just profiled—organized, methodical, a perfectionist with knowledge of forensics.

"Don't you think he might be leading us on, Doc?" Kay asked. "He wouldn't make such a blatant mistake."

"That's for you two to find out," he replied, shifting his attention to Alison's left leg. "I call them as I find them."

Kay stared at Alison's hair, carefully braided and tied neatly with leather hair ties adorned with small feathers. There was something familiar about her braids, about the way they ran the length of her chest, coming from behind her ears. Her hair had been parted perfectly at the center of her head, and the braids were executed well, without leaving loose strands anywhere. She'd seen Native braided hair on many occasions, from TV and media to her personal experience growing up close to Native communities, attending powwows, visiting her Native friends and meeting their families.

And yet, studying Alison's braids under the powerful exam lights, she couldn't stop thinking about the spiritual value Natives placed on their hair, the sacred meaning of it, the customs surrounding it. How was that relevant to the unsub? Did it have any meaning, other than trying to recreate the object of his rage in the women he abducted, tortured and killed?

"Anything else you can share with us, Doctor?" she asked, getting ready to leave. She'd seen enough. Kay could visualize what Alison had gone through, just by looking at the wounds on her body, at the numerous marks her skin bore in testimony to what she'd endured. If she closed her eyes, she could almost hear Alison's screams.

They'd been too late for her.

But the unsub was about to take someone else, and they didn't have a way of knowing when he would.

"As with the other victims, there are signs of sexual assault, prolonged and forceful," Dr. Whitmore said. "I'll give you more when I finish the exam." He left the table and peeled off his gloves, then discarded them into a sensor trash can and removed his face shield. "I have something else, though. It just came in, moments before you arrived." He typed in his password and unlocked his computer, and two missing person reports were displayed on the wall screen. "IDs came back on the two Jane Does. The first one is Lan Xiu Tang, a thirty-one-year-old tourist from Seattle, traveling with her daughter Ann. The other one was Janelle Huarez, twenty-six, who was born here, in Mount Chester, but moved away as a little girl with her mother. She lived in San Jose, and, thankfully, had no children. She was traveling to close on her grandfather's house, after he moved to the city to live with her."

"So, now, we have three kids missing?" Elliot said, his voice angry, tense. "Can't we get ahead of this guy?"

"We haven't found any additional bodies," Dr. Whitmore replied. "That means yes, there are three children missing. Ann Tang, eleven; Matthew Hendricks, five; and Hazel Nolan, eight."

Heavy silence engulfed the morgue, mixing with the chill in the air and the smell of death, sending ominous shivers down

Kay's spine. What was the unsub doing with the children? Had he let them go, and they just hadn't been found yet? Or were the children part of a sick game he was playing, unwilling actors in his twisted fantasy?

CHAPTER THIRTY-FIVE
Eye Candy

The sound of a wheelie being dragged on the carpeted hallway woke Wendy up, but she refused to open her eyes and face the piercing rays of the sun. She clung to sleep, to the sweet numbness in her limbs, wishing she had time for more. After all, it had been after two in the morning when she'd finally dozed off, spent, satisfied and so alive.

Opening her eyes just a little, she smiled as she disentangled herself from the sleepy embrace of the man she'd met the day before at the airport lounge, careful not to wake him. Her smile widened as she recalled last night. Who knew getting a flight bumped to the next day could be such a rewarding experience? The airline provided the hotel room, and the tall, dark stranger with fiery eyes and a smooth tongue provided the meal, complete with drinks and entertaining conversation. By the time they made it to the room, they were ready to rip the clothes off each other.

She sat on the side of the bed and frowned a little when the man shifted in his sleep; she hoped she'd skip the morning-after conversation and just disappear. Looking at his sweat-covered body and remembering how that body had brought hers back to life after so many years made her feel grateful for the warmth she felt inside. If she weren't booked on an early flight, she'd wake him up for another serving of feeling alive and living dangerously. Part of him was already awake, anyway.

She placed a gentle kiss on the man's lips, noting in passing she didn't even know his name. He'd mentioned it, sometime last night, while they were waiting for the first round of drinks at the airport brewery near Terminal 2, but she'd immediately forgotten it. To her, he'd always be the guy from the LAX stopover. Unforgettable... why bother with names?

Her life was just beginning.

Screw the bastard, she thought, remembering her husband's face when she told him she was leaving him. Of course, he'd been shocked to hear. He'd been taking her for granted for years.

"Hey, baby," the stranger said, stretching and reaching for her, and the memory of her husband's face disappeared with the touch of his fingers on her skin trailing streaks of fire. "Why don't you get us some breakfast, huh?"

She barely contained the roar of laughter that was about to explode out of her chest. Instead, she smiled, caressing his naked thigh until she obtained the desired reaction, and said in a sultry whisper, "Sure, I'll get right to it." Then she stood and started getting dressed.

Satisfied, the guy from the LAX stopover who was dangerously close to being remembered as the entitled asshole from the LAX stopover closed his eyes and dozed off.

She looked at him one more time before leaving the room and almost thanked him for the memorable night. Laughing quietly, she rolled her wheelie out of there and headed for the airport shuttle terminal downstairs.

Let the sexy bastard get his own damn breakfast.

The second leg of the trip was short, and she'd barely had time to finish her coffee, lost in memories and plans for the future, when the descent to San Francisco began, and she avidly stared out the window at the city she'd always wanted to visit, at the blue ocean glimmering in the distance, and the snow-capped mountains she was about to see from up close, in only a few hours.

She picked up her rental from Budget, a red Ford EcoSport that suited her new life. Small, compact, but quick on its wheels and responsive to her touch. She drove straight north, eager to feel the mountain air fill her lungs after having spent the summer in sweltering Phoenix. She couldn't wait to feel free, young and beautiful, not just a household implement meant to wash, clean, cook and be yelled at.

"Screw that son of a bitch," she said, louder than the blaring music. Not fully satisfied, she opened all the windows, and honked long, stepping on the gas and shouting, "Woo-hoo! Screw you, motherfucker! Whew!"

She drove with her windows down for a while, the feeling of the cold wind lashing through her long hair not something she wanted to part with too soon, and sang with the radio until she was out of breath.

She was about an hour away from Mount Chester when she saw the Miramonte diner, a place advertising baked potato soup and outdoor seating on a highway billboard. What an irresistible combo!

She got seated on the patio, even if it required her to unzip her wheelie and fish out a thick sweater. But it was worth it. The mountains were so close she felt she could touch them, the air so crisp she felt dizzy, unable to fill her lungs despite how hard she tried. She kept staring into the distance, at the snow-covered peaks, wondering if she could see the resort from where she was. She was so focused on the landscape, then on her phone looking at the map, she almost didn't see the insistent gaze coming from the man seated a few tables away.

He had an unusual intensity in his loaded stare, a sense of urgency that triggered an immediate response from her young body, but she decided to break eye contact and look away.

He's probably bad news, she thought. *And, seriously, you've just had a slice of fun in LA. Pace yourself a little, woman.* She repressed a smile that the stranger might've misinterpreted, and delved into the amazing potato soup. It might've been one of those nameless roadside diners, but it was awesome. Everything was awesome that very first day of her newly found freedom, even the unwanted attention from the man a few tables over.

He seemed loaded, and a decent piece of eye candy. She gave him another passing glance and found him still staring at her, just as intently. Something unfurled in her gut, something beyond the delicious voice of her awakened body, something nameless and terrifying.

Ignoring that chilling uneasiness, she continued to feast on her soup, her eyes riveted on the distant, snow-covered mountain peaks. When she dared look again, the table was empty, and the stranger gone.

She breathed with ease and leaned back in her seat, staring at the perfectly blue California sky.

CHAPTER THIRTY-SIX
Fingerprints

"Howdy," Elliot said, leading the way into the motor pool garage. That was the official name for a twenty-by-forty corrugated metal structure at the back of the sheriff's office building, littered with tools and lined with tool cabinets and workbenches. At the center of the space and the service technician's attention was Kendra Marshall's rental Jeep, its hood missing, and the entire engine compartment taken apart. On a sheet of blue tarp laid down to the side, all the removed parts were neatly arranged, some with yellow Post-it notes affixed to them.

"Right back at ya," the technician replied, without lifting his eyes from the engine compartment. The rhythmic clicking of a torque wrench continued for a moment, then he finally looked up at his guests.

If it weren't for the sheriff's office logo on the name tag he wore affixed to an oil-stained NASCAR shirt, Kay could've easily mistaken the burly man for one of the Tenderloin's street residents. His salt-and-pepper beard and the hair escaping from underneath a dirty ballcap were long and untrimmed, more yellowish salt than pepper, with streaks of black where he'd run his greasy fingers through the rebel strands.

"Ma'am," he acknowledged Kay as soon as he saw her, his voice husky but hinting of a good nature and a sharp mind. "I'm hearing it's you I have to thank for this," he added, laughing quietly.

She approached the Jeep, smiling encouragingly, and swallowed her immediate comeback that it was, in fact, the unsub's fault for the added workload.

"Tell me, Mr. Willie," she said, reading his name tag, "what have you found? How did the unsub disable those vehicles?"

"Just Willie, ma'am," he replied. "I'm a lowly service guy, not some fancy detective. I get to use my given name," he quipped, and Elliot was quick to mock punch him in the shoulder. "Some people call me the car guy, the pad slapper, or the Interceptor Inspector. But no one's ever called me the idiot in the garage or the clueless mechanic, not in thirty years of turning wrenches." He took off his ballcap and scratched the roots of his gray mane, then put it back on.

Kay wondered what had caused his defensive statement.

"Let me show you what I found and what I haven't."

He went over to one of the workbenches with a pained, crooked gait, and came back carrying a handheld device. He showed it to Kay and Elliot, flipping through various screen settings. The small LCD screen of the device showed a series of alphanumeric codes that meant absolutely nothing to her.

"This gizmo here is called an OBD2 scanner. It connects to the cars' internal computers and retrieves the error codes it finds, helping people like me figure out what happened. These vehicles," Willie said, gesturing at the Jeep first, and then at the Nissan Altima and the Subaru parked outside, "returned code P-0-2-1-7." He probably noticed her puzzled face, because he quickly added, "Overheated engine."

"I see," she replied, wishing she knew more about how car engines worked. "Any idea how that happened?"

A quick burst of laughter escaped Willie's lips before he stifled it and said, "Of course, I know how it happened. I wouldn't belong here if I didn't." He played with the OBD2 device for a moment, each key he pressed returning a subdued beep. "Most times, it's because the coolant level is low. That happens when the radiator springs a leak, or the hoses are cut."

"Were they cut, Willie?" Elliot asked, approaching the dismantled radiator on the tarp and crouching next to it.

"Nope," he replied, the tension in his jaw showing how frustrated he was with not having a better answer. "The Subaru, which is the most advanced of these vehicles, also returned P two five six zero, which is the code for low coolant level. That means, at some point in time, the coolant level in the Subaru was low enough to overheat the engine."

"At some point?" Elliot replied. "What do you mean?"

"Well, it's fine as heck now," Willie said, wiping his hands against the sides of his pants and walking toward the vehicle. He popped the hood and pointed at a white, semitransparent reservoir, tapping his finger on the fluid level line. "It's up to spec." He muttered an oath under his breath and lit a cigarette, his oil-stained fingers handling a Zippo lighter with the dexterity of a lifelong smoker. "That's what I didn't find. The reason why the engines overheated."

"What happens when an engine overheats?" Kay asked. "Billowing smoke or something?"

"First, the check engine light will turn on, and if you care enough to know what the gauges on your dashboard mean, you'll notice the engine temperature is climbing beyond the red line. If you still keep on driving, at some point these smart cars will stall and force you to stop, to protect the engine."

"That's how he forces them to stop," Kay said. "And it's relatively precise, right? Did all the cars stop in the same general area?"

"I checked all three navigation systems and yes, all three vehicles stopped in the same valley, just down from Katse, where there's no cellular service," Willie replied. "But then, later, when this killer of yours was done with them cars, they just miraculously functioned again."

"Did you figure out what he did to erase the GPS return trip from the navigation history?" Elliot asked.

"That's another thing I didn't find," Willie replied morosely. He seemed to be taking his lack of findings as a personal failure.

"Do you think it's possible he somehow tampered with the cars' computers, and made them *think* the engines were overheating?" Kay asked. "Maybe he has one of these devices, modified to—"

"Nah," Willie replied after inhaling a lungful of smoke and holding it in for a second or two. "Do you know the level of skill you'd need to have to pull that off?" He flicked the cigarette butt, sending it into a small rain puddle. "No, it has to be this other thing."

"What other thing?" Kay asked, a little irritated he'd left some information out.

"Something I found on the Jeep's radiator, like a deposit of hard resin or something. I took a scraping and gave it to Deputy Hobbs. He said he'd send it over to the San Francisco lab, to tell us what it is."

"What could it be?"

He scratched his chin, thinking, then walked inside and stopped by the blue tarp. "No one repairs radiators anymore; they just replace them altogether. But back in the old days, if you took a stone in your grille at high speed, and it chipped the radiator, causing a leak, the mechanic would solder that hole, patching it up." He kneeled on the tarp and pointed at a certain spot on the radiator, where recent scrapes were visible in the thick layer of dust. "See here? Someone has done something to these fins."

"And why aren't you certain this is the unsub's handiwork?" Kay asked, frowning slightly.

"Because it doesn't seem new," Willie replied. "It's covered by a dust layer as if the car had been driven for a few months at least, after it was done. There's no trace of recent leakage in the dust settled on the fins, like you'd see if coolant had leaked at high temperatures, washing some of the dirt away. And it's not what's typically used to patch up a radiator hole either. It's not soldering material; it's a resin of some kind."

"So, you don't know what happened to these vehicles," Kay concluded, her voice sounding bitter, disappointed.

"I don't," Willie replied, looking at her straight. "That's the god's honest truth. But sure as hell I won't stop looking until I have an answer for you. I'll take apart the other two radiators, and if I see the same resin blob, I'll know it's his doing."

She thanked him and walked out in the gloomy air, then, feeling the chill in her bones, climbed into Elliot's SUV.

"He's trying hard, you know," Elliot said as soon as he joined her. He started the engine and let it idle for a moment.

"I don't care if he's trying hard," Kay snapped. "I care those kids are still missing, and every day they spend with that monster is a day they'll never forget, no matter how long they live. I care that by now he's probably taken another woman, someone to keep his sick urges satisfied, and she won't live long, but no matter how long she lives, she'll wish she was dead already. Meanwhile, we have a lot of ifs and maybes, nothing certain, and we're nowhere closer to catching this guy. *That's* what I care about!" Her voice had climbed and climbed until it had turned into shouting. Feeling ashamed for her outburst of emotion, she lowered her head and said, "I'm sorry."

"It's okay," Elliot replied, touching her hand for a brief moment, then pulling away. "We're all tired, disappointed, ticked off like a hungry, wild pig in spring."

She breathed, exhaling long, easing the air out of her lungs slowly, while gathering her thoughts and remembering her basics. "Let's go back to victimology," she said. "There has to be something we missed."

"Okay," he replied. "We've been through it a couple of times already."

"Doesn't matter," she replied. "We'll keep going back to this until we understand how he hunts. That's our only chance." She breathed again, just as slowly, and started to correlate information in her mind. "There are now five victims we know about, different races. Three were mothers, two were not. Two of them drove to Mount Chester in their personal cars, three in rentals originating from San Francisco International Airport. By the way, are we getting Lan Xiu's and Janelle's vehicles brought over to our Mr. Willie?"

"That's happening today," Elliot replied, after checking something on his phone.

"I'm willing to bet those two vehicles will show the same—what was it—code for overheated engine. He's got a good method to get them to stop in the middle of nowhere; why change it?"

"Maybe it evolved over time," Elliot replied. "Lan Xiu and Janelle died last year."

"Maybe, but I believe this man's been killing for more than a year. After this is over, we'll have to consider expanding the cadaver dog search on the entire Silent Lake shore."

Elliot shifted into gear but didn't pull away, listening, waiting for her to continue.

She made an effort to focus, while her thoughts obsessed over the potential bodies they hadn't unearthed yet. Were they real? Or just a result of her imagination, of her experience reading clues into the organized and precise manner in which he grabbed, killed and disposed of his victims? There was no hesitation in anything he did, nothing left to chance. Did it matter now? No... the only thing that mattered was finding and stopping him, finding those kids. Then they'd have all the time in the world to find the other bodies, if they existed.

"We know at least two of his victims stopped at Katse Coffee Shop, either before or after their vehicles were disabled," she said, speaking slowly, piecing together the puzzle in her mind. "But, to me, it seems too close to the grab area," she mumbled. What if what he did to those vehicles needed more time to kick in? "Let's assume Willie is right and he messed with their radiators or something. What's before Katse, when driving from San Francisco?"

"Winding mountain roads," Elliot replied, looking at her with a raised eyebrow. Then he seemed to grasp the idea. "Seriously steep, curvy mountain roads, when cars overheat anyway. Some areas are at twelve percent."

"Exactly," she said excitedly. "Regardless of where these women came from, they all drove the same road, for at least one hundred miles or so before arriving at Mount Chester." She frowned, staring into the distance, trying to recall the landmarks along the way. "At Katse, he would've drawn attention to himself; he's too smart for that. So, then, where does he see them?" She paused for a beat, thinking of the best way to track down the movements of all the women. "We'll need all the victims' financials, credit card statements, everything. Somewhere along the way, all five women stopped somewhere, and chances are they spent a few dollars where they stopped."

Elliot's lips stretched into a smile. "Let's figure it out." Reversing out of the garage yard, he stopped again when his phone rang. Seeing Sheriff Logan's name on the caller ID, he took it on the media center with a quick tap of the green button.

"Take me off speaker," Logan said, and Elliot executed with a frown, putting the phone to his ear.

Kay wondered what that was about, but she wasn't officially a member of Logan's team. He had the right to keep some things closer to the vest.

When Elliot ended the call, he was tense, his brow deeply furrowed, and his jaw clenched. He turned onto the road and drove fast, heading across the mountain.

"I'm taking you home," he said, a chill seeping in his voice she'd never sensed before.

"What's going on?"

"Nothing, I just have to take care of something, that's all," he replied just as coldly, obstinately keeping his eyes on the road.

"Elliot Young, you make a terrible liar," she replied, trying to instill a little humor into the situation. Whatever was bothering him, they could work it out together. Had there been another victim taken? If yes, why would he keep that from her?

"Cut it out, Kay," he reacted, gripping the wheel tighter and flooring it. "You'll be home in five minutes."

As if he couldn't wait to drop her off. As if she'd done something to upset him.

"Please, tell me what happened," she insisted, her voice calm, steeled, communicating without words that she was ready to listen to whatever he had to say.

His jaw stayed clenched for another long moment. She respected his choice and let the silence between them fill the space, become just as uncomfortable for him as it was for her.

When he eventually spoke, his voice was strangled, filled with pain. "Remember the rusted knife we found buried with Alison's body? The one we found fingerprints on?"

"Uh-huh," she replied. "What about it?"

"Those fingerprints came back. They're your father's."

CHAPTER THIRTY-SEVEN
Knife

Gutted.

That's how she felt, fighting a sudden wave of nausea and dizziness that had her grabbing onto the armrest with white-knuckled fingers, breathing shallow and fast while blood drained from her face.

Could it be true?

She closed her eyes, recalling memories she'd tried so desperately to bury for the past sixteen years. The sound of the gunshots, piercing the panicked silence. Her father's body, lying on the kitchen floor, the knife still clutched in his fingers, covered in her mother's blood.

And his fingerprints, clearly on the handle.

The black plastic handle secured with three silver rivets, the typical cheap carving knife that came in kitchen knife sets of the kind that her mother could afford, that stores offered coupons with heavy discounts for, each year before Christmas.

That knife's plastic handle would've survived in the ground, intact, undamaged by the passing of time, buried by her father's decaying body yet coming back to haunt her sixteen years after she'd taken his life.

After someone had dug it up from his grave.

A fresh wave of nausea had her dry heaving, but she managed to feign a cough and go unnoticed by Elliot, as he was pulling into her driveway.

"This is where you get off," he announced in an uncompromising voice, as if she were some hitchhiker he was eager to be rid of.

She opened the car door, but then turned to him and said, "That's impossible. He's been gone for sixteen years. No one's seen him since he went to Arizona."

He pressed his lips together, refusing to look at her. "It's convenient as heck how you showed up here just when your father started getting busy raping and killing again, isn't it? Doing who knows what to those kids?"

"Oh, God, no," she reacted. "You obviously haven't met my father."

"I'd like that very much," he said in a low, menacing voice, grinding his teeth. "Would you please introduce us?"

She sighed angrily, aching with the need to tell him he was dead, buried, rotting in the ground where her brother had put him all those years ago. Yet the liberating words died on her lips, and all she could say was, "He's a drunk who's barely had any schooling. The best day of my life was when he slammed that door and left, sixteen years ago. No one's ever heard from him since." She paused for a beat, then continued, in a calmer, more persuasive voice. "Remember what we said, when Dr. Whitmore told us about the knife. This unsub is way too smart to leave a weapon with fingerprints on it, and he's leading us on to where he wants, playing us like puppets."

"Yeah, Kay, that's exactly what I'd have said if I'd returned here to cover for my father's crimes," he replied angrily, shooting her a fiery glance. The bitterness in his voice made her cringe. "You must believe the hillbilly cop from Austin, Texas, is some new level of idiot, don't you? Wrapped around your little finger, unable to think for himself? Well, even a blind hog gets the occasional acorn. You tricked me, lied to me since the day we met."

"What? I never lied to you," Kay replied, her surprise genuine. She'd omitted to tell him about her father and the real reason why she'd returned home, but other than that, she hadn't lied to him. She didn't think so… her head was spinning, her nausea still strong.

Who was playing tricks with her mind? Who knew she'd killed her father?

He laughed, a quick, bitter laugh. "You conveniently forgot to mention you'd visited the body dump the day before we officially met," he said. "But I saw you that night. I saw you circle Kendra's grave, looking for evidence that we might've missed, or maybe planting some, who the hell knows now?"

"Oh," she replied quietly. She'd forgotten all about that night. "Well, you haven't been exactly forthcoming either now, have you? Why didn't you tell me you saw me?"

He whistled angrily. "Women! Leave it to them to turn any argument against you and make you look like a fool."

She repressed a long slew of curses. The man was being obstinate as only men could be when an idea grows roots in their minds. "Listen, someone would've said something about my father, if they had seen him in all these years. Have you heard his name since you moved here? He wasn't exactly a law-abiding citizen; that's how you had his prints in the system. He'd been collared a couple of times for drunk and disorderly. Really, is this who our unsub is? Do you really see my father, the now sixty-year-old drunk, being able to alter cars' navigation history or cause vehicles to stall and stop where he damn well pleases?"

Elliot stared ahead, at the garage door in front of him, not saying a word. Only yesterday morning he'd driven her lawn tractor out of that garage, smiling, waving at her. Caring.

She gave him the space to make up his mind, to find his bearings.

But he turned to her and said, "I'm sorry, Kay. The sheriff was clear about this. You're off the case, and I have to get back to work." The sadness in his voice was unmistakable, while his entire demeanor communicated a different feeling.

Shame. Guilt.

Without another word, she got out of his vehicle and closed the door. She watched him pull away from her driveway and drive off, and kept her eyes on his brake lights until they vanished behind the edge of the woods as the road curved left toward the mountain.

Then she shifted her attention to the willow trees in the backyard.

A wave of nausea grabbed her again, and this time she gave in, falling to her knees on the freshly mowed lawn and heaving, the memory of that night dancing in front of her eyes like a nightmare she couldn't escape.

CHAPTER THIRTY-EIGHT

The Hunt

Out of all places where he found them, Miramonte Restaurant was his favorite. The patio was large, and everyone's gaze was on the landscape, not on him. From the side of the patio, where he liked to sit, he could see the interstate ramps, knowing instantly which travelers were headed north toward Mount Chester. A little attention paid to the small talk ensuing between travelers and their servers, and he'd know if the woman was headed to Mount Chester or the ski resort. Only those were worthy of his attention.

It didn't make much sense, he knew that. Why would it matter if the girls were headed to Portland, for example? Why would he care enough to let them pass through, to let them live? But it somehow mattered, as if their destination, the place where he was born, grew up in and then was shunned from, was marking them somehow, as if their destinies were intertwined with Mount Chester as the only common denominator he cared about.

He'd seen a few others, over time, who felt just right, but then he'd let them go, finding they were headed to Seattle, Portland, or just over the Oregon state line, to camp in one of the state forests. But he liked the game of catch and release. It was as if he was asking fate to choose for him, to make sure he chose right, he made no mistakes, and he could still control his urges. It wasn't easy to let go of someone amazing just because she was going someplace else, but delayed gratification had its rewards. The intensity of the release, once it came, was unparalleled. The excitement building up in his entire body, the way it prickled his skin and lit his blood on fire, the way it turned his nights into sleepless visions of exhilaration led to a superlative experience, once it came to be fulfilled.

If he couldn't live there, if his own mother had forced him to leave, these women, who chose freely to be in Mount Chester and were allowed to, had to be punished for their freedom, for their undeserved right to set foot where he was no longer welcome. The place he could no longer call home was to become their grave.

A red Ford crossover exited the northbound interstate and signaled the turn into Miramonte's parking lot. A quick grin fluttered on his lips. The car was the typical rental, new, compact, sparkling clean, easy to spot. Behind its wheel, a young woman, whose long hair was blowing in the wind. She drove with all the windows down, music blaring, and over that music, her voice occasionally hit high notes sung vigorously. A tourist.

If only she'd be going to Mount Chester.

He turned his chair slightly to face the patio, then perched his left ankle across his right knee and undid the button on his jacket. He munched casually on the remaining fries on his plate while the woman got seated, her back to the restaurant entrance, her face lit by the sun and turned toward the distant peaks of Mount Chester.

She was stunning. About thirty years old, with beautiful skin that glowed in the afternoon light. She smiled almost incessantly, probably thinking of something exciting, maybe her upcoming vacation. Her features showed strength, determination and grit.

She'd be a pleasure to possess. To spend winter with.

The woman's first exchange with the server brought little clarity as to her destination, only her choice of soup and salad. Yet soon after the server went away with her order, she noticed him, making lingering eye contact that he found promising, enticing.

Yes, she could bring him lots of pleasure over the long, frozen months to come.

Breaking off eye contact, she turned away, looking at the snow-covered peaks, but a smile hovered on her lips. He could only see her profile, but he could tell. She'd seen something she liked. Wouldn't it be interesting if she were to make a pass at him?

He looked at her intently, unable to take his eyes off her broad shoulders, the curve of her full breasts pushing through the fuzzy cashmere of her sweater, the line of her neck, and the way her hair flowed around her head, shining like a halo against the sun.

He'd love to braid those long, silky strands. The sensation of her hair touching his fingers, even if only in his mind, stirred him below the belt. She was perfect.

The server brought her soup and a tall glass of iced water, and quickly went away. The woman started eating, apparently having forgotten all about him. He leaned forward, elbows on the table, his eyes drilling into her as if sheer willpower would make her disclose her intended destination somehow or would grant him the ability to see inside her mind.

She was the one, he knew that clearly now. He could feel it in the heat spreading inside his groin, in the dark urge swelling his chest.

And each time, he wanted it to be better than last time, more intense, an addict to his own body and its brutal demands.

Briefly, for only a split second, she made eye contact again, but quickly turned away. Yeah, she was interested.

He'd love to hear her scream. See her fighting him off, kicking and clawing, only to be defeated, subdued, taken.

The server came by his table, but he waved her off with a smile. From there, she walked to the woman's table, asking how everything was. They chatted for a short while.

"Oh, this soup is amazing!" the woman said in a crystalline, joyful voice. He loved the sound of her.

"Can I get you anything else?" the server asked, ready to offer the check.

"I'm still working on the soup, but let me think for a moment," she replied. She dipped her spoon and stopped midair. "How much longer to Mount Chester, do you know?"

Hiding a satisfied smile, he pulled a twenty-dollar bill from his wallet and placed it on the table under the soda glass, so the wind wouldn't blow it away. Then he left, using the patio side door that led to the parking lot. Before turning the corner, he gave the woman one last look.

Yes, she was the one.

He stopped briefly by his car and opened the rear door, where he kept a scratch awl tucked under the rear passenger seat. He took the tool, holding it so that the handle was hidden in his fist and the long, sharp steel spike was along his arm. From a distance, no one could tell he was holding anything in his hand.

A few empty spots over, the red Ford she'd come in, facing the alley, was easy to get to. The grille posed no problems, its openings wide enough for him to do his job. He checked the surroundings casually, then walked past the car, barely slowing as he pierced the radiator discreetly with one quick, strong stab of the awl. Then he continued walking to the front of the parking lot, as if looking for someone. He then turned around and climbed behind the wheel of his Cadillac.

Smiling.

Soon, after she left the interstate, taking the road to Mount Chester, and drove about twenty miles of steep, curvy mountain roads, the loss of coolant would be severe enough and the engine would overheat, forcing her to pull over.

And he'd be close by, waiting.

He loved this manner of disabling vehicles. He didn't want to put her life at risk with a cut brake line or something that extreme. A forensic team would spot tampered brakes in a minute, and it would also be difficult to do in plain sight. And he wouldn't want her hurt, damaged in any way when she came to him.

He wanted to be the one to make her scream, not her stupid car.

With a little bit of luck, when her Ford would force her to stop, she'd be over the ridge, where even the most expensive smartphones couldn't get a single bar. That would be fate's final say about her.

Then he'd get to meet her, to run his fingers through her silky hair.

To take her home.

CHAPTER THIRTY-NINE
Brother

Kay approached High Desert State Prison with a sense of dread like she'd never felt before. During her FBI days, she'd visited inmates routinely and thought she was used to it, calloused even. Knowing her little brother Jacob was inside those gray walls changed things, unsettling her in ways she didn't think possible, making the bile rise in her throat and filling her with unspeakable rage.

At the same time, she bowed her head under the burden of her own guilt. She'd promised herself she'd reach out to the judge who'd imposed such an unreasonably harsh sentence on her brother for his first offense. A bar brawl, no injuries, and it landed him six months in High Desert? If that were the norm, the bars would be all empty, and the prisons filled to the brim with drunk and disorderlies.

She passed through security with the familiarity of repetition, but without the preferential status offered by an active law enforcement badge. She was just a family member visiting an inmate, and no one on duty that day at the front gate remembered her from prior visits. After she cleared security, she was escorted to the visitor room, where she was assigned a booth and took her seat.

When Jacob approached, at first she didn't recognize him. He looked frail and weak in the oversized orange jumpsuit. His beard had grown since she'd last seen him, and a fresh bruise adorned his right cheek. Another punch had clearly landed squarely on his jaw, leaving its mark, now yellowish, the swelling still tugging at his swollen lip. And he'd only been locked up for ten days.

Paralyzing fear unfurled in Kay's gut. He wasn't going to last in there.

"I told you not to come," he said, skipping over pleasantries.

He avoided her scrutiny, keeping his eyes lowered or shooting sideways glances, checking to see if anyone could overhear their conversation.

"I had to," she whispered, putting her hand on the glass divider, wanting to touch his bruised face, to hold his hand. She stopped short of asking him how he was. "Tell me what happened," she said instead. "I need to know everything, step by step."

He looked at her briefly, with the pained gaze of a beaten dog. "Leave it alone, sis. There's nothing you can do."

"There probably isn't anything I can do," she admitted. "I still want to know how this happened." Then she noticed the cameras above their heads. "Be careful, there's no privacy to inmate family visits, not unless I'm your lawyer."

He cursed under his breath. "Figures," he eventually said. "There's no privacy anywhere." He shifted in his seat, clasping and unclasping his hands in his lap. "What's there to tell?"

"How did it start?" she asked. "That night, at the bar."

"I—I don't know," he said, lowering his head. "It's not the first time I've been there to grab a couple of beers after a shift. But he came at me, this guy." He stopped talking for a while, a deep frown furrowing his brow while his eyes flickered with anger. "He was in my face, all the time, picking on me. Every time he passed by, he shoved me. Then he mocked me for being, um, you know."

"No, I don't know. What?"

"A pussy," he whispered. "I punched him. Once. He fell like a log."

"Did the ambulance come?"

"No, only the cops," he said with a sad chuckle. "Someone was in one hell of a rush to call them. They were there in five minutes, but he was fine by that time, drinking with his buddies and calling me names."

It made absolutely no sense. That type of intoxicated dust-up almost never involved cops.

"Sis, I've been an idiot," he said. "I know better, and I just... I don't know what came over me that night."

"What did they charge you with?" she asked, ashamed she hadn't found the time in the ten days since she'd returned to Mount Chester to look up that information or to ask Elliot to pull the arrest record. Instead, she'd immersed herself in the Silent Lake murders investigation, forsaking her own brother. Now Elliot definitely wasn't going to do her any favors, and she'd wasted ten days in which she might've been able to do something. Like make law history for example, because once a sentence was imposed, it wasn't going to be changed only because a family member said please, banging on the judge's door. Not ever going to happen.

He inhaled before replying, his breath shattered. "Felony assault with premeditation," he said, his voice loaded with frustration. "There was no premeditation; I don't know why they said that."

"Did you know this man?"

"Rafael? The guy I decked?"

"Yes, him. What's his full name?"

"Rafael Trujillo," he said, then spelled the last name for her as she took notes. "He and I used to work together on a construction site, but I hadn't seen him since July."

"Did you ever exchange words with him or fight with him until that night?"

"No," he replied quickly, looking at her briefly. "He kept with his buddies, and I'm a loner. We barely talked." He scratched his beard, then sighed. "He's got a record too, and it still didn't matter. And my lawyer was one of those court-appointed idiots, who didn't argue much in front of the mighty DA. I was surprised he didn't drop to his knees, right there in court, to kiss—"

He stopped himself and blushed like a teenager. Jail was rubbing off on him; her little brother didn't use to speak like that, not before. Memories of their father's sickening oaths had probably been enough to keep him from swearing for as long as she could remember.

"Who was the judge?"

"Judge Hewitt," he replied, staring at the floor again. "He preached like the pastor at Sunday sermon before handing me the sentence. How this cannot happen in our community, how elements like me cannot be walking free, endangering people, and that kind of crap. He spewed the words as if they were snake venom, although he knew nothing about me."

The more Kay listened, the more she realized something was off with Jacob's story. Maybe there was a detail, an apparently insignificant aspect of his case that he didn't think to mention, and that had changed the way the judge considered his sentencing. But, even before that, why was he arrested in the first place, and why was he indicted with such a trumped-up charge? And what the hell did that lawyer do, instead of defending her little brother?

That's where she needed to start.

"Who's your lawyer?"

"Mr. Joplin, Shane Joplin, I believe. A smug son of a bitch. He just as soon sold me out, that's what he did."

"Court appointed?"

"Yeah," he replied, smiling shyly. "I can't afford lawyers, sis. I haven't won any lottery since you left."

A bulky guard approached them stepping heavily on crooked legs, his face bearing a permanent scowl. "Five more minutes," he said, pointing at the clock on the wall above the entrance. "Wrap it up."

Jacob looked at her intently, his eyes pleading.

"Don't worry, sis, I'll manage somehow. Thanks for... you know, coming here, living at the house. Watching over things," he added, lowering his voice to a barely audible whisper.

She felt herself breaking into a sweat. "About that," she said in a low voice, keeping her head turned away from the cameras, "are you, um, sure, everything is still there?"

His eyebrows shot up. "What do you mean?" he asked. "*Him?*"

"Uh-huh," she replied with a quick nod. "And the, um, hardware. Is that still there?"

"The knife?" he mouthed silently, staring at her in disbelief. "Sure, it's in there," he whispered. "Why the heck would you ask me that now, after all these years?"

"Oh, nothing," she replied with a pained sigh. "Just being there, at the house, does weird things to my mind, that's all. I thought I'd seen that object in the house somewhere."

"Nope, no way," he said, shaking his head strongly. "Must've been something else you saw." He continued to stare at her. Since that fateful day sixteen years ago, they'd never spoken a word about it.

"Sorry about the mess," he said after a beat, smiling sheepishly.

When he smiled, his swollen lip cracked, and a tiny drop of blood appeared. Her heart twisted inside her chest, ripping the breath from her lungs.

"Jacob, listen to me," she added hastily, seeing the guard approaching. "Keep your head low, and just wait it out, okay? I'll wait for you. I'll be here."

The guard had laid his heavy hand on Jacob's shoulder, and he stood, ready to go back. He signaled he'd heard her by holding his thumb up and smiling weakly, then disappeared through the side door.

She sat there, looking at that closed door, unable to believe he'd been taken away, locked up, and she couldn't run to him and hold him in her arms. A sense of doom wrapped around her entire being, chilling the blood in her veins. What was that gut of hers trying to tell her?

Standing, she shook off the sense of foreboding and remembered that someone had put her brother in there for something not worthy of being called a crime, and that someone had some explaining to do.

"Okay, Mr. Joplin, let's see what you have to say for yourself," she mumbled, looking him up on her phone.

It turned out that he wasn't the typical court-appointed lawyer. He was a successful attorney, a partner at a major San Francisco law firm, where his name was billed second. Her brother's defense couldn't have been handled by a better lawyer, one who could've kept Jacob out of prison without lifting a finger.

And still, there she was, visiting her brother in prison.

It was pitch dark when she arrived home, after having spent two hours driving and thinking. Of Shane Joplin, the hotshot lawyer who couldn't salvage her brother's case. Of her father's fingerprints on that knife, showing up after spending sixteen years in the ground. Of the unsub who was playing tricks with her mind, forcing her off the case. That meant she was getting close, and he was getting desperate to throw the investigators off his scent and onto hers.

Nevertheless, that also meant he knew about what lay buried between the willow trees, and somehow, he'd gotten to it. The ground was undisturbed, but he could've dug it up some time ago, or maybe he knew how to lay it down perfectly, so she wouldn't know, so she'd slowly go insane wondering. There was no peace to be had unless she could be sure. Unless she found out how much the unsub really knew, and how much he'd taken from what Jacob had buried there.

She grabbed a shovel from the garage and went to the backyard, deciding to find out once and for all. Rushing to the back of the yard, she stopped in her tracks, frozen, as the moonlight shone through the immense crowns of the willow trees, their silent shadows menacing.

Dropping to the ground, she hugged her knees, rocking back and forth, sobbing hard. She couldn't do it.

She had to find out a different way.

CHAPTER FORTY
Hilltop

It was past dinner time when Elliot left the sheriff's office, after having spent the afternoon chasing evidence with little to show for it. One of the most promising leads, the blankets, had transformed into a dead end, but not before taking precious hours of his time.

He'd hoped the blankets the killer had used to wrap and bury the victims were a traceable item, considering the Native American motif, and the fact that he'd never seen that particular design before. He'd expected to track them down to a local weaver, maybe someone who lived on the reservation, someone who might've remembered the customer who bought several identical blankets.

He'd shown the photo of those blankets to tribal elders and various Natives, both on and off the reservation, even to tribal police. No one had seen that particular model or heard of a weaver who worked custom designs. While most of them agreed the motif was of Shastan inspiration, others said it didn't *feel* genuine. Whether he could believe them or not, that was a different story. At the end of the day, he stopped by Dr. Whitmore's and asked him to send blanket fibers to the lab, to gain some idea as to where the blankets were coming from. That was the easy part.

The difficult part of his day had been fielding everyone's questions and having to tell them, "No, we haven't found those kids yet. No, the FBI doesn't know either." The sense of powerlessness filled him with anger so raw it threatened to turn into rage at the slightest provocation.

All that powerlessness, and Kay.

Muttering an elaborate oath in his long Texas drawl, he pulled over in the Hilltop Bar and Grill parking lot. It was a popular watering hole for the local deputies, and he hoped by now everyone's questions would've been answered by other cops. He only wanted to sit down somewhere, eat a burger and down a couple of beers, no questions asked. By anybody.

He took the far-end stool at the counter and beckoned the bartender. Elliot wasn't a regular, not in the truest sense of the word. In a small place like Mount Chester, everyone was bound to become known in such places, just because there weren't that many options to begin with. Up on the mountain, near the ski resort, there were dozens of restaurants and bars, but here, in town, Hilltop and a couple of others were all he could choose from.

"Heya, Detective," the bartender greeted him, then quickly parked a coaster in front of him on the scratched and grimy counter. "What can I get you?"

"Bud Light," Elliot replied, "and a burger with fries, hold the onion."

"You got it," the man replied, wiping his hands on his apron. He placed a sweaty, ice-cold bottle in front of him, then disappeared.

Elliot took a sip, savoring the taste, then took a few more swigs. He kept his eyes fixed on the counter, avoiding everyone, but, unfortunately, not everyone was avoiding him.

"Detective, what a pleasure," a man said in a baritone, then followed up with a slap on his shoulder.

He turned and saw the chubby Deputy Hobbs grinning widely.

"Hey, Spence," he muttered, returning his focus to the dirty surface of the counter.

A couple of other deputies appeared out of nowhere, all seemingly entertained by something, with at least a couple of drinks in them by that time.

"How does it feel to be on your own again?" one of them asked with a wink, and the others burst into laughter.

Elliot realized he missed the structure of the Austin sheriff's office, where deputies knew their place in the food chain and thought twice before getting too casual with a detective. But Mount Chester was rural and small, and the local sheriff's office was more like a family, complete with rude kids, bullies and the redheaded child in the basement. Add alcohol to that mix, and Elliot wished he'd gone home instead, to cold cuts on stale bread and a shot of much-needed bourbon.

He didn't reply, hoping they'd go away, searching for better entertainment elsewhere.

"Sorry, Detective," Hobbs apologized, "these schmucks don't know their place."

He waved away the apology, choosing to not engage.

"But we do want to know," Hobbs continued, "what exactly happened with you and Dr. Sharp?"

A couple of snickers accompanied the question that Elliot initially misunderstood.

"Nothing happened, damn it," he snapped, before realizing they were asking where Kay was, not if he'd slept with her. "The boss took her off the case, that's all," he added, hoping they didn't notice how defensive he'd got for a moment.

The snickering continued, and so did Hobbs's endless questions.

"Why?" Hobbs asked. His round face was sweaty and looked pale in the fluorescent lights of the pub, his beady eyes restless. "I thought she was the best we could hope for, considering her background, given how she's an FBI profiler, and all that." He paused for a moment, but when Elliot didn't reply, he added, "Is she coming back?"

Elliot didn't know, and that question had been on his mind all afternoon. After how he'd treated her, she wasn't going to come back. He'd been an idiot; not once, but twice.

He thought she deserved it, but what if she'd been telling the truth? What if her father had vanished sixteen years ago, and the killer knew the story of his disappearance? He'd asked around, after dropping Kay at the house, hoping he'd be able to forget how she'd stood there on the driveway, staring after him, probably wondering what species of moron Detective Elliot Young from Texas was.

He'd asked around, hoping and fearing, at the same time, to learn that there was evidence or testimony to support how he'd treated her. He couldn't make up his mind what was worse. The fact that he'd treated her like a suspect, based on the assumption that she'd been insinuating herself into the investigation to cover for her father's unlikely killing spree? Or the fact that he didn't believe his partner, a seasoned investigator and recognized FBI profiler, when she'd provided him with a reasonable explanation for what was going on?

And why hadn't he believed her, really?

He downed the rest of the beer, and the bartender immediately replaced the empty bottle and put a burger with fries in front of him, filling his nostrils with mouthwatering scents of sizzling bacon and molten cheddar, but he remained indifferent.

Because he couldn't stop thinking about her. That's why he didn't believe her. Because it was easier to believe he'd fallen for a woman who was bound to destroy his career one way or another, than be faced with the fact that it was his move now. He needed to let her know how he felt about her or walk away.

Or, even worse, make a complete ass of himself and move to Alaska.

He poked a fry with the fork but stopped midair. He wasn't that hungry anymore, and Hobbs's clique was as annoying as a dry, prickly burr under a stallion's saddle. He glared at Hobbs for a moment, then said, "Do you think I could eat dinner in peace, *Deputy*?" He accented the word, dipping his voice in sarcasm. "Do I have your permission?"

The laughter came to a sudden stop and the three deputies hurried away, Hobbs being the last one. "So sorry, Detective, we didn't mean anything by it." Then they were finally gone, leaving him alone with his warm beer and cold burger, the background noise of the place a distant, faint dissonance of chatter, laughter and the occasional drunken shouting against a curtain of old country music.

He'd sworn to himself he'd never get involved with a woman on the job. He'd sworn it, and just as soon forgot all about the bitter oath he'd taken while packing his belongings and leaving his dear Texas in the rearview mirror, the moment Kay Sharp walked into his life.

Another swig of now-stale beer reminded him he wasn't actually involved with Kay. Only in his mind, wishing for it. But one thing was for sure. They had exactly zero chances to find that unsub without her. Zilch. Nada. Diddly-squat.

Only she understood how that murderer's mind worked, and the fact that she did was chilling, disturbing to a level he didn't comprehend. She'd been the one who asked all the right questions, while he and the sheriff had been chasing shadows, not even getting close. Maybe Logan would reinstate her status, after he presented all the evidence he'd just uncovered about her father. The man hadn't been seen in the past sixteen years, and, before vanishing, had stabbed his wife within an inch of her life. There was a warrant out for Kay's father, for attempted murder, and that's why he must've taken off that night, never to be seen again. And the killer somehow knew about it, and had decided to plant a knife with the man's fingerprints to get rid of Kay, to cast a shadow of doubt over her.

Because the unsub knew just how much of an idiot Elliot was.

Because they were getting close to finding him.

Because he was local, just like Kay had profiled. That's how the unsub knew about her father, and how he'd managed to get his fingerprints. Where from, exactly, that was still an open question.

He downed the remaining beer and walked out in the crisp, evening air, then rushed to his SUV. If he drove quickly, he could still catch Logan at his desk.

He'd been less than a minute on the road back to the White House when he saw red-and-blue flashing in his rearview mirror. Maybe another unit was rushing to respond on a case, although the radio had been silent. He signaled right and slowed down, waving the other car to pass him. But the pursuing vehicle slowed as well. He pulled over and stopped, then flashed his lightbar for a brief moment, to let the other cops know he was on the job.

They still approached, flashlights in one hand, the other on their weapons, ready to draw, as they would any other traffic stop in the dead of the night.

They were California Highway Patrol officers, and they weren't smiling. There was no hint of professional courtesy whatsoever.

Almost an hour later, in total disbelief, Elliot found himself charged with driving under the influence and thrown in the back of the CHiP Interceptor, in handcuffs.

CHAPTER FORTY-ONE

Judy

She'd woken up with the dawn, then counted the minutes until eight thirty, when she learned that "Mr. Joplin's not in the office yet," in the words of a receptionist with an affected, nasal voice. Half an hour later, he was already in a meeting with a client and could not take Kay's call.

Of course, he couldn't.

Exasperation swelling inside her like the Pacific tides, she dialed the law office again, this time opting to leave a message. She made it short and to the point, and, instead of being truthful as to her intentions, she dipped a carrot in honey and advised Jacob's lawyer that she was interested in pursuing the legal avenues of having her brother's sentence reduced, and that she didn't expect him to continue to represent him pro bono. Maybe good old-fashioned greed could get her a conversation with Shane Joplin.

Once that was done, Kay reverted to her earlier activity, which was to study all the possible routes the victims might've taken from San Francisco to Mount Chester, trying to pinpoint where the unsub might've spotted them. For at least one hundred miles, they all took the same road, first on the northbound interstate, then on the winding, sloping mountain road.

She'd identified a few places where the perpetrator could've stalked his victims, but one question was at the center of her thoughts. If he'd stalked them miles away from Mount Chester, and she knew that for a fact, because he'd tampered with their vehicles out there somewhere, how could he possibly have known they were headed to Mount Chester? From there, the state highway continued north to the Oregon border and beyond. And why was that important to the unsub?

Those questions faded for a moment, while another gnawing mystery occupied her mind. Why was the killer setting her up? Why the knife? To make her back down from the investigation? To compromise her in the eyes of the local law enforcement? Or was he planning something else for her? If the unsub knew about her father's resting place, he had her life in his hands just as he'd had Alison's and Kendra's, and he was about to tighten his grip and crush her.

Well, she wasn't going to back down, knife or no knife.

In the absence of financial records, and refusing to give into the urge to call Elliot and ask him to come to his senses, she decided to take the road trip to San Francisco, carefully observing every detail, stopping at every diner and gas station, and showing photos of the victims. Maybe someone remembered something.

She drove the mountain road to the interstate, counting the very few places the victims could've stopped. Katse Coffee Shop for one, but they'd already been there and talked to the owner. Yes, some of the victims had stopped there, but it seemed that by that time, their cars had already been tampered with. It had to have been farther south from Katse. How much farther, she didn't know.

A Chevron gas station, a small diner, and a Subway store returned zero information about the victims. No one had seen them, nor remembered anything about the women and their cars. Disappointed and increasingly wary with the passing of every minute, she stopped to yield to traffic before taking the interstate ramp.

From that vantage point, a tow truck driving north at full speed caught her eye. There was something about the angle of its empty platform and the hardware on it, the discolored lettering on its door, familiar but also not really.

She stepped on the gas pedal and, swerving to avoid a honking pickup, took the ramp and chased the tow truck. When she got closer, she recognized it. She'd played on it as a child, hung from its chains like a monkey, squealing and jumping off on a cracked driveway she remembered well. But it was weathered, the passing of time leaving rusty scars on its panels and peeling off some of the stickers. The arm with the clenched fist in a circle, the towing company logo, she'd remember that anywhere, as she would the name written below in bold, straight font, THE RIGHT HOOK. But the logo and writing were so discolored by the long winters and bright sunlight of the California mountain summers that they were barely legible. Driving parallel with the truck, she stared at the familiar logo, wondering. Could the unsub have towed the cars to San Francisco International Airport, but unloaded them before entering the parking structure, and only driven them inside the garage? That would explain the missing return trip from the cars' navigation systems in a much simpler way.

Occam's razor never let her down. It made much more sense to assume that, than to imagine the unsub was that one-in-a-million person who knew how to override a car's navigation history.

She hit the brakes and took the first exit, then found a spot where she could stop safely and check her email. The videos that the SFPD Airport Bureau had sent included footage of the man as he'd walked out of the parking garage, heading toward the cluster of highway ramps that continued past South Airport Boulevard and connected the facility with Highway 101. Then, the video feed from the next camera, providing views to traffic entering the highway, didn't show any pedestrian traffic.

She pulled up the footage again and watched it carefully. The bulky silhouette of the man who'd driven Kendra's Jeep into the long-term parking garage came into view, walking briskly along the side of the road. Then, in the next view, not a trace of him. She watched as the recording ran from the time code where the man exited the frame of the last recording, all the way to the end. Then she watched the last three minutes again, this time noticing a tow truck she'd missed before, barely visible in the lower, right corner of the screen, as it took the northbound ramp to Bayshore Freeway. Yet the image was too distant and blurry for her to be sure it was the same one, the tow truck flickering in and out of view within a fraction of a second.

If the unsub had been driving it, he'd known exactly how to avoid the traffic cameras.

She needed to watch the video on a larger screen.

In a fearful frenzy, she returned home where she pulled up the video on her laptop and, with infinite patience, scrolled through that section of it frame by frame until she caught a partial glimpse of the truck. Unfortunately, no matter how carefully she examined every frame, the truck's tag never made it onto the screen; only its bulky, blurry silhouette. Nevertheless, she printed it to have handy, wondering if it could be the same truck she remembered from her childhood.

Printout in hand, Kay rushed to her SUV and sat behind the wheel. Then her hand froze, hesitant to start the engine. The man driving the tow truck she remembered so well had been the closest thing she'd had to a father, a better parent than her own flesh and blood ever was. There was no way that Roy Stinson, a kind and fun-loving man who used to bounce her on one knee, and his daughter and Kay's best friend, Judy, on the other, could be capable of such heinous crimes. Fear coiled inside her gut like a snake, injecting its venom and chilling her blood.

But it couldn't be him, she realized as her panicked thoughts subsided, and she found the strength to draw air again. He didn't fit the profile; first of all, he was over sixty years old; she remembered vaguely he was a few years older than her father. He wasn't technically savvy, although he had access to the tow truck and had worked around cars all his life; he probably knew fifteen different ways to disable a vehicle without leaving too much evidence behind. But it wasn't him. It couldn't be. She knew it with every fiber of her being.

She typed a quick message to the SFPD Airport Bureau, indicating the date and time code where the tow truck was visible, and asking if someone could check the other videos to see if the same truck showed after all the other vehicles had been dropped at the garage. Hopefully, the SFPD Airport Bureau was unaware of her falling from grace with the Mount Chester sheriff.

Then she finally started the engine and drove off, heading to see her old friend, Judy. Kay had been back for almost two weeks, and each day she'd promised herself she'd find the time to visit with her best friend, but it just hadn't happened yet.

She found Judy the same place she'd known her to be working, waiting on tables at the Chesterfield, a restaurant that catered mostly to tourists with not-so-exotic foods and spiked-up prices. Taking a seat at a table by the window, she waited, smiling, for Judy to notice her after she finished with the customers she was helping. Her smile was heartfelt yet tense. No matter how she felt about it, she had a duty to those missing kids, to the women who had been buried at Silent Lake. How was she going to ask Judy about her father? How can anyone ask a friend if their loved one was a murderer?

"I don't believe it!" Judy squealed, then rushed to her. She stood and hugged her old friend tightly, then kissed her on both her cheeks.

"Look at you," Kay said, taking a step back and admiring Judy's thin figure and lean legs. "You haven't aged a bit."

"Ha!" Judy reacted. "Look who's talking. You're like a power-woman supermodel, as if you've been posing for some magazine in the big city," she added, referring to San Francisco by the name all locals used. "I heard you've been back, and I was wondering when you'd—"

"So sorry, Jude," she said, hugging her again. "I got overwhelmed with stuff. With life."

"I heard about Jacob. I can't imagine him in jail."

"I can't either," she replied. "I just keep hoping it's a nightmare and I'll wake up."

"Can you do something for him? You're a fed, right?"

"A fed on leave," she replied, turning her eyes away from Judy's scrutiny for a split moment. "I'll stay here at least until Jacob is out. Take care of the house and everything."

"We could've done that for him," she said. "It wouldn't've been a problem."

"I know," she replied quietly. "We both do." She paused for a beat, avoiding Judy's kind eyes. "I still felt I should be here for him, that's all."

Judy smiled, and it lit up the room. Kay's heart tightened in her chest. "So, how's your dad?" she asked, happy to change the subject. "I miss your parents, almost as much as I missed you. They practically raised me."

"They're fine," Judy replied, taking a seat at Kay's table but on the edge of the chair, ready to jump to her feet if a customer beckoned her. "They're divorced now," she added with a shrug tinged with sadness.

"Really? I can't believe it. They seemed so perfect together," Kay replied, remembering the gentle blissfulness of dinners at the Stinson family's house.

"Until one day they weren't," Judy replied. "When Mom retired, they started spending more time together, and it didn't work that well. They kept bickering, and one day, Mom just told us she was leaving. She lives in town now."

"Where? I'd love to stop by and say hi. I hope she remembers me."

"Are you kidding? Every time we meet, we talk about you. You're my sister," Judy said, squeezing Kay's frozen hand over the table. Then she wrote down an address on a piece of paper torn from her order pad.

"How's your brother?" Kay asked. "Married, kids?"

"Nah," she laughed, "not Sam. This one doesn't want a family; I don't know why. He's happy on his own, or with the occasional girlfriend." Her smile waned, replaced by melancholy. "He drives the tow truck these days. He took over from Dad when his back gave."

Kay's breath caught. Could the unsub be Sam? The cute, blond kid, two years her junior, who used to chase Judy and her, screaming like a banshee until his mother told him to keep quiet or sleep in the chicken coop? He was twenty-seven years old now, but still. It couldn't be him... just couldn't.

Her heart sinking, she pushed herself to ask the questions she needed to. "What happened to Mr. Stinson's back? Is it serious?"

"We didn't think so at first, but it became so bad he couldn't work anymore. He just tinkers with stuff at the garage, but can't really do much. He's too proud to admit it though. He could go on disability for a few years, and then retire. No one would judge him. He's worked hard all his life, and now he can barely lift a bottle of beer."

"How come?" she asked. The Mr. Stinson of her childhood used to be a bear of a man, tall, strong and proud, seemingly invincible. If he'd become a cripple in his old age, there was no point in questioning Judy about him as she'd planned to do. The thought brought relief to her mind, tinged with disappointment. One less lead she could follow.

She noticed the sadness in her friend's eyes as she explained.

"Nerve damage from slipped discs," Judy replied. "He needs surgery, but can't afford it. And he's too scared to get it."

"I can help you," Kay said, lowering her voice. "Just say the word."

Judy squeezed her hand again, her eyes filling with tears while she gazed at her friend. "It's so good to have you back," she said. "Thank you. I'll try talking some sense into him."

"How about Sam?" Kay asked. "Any mountain cabin up there, on those slopes, to take the girlfriends for the weekend?"

"Sam? Nah," Judy replied. "When he's not working, driving the tow truck, he's helping Dad in the garage, changing oil and tires for the locals. The business isn't what it used to be. Now all these cars run forever; they hardly ever break down, and when they do, the boys can't fix them anymore. They have computers and stuff. Different times, you know." She veered her eyes away from Kay's and stared out the window for a moment. "We're not doing that great. We're struggling to make ends meet."

A few moments later, Kay hugged Judy one more time and promised she'd come over for dinner. Then she walked out of the restaurant, squinting in the bright sunlight and wondering how the family tow truck was connected to the unsub, if at all. Relieved that neither Mr. Stinson nor Sam Stinson met any of the critical components of the killer's profile, she feared for each passing moment, and what that time meant for the missing children and for the woman the unsub was most likely hunting for already.

All she had was a thin lead, so thin it might've not been real after all, like spider silk carried by November winds. But she had to follow it.

Perhaps someone else drove the truck to help with the business or maybe Sam Stinson loaned it out sometimes.

Those were much easier questions to ask.

CHAPTER FORTY-TWO
Plan

The girl's body bounced on the four-wheeler's back seat, and he slowed down somewhat after a series of thumps told him her head was rhythmically hitting the side safety bars. He didn't want her to be brain-dead by the time they got to the cabin. Bruised and a little dizzy, that was fine, but he wanted her in good shape, strong, fiery, able to keep him company throughout the long months of winter, until the ground thawed, and he could lay her to rest properly at Silent Lake.

He was thrilled, barely able to contain his excitement about her. From up close, she was even more beautiful, and scared out of her mind when he'd appeared out of the thicket and said hello, before she recognized him. He wasn't wearing his work clothes anymore; he'd changed into camo coveralls and hunting boots, guaranteed to make him invisible against the late-October foliage.

No matter how fast he moved after piercing their radiators, it still took him a lot of time to get ready. Dropping off the Cadillac, getting changed, picking up the ATV, all those things took time, and most girls had already gone back to the coffee shop before he was ready for them.

He'd driven his four-wheeler through the woods and stopped close to the girl's red Ford, then waited until she returned from Katse, where she'd most likely gone to call for help. The girls usually asked Tommy, the owner, for a tow truck number or called their car rental company, who, in turn, dispatched someone. Then they usually spent some time drinking coffee, eating or just waiting for the mechanic's arrival.

Sometimes, the tow truck would offer to meet them at Katse, and that complicated things. He knew when that happened because more than fifteen minutes would pass, and the girls wouldn't leave the coffee shop. When that happened, he had to call the coffee shop himself posing as the tow truck driver and ask them to meet him at the vehicle instead. He'd say inconspicuous things in a feigned hillbilly accent, like, "Ma'am, my name is Jim, and I've been dispatched to take care of your car. I'm ten minutes out. I'll meet you at the vehicle. Did you leave it with the four-way flashers on?"

That call usually sent them rushing out, not even asking why the call hadn't arrived on their cell phones. They'd simply assume the service was bad or, in the rare case someone would ask, he'd say, "Sorry, ma'am, your phone goes straight to voicemail. It must be the spotty coverage in that area."

Kendra had asked. She'd been the only one.

Nevertheless, even Kendra had come out of Katse running, paper cup in hand, in a rush to get to her car before the tow truck's arrival, while he was trailing her on his four-wheeler, twenty yards into the forest, silent and invisible.

When he was hunting, he didn't have the luxury of time, and had zero room for errors.

He made all his calls from burner phones, each one from a different device. Then they all found their final resting place at the bottom of the river, thrown while he drove over the bridge in the next county over.

The usual response time for a tow truck in that area was sixty to ninety minutes; that was all the time he had from the moment the girls reached Katse Coffee Shop and called for help. He waited fifteen or twenty minutes to give them time to leave Katse on their own. If not, he made the call, then followed them closely as they rushed back to their car.

Then he appeared out of the brush, smiling, offering help.

She'd recognized him from the restaurant, and that was because she really liked him. He felt that deep inside, and was intrigued by it, fascinated even. She'd be the first one to show real interest in him, beforehand. Before she knew who he was. He wondered how that was going to change things.

She even told him her name, Wendy. How wonderful. He'd enjoy calling her by her name all winter long. It rolled off the tongue in a sensual, promising way.

From there, from that initial smile and handshake, it was easy.

A quick blow to the back of her head rendered her unconscious, her slender body an easy load to carry to his ATV. He grabbed her car keys from her pocket, bound her wrists and ankles with cable ties, then drove the ATV deep enough into the woods to not be seen from the road. He then took a bundle of camo tarp and a half-full, five-gallon can from the four-wheeler and rushed to her car. He popped the hood, poured water into the coolant tank, then started the engine and drove it downhill for about a hundred yards, where the first of many side paths opened. He took it, driving slowly on the rutted path, until he could barely distinguish the asphalt of the highway behind him. He found a place where he could go deeper into the brush, then cut the engine, locked the vehicle, and quickly covered the Ford's conspicuous red with the large tarp in hunting camouflage colors, securing the fabric in place with a few boulders. Standing only a couple of yards away, he couldn't see it anymore.

Perfect.

Later, when Wendy would be safely at the cabin and the sun had set, he'd go back to the Ford, fix the hole in the radiator quickly and douse a layer of dust-colored, grainy spray paint to hide the resin patch and the traces of spilled coolant. Then he'd haul the car into the San Francisco airport long-term parking garage; a tremendous risk he was still weighing. Was it worth it? Maybe he'd take the Ford to a different terminal this time. The cops had found three of the girls' cars already, and they might be watching, waiting for him. Should he go to San Jose instead?

But that was later. For now, he focused on getting Wendy home, on spending his first exhilarating hours with her.

With her Ford secured, he rushed back to the ATV. It was more difficult to run back to the four-wheeler through the woods, but much safer. He didn't want to chance being seen trotting on the highway on foot, probably the only pedestrian to walk on asphalt in that ZIP Code, and be remembered like a sore thumb sticking out at the precise time and place that Wendy vanished. It was bad enough that the cops still swarmed the area with bloodhounds, looking for evidence. But they weren't going to find him; not unless he made stupid decisions like walking on the highway or going back to San Francisco airport.

When he reached the ATV, Wendy was still unconscious, but he waited a moment before driving off. The red tow truck was passing by, its driver probably swearing mouthfuls at the no-show call that burned his fuel but made him no money.

Well, it happened. Tough luck.

He drove straight into the woods, and after about twenty minutes, he'd crossed over into the next county, where his cabin was, tucked in a ravine behind the snow-covered peaks of Mount Chester. He still had a ways to go and let his mind wander, driving slowly across the acres of woods carpeted in turning foliage, careful not to hit a tree stump and flip over.

Sweet Wendy was going to make a great companion for the long, dark winter nights to come. She was young and seemed sensitive yet gritty, a fighter, promising night after night of pleasure and deeply satisfying screams.

And still, the stirring, anticipating visions disintegrated under the pressure of more practical matters.

The cops were getting closer, regardless of how cautious he'd been. They'd found a few of his girls and disturbed their final resting places. They'd correlated the murder cases and already knew too much of what they had in common. Three of the girls' cars were in the sheriff's impound, right there in Mount Chester, and that meant soon they'd know how he immobilized them. How he hunted. They already knew about Katse, and taking Wendy under those circumstances had been a huge risk, the biggest chance he'd taken since that night on a fog-engulfed alley in the San Francisco Tenderloin. Because he couldn't bring himself to spend the winter alone.

They were getting dangerously close.

He'd managed to put the Texas detective's ass in a sling with that DUI charge and everything else that came with it. That was going to keep him busy for a while, and, in itself, had been yet another risky maneuver to pull. Anything involving asking favors of other people was treacherous; no one could count on anyone else but themselves.

But Kay, as she liked to call herself these days, was another matter altogether. He thought he'd taken care of her sleuthing with that knife bearing her father's fingerprints. He thought the piece of evidence would stop her dead in her tracks, rendering her unwilling to have anything else to do with the investigation.

No; Kay Sharp kept going, undeterred, and he couldn't stop thinking about her. He'd never really stopped thinking of her, not since the day he'd first seen her.

A federal agent, albeit former, obsessing over the Silent Lake murders just as much as he was obsessing over her was a powerful, heady mix, a recipe for disaster. And yet, while he drove across the pristine acres of national forest, the intoxicating thought he'd been avoiding for a while wriggled its way into his mind, lighting it on fire.

What would winter be like when Kay would join him and Wendy at the cabin?

CHAPTER FORTY-THREE
Alone

When Elliot entered Sheriff Logan's office, he was anticipating the long glare the man greeted him with. He was ashamed and frustrated at the same time, after having spent the night in the Redding police lockup, no professional courtesy shown to him whatsoever. He stunk of stale booze and human excrement, the typical stench of someone who'd spent the night on the floor of an overcrowded holding cell. But he'd wanted to see Logan first of all, even before getting a shower and a meal.

He sustained Logan's glare without bowing his eyes. When the sheriff pointed quietly at the seat in front of his desk, he sat without saying a word.

"Well," the sheriff eventually said, after a long sigh escaped his lungs. "It isn't every day that my best detective spends the night in jail for drunk driving." He crinkled his nose with disgust. "And you stink. You could've paid me the courtesy of getting yourself cleaned up first."

"I wasn't drunk, sir," Elliot replied calmly. "I insisted they do a blood test last night, as soon as we reached the Redding lockup. They wouldn't hear of it, but the cops who came on duty after midnight agreed to do it."

"You're the joke of the department, Young. Nothing short of an embarrassment. If you need to get soused, do it at home, willya?"

"It was one lousy beer, boss. The blood test cleared me. I don't know why—"

"How about the bribery charge that I had to pull serious weight to make it go away?"

"What bribery charge?" Elliot sprung to his feet, as if the accuser was about to enter the office and he wanted to be ready for a physical confrontation, fists clenched and guard up.

"The two California Highway Patrol officers who pulled you over said that you offered them money to make the DUI go away. They said they'd testify to that."

"That's not true!" he shouted, feeling his blood boil inside his veins. "Let's have their bodycam recordings. You'll see I wasn't drunk, and I never offered them anything. I knew once I had my blood tested, they'd let me go." Angry beyond words, he ran his hands against the sides of his jeans, then crossed his arms at his chest.

"Those recordings are conveniently unavailable," Logan replied in a somber tone of voice. "Corrupted, I believe they said. That's how I got the charges dropped. Something about this entire situation smells bad."

"See? I told you it wasn't true," Elliot replied, running his hands quickly through his hair. "And they lost my hat," he mumbled, "scum CHiP assholes." His eyes met Logan's scowl. Swallowing the long slew of expletives that were going through his mind, he added, "This was no random DUI stop, boss. I was targeted."

"Why? Did you have a run-in with CHiP?"

"No," he replied quickly. He hadn't worked a case with CHiP for years. "If I pissed someone off at CHiP, I have no idea who and why."

Logan closed the personnel file folder he had been reviewing, then steepled his fingers on top of it. "I'll look into it, ask around. It's bad taste to go after other cops. Only rats do it without a reason, and I won't tolerate any rats on these highways." He frowned and paused for a beat, thinking. "If someone has a hard-on for one of my cops, they better run through me if they want a late-night date."

"Yes, boss," Elliot replied, his usual sense of calm slowly returning. He felt redeemed by Logan's confidence in him, but still wished he could've watched those bodycam videos. Now all he needed was a shower, a meal and another hat, and he was ready to get back to normal. "I was thinking maybe it has something to do with the Silent Lake murders."

"What do you mean?" Logan asked.

"Not sure," he replied, lowering his gaze for a moment. "I know just who to ask, but—"

"You think the killer is CHiP?" His voice was tinged with a hint of sarcasm; he was testing him.

"N—no," he replied. "Not like that. It's just that I don't like coincidences. First, that knife is conveniently buried with a body for us to find. Then I get busted for a DUI and a bogus bribery charge. It just stinks. In the past twenty-four hours, the top people working this case were conveniently sidetracked."

"You should be happy," Logan said with a hint of a smile. "You're getting close to the killer. He's bound to make a mistake." He wrote a couple of words on a piece of paper, then buzzed in his assistant and handed her the note. "I want to see these people today." After she left, he added, "I'll be questioning the two CHiP officers who pulled you over; see who's pulling their strings. I'm not expecting they'll talk, but still want to do it. You grab Dr. Sharp and keep working the case. Those kids are still out there, and we just wasted precious time."

"About that, sir," Elliot started, but Logan quickly interrupted.

"You assumed she was covering up her dad's criminal activities? That's why you thought she wanted to be a part of the investigation?"

"Well, um, I might've said that to her, in other words, but in essence—"

"You're an idiot, Young; you jumped to conclusions. She must've told you you're being played. And you didn't listen."

"We don't know that much about her, boss. What's the story with her leaving a job like that to come live in this town? I know she's a former fed and all that, but do we really know her? Can we be sure?" As he spoke the words, he realized he *was* sure. She wasn't covering up for anyone, and he'd been a major idiot for thinking that for a single minute. Charlene and Texas still haunted his thoughts, instilling the fear of making the same mistake again. He'd overreacted.

"You never met old Mr. Sharp," Logan replied. "He was a sorry-ass drunk who could barely stand half the time, who beat on his wife and kids every chance he got. We locked him up a couple of times. I bet he's rotting away someplace by now, probably in an Arizona jail or six feet under that desert somewhere."

"I see," Elliot replied, wondering why he hadn't asked Logan about Sharp before ripping Kay to shreds with his suspicions. He'd be lucky if she ever spoke to him again.

"As for Dr. Sharp, I hope you don't believe I'd let someone work cases for us without doing background checks and speaking with her old boss at the San Francisco field office."

"You did?" he replied, surprised. He'd thought it was his persistence that got Kay Sharp accepted to consult for the sheriff's office, his vouching for her. Turned out, his word had not carried that much weight after all.

"She didn't quit, first of all," Logan said, chuckling slightly when he noticed Elliot's expression. "Yeah, son, big surprise, she lied to you. Women do that." He chuckled again, rapping his fingers against the desk in a quick gesture that Elliot had learned to mean he was running out of patience. "She's on leave for personal reasons, something to do with her family, and she's welcome to return to work at her earliest. She's the best they've ever had." He stared at Elliot for a moment. "Now get back to work."

"Yes, sir," he replied, smiling. "Thanks for calling me your best detective, boss. I know I'm your only one, but still, I appreciate it."

"Not for long," Logan replied cryptically. "Now get out of here."

Elliot left the sheriff's office wondering what he meant, but soon forgot all about it.

Were they getting close to catching the unsub? Enough to make him desperate enough to set him up?

How the heck were they getting close, when it seemed they didn't have a single lead left? Every turn he took, everywhere he looked, nothing. Leads disintegrated like smoke in the wind, evidence led nowhere, and the remaining lab tests took forever. He still waited on advanced tox screens on the victims, on fiber analysis for those blankets, on something, anything that could point him in the right direction. Because he was counting the things he was still waiting for, that included the vehicles that had been driven to Mount Chester by Lan Xiu Tang and Janelle Huarez, the unsub's oldest victims.

Instead of going to his car, he walked over to the maintenance garage and called out. "Heya, Willie!"

The mechanic grinned widely, his teeth white against the grime-covered face. "Was just about to call you," he said. "Come on over here, let me show you what I got."

Elliot approached the tarp where Willie had kneeled down, running his fingers over the thin, metallic fins of a radiator.

"I know how he did it," he announced proudly. "See here?" he pointed his finger at a place on the radiator, but Elliot didn't see anything out of the ordinary. "He pierced the radiators, then waited for the coolant to drain. Then he patched them up with fast resin, and topped the fluid with water. The coolant was diluted in all the cars. I should've seen this earlier, but—" He spat on the floor angrily. "I'm getting old, I guess."

"I don't see any leaks on this radiator," Elliot replied.

"That's 'cause this ain't dust," Willie said. "It looks like dust, but it's spray paint. See?" he ran his finger against the radiator fins, then showed him the finger. None of the apparent dust had rubbed off the metallic surface and onto his skin. "Smart, this feller you're trying to catch. He sprayed over the radiators to cover the resin plug and all the leaks."

"He took them apart, like you did?"

"Nah," Willie replied, standing up with a groan and pointing at the inside of the Jeep's grille. "He stuck the spray nozzle through these holes, and that did the trick. It didn't have to be perfect; just enough to make me think nothing was leaking."

Yeah, he was smart, Elliot thought, heading to his car. At every juncture, the unsub had proven to be methodical, organized, carefully planning every detail with advanced knowledge of forensics. Of how murder investigations were conducted. Of how evidence was collected and examined.

Just like Kay had said he would be.

He called her cell, but it went straight to voicemail. "Damn it," he muttered, then floored it, flashers on, heading to her place. If she wanted to pout and make him eat crow, that was well within her rights, but not before they caught that sick son of a bitch who was still out there.

Her white Explorer wasn't at the house, and he almost drove off, but didn't know where to find her. He tried her cell again, then remembered she never locked her front door. Knowing just how much worse his actions would make things between them, he entered the house and headed to the kitchen.

"Kay?" he called out, hoping she'd reply. "Kay? It's me, Elliot."

She wasn't home. Silence spelled that out for him.

But her laptop was on the kitchen table, still running. He looked at the screen and froze. A blurry, low-resolution video recording from the SFPD Airport Bureau had been paused at the exact moment when an empty tow truck was leaving the facility and taking the northbound ramp to Bayshore. Behind that window, another blurry, poor resolution image, a scanned photo of two little girls and a boy, taken in front of a red tow truck. He zoomed in the photo, and in one of the little girl's eyes, in the color of her golden hair, and the line of her stubborn jaw, he recognized Kay Sharp.

She was going after the unsub alone. She hadn't listened to anything he'd told her. Stubborn, stubborn woman.

"Damn it, Kay," he muttered, storming out the door. "You could've at least waited for me."

CHAPTER FORTY-FOUR

Lesson

Darkness.

Complete, absolute, and terrifying darkness.

Wendy blinked a few times, as if to make sure she was awake. Then she tried to move, to get up from the cold floor, but had to hold on to the wall for support. She was dizzy and felt faint, and a throbbing headache pounded at her skull mercilessly. She rubbed her temple with an ice-cold, trembling hand, trying to ease the pain.

In her hair, her fingers got entangled in something unfamiliar. Her hand froze in midair for a brief moment, then explored the unfamiliar shape. With the sensory recognition came the faint memory of the man braiding her hair and humming an obsessive tune she couldn't name although she thought she recognized.

Then a flood of forgotten memories flushed over her. His hands on her naked body. Her helplessness, her screams, his laughs. His face, so familiar... where had she seen him before?

As headlights in the fog, a glimmer of recognition found its way into her weary mind. The man at the restaurant where she had that soup. The way he'd looked at her, his eyes riveted on her face. How naïve she'd been, feeling flattered by his attention. How stupid, to stay there and make casual conversation with the server while sipping her soup, instead of running for her life.

Where was she?

She felt her way along the walls, looking for a door, a window, anything. All she could sense were cinder blocks cemented tightly against one another, not a crack in between. Finally, her fingers stumbled across a doorjamb, and felt the uneven, splintery surface of a wooden door. She found the handle and grabbed at it with both hands, then turned it downward and pulled hard.

It didn't budge.

Leaning her body against the wood panel, she tried pushing outward instead, but that didn't work any better.

Feeling a heavy, bitter sob rising from her chest, she let herself drop to the floor, hugging her knees tightly. As her head hung lower, the two braids touched her cheeks and the unfamiliar sensation startled her.

Gasping for air as if it had suddenly vanished from the room, she tore the hair ties and unbraided her hair quickly, then ran her fingers through her tangled strands until they didn't feel like they belonged to a stranger anymore.

Then she stopped moving, blinking away panicked tears. Not a shred of light was coming from anywhere, nothing. Not a sound. The coldness of the floor under her feet, the chill of the air brushing against her skin and sending shivers down her spine, the pain in her body, those were the only indications that she was still alive.

When the door opened, light tore at her eyes like sharp darts and she squinted, throwing her hand in front of her face. Then the blow came, hard, sending her to the ground, seeing stars.

"No, no," the man said, anger seeping in the tone of his low, threatening voice. "Now we have to do it all over again." He grabbed her hair roughly and started braiding quickly, humming that unnerving song that sounded so familiar. "It's all right, you didn't know. Next time you'll do better than to disobey me."

CHAPTER FORTY-FIVE

Sam

Kay found Sam Stinson on the front porch of the house she knew well, smoking and flipping through some receipts. He wore jeans, a black T-shirt, and a work vest with yellow-and-gray reflective stripes. A pair of black-rimmed glasses completed his appearance; that was new. She didn't recall that about him, nor the neatly trimmed goatee that showed early signs of turning gray.

When she pulled alongside the tow truck and stopped, he stood and dropped the pile of crumpled papers on the Adirondack, then rushed to meet her, smiling like a child on Christmas morning.

"Hey! Look who's come to visit," he said, lifting her up in a bear hug that knocked the air out of her lungs. "Judy told me you'd be coming by."

Kay let the warmth of the reunion swell her heart for a moment, savoring it with her eyes closed and a wide smile on her lips. Beyond the evidence pointing toward Sam's tow truck as the unsub's method of choice in disposing of the victims' vehicles, that was Sam Stinson hugging her, Judy's younger brother, the kid she grew up with, the freckled boy whom she'd always saved her homework for. He was her little brother too, not just Judy's. Kay had been the one to punch the class bully in the nose for tripping Sam in the school hallways. She and Judy taught him how to ask a girl to prom, or how to behave when showing up at her door to take her dancing.

He was family.

"How about a beer?" he asked, as soon as he let her go. "I don't have much food, but I can always pop a cold one for you."

"Sure," she replied, realizing she was thirsty. It wasn't even one in the afternoon yet, but beer was a guaranteed icebreaker and lubricant of potentially difficult conversations.

When Sam came back outside, he was only holding one bottle. He popped the cap and handed it to her.

"And you?" she asked, surprised he wasn't going to join her.

He shrugged, then gestured toward the tow truck. "Customers frown when they smell alcohol on my breath, even if it's just a lousy beer. They don't tip me as much," he added with a sheepish grin.

"Cheers, then," she said, raising the bottle as if he had one in his hand too, then downed a few thirsty gulps. "This is good," she added with a satisfied sigh. "I needed this."

"There's more where that came from," he replied with a wink. "Come, sit down," he invited her, clearing the Adirondack of the scattered paperwork. He collected all the receipts and shoved them in his vest pocket. "Damn accountant has me on a tight leash," he muttered. "Every quarter he wants the receipts, as if I need him to tell me I'm not making enough money."

She sat on the rocking chair, remembering Mrs. Stinson sitting there, knitting scarves and sweaters while Judy, Sam, Jacob, and she played in front of the house, the smell of fresh cookies baking in the oven filling her nostrils and seeding cravings in her belly. She let the chair rock back and forth for a while and closed her eyes. She could almost smell the sweet scent of those cookies, of molten chocolate, of home.

"How's the towing business?" she asked casually, regretting the cherished memory as soon as she opened her eyes and it dissipated. "Do you get enough customers to keep you going?"

"Barely," Sam replied, lowering his gaze. "Winter season is the best, when tourists fill the slopes and do stupid shit. California drivers have no clue how to drive on ice, thank goodness for that. Otherwise, I would've been broke by now." He leaned forward, his elbows resting on his knees, his fingers intertwined. "I'm not far from it as it is."

She threw the tow truck another glance. Rust was popping up here and there, piercing through the metal below the fenders and at the lowest edge of the door panels. The color was faded, burned by winter salt and the brutal summer sun, and the decals were barely legible.

Feeling the threat of tears burning her eyes, she inhaled sharply. "What kind of customers are you getting?" she asked, aware her voice sounded strangled. She cleared her throat, then took another swig of beer. "Do you get a lot of rental cars breaking down?"

He chuckled. "Yeah. Tourists don't know how to drive these steep mountain roads. They overheat the engines climbing up, and burn through brake pads going back down." He stared at the truck for a while, as if he'd never seen it before. "But I don't get all those calls, unfortunately. Sometimes the rental companies dispatch their own road assistance or send a mechanic with a replacement vehicle for the tourist, then fix it themselves." He paused for a beat. "It's tough."

There was tension in his shoulders, and ridges ran across his forehead. He began bouncing his right foot, as if waiting impatiently for something.

"You're just, um, expecting calls to come in?" Kay asked, starting to understand his situation. He waited his life away, some days better than others, in the hope that calls would come, and he'd be able to make ends meet. Not making nearly enough to call it a decent living, making just enough to not have the heart to kill his father's business and find a different line of work. Stuck in his rut, with no way out.

"That's pretty much it," he replied, looking briefly at her with a sad smile. "Triple A sends me some business, but it pays bottom dollar. Some car rental companies dispatch me when they're out of options, but I've seen a couple of Enterprise and Budget trucks towing loads from around here." He sucked his teeth and ran his fingers across the back of his head, probably a subconscious effort to relieve the tension nestled in there. "The one-off calls are the best, when the customers call me directly. Locals know they get ten bucks if they refer business to me."

"That's smart," she said, finishing off the bottle and setting it down on the discolored deck. "I bet these customers ask locals for referrals, like servers and baristas and such, right?"

"Uh-huh," Sam replied. "Tommy sends me a lot of business. Remember him? He was a senior when you were a sophomore, right?"

"Which Tommy? The coffee shop guy?" she asked. She had no recollection of having been in school with the bulky owner of the place.

"Yeah, he owns Katse now; his dad passed."

"I didn't know that," Kay replied. "I've been there, but I didn't recognize him," she confessed. "I thought he was much older than us. He looks fifty, not thirty-something."

Sam chuckled sadly. "Life does things to us. Look at me," he said, holding out his hands with his stubby fingers fanned out. "You'd think I'd been working construction for twenty years. A couple of winters will do that to you, the cold and all that rusted hardware."

She wondered if there was anything she could do to help while she was there, while she waited for Jacob's release with not much else to do. Maybe she could advertise or get him new decals for his truck. She'd think of that later; for now, she still had a few questions in need of answers.

"Do you ever get canceled calls, or you go to the location and there's no one there?"

"Yeah," he groaned. "Damn those people. I wish they'd just have the decency to call me and cancel. At least I wouldn't burn the fuel for nothing." He pulled out his phone and looked at the screen for a moment, then said, "Just last night I had one of these no-shows."

Kay felt a pang of fear driving a blade through her gut. "Where was that call?"

He reacted to the intensity in her voice, looking at her with an unspoken question in his eyes. "Just over the ridge from Katse. Why?"

She didn't reply; turning her loaded gaze away from his, feeling the urge to spring to her feet and rush out of there, to see if she could catch up with the unsub.

He'd taken another woman yesterday, a woman they knew nothing about.

And he was long gone by now.

"When was that call, Sam?" she asked quietly.

"Yesterday, at about four," he replied, intrigued. "Does this have to do with, um... I heard you are a federal agent now."

"I am, yes. Well, I was," she replied. "I'm not on the job, if that's what you're hinting at," she said, and noticed he seemed relieved. "I'm asking because there are three children missing, and several women were found buried at Silent Lake. Murdered."

"Yeah, I know. The entire town talks about that. I live here, remember?" he added, a trace of his old sense of humor surfacing under the sadness that seemed to engulf him like a shroud.

"I thought that maybe there was a connection, that's all," she said, leaning back into her chair and making it rock gently. It was soothing to her frayed nerves, and allowed her to think clearly.

Sam wasn't the killer; that was a certainty, especially after seeing him, after speaking with him and noticing his reactions. The only thing he had to hide was his own despair, nothing more. But if he wasn't involved in the murders, then who was?

"Nah," he replied, "I don't think there's any connection. Cops asked me about that too, last week I think it was. Tourists drive up the hill in the wrong gear and overheat the engine. They stop for a while, call me, then they notice their engine is cooled off and they can keep on driving. And they leave. That's it. They just don't care," he added, a loaded breath leaving his chest. "They're quick to get out of there, happy they saved the tow money."

"How's your dad?" Kay asked, changing the subject. "Judy told me he's got back problems."

"Yeah." He stood and started pacing the porch slowly, back and forth. "He's pretty much screwed, and he's not on Medicare yet. A few more years to go."

"I told Judy I'd be happy to help. I make, um, made a good living. It would mean a lot if you'd take me up on this offer."

He stopped his pacing by her side and put his hand on her shoulder. He stood like that for a long moment, while silence filled the space, heavy, connecting them yet unable to bring peace to either of them, each lost in their own thoughts.

"Is this the same old truck?" she asked, trying to infuse some normal curiosity in the tone of her voice, instead of it sounding like a suspect interrogation. "The one we were climbing on as kids?"

"Yeah." He laughed fondly at the shared memory. "Dad used to drive it, then I took over. He doesn't drive it anymore. He just tinkers in the body shop, wandering about, hoping clients will come."

"It needs new decals," she said, pointing at the half-torn logo on the left side of the truck. "Saw it earlier today on the interstate, almost didn't recognize it."

"It needs a lot of new stuff, this jalopy," he replied. "No can do, though."

She didn't reply, feeling there were things he'd left unsaid. He was staring at the truck with disappointment, pressing his lips together. The seven-ton chunk of rusted metal had been a staple of the Stinson family's existence for decades. It couldn't've been easy for Sam to watch it break down and be unable to fix it, to maintain the lifeline of his business.

"One day it will crap out on me," Sam continued, still staring at the truck. "Then what?" he said, throwing Kay a quick glance. He was smiling, but it didn't fool anyone. The torment of his own powerlessness was tangible in the unspoken words, in the air between them.

"Sam, if I can—"

"It drives me crazy sometimes," he said, as if he didn't hear her words. He glanced at her again, his brave smile still pasted on his lips. "I swear to you, this thing has a life of its own."

She frowned slightly. "What do you mean?"

He hesitated before speaking, even checked the surrounding area as if fearing someone could overhear their conversation.

"It's playing tricks on me," he eventually said, keeping his voice low. "You know me, you know I'm not crazy, right?" he asked, seeing her raised eyebrow and long stare.

"Yeah, sure," she replied, nodding a couple of times. Sam was one of the sanest people she'd met. Unable to climb out of his rut, if that meant throwing away his family business, yes, but nevertheless he was practical, of solid judgment, someone whose words she believed. Yet she was thrown off by what he'd just said.

Trucks didn't play tricks on people.

Something was going on, and the thought of it lit a glimmer of hope in her heart.

Maybe it wasn't the truck who was playing games with Sam's mind. Maybe it was the unsub.

"Tell me, what did the truck do?" she asked, instilling just enough humor in her voice to encourage her old friend to open up.

"It's like it's cursed, or something," Sam replied grimly. "Haunted even."

"Why?"

He scratched the back of his head. "Last night, for example, I left it with the radio off. I know that for sure, 'cause there was too much talking about politics on the air, and I can't stand it anymore.

But this morning, the radio was back on." He swallowed hard, then looked at her over his shoulder. "That thing doesn't turn on by itself. It's minor things like that, but it drives me nuts."

"What else happened?" she asked. "And when?"

"About a month ago, I left it with the wheels straight, like I always do, but in the morning, I found it with the wheels steered left. All the way left. See, when you come up this driveway, you have to steer left to align with the house, but I always straighten my wheels, so I don't trip over them in the dark."

Approaching him, she leaned against the porch railing by his side, then looked at the truck. She believed she knew exactly what was going on; but didn't have it in her to tell Sam. It would break his heart to know his truck had been involved in such horrible crimes.

"Has anyone been by the house lately? Friends, relatives, anyone?"

"No," he replied, "no one ever comes here." He smiled awkwardly, seemingly embarrassed of his solitary lifestyle.

"Where do you keep the keys?"

"In the ignition. No one's gonna steal this piece of—" He stopped mid-phrase and slapped his hand against the railing. "Someone's messing with me, huh?"

"Yeah," she said quietly, squeezing his hand. "Someone is messing with you."

CHAPTER FORTY-SIX
Cabin

He stood in the large room, looking at the children, deeply disappointed.

It wasn't how he remembered it. His sister and brother used to laugh all the time, chasing each other around the dining room table until Mother sent them outside, mock-threatening them, and they obeyed, taking the squealing and the giggles away with them.

While he wasn't allowed to participate or come anywhere near them.

But he wanted to prove that the children were safe with him, that he wouldn't harm his sister in the way his mother feared. It wasn't his fault his body reacted the way it did when her skirt rode up her legs exposing her panties or when her girlfriends came by the house and played.

He would *never* touch his sister, not like that. He only watched, looked at her with yearning eyes, not understanding why the sight of his sister's bare skin would stir him that way or why his eyes clung to his mother's plunging cleavage, unable to look elsewhere, attracted by the sight of her full breasts touching, like a moth to an unforgiving, deadly flame.

He would've never touched his sister, not like that.

He wasn't an animal, out of control, driven only by the urges of his body. He'd proven that already, refusing himself the gratification his entire being craved, until it was safe to act. Even if it had taken years.

Now he wanted to prove to Mother he could play with his younger siblings, but the children wouldn't engage. They weren't laughing, they weren't chasing each other around the living room, they weren't even talking. Not to him, not to each other.

The girl sat on the edge of the bed, her little arms wrapped around her thin body, shivering. She whimpered sometimes, but immediately stifled her own sobs, probably knowing how much it pissed him off to see her like that. She kept her eyes riveted to the toy-littered floor, unwilling to look at him, unwilling to smile and make his day.

The boy stood by the window, staring into the distance at the edge of the woods, barely acknowledging his presence. When he'd entered the room earlier that day, that's where he found the boy, standing, staring at the far end of the stony ravine, where he'd buried Ann's body.

It wasn't his fault Ann had died last spring.

The little girl didn't obey his rules, and his rules were clear. The children could do anything they wanted, except go to the basement or try to leave the house. They had plenty of food, water and toys while he was gone. He had to go to work every day; it wasn't as if he had nothing else to do but watch those kids.

Everyone obeyed the rules, Tracy and her brother Matthew, Hazel, even Ann at first. But Ann was untamed, restless, a wild child who always sought ways to free herself from captivity. One day, when he was away, she'd managed to squeeze her thin body through the bathroom window, the only window he hadn't nailed shut, just because it was a tiny hole in the wall, six feet above the ground.

She must've climbed on Tracy's shoulders to do it, and must've gone through the opening headfirst, unaware the window opened twenty-five feet above the ravine.

He'd had the cabin built there, on a rocky ledge above the ravine, to enjoy the elevated vantage views and the absolute solitude. There was a single road leading up to it, barely a path, and only his four-wheeler made it that far into the woods. The entire versant belonged to him, and a mile down the road he'd built another house, that one larger, complete with a two-car garage, where he changed vehicles. That's where he left his Cadillac when he needed the ATV to drive up to the cabin or go hunting.

No one knew the cabin existed; he'd made sure of that. Not even the park rangers who patrolled the area sometimes; they always stopped at the edges of his property, marked clearly with NO TRESPASSING signs affixed on top of a wire fence every twenty yards. Of course, everyone knew about the house, a modern Craftsman with vaulted ceilings and stone-accented exteriors. He entertained guests and political allies there; he'd even held a press conference at that house, when he'd just won a capital murder case that had made headlines for weeks in a row.

But the cabin no one knew about. The general contractor who'd built it and his two workers had a terrible accident coming down the winding, sloped roads of Mount Chester, when the steering froze and the contractor's truck flew through the side railing into the steep rocks of the mountain, where it instantly burst into flames.

No one survived.

He'd designed the cabin to be completely off the grid, knowing that someday it could be possible he'd have to hide up there for a longer period of time. Heated solar panels covered the roof, instantly melting the snow that would cover them during winter. A backup powerline had been drawn from the house, and water was pumped up from the stream running through the ravine. He could live up there for months, years even, unseen and unknown by anybody, hunting for food and enjoying all the comforts of a well-equipped log cabin. No one knew that if one took an ATV and circled the house downhill, in the back there was a path that led to the cabin. No one knew, and no one could accidentally stumble upon that path either. It was hidden from view by low-hanging fir branches and shrubs, an apparent wall of green hiding the ATV's barely visible tire tracks on the foliage-covered rocks.

When Ann had ventured to escape through the bathroom window, she had no idea there was nowhere she could run, even if she'd survived the twenty-five-foot fall to the bottom of the rocky ravine. She would've gotten lost and surely met her death when a bear or a coyote would've picked up her scent.

Either way, it wasn't his fault she'd died, but he wanted the other children to learn something from it. He was mad as hell over the senseless death of that girl. What would Mother have said? That he couldn't be trusted to take care of his siblings, that one way or another he ended up harming them, maybe not with his body's urges, but with his carelessness. It didn't matter that Ann had grown increasingly restless after her mother, Lan Xiu, had vanished from the cabin. Little Ann had listened for her mother's voice for days, and had even asked him about her. But Lan Xiu was gone already, resting peacefully at Silent Lake. There was nothing he could say to her daughter to make her feel better.

Then she'd made her escape attempt, and had probably lost her footing and broken her neck in the fall. When he arrived at the cabin that night, after finding out what had happened, he didn't rush downstairs, as he usually liked to, for a visit with his latest guest, a stunning blonde named Shannon. Instead, he took Shannon's two children, Tracy and Matthew, and gave them each a shovel, then took them down into the ravine, to see Ann's body with their own eyes.

And bury it themselves.

They'd remember Ann's fate for the rest of their lives, and they would never, ever try to escape again.

A few days later, he had to drive Tracy to the city and set her free near the Tenderloin somewhere. After having seen and buried Ann's body, the girl wouldn't stop screaming, and it drove him crazy. The children weren't supposed to scream; only Mother was. Only the mother's wails soothed the pain eating him from the inside out.

But Matthew had stayed behind, quiet, absent-minded, as if not even really there, refusing to engage with him. He hadn't spoken a word since his sister had been taken away, not even after Hazel had joined him. There was no laughter to be heard in that room, no playfulness, no giggles.

It wasn't like he remembered it. Not even a bit.

He tried approaching Hazel holding a new toy in his hand, but the girl whimpered and withdrew into a corner. Right then, a distant scream came from the basement, where Wendy was slowly coming to grips with her new reality. Matthew flinched, but his eyes stayed riveted on Ann's resting place, while Hazel's whimpers turned into sobbing, her little shoulders heaving while she crouched on the floor, away from him.

That's not how family life used to be, before Mother screwed everything up.

These kids weren't good for anything. He didn't know what was wrong with them, why they didn't want to play with him. His sister and brother always wanted to play with him; only Mother wouldn't allow it.

He'd have to deal away with them, and soon.

He didn't know how yet, because taking them back was dangerous. Everyone was looking for those kids. There were AMBER Alerts active, and, most recently, a description of his car had been added to the alerts. How the hell did they find out he was driving a blue Cadillac? What else did they know, and how close were they to finding him? He needed to manage that, to do something. To derail Kay Sharp and that detective off his scent, before it was too late.

It was about damn time Kay Sharp joined him at the cabin.

And no, he couldn't take the children back. Someone could recognize him, now that he was a public figure who'd been interviewed on local television a few times.

Maybe the ravine would be a good resting place for the children who wouldn't play. Or, perhaps, joining the others by Silent Lake would be better.

He had to decide quickly, before the ground froze completely.

Unable to make up his mind, angry, dissatisfied, he closed the door to the large room and went downstairs, where Wendy was sobbing hard. Her fingers were bleeding from senselessly scratching at the door like a caged animal. There was nowhere to go; he wished she'd listen to him.

When she saw him enter, her pupils dilated in fear, and she stumbled backward until she hit the concrete wall.

"No, no, please," she whimpered. Tears were streaking down her cheeks, staining her beautiful skin.

Feeling the tremor of anticipation kindle his entire body, he took a whip, his hand welcoming the sensation of the braided leather handle against his skin. Then he closed his eyes and saw the image of his mother, tied up in chains in front of him, naked, begging his forgiveness, screaming with each strike of the whip against her trembling body.

CHAPTER FORTY-SEVEN
Conversations

Kay gave Sam Stinson a hug and placed a kiss on his cheek, then climbed behind the wheel of her Ford, noting in passing that it had been hours since he'd received a service call. From that morning around ten, when she'd seen him driving on the interstate, until now, at two in the afternoon, when Triple A had texted a work order for him, almost four hours had passed during which time he hadn't earned any money.

She let him leave, waving him off with a smile. As soon as the truck disappeared from view, so did Kay's smile, replaced by a flurry of mixed emotions.

The unsub had taken another woman. Who was she? Was she traveling with a child?

And if she'd been right in profiling the killer, he wasn't going to take anyone else until the ground thawed, and that meant he wasn't going to need Sam's truck until spring. Her best lead had proven to be fruitless, at least for now. Yes, the unsub was using the tow truck, just as she'd anticipated, but he was wearing gloves in all the videos she'd seen. After Sam had taken off, she realized that, regardless, the forensic team should've probably gone through that truck's cabin with a fine-tooth comb, just to cover all bases. Although she knew the perpetrator well enough to know he would've never made the mistake to leave any evidence behind.

A knock on the window made her jump out of her skin.

It was Elliot.

She breathed out and lowered her window.

"What the hell are you doing here?" he asked, no greeting, no apologies for the previous night's outburst.

"Visiting an old friend," she replied coldly. "Why? You ran out of people to accuse?"

He lowered his gaze for a brief moment. "Don't lie to me, please, Kay."

"I'm still mad at you," she said, instead of answering his question. She rested her elbow on the door and looked at him, studying his reactions. That shame was still there, the guilt for whatever he thought he'd done wrong. "Isn't your boss telling you we can't work together anymore?"

He ran his hand over his forehead, shielding his eyes for a brief moment. "No. He, um, checked you out, and he said no way your father is mixed up in all this." He cleared his throat, and shifted his weight from one leg to the other. "I'm sorry I didn't believe what you said about him. You would've probably done the same."

She shrugged, feeling a little vindicated, but not entirely. "No," she replied candidly. "I would've probably chosen to believe my partner instead of applying statistical fallacies without thinking."

"What statistical fallacies?"

She sighed and repressed a smile, but decided to explain. He seemed miserable enough without her making it worse. "Yes, it's statistically true that perps have a tendency to insert themselves into investigations, so they can keep an eye on things and even derail the outcomes if they can. But that doesn't mean *everyone* who becomes involved in an investigation is necessarily the unsub or is protecting the unsub."

Silence fell heavily between them for a moment.

"I see," he replied, the look in his eyes heavy, burdened. "Well, I've had me plenty of time to think about it. I spent last night in jail."

That explained his attire and disheveled look, maybe even the absence of his wide-brimmed hat. She realized she had never seen him without it. He had a tall forehead and light hair. "How come?"

"Technically, a DUI, but I wasn't drunk; I was set up. Not sure how, but I'm willing to bet my gold star against a pile of steaming manure he pulled the strings and framed me." He lowered his gaze again, only for a split second. "We must be getting really close to him."

She mulled things over for a brief moment. The unsub had managed to come after both of them, effectively, without either of them seeing him coming. "He's not only local," she said, "he's also connected."

He nodded once. "I got the results from Doc Whitmore on the blanket fibers. We struck out again. The blankets look Native, but they were made in China, and there's no telling where or how they were shipped here. To whom."

There could be some telling, but it required the best analysts from the FBI pulling mountains of Chinese import data together, gathering customs declarations, and cross-referencing them nationwide to registered owners of blue Cadillac Escalades. It would take time. Too much time.

"He took another woman, Elliot," she announced grimly, her own powerlessness suffocating.

"How do you know?"

"Sam Stinson had a no-show call last night, over the ridge from Katse, and this morning, he found someone had messed with his truck while he was sleeping. Left it with the radio on."

"So that's how he does it," Elliot exclaimed, raising his hands in the air. "So, where to next, partner?" he asked, venturing a tense smile.

"You'll get video surveillance installed here, so we'll catch him when he takes Sam's truck again."

"But you said—"

"Yes, it could be months until he does." She pressed her lips together, determined to not let her discouragement seep out. They'd lost Alison; regardless of everything they tried, they'd only found her body. Not her, alive, and not her daughter Hazel. The unsub still had Hazel. But maybe this new woman had a chance. "You do that, Elliot, and I'll keep asking questions, see who could've got so close to Sam Stinson without anyone noticing."

"You don't have a badge anymore," Elliot pushed back. "You shouldn't be conducting investigations on your own."

"I'm not," she replied firmly. "I'm just visiting old friends, catching up."

They stared at each other for a brief moment, then Elliot walked away with a heavy sigh. Kay was about to start her engine, when her phone buzzed. She took the call on her car's media system, and a man's voice filled the space.

"Dr. Sharp? This is Shane Joplin, returning your call. Your brother's attorney?"

That was a call she hadn't really been expecting. "Yes, hi," she said, thinking quickly how best to approach the conversation. "I was wondering if we could speak for a moment about my brother's sentencing, which seems significantly more severe than the norm."

She paused, giving him time to respond.

"Um, yes, well, this is entirely up to the judge in these cases, and Judge Hewitt is famous for imposing harsh sentences in physical assault cases. I defended the case to the best of my abilities, but—"

She'd looked Judge Hewitt up on the internet, right after Jacob had mentioned his name, and Joplin's statement was correct. But even His Honor should've seen the trumped-up charge for what it was.

"Felony assault with premeditation?" Kay said, allowing her frustration to become apparent in her voice.

"The DA wanted to, um, make an example out of him. Your brother could've pleaded it out, but he refused. Jacob insisted he wasn't guilty of any premeditation, and that we'd be able to prove it in court. But juries are finnicky, as you well know, and they found him guilty after all. Then the judge—"

"What could we do for Jacob at this point?" she asked, unwilling to hear him make any more excuses. "I will pay for your services." She waited for an answer, but none came. "And I'd really want to understand how a simple bar brawl ended in a six-month prison sentence for a first-time offender. I don't believe I'm getting the full picture here."

"Dr. Sharp," Joplin said, his tone lower, as if he was trying to keep his words from being overheard. "Let's meet face to face. I believe the conversation would be better handled that way."

She wholeheartedly agreed, yet there was no time. Not until she found the unsub. But it was her own brother whose every day behind bars could be his last. "Yes, I believe it would be better if we met in person."

"Excellent," Joplin replied. "When can you meet? Time is of the essence, I'm sure you understand. I could meet with you right now, if you'd like."

She hesitated for a beat, then replied, "How's tomorrow around lunch? Should I come to San Francisco?"

"No, Dr. Sharp, I'll meet you up there, where you live."

She thanked him and ended the call, then started the engine and drove off Sam Stinson's property, turning onto the state highway and heading to town. She replayed her conversation with Joplin in her mind, wondering what secrets lay beneath her brother's unusual charge and harsh sentencing, and if there was a coincidence anywhere, with Elliot having spent his night in jail over a bogus charge. Was the unsub someone who held power or influence in law enforcement, or maybe somewhere else in the justice system?

As she drove away, deeply immersed in her own thoughts, she failed to notice the dark Escalade trailing her from a distance.

CHAPTER FORTY-EIGHT
Meg

Meg Stinson lived in one of the newer ranches, a small one over-looking the snow-covered peak of Mount Chester. She looked just as Kay remembered, the only traces of time passing showed in the laugh lines at the corners of her eyes. Her hair was still chestnut, wavy and wild, not a visible trace of gray anywhere. She wore it long, like a teenager would, and her turtleneck, white sweater was youthful too, loose over skinny jeans.

Kay teared up in Meg's arms. She'd missed her dearly, the smell of rising bread in her hair, the sound of wind chimes on her porch, the touch of her warm hand against her cheek. Meg was like a second mother for Kay, and since Pearl's passing, Meg had been in Kay's thoughts many times. But she'd stayed away, more afraid to come to Mount Chester and open old wounds than eager to see the people she loved.

She sniffled and withdrew from the embrace, afraid the flood gates would open, and she'd end up breaking down in Meg's arms, all the unwanted tears accompanying the recent anguish in her life threatening to burst out.

"I missed you," Kay confessed, then turned her head to hide her face as she wiped another rebel tear. "You look amazing," she added. "You haven't aged a bit."

"Only on the surface, my dear," Meg replied. "Come, sit with me," she said, patting a spot next to her on the cedar swing.

She gladly accepted, and they sat there together for a while, silently, looking at the mountain peak in the distance, enjoying the serenity of the breezy afternoon.

"New wind chimes?" Kay asked.

"Yes, you noticed," Meg replied, smiling. "Every now and then I drive to the Pacific coast and collect some shells from the beach. That gives me something to do. A divorced schoolteacher has a lot of free time on her hands." She slid off the swing, setting it into a slow, relaxing motion. "I'll get us a cup of tea."

Kay followed her inside while she made the tea, eastern hemlock, her absolute favorite for chilly days. Meg had introduced her to the tribal tradition of drinking the brew when she was barely tall enough to reach the counter. It smelled of mountain air, of pine forests, of evergreens uncovered by thawing snow.

Meg had arranged the small house neatly, with little furniture, all of it functional and reminiscent of Native interiors. Sheepskins covered the couch and one of the armchairs, and another lay on the floor, by the couch, in front of the fireplace. An area rug with a geometrical pattern covered a section of the wooden floor, a small dining room table with four chairs centered on it. Another hung on the wall, behind the couch, bringing color and warmth to the interior. The house smelled faintly of sweetgrass and fresh cookies, the scents of her childhood, the ones she loved to remember. Others, she still struggled to forget.

Kay noticed some framed photos on the wall by the kitchen and walked over there to take a look. One of the photos showed Judy, Sam, and her in front of the Stinson house, taken the summer the girls had turned twelve. Another showed Judy and Kay, older, all dressed up for prom, and Sam threatening to shoot his water pistol at them. That one made her chuckle; she still remembered how terrified she was that Sam would pull the trigger and she'd end up going to the prom wet as a cat caught in the rain. A third one, a little to the side, showed young Meg and Mr. Stinson, holding hands. Meg was about twenty-five years old in that photo and smiled happily, the smile of a woman in love. Yet Kay's heart froze when she noticed Meg's hair in the photo. It was braided tightly, not one loose strand anywhere, and the two braids were tied with ornamental hair ties made from leather and small feathers.

Just like the girls from Silent Lake.

Slack-jawed, she stared at the photo, taking in every detail, barely aware her throat was parched dry and words weren't coming out. She swallowed with difficulty, then asked, pointing at the picture, "When... what was this about?"

Meg wiped her hands off her jeans and approached to see which photo Kay was asking about.

"Roy and I met at a powwow, don't know if you knew that," Meg replied, a fond smile stretching her lips. She handed Kay a hot cup of tea. "This is one of the last times he and I went to a powwow together," she added, a hint of sadness in her voice. "His parents demanded that I convert to Catholicism if we wanted to be married, so I did." Meg paused for a moment, and Kay didn't interrupt her thoughts. "Different times, back then." She looked at Kay with an apologetic smile. "I would've acted differently today. But thirty years ago, I said yes, and left my tribe behind."

"Did you miss it?" Kay set her teacup on the dining room table and pulled herself a chair.

Meg sat next to Kay and squeezed her forearm gently. "More than you'd think. Truth be told, I never really converted, not deep inside," she said, touching her chest briefly. "In my heart, I'm still Pomoan." Her smile was loaded with sadness, with unspoken regret. "But if you want to look at old photos, I have some right here," she said, her voice a bit more cheerful than before.

She stood and went over to a dresser, then opened a few drawers, looking for something.

Kay was drawn toward the photo, as if it was a window into the unsub's twisted soul. Yet asking about it, talking about it with

Meg seemed surreal, sending shivers down her spine as if she was about to conjure evil and look it in the eye.

"Is there a significance to the braided hair, the way you wore it in that photo?" Kay asked, her tense voice barely above a whisper.

"Some say the braiding represents the connection with the infinite," Meg replied, approaching the table with a large photo album. She set it on the table, while Kay moved the teacups over to make room for it. "But I believe it was more practical than anything else, not having hair in your eyes when working or cooking. Or dancing," she added, laughing quietly. "Because Pomoan Indians never cut their hair unless they're grieving the death of a loved one."

"I knew that," Kay replied. "I just didn't know about the braiding. And those hair ties? They're so beautiful," she added. "Do you remember where you got them from?"

"I made them," Meg replied proudly. "Before I got married, I used to make all sorts of things and sell them at powwows. It was a little bit of money my family needed." She opened the album and turned the transparent, protective sheet between the pages. "This is me and my Native family, my mother and father," she said, showing her the yellowed photo of Meg as a young girl, maybe fifteen or so, with both her parents dressed in ceremonial attire. "It was someone's wedding; I don't remember whose."

Kay saw Meg growing up in one photo after another, then a photo from her own wedding.

"Wow, you were an amazing bride," Kay said, looking at the weathered image.

"Thank you, my dear. That was thirty-seven years ago."

Kay thought to ask about her divorce, but bit her lip. If Meg wanted to talk about it, she'd bring it up.

Meg turned another page in the album, then almost rushed to turn another. Kay stopped her, and caught her frown in the corner of her eye, while she stared at a photo that brought back forgotten memories. It was a picture of Meg and three children: Judy, Sam, and an older boy, taller than his siblings, almost as tall as his mother.

"Who's this? He looks familiar, but I can't remember, I'm sorry," Kay whispered, running her hand over the photo's protective sleeve. There used to be another boy, but she realized that she'd forgotten all about him. He was older, and they never really played together. Judy must've been eleven or twelve in that photo, and Judy was her age. One summer he'd just vanished.

Meg averted her eyes. Her expression had changed, showing lines of sadness that flanked her mouth and cast shadows over her eyes. "We don't talk about him," she replied in a cold, firm voice. "He's gone."

Kay wrapped her arm around Meg's shoulders. "I'm so sorry, Meg. I had no idea. Losing a child must be terrible."

"It is," she said, keeping her eyes shielded. Kay heard the threat of tears in her voice.

"How did he die?" Kay asked, her voice barely a whisper.

Meg didn't speak for a while, staring into the distance, as if somewhere in the sweetgrass scented air of the living room was the answer she was looking for.

"He didn't," she eventually said, while a tear rolled down her cheek. "Nick left the year we took that photo. He argued with us a lot. He had… a difficult time growing up."

"How, exactly?" Kay asked, embarrassed to be pushing Meg into a difficult conversation. Her instinct unfurled a sense of foreboding in her gut, seeding goosebumps on her skin.

"At first, I thought it was all a coincidence," Meg replied, stifling a shattered breath. "I kept finding dead animals in our barn. Mrs. Wilkinson's cat, a stray dog one time, strangled. It was awful." She stopped for a moment, visibly struggling to continue.

Kay squeezed her frozen fingers, wondering how come she knew nothing of what had happened to her closest friends. She guessed that nobody thought it necessary to share such things with twelve-year-old girls.

"I—we confronted him," Meg continued, "and he denied everything. We argued badly, then a few nights later, the barn caught fire when we were at work, and the children, supposedly, at school. Later, we learned he'd skipped geography class that afternoon and couldn't account for his time."

"Did he say why?" Kay asked, although she believed she knew the answer.

"No," Meg whispered, "he didn't. Then, later that same month, he did something unspeakable."

Kay looked at her, insisting without words that she continue her story, but Meg shook her head gently, letting silence engulf the room for a long moment. After a while, the silence became heavy, unbearable to the weary heart that had kept secrets all those years.

"I caught him touching himself when watching Judy and you," she added, averting her eyes, her voice strangled with embarrassment. "Then he came to my bed one night, when I was asleep. I nearly... I almost didn't realize—" She choked and shook her head, as if to rid herself of the nightmarish memory. "I threw him out," she eventually said, then burst into bitter sobs. "I told him he wasn't my son anymore. No one was to speak his name again in our house."

Kay wrapped her arms around Meg's heaving shoulders. She understood her turmoil. "It's okay," she whispered. "You had reasons, two other children to protect. Don't forget that."

"I never forgave myself," Meg whispered between tears. "But I had no idea what to do. His sexual urges were scary... As soon as he entered puberty, he wasn't my little boy anymore. He turned into an intense stranger who looked at me as if I were—" She pressed her lips together for a split second, then continued. "We didn't know how to handle him. We just didn't." She wiped her tears, then looked at Kay with guilt in her eyes. "We were simple people; back then I didn't know what else to do."

Kay allowed Meg the time to gather her thoughts. It must've been tough for her to revisit the most painful moment of her life as a mother. But the more she thought about it, the more Nick Stinson fit the unsub's profile, and the thought of that energized her.

She looked at the photo again, then flipped the page over. There was another image taken inside the house, showing Judy wearing the ribbon she'd won in the seventh-grade spelling bee. But that wasn't what had caught her attention.

On the wall behind the couch there was a blanket, hung in traditional Native decor style. It was a geometrical design on dark brown, framing around a bundle of feathers tied together with a blood-red leather twine and carried by an arrow. She'd seen it before.

All the Silent Lake victims had been buried in one just like it.

"Do you still have this?" she asked Meg, pointing at the blanket.

She smiled between tears, a sad, loaded smile. "Funny you should ask about it now. Roy bought it for me, seeing how upset I was for not attending the annual powwow with my people, the first year after we got married. But it's Shasta, not Pomo; he screwed up." She sighed and wiped a tear with her finger. "I gave it to Nick the night I—the night he left. I figured he wouldn't know the difference. It was chilly that night, and I—" A new wave of sobs overcame the poor woman, her breath shattered as she tried to control herself.

Kay held her hand the entire time, squeezing it gently, reminding her she wasn't alone and giving her the time she needed to sort through the painful emotions that her questions had unleashed.

"I heard he's doing okay for himself," Meg added when he could speak again. "I don't know anything else of him and it's better this way. He's not my son anymore."

Kay stood, a strong sense of urgency driving her away from there, even if they didn't finish looking at the entire photo album.

She apologized profusely and promised both Meg and herself that she'd return the next day, when, under no circumstances, was she to open the painful subject again. She cringed, though, hoping she'd finally identified the unsub, while at the same time dreading having to break to Meg Stinson the news that her firstborn son was a killer.

But how did Nick, the boy who'd vanished from Mount Chester all those years ago, know about her family secret? How did he find out about her father's demise, and how did he figure out where to find the knife with her father's fingerprints on it?

Pushing the turmoil out of her mind, she focused on her priorities, simple and urgent: finding the missing children and the woman the unsub had taken the day before. Finding them alive.

Back in the car, she speed-dialed Elliot's number, barely waiting for him to pick up.

"Elliot," she said, as soon as she heard his voice. "I think I know who the unsub is."

"Shoot," he replied.

"Sam Stinson had an older brother, Nick. He disappeared when I was about twelve, so that's—"

"Eighteen years ago," he said. "What about him?"

"Have you heard of the homicidal triad?" she asked. "You might know it as the Macdonald triad," she continued, seeing he wasn't replying.

"No, I haven't. What's that?"

"A set of three predictive factors of future violent antisocial behavior: bed-wetting, cruelty to animals, and fire-setting. Any two of these three factors are strong predictors of serial violence later in life. Well, Mrs. Stinson just told me Nick used to strangle animals and he also set the barn on fire before he was kicked out of the house. His own family ousting him could've been the main stressor that led him to kill, with his mother as the central object of his rage. She'd been the object of his sexual fantasies, but she rejected him firmly and made him feel insignificant, inadequate. From deep desire to burning rage, all it takes is the word no."

"That's it? He strangled animals and set the barn on fire? And dreamed of sleeping with his mother? That's all you got?"

"There's more evidence pointing at him. Everything correlates, Elliot. The blanket, I saw it in a photo dating back years; it used to hang on his childhood home's wall. And his mother braided her hair just like the unsub did his victims'. Just run a full background on Nick Stinson and let me know what you find."

"On it," Elliot replied, and for a long moment, all she could hear was the keyboard clacking under Elliot's rushed fingers. "Huh… He graduated from law school *cum laude*, then had a legal name change to—"

Silence filled the air, taut as a wire before snapping.

"Oh, hell, Kay. He's the district attorney," Elliot said. "*Our* district attorney, Nicholas Stevens. He can't be the unsub."

But Kay knew in her gut it had to be him. The blanket his mother had given him the night she'd banished him was a symbol of his rage. He'd probably found a company in China that could replicate the design and had several made and shipped to him, an essential part of the ritual he performed with every killing and every burial. The braided hair, just like his mother's, was another symbol.

"Check his DMV records, Elliot," she suggested, knowing precisely what Elliot was about to find.

Another moment of keyboard clacking, then a whisper. "Jeez… He drives a Cadillac Escalade, dark Adriatic blue metallic." He paused for a moment, then added, "Running a property check. He's got a house at the base of the mountain, in the next county over, and an apartment in San Francisco. I'll send you the address for the house and I'll meet you there."

She peeled off from Meg Stinson's driveway in a cloud of dust and gravel. "Heading out there now."

CHAPTER FORTY-NINE
Hunted

Kay vaguely remembered Nick, from all those years ago. She had one foggy memory of him, one time when he was watching Judy and her playing from behind the fence, looking at them with a strange intensity in his eyes, slightly trembling. She recalled how Judy's mom had told him to go work in the barn, the fearful tone in Meg's voice etched in her mind. That part she remembered clearly, because she still had a recollection of her own thoughts at the time. *I'm not afraid of Nick. Nick is cool.*

She closed her eyes, subjecting herself to a silent cognitive interview. She invited the distant memories to return, rewinding through them as if they were a video stored in the deepest recesses of her mind.

*

Kathy threw the pebbles carefully, weighing them in her hand to make sure she hit the right spot. Still, a pebble bounced right out of the green circle, in defiance of her best intentions.

"No," she squealed, then looked at Judy, waiting for her orders.

"Lay flat in the dirt," Judy commanded, laughing heartily.

Resigned, she lay on her back by the driveway, her arms folded under her head, pretending she didn't care she lost again. Stupid pebbles had a mind of their own.

"Face down," Judy insisted, laughing. Winning was fun. Yeah.

"You didn't say!" Kathy replied, jumping to her feet and brushing some of the dirt off her dress.

She picked the pebbles from the chalk circles and gave them to her friend, then took her position to the side. Judy missed, and Kathy was quick to order, "Do a cartwheel."

Her eyes wandered while Judy threw her pebbles, and saw Nick in the distance, behind the fence, by the barn. He was looking at the two girls, and Kathy waved. He was tense, rigid, and his eyes burned strangely when they met hers. He seemed to be trembling a little, although it was hot outside, his entire body shaking, his jaw clenched, his brow scrunched in effort. Or maybe she was wrong; she was imagining things. Or was she? What was he doing behind that fence? In her memory, she couldn't see Nick's hands, hidden from view by the pickets. Was he touching himself, while looking at them? Was he trembling with arousal?

"Why can't Nick play with us?" she asked.

"Mom said he has to do chores," Judy replied indifferently.

Her smile waned. She liked Nick. He must've been about sixteen; he kept the girls supplied with his old stash of school homework. All his notebooks were saved in a box under his bed, and he readily shared when asked. Nick was cool. She wasn't afraid of him; had never been.

She waved at him, but he didn't wave back. The tension on his face had waned, and the shaking was gone. His eyes still burned though, his gaze intense, fixated, making her eyes veer to the side.

He showed her the rake he was holding, lifting it up in the air and pointing at it in an exaggerated way, then went toward the barn, to work. He threw her one long, loaded stare, probably feeling sorry he couldn't play with them. Or maybe there was something else in that look, an intensity her child mind hadn't picked up on at the time. An urgency, a longing that could not be denied.

"Nick!" Mrs. Stinson called. "Get in the barn and lay the straw already. It's almost dark."

That's where her childhood memories of Nick ended, with him going into the barn, and her regret for not having played with him.

*

Well, apparently, developing good instincts about people doesn't happen in early childhood, she thought bitterly, wondering how she'd forgotten all about that boy. Meg was keeping him at a distance, not allowing him to play with the girls. Back then, she hadn't shared why, but now, in retrospect, Meg's decision to keep Nick away from the two little girls made sense.

And that visit he'd paid his mother one night, that had scared Meg Stinson into throwing him out of the house, her own flesh and blood, that must've been the culmination of his sexual urges seeking relief.

Her experience as a profiler painted a clear picture of what had happened that night. In all the serial killer cases she'd studied, the homicidal triad was just the beginning, sending the pubescent teen into a rapidly evolving rash of urges and hormone-based drives he could not understand nor control. Maybe he'd become aroused by Judy or even by his own mother. Maybe that day, behind the fence, he was masturbating while watching the two little girls play. And then later one night, when he couldn't control his urges anymore, or when masturbation wasn't satisfying enough, he took it one step further. One step too far.

But not all children who display at least two of the three factors of the triad end up evolving into serial killers. For some, the parents seek professional help, and that is sometimes able to detour them off the path to killing people. In Nick's case, his family had banished him, seeding in him a rejection-fueled anger that must've been all-consuming, devouring him from the inside out, a wound that could never heal.

His trigger.

Exacerbated by whatever challenges his life as a homeless teenager might've thrown at him.

Engendering an unsatiable urge to soothe his pain, to soak it in the blood of strangers who reminded him of his mother, the woman who rejected him instead of showing him unconditional love.

But how does one get from homeless teenager to district attorney? Less than ten percent of all serial killers were high-functioning, successful and perfectly integrated individuals. Those who were, in one hundred percent of the cases, were pure psychopaths, people who never had to carry the burden of a conscience weighing them down. People who could manipulate, lie and claw their way into whatever place they desired to hold in society. And kill.

Immersed in her thoughts and rushing to the address Elliot had sent her, she floored it the entire time, the winding, sloped road over the mountain no longer a challenge for her. She almost didn't notice when she passed by Katse Coffee Shop, the sight of the place making her think briefly of Tommy, another kid she didn't remember. He was thirty-two, but looked fifty-something, and had a rap sheet for assault and battery. How did that happen to otherwise normal children?

Then again, how did Jacob's rap sheet happen?

Then another thought crossed her mind, this one making her stomach sink. She scrolled quickly through the phone numbers stored in her phone's memory, almost missing a curve, then dialed the number. This time, Joplin picked up the call himself.

"Who was my brother's DA?"

"Nicholas Stevens himself, not one of his errand boys," he replied, his voice cutting off badly. "I found that strange, for a low-profile case like that. Why?"

She heard a chime when the check engine light came on the dashboard. She'd just driven by Katse, heading into the valley. The temperature gauge on her dashboard was at the max, and there were two warning messages displayed, "Engine coolant low. Engine malfunction."

Another buzz announced the call with Joplin had dropped. She looked at the media screen and saw she'd entered the cellular dead zone of the valley.

She knew exactly what was going on.

Nicholas Stinson was coming after her.

Her heart racing, she slowed barely enough to pull a one-eighty with screeching tires, knowing she was merely a few hundred yards downhill from where she had a couple of bars on her phone. Unlike others before her, she didn't need to stop to check what was going on with her car; she already knew. Yet she wondered why Nick was coming after her. Was it because she was getting close to him? And where did he get so close to her car to damage it? Where and when?

Just as her engine stalled, she realized exactly why he was coming after her.

She'd visited Meg Stinson that morning. His mother. He was probably out there somewhere, watching as she basked in the motherly love that was forbidden to him, while she sat by Meg's side on the porch swing, chatting, holding hands. Then Meg and she had gone inside the house, to make tea, giving him the chance to damage her car, unseen, unheard.

The Ford's engine sputtered and came to a stop, while she barely had enough momentum to pull the SUV off the road, dangerously close to a deep ditch. Out of habit, Kay felt for the weapon that used to be at her hip, but found nothing. She remembered how she'd decided to leave it at home, thinking she was going to visit old friends.

He could come at any time, from any direction, and she had no defense, nothing she could use. Nothing, except knowledge of what he'd done to the other women. Mostly all of them had

had the time to walk back to Katse and call for help. For some reason, he never snatched them right away, right after their cars had stalled. She could, most likely, make it on foot to Katse and call Elliot. Knowing that the unsub was close, hunting for her, turned her blood to ice, while fear coiled in her gut, awakening her senses. She felt the urge to run all the way to Katse, although she knew well that was exactly what he wanted her to do. What all the others had done.

But more than anything, she wanted to see him, to put a face to the monster she'd been trying to catch. Curiosity got the best of her, and instead of rushing to the coffee shop, she found some shrubs behind a large oak and crouched there, hidden by the thick foliage, and waited. She wanted to know how he took them, why he let them go to Katse in the first place. To her, it seemed an unnecessary risk he was taking; they could run into traffic, another driver who would stop to help or even a cop.

Soon she'd be able to sketch another missing part of the profile, and that, in itself, was worth the risk.

She'd been waiting for about thirty minutes when she heard the ATV engine, approaching from the opposite side of the road, through the woods. She peeked from behind the tree trunk, hoping she'd see his face and recognize him, but he was too far away. He'd stopped his vehicle a few yards into the woods and had crossed the road on foot, approaching her car. He was dressed head to toe in hunting gear, the fall camo pattern making him barely distinguishable against the foliage.

Circling the SUV, he looked inside, then paced up and down the road, waiting for her. Then he made a call, pretending to be a tow truck driver looking for his customer. By his responses, the call hadn't gone as expected.

He swore out loud, then started looking for her. She held her breath, afraid he'd hear it from only a few feet away, fear clouding her judgment while her heart thumped in her chest. She hated being afraid; it wasn't a feeling she was used to. *Think*, she willed herself, letting out air slowly and quietly from her lungs and watching the unsub's search drawing nearer.

Checking the opposite side of the road, he went a few yards deep and several yards up and down from where she'd stopped. Then he crossed the road again, after waiting in hiding until two passing cars were out of sight. He searched skillfully, every few steps stopping and listening for any noise that didn't belong, looking at the ground for tracks, everything a hunter would do.

Stepping backward, she tried to hide herself better, and let herself slide all the way to the ground, curled on her side. A twig snapped under her knee and the man stopped in his tracks, listening. She held her breath, her heart racing, pounding forcefully against her ribcage as he approached her hiding place. It took all her willpower to resist the urge to run, knowing she didn't have a chance against the man and his ATV.

He stopped a few feet away from her, so close she could hear his raspy breath. She could only see his boots from her vantage point. She froze, afraid he was close enough to hear her heartbeats, and stared at those boots, anticipating how the incapacitating blow would come.

But he moved on, searching for her a few yards farther north.

Breathing silently, she kept her eyes riveted on the man until he climbed on his four-wheeler and drove off, heading east. She waited another moment, illogically fearing he'd return if she made the tiniest sound.

Then a vehicle approached at high speed and stopped near hers with a screech. She heard her name being called out loud.

"Kay?" Elliot shouted. He opened the door of her SUV and honked a few times. "Kay?"

CHAPTER FIFTY

Where

He drove back in a frenzy, chaotic thoughts swirling in his turmoiled mind. He'd been close, so close he could feel her, he could smell her, but he was returning alone, defeated.

Where the hell did she go?

Had she been expecting him?

She probably had, considering the cops had at least three of the cars he'd tampered with. When her engine stalled, she must've known it was him, coming for her, and she managed to do something completely unexpected.

That was the girl he remembered, the girl who'd set his blood on fire when he was just a kid and had no idea what was going on with his own body. Fearless and proud, a girl whose arms bore the signs where her father had touched her in black-and-blue marks, yet laughed and danced in the sun with his sister, until they were both out of breath with laughter. A girl who fought back, and who'd resist him in ways none other had. A girl who'd known pain, and pain hadn't defeated her. Not yet.

He ached for her body, for her presence in his life. It was her fault, all of it, and it was high time she paid her dues. She'd always been there, in his home, in his backyard, leaving no place where he could withdraw except that dreaded barn. She'd always been there, with her short, windblown skirts, her bare thighs and the sight of her pink underwear when she climbed up in the walnut tree with his sister. Hers were the first breasts he'd noticed, through the thin fabric of her blouse, against the setting sun. And from that moment, all he could think of was those soft mounds of delicious flesh he craved sinking his teeth into.

She'd always been to blame, the Kathy of his youth, the girl who'd haunted his dreams for the past sixteen years, alongside the memory of his mother. She'd been the one who had kindled the first fire in his groin and seeded restless thoughts and haunting images in his mind. She'd always been the one to blame for his unrelenting desires, thoughts, and urges he didn't understand then, but had turned his life into a waiting game for the supreme moment of vengeance, of absolute, earthshattering release.

Yet she'd slipped through his fingers. Where had she gone? And how much did she know?

She got too close, if she talked to Mother.

She shouldn't've talked to Mother.

The sight of them, sitting together, enjoying each other's company, had left him raw and aching inside, the rage buried deeply in his heart screaming for their blood. Even if he willed himself to, he couldn't erase the memory of the two women on that swing, not a care in the world, not a single thought about *him.*

The son without a mother.

The forgotten friend no one talked about.

While she, the imposter who'd taken his rightful place, was welcome to hold Mother's hand and wrap her treacherous arms around her.

He drew air until his lungs hurt, then released it forcefully in a long, wailing, rage-filled cry that echoed against the mountain, then died, leaving behind the silence of all the creatures he'd terrified with his roar.

Where on earth had she gone?

And how could he get near her again?

By the time he got to the house, he still didn't have an answer, but he was starting to have an inkling of a plan. He put the ATV inside the garage, then climbed behind the wheel of his Cadillac and started the engine.

CHAPTER FIFTY-ONE
Strategy

"I know what's wrong with the stupid car, and it's an easy fix, remember?" Kay snapped at Elliot, only moments after she'd breathed in relief. The thought of her own fear, of her own weakness filled her with shame and anger. *Just like a bimbo, for crying out loud*, she admonished herself, her cheeks burning when she recalled how she'd run out of hiding straight into Elliot's arms.

"Hobbs can be here with another vehicle in thirty minutes," Elliot insisted. "And I can't understand, for the life of me, why you don't want to ride in mine."

"Because *I'll* go talk to him, not us," she said, climbing behind the wheel. "Not both of us."

"Why the heck not?" he shouted. "You're making no sense at all."

She grabbed the wheel tightly, squeezing it, an effort to calm her taut nerves. "If he sees you—law enforcement—he'll lawyer up. He'll demand a warrant to give you access to the premises. We'll botch the whole thing, and while we fumble with it, he could kill those kids. What's to keep him from tying up all the loose ends?"

"We'll get that warrant really quickly," Elliot replied, his hands propped on his hips. Every few minutes, he ran his hand through his hair, probably missing his hat more than he realized. "He won't have time to kill a woman and three kids and dispose of their bodies before we come back."

"Listen," she said, putting Nick's address into the GPS, "there's no way he's been holding those women in this house. No way. Have you seen their bodies on Dr. Whitmore's table? Do you think that kind of torture didn't make them scream? His closest neighbor across the street is fifty yards away!"

"The land deed said two hundred and twenty-two acres," he replied, seeming a little embarrassed. "I thought—"

"That the house was smack in the center of it? No, his land extends *behind* the house, probably on the entire side of this mountain," she replied, looking at the map intently. "I'm willing to bet there's a place somewhere between his house here," she tapped the GPS screen with her fingernail, "and the dead zone valley, the place where the victims' cars broke down, and that place is where he does his torturing and killing."

"I ran a property search, and there wasn't—" Elliot said, then whistled, his signature reaction to something unexpected. "But he's the district attorney, right? He knows what people he puts in jail and for how long, and he knows their assets. Maybe someone gave him a hunting cabin or a lodge or maybe he's just using one while the owner is locked up."

"Bottom line is, he'll never tell *us*, but he might tell *me*."

"What, he's just gonna pour you some coffee and say, by the way, let me tell you where I've been killing people?"

She rolled her eyes, exasperated. "Not like that. But he might have his guard an inch lower with me, that's all." She looked at him, holding the stern gaze of his blue eyes without blinking. "I'm not a rookie, Elliot. I know what I'm doing. What would it take for you to trust me on this one?"

"Kay, this man screwed up your car and tried to kidnap you! He wanted you locked up in the hellhole where he tortures and rapes his victims. He's not someone you can toy with!"

"I know," she admitted, his words stirring primal fear in her gut. She hated him for that. "But I need you to trust me on this one."

Elliot groaned, visibly frustrated. "I have to call Sheriff Logan anyway," he replied, his voice carrying tones of the doubt he was probably feeling. "I have to get approval for all this, and get the team ready for a breach, once we have a location. We're dealing with the district attorney and he lives in another county, so there could be a jurisdictional issue here."

"For you, maybe, but not for me, his childhood friend."

"Now I know," he reacted, "you're insane!"

Kay smiled sheepishly and started her engine, ignoring the dashboard chimes and the engine failure messages. "I've got to get to Katse before it stalls again. If I keep pouring water into the damn thing, it will work."

Elliot leaned over, holding on to the door frame, to be on the same eye level with her. "If you're right, and you seem to be annoyingly right just about every darn little thing, this man's a serial killer, and you want to have a chat like old friends?"

She smiled, thinking his concern exceeded the professional level and crossed into personal, and she liked it. She liked the thought of that, of someone caring about her enough to worry.

"You know where I'll be," she replied sweetly. "I'll be safe. If I don't come out in an hour, and I don't pick up my cell either, you can go ahead and break down the door. *After* you try calling me, all right?" She squeezed his forearm. "But we have to get there in separate cars. He can't see yours anywhere near his property."

He nodded; his jaw clenched so tightly she could see the knotted muscles under his skin. "All right. Have it your way."

"I just need one favor. Could I borrow your backup weapon?"

CHAPTER FIFTY-TWO
Visit

Nicholas Stevens, formerly Stinson, must've been highly successful in his law career. District attorney jobs weren't famed for their paychecks, yet the once-homeless boy had done well for himself. The Cadillac Escalade, brand new, was one indication of his wealth. The house Kay was staring at was another.

Lots of windows faced the driveway, the south frontage of the property guaranteeing sunshine all day long, and a side peek of the twilight now shooting red-and-crimson arrows against the reflective panes of glass. The property had a three-car garage, built in, with gray doors that complemented the charcoal roof and the stone accents. She pulled in, onto the wide driveway, not all the way to the garage doors, but to the side, as any polite guest would've done.

Feeling her heart racing wildly in her chest, Kay breathed, settling her thoughts. Never in her wildest dreams had she envisioned herself thinking of someone she used to play with as a child as an unsub, ready to enter his property expecting to find clues to the many murders he'd committed and leads to the den of horrors where he kept the people he'd kidnapped. There was something deeply disturbing in that, as if Nick's actions had tainted her entire being somehow, just because he'd been there during her childhood and she hadn't sensed a thing.

How could she not have seen him for who he was, back then, when she was young? She'd always trusted her instincts to a fault, up until learning who Nick was. Then all her confidence had come tumbling down, a pile of rubble where once stood her undoubted ability to infer conclusions from data without second-guessing herself.

In her defense, she was twelve at the time, and she'd been protected by Meg and Roy Stinson, Nick's parents, her eyes shielded from the truth. Around that time, her own family was going through a different brand of hell, and those memories were the ones that burned the most vividly, her nightmares raw now, just as they had been all the years since.

But there would be a different time to process all those doubts and conflicted feelings. She wasn't going to waste another second, while a woman and three children were spending endless moments of terror in captivity. She touched the handle of Elliot's gun, tucked neatly in her pocket, and breathed slowly, steeling herself.

Climbing out of her Explorer, she shot a quick glance over the shoulder, in the general direction of where Elliot's car was, parked on the side of the main road and hidden behind a clump of thick firs. Then she walked quickly to the front door and rang the bell, reminding herself to breathe normally.

Nick opened the door. When he recognized her, his face lit up.

"Oh, my goodness, come in," he said in a friendly voice loaded with excitement that sounded heartfelt to her ears. He held the door wide open for her. "I can't believe it's you."

Kay stepped inside, then shared a blood-curdling hug with him, thinking it lasted longer than it should have. The proximity of a brutal killer, the sensation of his skin touching hers, the burn of his breath against her cheek made her shudder, repulsed. She walked through the tiled hallway, noticing the fine furnishings, hand-carved pieces in cherrywood that matched the rest of the decor.

Her eyes caught an unusual piece, hanging on the wall by a coatrack, but he guided her toward the living room with a hand on the small of her back, and she didn't resist.

She took a seat on a burgundy leather sofa and spent a moment looking around, noticing the many details of a perfectly decorated house. Gleaming hardwood floors from one end to another, oriental rugs here and there, stylish furniture again in dark cherrywood, including the large law bookcase and his home office desk, all in an open-plan layout that was breathtaking. Here and there, a perfectly matching art piece added to the room's decor. And, on the dining room table, a large bouquet of roses, still wrapped in cellophane.

Nick was about thirty-five, if memory served her, and had aged a little bit, gracefully. It was amazing how much better men aged than women; in his case, the success of his career instilling an air of power and self-reliance in his demeanor, the silver on his temples was becoming. He wore a suit and tie, the usual attire for court-appearing attorneys, and it flattered him, enhancing his image as a powerful prosecutor, one that should be feared in court.

And elsewhere, Kay thought bitterly, struggling to reconcile who he really was with who he appeared to be. She continued to smile, though, perplexed as he took the flowers from the table and brought them to her.

"You're not going to believe it, but these are for you," he said, his smile seemingly genuine. "I was planning on a surprise visit, later this evening. I heard you were in town, visiting old friends. I never expected you'd think of me."

She bristled, wondering why he would've come to visit her. Maybe because he'd failed to grab her earlier, when she'd slipped right between his fingers and he had to go home empty-handed. Had he planned to snatch her from her house, after dark?

But seeing him smile like that, a dozen long-stemmed roses in his hand, it seemed surreal that only a couple of hours earlier he'd been pacing the woods in full camo gear, looking for her, while she trembled for her life, crouched on the ground.

Yet she continued to play the charade, and accepted the flowers with her megawatt smile and whispered thanks, reminding herself

Elliot was out there, ready to bust through the door at the slightest sign of trouble.

"Where have you been all these years?" Kay asked, accepting a glass of wine from his hand and pretending to drink a little. She just moistened her lips in it, knowing from her time by Dr. Whitmore's side in the San Francisco autopsy room that a spiked beverage will numb one's lips in a few moments. But that was valid only for some drugs and poisons; not for all of them.

He laughed quietly. He'd taken an armchair and crossed his legs, elbows on the armrests, and the subdued laughter faded into a smile. "I've been working my tail off," he said. "I was in the private sector for a few years, making the big bucks, but the DA job suits me better."

"How interesting," she replied, leaning forward. "Tell me, how does one get from teenage runaway to this?" She gestured toward the far side of the living room, where his desk was.

A flicker of a frown clouded his eyes for the briefest of moments. He still reacted to having been banished from his childhood home, just as she'd profiled.

"You know what they say," he replied, "if there's a will, there's a way. And it was, for me. I worked two jobs, starting from the most menial you can think of. I loaded produce on shelves at the local market, and packed garlic in Gilroy. Onions too," he added, laughing as if he was telling someone else's story. But that laughter didn't touch his eyes, focused more and more intently on her, making her uneasy. "I taught myself to play ball, and fought hard to get into college, then got a scholarship. I was lucky, I guess," he added, his eyes drilling into hers, unyielding.

He licked his lips, and she fought the urge to run out of the house, screaming.

His gesture betrayed his arousal and brought back the memory of Alison's body on the autopsy table, her bruises fresh, her autopsy findings a terrifying story of what came out of that man's lusting urges.

And he was lusting now. For her.

She repressed a shudder. "And? After law school?" she asked, relieved to hear her own voice sounded normal, casual, with the right amount of interest. None of her internal anguish was coming through.

"Private practice," he replied, still smiling. "That's what paid for all this." He picked up his wine glass and held it in the air. "Here's to a happy and long overdue reunion."

Lifting her wine to her lips, she dipped them in the liquid again, then held on to the glass instead of setting it down on the table, an unspoken promise she was going to drink some more.

"Then why leave it?" Kay asked. "Financial success is the ultimate success, they say."

"And *they* are right," he replied, taking another sip of Cabernet. "But I've always yearned to deliver justice, to punish wrongdoers instead of defending them."

There was deep truth in his words. His entire being seemed to echo his words, sending a sparkle of something in his eyes, something reminding Kay of knife blades dipped in fresh blood. She believed him. She believed he still wanted the ones who'd done him wrong punished, again and again, even if by proxy, innocent women taking the place of the mother who'd shunned him away.

"I get that," she replied, repressing a shiver under his fierce gaze. Fear sent blood rushing through her veins, urging her to run. "More than you know, I get it."

Her words came out a little slurred and her lips felt swollen. Numb. She was running out of time.

"So, tell me, have you heard anything about the girls from Silent Lake?" she asked, forcing herself to speak clearly. "I'm guessing you have; it's your line of work."

Instead of replying, he stared at her for a long moment, while her breath caught, captive in her lungs. His eyes turned dark and his smile vanished. Tension locked his jaw as he stared at her with bloodlust in his heavy gaze, the air between them crackling with tension.

The time for charades had passed.

"Where are you keeping them, Nick?" she asked coldly.

"Who?" he replied, standing abruptly, the armchair scraping against the hardwood. "I don't know what you're talking about."

She stood also, relieved to see she was firm on her feet and not dizzy at all, the numbness of her lips the only effect of the spiked wine. She walked toward the front door and stopped by the wall-mounted coatrack, an antique piece that must've cost a fortune.

Next to it, at eye level, there was a matching, hand-carved key cabinet, six inches tall by at least twenty inches long, protected with two sliding panels of glass. Inside, hanging from individual silver hooks, there was a variety of car keys, some simple, others modern, smart, keyless remotes.

She counted fourteen different keys, all different brands, including Nissan, Jeep, Subaru, and Ford. Mementos of his victims, on display, to rekindle his urges and soothe his searing pain.

Pulling Elliot's gun, she pointed it at Nick's chest.

He didn't even flinch. "Who are you talking about, Kay?"

"Them," she said, gesturing with the gun toward the keys hanging on the wall display. "The women whose keys you kept as trophies. Some are at Silent Lake, others in the morgue, and one, one's still out there, isn't she? Where is she, Nick?"

"That's ridiculous, Kay," he replied, laughing lightly as if Kay's question was an old joke told by a friend. He approached her casually, clearly unafraid of the weapon she was holding aimed at his chest. "Those are from the cars I've owned, nothing else." He took another couple of steps closer. "I was hoping you were here as a friend, not as a federal agent."

"I'm not a fed anymore," she said, realizing she'd backed herself into a corner of the hallway, in a spot where Elliot couldn't see her through the large living room windows.

He took a few more steps forward, getting so close to her she could hear his calm, steady breathing. A stone-cold psychopath, whose pulse didn't climb under stress, a predator who never felt fear.

"Stop right there," she ordered, but Nick smiled and took another step closer.

"Or what, Kay? Shoot me at point blank?" He kept on smiling, he kept on drawing closer, inch by inch. "Because I have a collection of car keys?"

If she pulled that trigger, there was a risk they'd never find them, the vastness of the national forest an insurmountable impediment to any traditional search. Bloodhounds had been at it for several days already and had found no trace of the missing children. Even if she didn't kill him, if she only wounded him, he'd never cooperate; people like him, psychopaths, never did. Her bullet would kill four other souls, the missing woman and three children, surely prisoners without escape in a place where no one could ever find them. She only had one option, regardless of how scary it was. Regardless of how much it took to keep her fear under control, when it screamed inside her mind, seeding fire in her blood.

She could let him capture her. He'd take her where he held the others. And Elliot would follow them, would rescue her. *Please, Elliot, come find me.*

Her hand shaking a little, she lowered her weapon with a long sigh. She'd made her decision.

"You're right, Nick. I'm sorry," she said. "I—I guess being a fed changes the way I look at people. I hope you can forgive me."

"No worries," he replied, grabbing the Glock from her hand. "I won't hold that against you."

Then he struck her with the butt of the handgun, sending exploding stars in front of her eyes, while she fell to the ground. She was still falling when darkness engulfed her, thick and silent.

CHAPTER FIFTY-THREE
Breach

Elliot watched the brightly lit window through binoculars, crouched behind a clump of firs with heavy, low branches. Even so, he could barely see Kay, who sat on a sofa at the far end of the room, but at least he knew she was all right.

From a distance, the two seemed to chat and drink wine as if they were old buddies catching up, which, in fact, they were, at least officially. He didn't understand how Kay was going to make him divulge the location where he kept his victims, but she was the one with all those years of fancy education and experience catching serial killers.

He had to admire her guts, when he could stop for a moment from wondering how he'd let himself be talked into letting her go in there by herself. It couldn't've been easy for her to ring that doorbell, knowing who Nick Stevens really was, and walk into that house, after having seen, under the strong lights of the autopsy room, what he did to the women in his power.

A quiet buzz alerted him of a new text message. He pulled out his phone and checked the screen. Deputy Hobbs's message read, *We're in position.*

Everyone who could be spared from the sheriff's office, including Logan himself, were holding a mile out, ready to storm the property when he gave the signal. As Kay had instructed him, he wasn't supposed to breach unless more than an hour had passed, and she was unresponsive on her cell.

He counted the minutes, slowly dragging as Kay seemed relaxed, glass of wine in hand, talking and smiling casually with a blood-lusting psychopath. The woman had some seriously big, round stones, the size of pickup trucks; that was a fact.

She'd told him she'd be safe, because he couldn't take her anywhere without having to drive his Cadillac right under Elliot's nose, and he'd see that coming the moment the garage door would open. But was she, really, safe in the presence of a homicidal psychopath? Anything could go wrong in a situation like that. Absolutely anything. The district attorney, like a bucking wild bronc, could do whatever crossed his deviant mind; there was no way of knowing what and when.

"What the heck was I thinking?" he muttered, angry at himself and his powerlessness. It seemed his brain turned to mush whenever he worked with a woman. That had to be the reason why he'd always given into his female partners' demands, no matter how ludicrous. He'd let them talk him into just about anything. If Alaska was in his future, it was a long time coming.

Kay and Stevens stood, then disappeared from view, somewhere to the side. He didn't see any other windows lighting up, but with every moment he didn't see Kay through the living room window, he ached to break that door down, warrant or not.

He checked the time and groaned. Only thirty-five minutes had passed; he still had some time to kill, the slowest-moving seconds of his entire existence.

Eyes riveted to the window through binoculars, he watched for any indication as to where Kay could be. Were they still in the living room? Did they go to the back of the house? Why? Why wasn't she staying where she knew he could see her? Why risk her life pointlessly?

For the remaining twenty-five minutes, Kay didn't reappear in view, there was no indication of any movement and no sound to give him a hint as to what was going on. The moment one full hour had finally passed, he called Kay's phone, but the call went straight to voicemail.

"Damn it to hell and back, Kay Sharp," he mumbled, then radioed Hobbs. "Breach, now." He overheard Logan's voice, ordering him to wait until they got there, but didn't acknowledge. Weapon in hand, he left the cover of the firs with the gait of a prowler, hiding in the shadows and keeping to the left of the driveway, where the trees continued along the asphalt. He reached Kay's car and crouched behind it, waiting a few seconds, listening, checking his surroundings for any sign that he'd been spotted. Then, with a few rushed and silent steps, he approached the front door, then looked through the window, searching for Kay. She wasn't in sight, and neither was Stevens.

With one kick, the door flew open. He entered carefully, stopping for a moment to listen for any sound. Several blood drops and a smudge stained the white tiles, telling the story of what might've happened. Anger rising in his body like a tide, he cleared the living room, then proceeded to the kitchen as the rest of the team arrived, entering the property through the front and back doors at the same time.

"Clear," he heard Logan's voice from the back of the house.

"Clear," Hobbs said, leaving the dining room after opening a closet and checking inside.

"Clear," Elliot announced, after going through the living room one more time.

Kay, where the heck are you?

His next stop was the three-car garage. He opened the door and felt for the light, then switched it on and stepped back, in case Stevens was waiting in there, ready to ambush him. Then he looked inside. Outside of the blue Cadillac, a lawn mower, and some garden tools, the garage was empty. "Clear," he announced, then holstered his weapon with a long oath.

They couldn't have just vanished into thin air.

The Cadillac took the middle bay, and the left bay housed the ride-on mower and several power tools along the walls. The right bay was empty, but the most interesting detail was another door, narrower, leading to the backyard.

He pulled out his weapon and approached the rear garage door. There was no door opener installed above it, so it had to be manual.

Yanking it up to open it, he flinched when he found himself face to face with a man. He almost pulled the trigger.

"Don't shoot," Hobbs reacted, "it's me."

"Jeez, Hobbs," Elliot replied, lowering then holstering his gun, while sweat broke at the roots of his hair. "That was too damn close."

He took out his flashlight and examined the backyard, rushing from one end to the other.

The right side of the garage stood neatly against the rocky side of the mountain, not leaving nearly enough space for a vehicle to access the backyard by circling around the house, not even a ride-on lawn tractor. That was probably why he'd had the smaller door built at the back of the garage. It made sense.

But in that case, why was the ride-on parked in the left bay, not the right one? That part made no sense whatsoever, unless there used to be a third vehicle in that third bay, a vehicle that had disappeared with Kay and the killer who'd taken her.

The backyard was narrow, ending in thick woods and a steep, rocky ravine. There was nowhere to go, even if there had been a third vehicle in the garage. He kneeled by the rear garage door and studied the blades of grass, looking for tire tracks. They weren't visible at first, not from up close. But when he took a couple of steps back and aligned his line of sight with the direction of a vehicle leaving the garage, he spotted them.

He'd been looking for small tires, like a lawn tractor's, but the barely visible ones he saw were from large, wide wheels, the kind all-terrain vehicles had, especially those geared for rocky, uneven mountain slopes. And that all-terrain vehicle was now gone.

He followed the tracks to the back end of the yard, where they disappeared behind a curtain of low-hanging hemlock branches, and descended into a steep ravine on a barely visible path that disappeared after twenty yards or so into thick woods.

They could be anywhere on Stevens's 220-acre property, or beyond, far into the national forest somewhere or on the other versant of the mountain. Blood drained from his face when he realized how badly he was out of options, while with every moment that passed Stevens put more distance between him and Kay.

She was gone.

He turned around and looked at the house, every lit window projecting a yellow glow against the darkness of the woods. Logan and Hobbs approached quickly, but he was staring at the blue Cadillac, partially visible through the back door of the garage.

"He drove straight through there," Elliot explained, pointing at the ravine. "Get some ATVs from the neighbors; most people who live here have them."

"You got it," Hobbs replied, then rushed away, beckoning two other deputies to follow him.

"What are you going to do?" Logan asked, following him to the garage.

"I'm going after her," he replied, then headed toward the Cadillac. "When Hobbs gets an ATV, he'll catch up."

"That won't fit—" Logan started to say, but Elliot had already started the engine and forged ahead. The narrow door barely allowed the massive frame of the SUV to make it through, leaving deep, long dents on both sides and putting deep cracks in the garage wall.

Once he got to the edge of the lawn, he slowed down a little, then advanced through the curtains of low-hanging hemlock and fir, flooding the woods in the bright lights of the Escalade. The ATV's tracks were no longer visible, but here and there he could still see where the all-terrain vehicle had driven a few times before, leaving behind the makings of a path.

CHAPTER FIFTY-FOUR

Taken

She came to with a start, awakened by the thumping in her chest and the pounding of a blinding headache. She blinked a couple of times, trying to adjust her vision to the powerful light in the room, then she saw him. His back was turned to her, while he busied himself with arranging some small objects on a tray.

Kay breathed, steadying herself, and took a mental inventory of her body. She'd been hurt, hit in the back of her head, and the collar of her blouse seemed moist. Her nostrils picked up a familiar metallic scent. Blood.

She was seated on a wooden chair, her hands tied behind the tall, narrow backrest with what felt like a zip tie, already cutting into her flesh. Her ankles were tied to the chair legs, also with zip ties. She wasn't injured anywhere else except her pounding skull and her self-esteem.

How could she let herself fall into his trap so easily? What good would it do the others if she was tied up and about to be tortured, like the rest of them? Elliot was right; she was insane.

Elliot.

The thought of him rushed through her mind like a lightning bolt. Why wasn't he there already? Had he been caught? Killed? The idea of Elliot Young lying somewhere in a pool of blood brought a whimper to her lips.

"Ah, you're awake," Stevens said, turning to face her.

His eyes were cold and frenzied, as he was consumed by his compulsions and energized at the thought of what he was about to do. She'd seen on Kendra's body what that was, in gruesome detail, on Alison's too. Panic rushed through her entire being, making her pull erratically against her restraints.

"Don't even think about it, my dear Kathy," he said smiling, a cold smirk that didn't reach his eyes. "May I call you Kathy? That's what I used to call you, anyway." He caressed her cheek with his fingers. "To me, you'll always be Kathy. The girl who stole my heart."

She resisted the urge to pull away frantically, knowing that she'd only harm herself. She listened to her own breathing for a moment, pushing him out of her reality, distancing herself in a controlled dissociative state. Then she regained control over her senses, reminding herself she still had a fighting chance.

"Kathy, the girl who stole my family," Stevens continued, gathering a few objects from a distant table and putting them on the same tray.

Kay stopped herself from denying the accusation, no matter how ridiculous. For all intents and purposes, he was a hostage taker. The golden rule in hostage negotiations applied here; never say no to them. Never contradict them, no matter how insane their statements or ludicrous their demands.

She remained silent, inviting him to continue. He didn't.

"Tell me, was there any truth to the story you told me?" she eventually asked.

"Uh-huh," he muttered.

"Which part?"

He brought the tray over by her chair and set it on a nearby stool. It held scissors, a hairbrush, several combs, and a couple of braided leather hair ties adorned with small feathers. Then he looked at her as if he'd never seen her before.

"Why did you want to become a district attorney, Nick?" she asked, ignoring his distancing silence.

A lopsided grin stretched the corner of his mouth. "For the power it gives me," he replied. "I'm surprised you, the famed psychologist and criminal profiler, didn't figure that part out yet."

He ran his fingers through her hair, his touch sending shivers of dread down her spine. She managed not to flinch, not to gasp, and focused on what she needed to say to reach him, to throw him off his game.

To buy herself some time.

"I apologize for every harm I've done you, Nick."

He glared at her. "You have no idea." He grabbed a comb from the tray and started drawing it through her hair. "You took my rightful spot in my family," he added, grabbing another comb, one with a long, sharp handle. He used it to part her hair from the forehead all the way to the back of her head. When he touched her wound, she winced.

He didn't stop. He tied one half of her hair loosely with an elastic tie to keep it out of the way, then rolled his chair over to her right side and started braiding. "It was *my* family, Kathy! Mine, not yours."

She swallowed hard; her throat parched dry. "I had no idea, Nick. I was just a stupid kid, and you were my friend. I never wanted to hurt you."

He tugged harshly at her hair and continued braiding. "They loved you more than me."

She bit her lip, tempted to say that wasn't true. "You were my friend, Nick, and one day you disappeared. I had no idea why you left without saying goodbye."

He tugged at her hair again, the sudden move reigniting the pounding in her head. "I didn't leave!" he shouted. "But did you bother to care? To ask where I was?"

"That year was a difficult one," she started, and instantly wanted to kick herself. She knew better than to defend herself in front of a power tripper. It ticked them off worse than anything else. "I asked," she lied, "many times. But no one told me anything, and your mother, um, she said I shouldn't ask about you anymore."

He didn't say anything, continuing to braid her hair tightly, watching every strand carefully. Twice he went back to catch loose strands he'd missed, undoing his work and starting again.

"That year I lost two people," Kay continued, unwilling to let him take his mind down some rabbit hole she couldn't follow. "You, and my father."

"Your father," he repeated, speaking slowly, ominously. "What happened to your father, Kathy?"

"You don't know?" she asked, holding her breath. If he had the knife, he knew. He'd seen his body, what was left of it, and he'd known it for a while. The patch of ground between the willows hadn't been disturbed recently.

"How should I?" he replied calmly. "I was a homeless kid in San Francisco, eating from the trash and getting raped."

Her breath caught. That explained his violence against the women he substituted for his mother, the person he held responsible for his suffering. He wanted them to feel all the pain he'd once felt.

"I thought you knew," she continued calmly. "Because of the knife."

The lopsided grin returned as he finished one braid and secured it with a hair tie. Then he pulled it behind her ear and then to her chest, and arranged the feathers with delicate fingers that seemed incapable of doing the harm she'd seen done on his victims' bodies.

"Maybe I do know something," he replied. "Why don't you fill in the blanks?"

She paused for a beat, carefully considering every word she was about to say, and what impact it would have. What if, through some unexplained turn of fate, he didn't know everything about her father? It didn't make much sense; if he had the knife, then he knew everything there was to know about the man she and Jacob had put in the ground behind the house.

"My father stabbed my mother with that knife," she said quickly, blurting out a morsel of truth and glad when it was out there, in the tense air between them.

He didn't reply, silence heavy between them as Kay ached to hear what he knew, and since when. "Now you know," she said, then licked her dry lips and forced some air into her lungs. "Was that knife a message to me, Nick?"

He still didn't respond, seemingly lost in his thoughts, driven by his compulsion to build the perfect setting for her punishment. His intense gaze remained focused on his work. Shifting to her other side, he combed the remaining hair again, getting ready to braid it.

"It's funny how you choose women who don't have bangs," she said, forcing herself to smile. "I don't have bangs either. Is it because Native women don't cut their hair unless they're grieving? Is it that?"

That hit a nerve. He started braiding her hair with rash movements, tugging at her scalp and making her wince in pain. She felt blood trickling onto her nape and soaking her collar.

"She didn't grieve after I left," he eventually said. "She didn't cut her hair. My loss was nothing to her."

"No, she didn't cut her hair," Kay said gently, "but she's still grieving. I've seen your photo in her album. She cherishes that."

He slapped her across the face, bringing tears to her eyes. "Don't lie to me! Don't think I don't know what you're trying to do."

"I'm not—" she started to say, but stopped herself, hating the stinging tears that welled in her eyes. "I wanted you to know, that's all. I was there today, at your mom's place. I saw her tears when she mentioned your name."

His anger still showed in his movements, and for a moment, she didn't speak, afraid she'd trigger him again.

"Why did you change your name, Nick?" she eventually asked, hoping it was a safe enough subject to broach with him.

His breathing accelerated and his jaw clenched. "She filled the town with her lies," he said, grinding his teeth as he spoke, as if the words hurt him by leaving his lips. "Everyone despises Nick Stinson in Mount Chester. But they voted for Nick Stevens to become the Franklin County district attorney."

"What lies?" she asked calmly, hoping her voice would soothe the old injury even in the slightest measure.

He didn't reply, averting his eyes for the first time. Ashamed.

"You were aroused by me, weren't you?" she asked quietly, her voice barely a whisper, her tone understanding, compassionate. "I was just a little girl," she added.

"Yeah," he replied bitterly, "you and Judy both were. You always were Mother's little girls." He wrapped the second hair tie around the end of her braid, and arranged it neatly, like he'd done with the first one. "Well, not today, my dear. Today you pay for everything you've done."

Her breath caught while panic returned to stake claim on her entire being.

"What have I done, Nick?" she asked softly, willing herself to keep from trembling.

Silence fell heavily, while knotted muscles danced on Nick's jaw. He glared at her, the intensity in his eyes burning, threatening, urgent.

When he spoke, his voice was choked and bitter, strangled by unspeakable rage.

"You were always there, with your short skirts and your cartwheels and your pink underwear, flaunting your flesh in front of me, not caring what that did to me, to my body."

She waited a beat, but he didn't continue. She could picture his anguish in her mind, a teenage boy not understanding his sexuality, his urges driving him insane and burying him in guilt.

But he'd never been the typical teenager; he'd already demonstrated two homicidal triad factors. He'd killed animals and set fire to the family barn. The urges in him were raging, and his sexual drive merciless, obsessive.

But he'd gone to his mother's bed, not Judy's nor hers. Then why had he fixated on her? Probably because she'd been the absolute first to cause a sexual response in his young body. He must've blamed her for the sexual thoughts he had for his mother, for his sister, and for the guilt and shame he'd endured.

"I understand," she replied, her words almost unintelligible and her voice broken. "I get why you want to punish me. But why were you so harsh to Jacob? He didn't deserve to go to jail for a lame punch in a bar, Nick. You'd done worse than that by the time you were sixteen."

He burst into laughter, standing at a distance and admiring his work. His cackles echoed strangely in the room, and, in response, a woman's voice wailed loudly from another room. Loud pounding noises against a door sent a glimmer of hope through Kay's heart, but soon she realized it was probably the same woman, the one he'd taken the day before. Not Elliot.

At least Kay had found her in time. She was still alive, albeit Kay had envisioned her rescue a little differently.

Where was Elliot?

"You think I was harsh to your brother?" he asked, still laughing like a madman, his hands propped on his thighs. "You think that was it? An excessive charge prosecuted vigorously to earn him time in jail?" He clapped his hands together, visibly entertained. "Well, think again!"

Blood drained from her face while her heart raced, aching, remembering Jacob's black eye and swollen lip. "What have you done, you sick son of a bitch?" she asked in a low, menacing voice.

"*I* sent Rafael Trujillo to provoke your lame-ass brother, in return for dropped charges for his joy ride with a stolen car. *Then* I laid down an excessive charge and prosecuted it vigorously. Finally, Judge Hewitt, with whom I play poker every Thursday night, did me a solid and used Jacob Sharp's case to set an example in the community. I erased his poker debt, but what's two thousand dollars these days, right?"

She pulled hard against her restraints, not even feeling the pain where the zip ties slashed into her flesh. "Why?" she asked, her eyes drilling into his, her rage fueled by his amusement. "I swear to God, Nick, I *will* kill you."

He chuckled. "Why? The almighty FBI profiler can't even figure that much out?"

She stared at him, unable to think, unable to comprehend the depths of his viciousness.

"I knew you'd come rushing to his side," he explained, grinning widely. "I wanted you here, like this, keeping me company for the winter. I've been dreaming of this moment since I first saw you, in our backyard, doing cartwheels with Judy. You wore pink underwear, remember?"

She felt sick to her stomach and inhaled sharply to settle her nausea. "I was a child, you sick bastard!"

"I expected you to come testify on Jacob's behalf, and I would've let him slide easily, if only you'd come," he said, pacing the room slowly. "But you didn't. It's all your fault." He stopped in front of her and ran his fingers against her lips. "You're here now, Kathy. That's all that matters."

It took all her strength to remain calm.

"Why now, Nick? What's so special about now?" she asked, feeling the bile rise in her throat at the thought that she had somehow become a serial killer's apex target, the ultimate kill he'd been practicing for all those years. But why now, what was the trigger that had set in motion the course of events that had started with Jacob being set up?

"Lost time is never found again, is it?" he replied calmly, as if discussing philosophy over a glass of wine.

"Something happened, Nick, to remind you I existed."

"Oh, I never forgot you existed, not for one day. You were mine all along, and I wasn't going to let that change. I wasn't going to let you live happily ever after with anyone else than me."

She frowned. What the hell was he talking about?

He scoffed and pulled out his wallet, then fished out a folded newspaper clipping from the *San Francisco Chronicle*, dated a few weeks ago. The photo depicted her being awarded the FBI medal of valor by her mentor and longtime friend, Aaron Reese, the head of the Behavioral Analysis Unit.

He shoved the photo under her eyes, and she looked at it trying to see things from his perspective. She was beaming in the picture; she still remembered how she'd felt that day, proud and a little overwhelmed, being recognized for her service after a very difficult case. Aaron Reese was also smiling fondly; he'd always maintained she was the brightest of his students, destined for great achievement in the bureau.

But it took a twisted mind to imagine there was a sexual relationship between her and Reese, based solely on that photo.

"You misunderstood, Nick," she replied, "there's nothing going on between—"

"I believe you, yes," he replied calmly, a satisfied smile appearing on his lips. "Aaron Reese had an accident on the interstate a few days ago. Quite unfortunate," he added, his smile now unveiling his teeth. "Afraid he didn't make it, poor soul, so, yes, there's nothing going on between you two. Now you and I can fulfill our destiny."

"You'll pay for this, Nick Stevens, or whatever the hell your name is," she said, her voice filled with rage. "They know who you are, and they're coming for you."

He laughed again, almost kindly, the way someone laughs hearing a child's delusional fantasy. "Yeah? So, then, why aren't they here already?"

He undid the buttons on her shirt, slowly, taking pleasure in seeing her chest heaving with every shattered breath she took.

"Your mother was right to throw you out like a rabid dog," she said, looking him in the eye.

His hand landed hard across her face and she screamed before she could control herself. But she didn't lower her gaze. Blinking away burning tears, she said, "I will kill you, Nick Stinson, with my own hands, I promise you that."

The second blow came just as hard, and she screamed again, while he laughed. "I knew you and I were going to have fun together. I knew that a long time ago."

A child's loud crying came from a distant room, and he froze. Earlier, when the woman she'd heard sobbing before had started wailing, he didn't seem to care. But the sound of the child's tears had a different effect on him.

He stared at her for a short moment with lustful, bloodshot eyes, then left, slamming the door behind him.

CHAPTER FIFTY-FIVE

In the Dark

Kay listened intently for a few moments, following his footfalls as they faded away. Soon, another door was closed, and a moment later, the child's sobbing ceased.

She didn't have much time. She only hoped she had enough.

Cringing at the thought of causing more pain to her wounded skull, she threw herself on the side and landed hard on the tiled floor with a muffled groan, seeing stars again when her temple slammed into the hard surface.

On her side, she pushed her left ankle lower, as far as it would go, forcing the zip tie to slide along the chair leg with it, until it reached the end and became loose. She repeated the same movement with the right ankle, using her left foot to hold the chair in place while her right ankle slid lower.

As soon as both her feet were loose, she pushed away from the chair, sliding her tied wrists behind the backrest until they were free of the chair. Then she kneeled on the floor, dizzy and wobbly, her head pounding fiercely. As she lowered herself to her knees, she slid her tied hands under her buttocks and forward, then shifted her weight backward until she was seated on the floor, her tied wrists under her knees. She then folded her legs, one at a time, until she was able to get her hands past her feet and in front of her.

A door opened, then closed somewhere close, and she sprung to her feet. The zip tie holding her wrists had loosened a little, but not enough to let her slide out of it. She grabbed the end of the tie with her teeth and tightened it as much as she could without screaming, ignoring the blood tricking from where it had cut into her skin, and knowing it would get worse before it got better.

She'd done this before, in a training session at Quantico, with a seasoned SERE trainer. Back then, she didn't think she was ever going to make use of the man's thorough approach to survival, evasion, resistance, and escape strategies, but she'd been wrong. Now she recited his method in her mind, quickly, her heart pounding as rushed footfalls approached in the hallway.

Raise your arms above your head, and then bring them down quickly against your abdomen, pulling your elbows apart at the same time. The faster and more forcefully you do this, the less the pain and damage to your wrists. Do it right, and the zip tie will snap open. Do it wrong a couple of times, and you'll slice open your veins and bleed to death in captivity.

She filled her lungs with air as she lifted her arms above her head, just as the door handle moved. Then she brought down her arms forcefully, not caring it was going to hurt. The door opened and Stevens stopped for a beat, surprised, as the zip tie snapped, and she broke free. For a split second, they stared at each other, Kay sorely aware he was twice her size.

She looked around for something she could use as he lunged at her with a guttural sound. Moving out of the way and avoiding him for a brief moment, she saw the scissors on the tray. She reached for them and grabbed, just as he latched onto her waist and slammed her to the ground. He pinned her down under his weight and tried to get a hold of her flailing arms. Holding the scissors as tightly as she could, she brought down her arm forcefully and stabbed him in the back.

He gasped, blood gushing from his wound. She broke herself free of his weight and ran out of the room, disoriented. The wails and pounding coming from the lower level had resumed, and she could hear the child crying again. Soon she'd set them free, but first she had to see where she was.

With trembling hands, she found a light switch and turned on the light in what seemed to be the great room of a log cabin. Frantic, she looked for the entrance and found it. She opened the door and rushed outside, feeling instantly chilled by the freezing air and complete darkness. The faint light coming through the open door cast against the thick woods. She could see the dim shadow of the mountain peak against the moonlit sky, enough for her to realize she was close to the peak, on one of the versants.

How did she get there? She rushed to look around the house and almost fell to her death in a massive ravine that opened at the side of the cabin, a bottomless pit. On the other end she saw an ATV, but the keys weren't in the ignition.

He must've had them.

Kay was about to rush back inside and free the others, then find those keys and run, when lights flickered in the distance, through the thick woods.

"Hey," she shouted, waving desperately at the approaching lights. "Over here!"

Her blood froze in her veins when she felt Nick's hands around her neck, strangling her mercilessly, snuffing the air out of her lungs. She flailed erratically, unable to fight him off and free herself. Even wounded, he was stronger than she was, and she was losing her strength with each passing suffocating second.

As her knees were starting to give, she remembered another SERE technique. She reached out behind her and grabbed his head with all her strength, then threw herself forcefully to the ground. She brought him down hard, then rolled from under him as his fingers continued to choke her, crushing her trachea. She flailed her arms desperately, feeling for something she could use, and found nothing. Instinct made her pull at the merciless grip he had on her throat, but as darkness descended upon her, a flash of a memory came to her mind. Back at the house, he'd taken Elliot's gun from her hand and put it in his right pocket. He still wore the same clothes.

Reaching down, she felt for the gun with trembling, frozen fingers. It was there. She pulled it out of his pocket, and he felt that. He groaned, cursing, and released the pressure around her neck. She filled her lungs in a raspy, choked breath that hurt like hell, then pulled the trigger just as his hands were reaching for the gun.

The shot echoed against the rocky mountain slope, then another shot came.

Then everything went dark.

CHAPTER FIFTY-SIX

Another Woman

She'd woken up with a start, panic raging in her weary mind and rushing blood through her veins. Noises she'd never heard before had her springing to her feet and pacing the room silently, then pasting her ear against the door and holding her breath.

Somewhere nearby, the noise of a hard blow, then a woman screaming. A few moments of silence, then the same sounds painted the picture of what was going on, vividly, beyond any doubt, because she'd been at the receiving end of the beatings, and she'd screamed until her throat was raw.

The sick son of a bitch had taken another woman.

Tears burned her eyes and slowly rolled down her cheeks. She clenched her hands into fists and pounded against the door, uselessly, knowing it was for little else but a show of sympathy for the other woman if she could hear it, a wordless encouragement. She knew just how scared she had to be, terrified into a primal state of sheer panic, feeling the entire world had opened up and swallowed her whole, leaving her at the mercy of a savage animal.

Then silence ensued for a few moments, and Wendy breathed, slowly, afraid the sound of the air leaving her lungs would cover distant noises she so desperately needed to hear. For a while, nothing could be heard, silence filling the room like heavy smoke, choking her.

The distant sound of a child crying was faint, barely recognizable. She'd heard it before, coming from upstairs somewhere, almost as desperate as her own cries yet immediately subdued. Who was the child, and where was his mother? Had she fallen into the hands of the same brute, and somehow met her demise?

Wendy heard a door open nearby, and heavy footfalls rushing, approaching. She stepped back from the door, fearing the man's approach and putting as much distance between them as possible. But he walked right past her cell, then up the stairs, his shoes thumping against the steps in a fast, urgent rhythm. A few moments later, the child's sobs ceased, and silence reclaimed its territory.

She breathed again, this time deeper, her lungs hungry for air, deprived, eager to fuel her weakened body in the brief respite she'd been offered. Another woman, captive, meant he might not come that night. He might visit her instead. Wendy's head hung, ashamed for the relief she felt at the thought of another human being's suffering instead of her own.

The sound of a thump coming from the same room nearby caught the breath in her chest. She tiptoed to the door again and listened, her own heartbeats too loud, thumping in her ears. The sounds of someone scraping the floor, something being dragged across the tiles, then light footfalls rushing out of the room and up the stairs in rapid bursts of a few steps, then a pause, while she most likely watched and waited, fearing her captor.

That woman had escaped!

Exhilaration swelled her chest with renewed hope. The brave stranger would soon make it to safety and tell people about that place of horrors, and cops would come and find her, set her free.

Her entire body pressed tightly against the door, she listened, visualizing the woman as she lurched toward freedom, every second bringing her closer to the door, to the outside world. Then her footfalls faded away, leaving silence behind them like wet footprints in heavy snow. The man was somewhere else, probably upstairs, and had not heard the woman leave.

A faint squeak marked the moment the woman opened the main door, bringing a rush of frigid air inside, sneaking underneath the door and chilling Wendy's feet. She was outside… she'd made it!

Then Wendy heard the woman's voice, hailing someone in the distance, by the sound of it, and saying, "Hey! Over here!"

Tears streamed across Wendy's cheeks without her even feeling them. There were others… Other people out there who would soon come and set her free. That man would never touch her again. Never hurt her again. She'd soon go home.

But the woman's call must've been heard from upstairs, because a door swung open somewhere above Wendy's head, then the man rushed down the stairs and out the door.

Her blood froze in her veins and she covered her mouth with both her hands to keep the scream rising from her lungs trapped in silence.

When the first gunshot pierced the air, right outside the tiny window of her cell, she froze, hoping the man had met the fate he so deserved. But no matter how intently she listened, she didn't hear his body fall and hit the pavement. Nothing, just a subdued grunt, and a woman's cry of pain.

Then a second gunshot sent echoes in the valley, the sound ripping through Wendy's heart. The sound of a body hitting the ground was the last sound she heard, before fear rose in her chest, suffocating her.

She climbed to the tiny opening in the wall and peeked outside, struggling to catch anything in the thick darkness. The window faced the ravine, but it caught a tiny section of the paved driveway at the side of the entrance. In the dim moonlight, she saw a woman's leg lying on the ground, blood dripping from her ankle where she'd been tied up just like Wendy had been, the rest of her body obstructed from view by the corner of the house.

He'd killed her.

A wave of despair filled her lungs and she let it out, the cry searing her throat as she pounded against the door with both fists.

Nothing but silence met her agony.

CHAPTER FIFTY-SEVEN
Detective

The first thing Kay heard was Elliot's voice directing the collection of evidence from the cabin. He wanted deputies to inspect every room and pack everything they found in evidence bags, no exceptions.

She opened her eyes and blinked a few times until her double vision cleared and the two images of her reality overlapped in one clear picture. She was lying down on the sofa, covered with a blanket, and there was something at the back of her head that didn't belong. Lifting her hand there, she felt some gauze bandage and tape, probably put there by an EMS.

She shifted and tried to rise, then gave it up for a moment, overcome by dizziness and nausea. She tried to swallow, but the excruciating pain in her throat made her regret it.

"You're awake," Elliot said gently, crouching by her side. "How do you feel?"

Kay tried to reply, but only a hoarse whisper came out. She touched her throat and felt it tender under her fingers, painful with every breath and every move. Grabbing hold of Elliot's arm, she sat on the side of the sofa, pushing the blanket away. She recognized the pattern of the blanket and winced. "Are you kidding me?" she said, her words a strangled, raspy whisper.

It was one of the blankets the unsub used to wrap his victims in before burying them.

"Sorry," Elliot replied. "We didn't have anything else."

She stood, a little unsure on her feet at first, but then found her strength. The cabin swarmed with cops, and daylight was breaking, coloring the windows in misty pink and purple. She went to the door and looked outside, curious to see the location of the place in the light of day.

The paved patio was packed with ATVs and four-seaters, and there was a crew from the fire department getting ready to descend into the ravine. There was no access road leading to the cabin, only a path through the woods.

"The children?" she asked, looking at Elliot.

"We found them," he replied, after a brief hesitation. "We found Matthew and Hazel," he added, lowering his gaze to the ground. "Ann is dead." He gestured toward the ravine.

"He killed her," she said, wondering how she'd gotten that piece of the profile so wrong.

"Seems it was an accident, an escape attempt gone bad," Elliot replied. "But he made the other kids bury her."

"To silence and subdue them," she whispered, realization dawning. "Can I talk to them?" she asked, hurting with every syllable that left her mouth.

"Social Services has them, back in Mount Chester," he replied. "We took them out of here as soon as we could."

"And the woman?" she asked, remembering the wails and pounding against the door she'd heard.

"She's fine, as good as could be expected." Elliot said, sadness seeping in his voice. Then he cleared his throat and continued, "Wendy Doyle, a tourist from Phoenix, Arizona."

Kay stared at the rising sun, burning through the mist and promising a clear sky. She felt the cold air touching her soul, and wrapped her arms around herself, shivering, her teeth clattering. Elliot took off his jacket, and wrapped it around her shoulders.

Feeling the heat captured inside it warm her, she gladly slid her arms through the sleeves.

"I don't know how you do this," Elliot said. "How can anyone do this type of work for a living?"

She shrugged, the sudden movement igniting pain in her skull. "Someone has to," she said, smiling sadly. "As long as people like Stevens exist, someone has to."

"But why you?" Elliot asked.

She looked in his eyes for a moment, seeking the reason for his unusual question. Was he doubting her ability to do the job? After what had happened last night, she doubted it too. She'd thrown herself in harm's way without thinking it through, without playing it safe. She could've been killed. Stupid bravado... and yet, she'd do it all over again, if that would've cut those children's ordeal shorter, even if by a minute.

But what she saw in Elliot's eyes wasn't doubt; it was something personal and deep, something she was afraid to discover, unsure where it would take her. She veered her gaze away from his, deciding to give herself some time to heal before looking into those blue eyes again. "Because I'm good at it."

She watched the coroner's office load a stretcher over the top of a roll-caged four-wheeler and secure it in place with straps. As they were about finished, she approached the stretcher and asked, "May I?"

Climbing on the side of the ATV to unzip the body bag enough to see Nick's face, she barely recognized him. Color had drained from his face completely, but there was still some of his deep-seated rage forever burned into his features, as if he wore a grotesque mask.

"Why do you think he let the kids go?" Elliot asked. "Some he let go, others he kept, but they weren't hurt, not physically." He shoved his hands in his jeans's pockets, shivering. "You were right about that," he added. "How did you know?"

She smiled. "Can I offer you that blanket?"

"I'll pass," he replied, jogging on the spot to warm himself up.

"He was reenacting," she replied, taking a hand to her throat and feeling where it hurt the most. She could barely touch her skin; it would probably take her a while before she could feel normal again. As for forgetting what had happened on the eastern versant of Mount Chester, that was never going to happen.

"Reenacting? What, exactly?"

"His childhood," she replied. "He was shunned because Meg Stinson, his mother, feared for the safety of his younger siblings." She paused for a moment, wondering how much she wanted to share from the profile that had already served its purpose. "And me." She tried to swallow again, and this time it wasn't impossible. "His mother didn't trust him to be around younger children. He was trying to prove her wrong."

"So, he's trying to do what? Raise them as his own?"

It was an intriguing thought, but the unsub's pathology pointed toward a different explanation.

"He's reliving his past, recreating it in detail," she said, lost in thought. The theory made sense; everything Stevens had done pointed to reliving his childhood trauma. "Matthew Hendricks represented Stevens's younger brother Sam, and Hazel Nolan represented his sister Judy. I believe that's why he let Tracy go. Shannon's daughter didn't fit anywhere in the picture; his fixation called for one girl and one boy, and Tracy was extra. He wanted it to be as close to reality as possible, to prove to his mother he could be trusted with young children."

"Trusted?" he scoffed, eyebrow raised in surprise. "Like that, holding kids hostage in the middle of nowhere and killing their mothers? Seriously?" He looked away, in the distance, something obviously bothering him. "I sort of know him, as much as a cop can know the prosecutor who puts him on the stand at least twice a year. Nevertheless, he never struck me as delusional." He paused for a moment, while a frown settled on his brow. "Well, he never struck me as a serial killer either."

She patted him on the elbow. "That's why some don't get caught for years, or never. They're too good integrating into society, and no one suspects them. But somewhere inside, they have a totally different world, one fueled by trauma and rage, where values shift and reality melds with twisted urges and homicidal fantasies. They're compelled to act on them, and they do."

The ATV carrying Nick Stevens's body disappeared into the woods, going at slow speed. She was done with that place, ready to go home, take a shower, sleep. But she had one more thing left to do.

Jacob.

He didn't belong in jail, and she needed to tell someone he'd also been a victim, a prop in an entrapment play. Who could she call? His lawyer, for one.

"Dr. Sharp," she heard a voice call her. She turned and saw Sheriff Logan, a slight smile on his lips.

"Sheriff," she replied, her voice still coarse, barely audible over the background noise of the scene. "I wanted to ask you to set the wheels in motion for my brother's release. He was set up. I can testify to that."

His smile widened. "Already in the works, Doctor. Which brings me to the reason why I wanted to catch you before you leave."

He drew closer and took something out of his pocket, but kept his hand low. She couldn't see what that was.

"When Jacob is released, and I hope that will happen today, you'll probably want to go back to San Francisco, to your prestigious job with the FBI and the glamor of big-city living."

She nodded slightly. She hadn't thought that far. She glanced at Elliot, but his expression was impenetrable.

"I can't compete with that," the sheriff continued, "but I'll be damned if I'm not going to try." He opened the object he was holding and exposed a gold star affixed to a two-sided black leather holder. "I hope you'll accept to stay and be a detective here, in Mount Chester, for about a third of the FBI pay and none of the glamour."

Wide-eyed, she stared at the sheriff for a moment, then reached out and took the seven-point star, running the tip of her finger over the shiny metal.

"I'll let you think about it," Logan said, then took two fingers to the brim of his hat in a quick greeting and walked away.

"Well, Detective," Elliot said, grinning widely.

He was beaming, so visibly thrilled at the thought she might stay that it made her smile.

"Not yet," she replied. "I need to think about this. But I'm ready to wrap up here and hitch a ride on an ATV going to Nick's house, where I left my car. I'm dead tired, and I think all questions have been answered here."

"All except one," he said, showing her a photo on his phone. "Your father's knife."

Her heart stopped beating for a moment. With trembling fingers, she took the phone from his hand and stared at the photo.

At first, she didn't recognize the knife, photographed through the clear plastic of an evidence pouch. It was a hunting knife with a three-rivet metallic handle, engraved with his name, Gavin Sharp. It must've been a gift from someone, maybe his coworkers.

She closed her eyes, processing every implication of what she'd just seen.

The knife her father had stabbed her mother with was still buried, rusting near his bones, where no one knew about it. That was a plastic-handled kitchen knife, not an engraved hunting knife.

Then, how did Nick know about her father? Or did he? And where did he get the hunting knife from?

She remembered that Sunday morning, when she woke to find Elliot mowing her lawn, he'd sworn he'd found the garage door open. She knew she'd closed it the night before. Her father's knife must've been somewhere inside the garage, and Nick must've rummaged through the junk in there until he found something he could use. Then he'd left the door open... maybe because Elliot arrived so early, before the break of dawn, and surprised him.

"I can understand how, as district attorney, Stevens had me arrested, and I understand why," Elliot said, seemingly surprised she was silent. "Stopping the lead detective in his tracks can derail an investigation. As the case is handed over, details could fall through the cracks. But why did he bring your father into this?"

She didn't speak, still wondering the same thing. How much had Nick known?

"What is it you're not telling me, Kay?" Elliot insisted, a frown of concern appearing on his brow.

She repressed a shudder in the cold breeze. "Maybe he knew something I don't," she said. "He knew I was working the case with you; he'd known that all along. Probably he was hoping he'd throw me off if I'd worry my father was involved somehow." She breathed in the crisp morning air, enjoying the sun's rays on her face. "Too bad he can't talk now."

"Uh-huh," Elliot replied, and she felt a pang of sorrow descending over her heart. She'd always have to carry the weight of what happened that night. She'd never be rid of it, and neither would Jacob. But maybe there was a way to live with what happened, to live a good life, free of the ghosts of the past.

"Ready to go?" Elliot asked, pointing toward an ATV parked a few yards toward the forest. "We can grab that one."

She walked toward the four-wheeler quickly, happy she was about to leave that place, the seven-point star still in her hand. She tried to put it in her pocket, but it didn't fit, its holder too wide. Out of options, she slid the back cover over her belt and wore it the way most cops do.

She was almost at the ATV, listening to Elliot's account of how they'd found the log cabin, when Deputy Hobbs passed by them and grinned. "Well, good morning, Detective," he said, looking at her.

An involuntary smile tugged at the corner of her mouth. She liked the sound of that.

A LETTER FROM LESLIE

A big, heartfelt *thank you* for choosing to read *The Girl from Silent Lake*. If you enjoyed it and want to keep up to date with all my latest releases, sign up at the following link. Your email address will never be shared, and you can unsubscribe at any time.

www.bookouture.com/leslie-wolfe

When I write a new book, I think of you, the reader; what you'd like to read next, how you'd like to spend your leisure time, and what you most appreciate from the time spent in the company of the characters I create, vicariously experiencing the challenges I lay in front of them. That's why I'd love to hear from you! Did you enjoy *The Girl from Silent Lake*? Would you like to see Detective Kay Sharp and her partner Elliot Young return in another story? Your feedback is incredibly valuable to me, and I appreciate hearing your thoughts. Please contact me directly through one of the channels listed below. Email works best: LW@WolfeNovels.com. I will never share your email with anyone, and I promise you'll receive an answer from me!

If you enjoyed my book, and if it's not too much to ask, please take a moment and leave a review on a social media site or where the book was purchased. You can recommend *The Girl from Silent Lake* to other readers. Reviews and personal recommendations help readers discover new titles or new authors for the first time;

it makes a huge difference, and it means the world to me. Thank you for your support, and I hope to keep you entertained with my next story. See you soon!

Thank you,
Leslie

LW@WolfeNovels.com

www.WolfeNovels.com

wolfenovels

Follow Leslie on Amazon: http://bit.ly/WolfeAuthor

Follow Leslie on BookBub: http://bit.ly/wolfebb

Made in United States
Troutdale, OR
09/12/2023

12838153R00199